Will

Early English Prose Romances

Vol. III

SALZWASSER
VERLAG

William J. Thoms

Early English Prose Romances

Vol. III

Reprint of the original, first published in 1858.

1st Edition 2023 | ISBN: 978-3-37514-878-2

Verlag (Publisher): Salzwasser Verlag GmbH, Zeilweg 44, 60439 Frankfurt, Deutschland
Vertretungsberechtigt (Authorized to represent): E. Roepke, Zeilweg 44, 60439 Frankfurt, Deutschland
Druck (Print): Books on Demand GmbH, In de Tarpen 42, 22848 Norderstedt, Deutschland

EARLY

ENGLISH PROSE ROMANCES.

VOLUME III.

EARLY
English Prose Romances,

WITH

BIBLIOGRAPHICAL AND HISTORICAL INTRODUCTIONS.

EDITED BY

WILLIAM J. THOMS, F.S.A.

SECOND EDITION, ENLARGED.

VOL. III.

HELYAS.
DOCTOR FAUSTUS.
SECOND REPORT OF DOCTOR FAUSTUS.

LONDON:
NATTALI AND BOND, BEDFORD STREET,
COVENT GARDEN.
1858.

HELYAS,

KNIGHT OF THE SWAN.

HELIAS, KNIGHT OF THE SWAN.

THE History of Helias Knight of the Swan as related in the following pages is an old English version of a very early and very popular Romance.—It is supposed by Sir Francis Palgrave* that the most ancient form in which the story exists is in the "*Chronicle of Tongres*" by the "Maitre de Guise" much of which was afterwards incorporated into the "*Mer des Hystoires.*" There is also an Icelandic Saga of Helis the Knight of the Swan in which he is represented as a Son of Julius Cæsar; and a similar legend is introduced into the German Romance of *Lohengrin* of which an edition was printed at Heidelberg so late as 1813.† The tradition that the celebrated Godfrey of Boulogne was lineally descended from the Knight of the Swan is still current in the Duchy of Cleves, and forms one of the most interesting stories in Otmar's *Volksagen.*‡ It must have obtained an early and general circulation in Flanders; for Nicolaes de Klerc who wrote at the

* Mr. Utterson's Introduction to the *Chevalier Assigne.*

† Under the Editorship of Goerres, who has prefixed to it a long learned but somewhat too fanciful an Introduction.

‡ Note by Mr. Price the Editor of Warton, vol. ii. p. 107. ed. 1840.

commencement of the 14th century (1318) thus refers to it in his *Brabandshe Yeesten* :

> " Om dat van Brabant die Hertoghen
> *Voormacls*, dicke syn beloghen
> *Alse dat sy quamen metten Swane*
> Daar by hebbics my genomen ane
> Dat ic die waerheit wil ontdecken
> Ende in Duitsche Rime vertrecken."

i. e. because *formerly* the Dukes of Brabant have been much belied, to wit, *that they came with a Swan*, I have undertaken to disclose the truth, and to propound it in Dutch Rhyme. See Van Wyn, *Avondstonden*, p. 270. Maerlant too in his *Spiegel Historiael*, 4, l. 29:

> " Logenaers niesdaet an doen,
> Dat si hem willen tien ane,
> Dat tie *ridder met-ter swane*
> *Siere moeder vader was.*
> No wijf no man, als ic-t vernam
> Ne was noint swane, daer hi af quam
> Al eis-t dat hem Brabanters beroemen
> Dat si *van der swane* sijn coemen."

From these concurrent sources it seems probable that the original fable was fabricated in Belgium or at least on the borders of the Rhine and a further evidence of the correctness of such a supposition is to be found in the circumstances of the Legend forming the subject of a Flemish chap-book of frequent occurrence at the present day.*

There is also a French Romance upon this subject consisting of about 30,000 lines, which was begun by one Renax or Renaux and finished by Gandor de Douay. It is enumerated among the MSS. in the Royal Library at Paris by Montfaucon, *Le Roman du Chevalier au Cigne, en vers*—and in the British Museum Royal MSS. 15. e. 6. is a magnificent volume of French Romances and Fabliaux—in which is contained *L'Ystoire du Chevalier au Signe*—a romance upon the subject of our hero extending to nearly 3,000 lines. This is probably the original of a curious little poem entitled Chevelere Assigne, reprinted by Mr. Utterson, for the Roxburghe Club from a MS. in the Cottonian Library, (Caligula, a. 2.) which has been quoted by Percy and Warton as an early specimen of alliterative versification. It is contained in a small but thick folio volume of paper comprising several other interesting specimens of Early English Poetry; and although there may be some difference in the

* For the history of this chap-book, which is entitled *Historie van den ridder van avonturen Helias, welken genaemd word den ridder met de Zwaene, &c.* see Mone's valuable Essay on the Popular Literature of the Netherlands, p. 71. It forms No. 3 of the collection of *Volksboeken* edited by Snellaert, and published at Ghent in 1847.

respective periods, when these poems were transcribed, we may without hesitation give to **Chevelere Assigne** a date at least as early as the reign of Henry the sixth, and, perhaps, in attributing to it a still more remote æra, we might be nearer to the truth. It is but a meagre epitome of a portion of the French original which continues the story of the Knight of the Swan and his descendants down to the Capture of Jerusalem by Godfrey of Bullogne, but its rarity and the peculiarity of its style will justify a few extracts from it. It begins:

"All weldynge God whenne it is his wylle
Wole he wereth his werke wth his owne honde:
For ofte harmes were hente y^t^ helpe we ne myghte,
Nere the hyznes of hym y^t^ lengeth in hevene.
For this I saye by a lorde was lente in an yle
That was called Lyor, a londe by hym selfe;
This kynge hette Oryens, as ye book telleth,
And his qwene Bewtrys y^t^ bryzt was & shene:
His moder hyzte Matabryne, y^t^ made moche sorow,
For she sette her affye in Sathanas of helle;
This was chefe of the kynde of Chevalere Assygne."

And the journey of the hermit and his godson to the court is thus described.

"Then grypte eyther a staffe in here honde and on here wey strawghte
Whenne the heremyte hym lafte, an angell hym seemethe
Ever to ride ye chylde upon his ryzte sholder,
Thenne he seeth in a felde folke gaderynge faste,

And a hyz fyre was ther bette, that the qwene sholde in bren,
And noyse was in y[e] cyte felly lowde
With trumpes and tabors, whan they here up token
The olde qwene at her bakke betynge full faste,
The kynge come rydynge afore a forlenge & more.
The chylde stryketh hym to, and toke him by y[e] brydell
What man art y[e] q[d] y[e] chylde & who is that ye sueth ?
I am y[e] kyng of y[is] londe & Oryens am kalled,
And y[e] yonder is my qwene—Beatryce she hette,
In y[e] yonders balowe fyre is buskedde to brenne ;
She was slawndered on hyze y[t] she hadde takene howndes,
And zyf she hadde so don here harm were not to charge.
Thenne were you nozt ryzlye sworne, q[d] y[e] chylde upon ryzte juge
Whenne you tokest ye thy croune, kynge when y[u] made were
To done after Matabryne for thenne you shalt mysfare,
For she is fowle, fell & fals, and so she shal be fownden,
And by lefte with y[e] fende at here last ende,
That styked styffe in here brestes, y[t] wolde y[e] quene brenne,
I am but lytull & yonge, q[d] y[e] chylde, leeve you forsothe
Not but twelfe zere olde even at this tyme,
And I woll put my body to better and to worse,
To fyzte for the qwene, wth whome y[t] wrong seyth.
Thenne granted y[e] kyngé, and joye he begynneth.
If any helpe were y[er] inne y[t] heré clensen myzte."

The next form under which this Romance presents itself to our notice is the one from which the present version is translated, and for the opportunity of using it I was indebted to the kindness of the late Mr. Utterson, the then possessor of this very rare volume, which is entitled "LA GENEALOGIE AVECQUES LES GESTES & NOBLES FAITZ DARMES DU TRES PREUX & RENOMME PRINCE GODEFFROY DE BOULION: & DE SES CHEUALEREUX FRERES BAUDOUIN ET EUSTACE: YSSVS & DESCENDUS DE LA TRES NOBLE & ILLUSTRE LIGNEE DU VERTUEUX CHEVALIER AU CYNE. AVECQUES AUSSI PLUSIEURS AUTRES CRONICQUES HYSTOIRES MIRACULEUSES: TANT DU BON & ROY SAINCT LOYS COMME DE PLUSIEURS AULTRES PUISSANS & VERTUEUX CHEVALIERS."

The Colophon on the recto of the 158th leaf is as follows—

"CY FINIT LE CHEVALIER AU CYNE AVECQUES LES FAICTZ DE GODEFFROY DE BOULION & DE PLUSIEURS AUTRES PRINCES & BARONS CRESTIENS. IMPRIME A PARIS POUR JEHAN PETIT LIBRAIRE DEMOURANT EN LA RUE SAINCT JACQUES A LENSEIGNE DU LYON DARGENT. & FUT ACHEVE LE DIXIESME IOUR DOCTOBRE LAN DE GRACE MIL CINQE CENTZ & QUATRE.

The following extract will at once serve as a specimen of this very rare work, and of the state of the French and English languages at the time when the translation was made. It is the seventeenth chapter in the edition of Jehan Petit, and the twentieth in that of Copland.

"COMMENT LE ROY ORIANT FIST DELIURER DE PRISON LA BONNE ROYNE, BIETRIS SA FEMME & PUIS FIST ORDONNER POUR COMBATRE LE JEUNE FILZ HELYAS CONTRE MAUQUAIRE SON ENNEMY."

Apres que le noble roy Oriant fut retourne de lhermitage et quileut sceu la verite des sept enfans il fit incontinent delivrer la noble royne Bietris de prison et captivite en la restituant du tout a sa franchise et liberte : pour la plus aymer et honorer sans comparison que jamais par avant nauoit faict tellement que a son bon vouloir peut aller ou bon luy semble, comme innocente et non couspable, de ce que on luy veust imposer. Donc treshumblement elle rendoit graces et louanges a dieu. Et aussi de sa delivrance fut tout le peuple tres ioyeulz en louant dieu nostre seigneur. Apres fist prendre Matabrune et la tenir en prison fermee avecques la garde de quatre sergens, pour icelle songneusement garder de fuyr jusques ad ce que justice fust determine de son cas. Puis consequement envoyer querir le desloyal chevalier Mauquaire pour soy trouver a la journee que le dit Roy avoit ordonne pour combattre avecques son filz le jeune Helyas, lequel dieu avoit envoye pour soubstenir la iuste querelle de sa bonne mere la royne Bietris. Si fut alors par les deux chevaliers, que le roy luy avoit ordonnez bien arme d' toutes haustes pieces darmure, tres bien assereez. Le heaulme de mesmes comme il appartenoit honnestement a filz de Roy.

Puis fut richement acoustre de devise a luy condescente, lescu au bras. Et la lance en la main, la quelle il coucha en larrest comme tout inspire de la grace de dieu. Apres luy donnerent une belle espee darmes bien asseree et de bon trenchant. Puis fut saseurement monte sur ung bon & puissant Courcier bien barde & habitue ainsi que en tel cas appartient. Et dautre parte fut appointe le desloyal Mauquaire. Le quel nestoit pas trop ioyeulx de ce que luy convient faire, car consederoit assez quil navoit pas bonne cause ne juste querelle ce ce quil soustenoiet a lencontre de la juste et loyalle royne la royne Bietris. Et dautre part quilla veoit ja delivree de captivite a sa pleniere et franche liberte et la fausse Matrabune estroictement detenue en prison, mais nonobstant toute ces choses faisoit il bien la manière davoir juste cause en son fait, mais il nest nulle sapience contre la voulente de dieu. Et quant ilx furent tous deux preparez dune part et dautre, se assemblerent incontinent plusieurs chevaliers lesqlz leur firent jurer que chacun deulz pencoit avoir bonne cause, en la querelle differente que lung contre lautre vouloit soustenir, laquelle chose afferma le dit Mauquaire tout ainsi que fist le dit Helias, mais avant que partir du champ luy mesme confessa lopposite devant le roy et la bonne royne accompaignez de plusieurs nobles chevaliers et damoiselles.

Du Fresnoy in his *Bibl. des Romans* mentions the following editions of the French Romance of

"LES FAITS & GESTES DU PREUX GODEFROY DE BOUILLON ET DES VALEUREUX FRERES BEAUDOUIN ET EVSTACHE, ISSUS DE LA NOBLE LIGNEE DU CHEVALIER AUX CIGNES AVEC LEUR GENEALOGIE PAR PIERCE DERREY DE TROYES EN CHAMPAGNE."

in fol. gothique sans date: in 4to. gothique sans date, and in 8vo. Lyons 1580.

It is from the first thirty-eight chapters of the above work that the following Romance was by Robert Copland, "newly translated out of Frenshe into Englyshe at thinstigacion of the puyssant and illustryous prynce, lorde Edwarde duke of Buckynghame"—This nobleman was beheaded upon Tower Hill, 17th May, 1521, and as Helyas "of whome linially, is dyscended my sayde Lorde" is represented to be the grandfather of Godfrey of Boulogne, it is to be supposed that it is through this latter that the duke made out his relationship to our hero. Percy, *Reliques*, vol. 2. page 277, speaking upon this subject says "A curious picture of the times! While in Italy, literature and the fine arts were ready to burst forth with classical splendor under Leo X, the first peer of this realm was proud to derive his pedigree from a fabulous *Knight of the Swan*."

Ames speaks of **The Hystory of Helyas Knight of the Swanne, Imprynted by Wynkyn de Worde, &c. M.CCCCC.XII.** 4to. but does not state in whose possession it was, merely describing it as having figures and being printed on parchment. Of the edition by Copland, the copy in the Garrick Collection in the British Museum from which the present is reprinted is the only one known.

It may be proper to remark that the History of Don Flores of Greece, *Knight of the Swan*, is totally distinct from the present work.

THE KNIGHT OF THE SWANNE.

HERE BEGINNETH THE HISTORY OF THE NOBLE HELYAS KNIGHT OF THE SWANNE, NEWLY TRANSLATED OUT OF FRENSHE IN TO ENGLYSSHE AT THINSTIGACION OF THE PUYSSANT AND ILLUSTRYOUS PRYNCE LORDE EDWARDE DUKE OF BUCKINGHAM.

FROM THE EDITION PRINTED BY COPLAND.

PROLOGUE

OF

THE TRANSLATOUR.

VERITABLY it is that all vertues and noble entencions ben nourysshed and engendred in the hertes and courages of gentyl persons, the which causeth them to enclyne to all perfeccyon of bounte. Endeveryng them to heare, se and avaunce the gloryous renoune of theyr foregoers predecessours replenisshed with the grace and love of God. Amonge all other endewed with bountie and noblesse the hygh dygne and Illustryous prynce my lorde Edwarde by the grace of god Duke of Buckyngham Erle of Hereforde, Stafforde, and of Northampton desyringe cotynyally to encrease and augment the name and fame of such as were relucent in vertuous feates and triumphaunte actes of chyvalry. And to encourage and styre euery lusty and gentell herte by the exemplyficacyon of the same havying a goodli booke of the highe and miraculous histori of a famous and puyssaunt kinge named Oryant somtime reynynge in the parties of beyonde the sea havynge to his wife a noble Lady of whome she conceived sixe sonnes and a doughter and chylded of them at one onely tym at whose byrthe echone of them had a chayne of Sylver at their neckes the whiche were all tourned by the provydence of god into whyte Swannes (save one) of the whiche this present Hystory compyled, named Helyas the Knight of the swanne of whom linially is dyscended my sayde Lorde. The whiche ententifly to have the sayde history more amply and unyversally knowen in thys hys natif countrie as it is in other hath of hys hie bountie bi some of his faithful and trusti servauntes cohorted mi mayster Wynkin de Worde to put the said vertuous hystori in printe. And he as willing and glad to content accomplish and obey the gracious mynde and pleasure, hath sought and found a true approved copie, enprinted and corrected in the frenssh language, at whose instigacion and stirring (I Robert Copland) have me applied moiening the helpe of god to reduce and translate it into our maternal and vulgare english tonge, after the capacite and rudenesse of my weke entendement. Beseeching my sayd lorde and consequently al them that redeth or hereth it red to take no regard to the languag misorned and rude, for wythout hygh style and enerve industry I have al onely verbated and folowed mine auctour as nyghe as I coulde with the profoundite of good herte, and where as oni faute bi me or wrong Impression be found intelligibly after their science to correct and amend in pardoning al ygnoraunce. In the whyche doynge I shal be oblygate and bounde to praie for them to almighti God that he geve unto them his realme celestiall unto the which we al mai come. Amen.

Explicit prologus.

HERE BEGYNNETH THE TABLE OF THIS PRESENT BOOKE.

Explicit tabula.

KNIGHT OF THE SWANNE.

CHAP. I.

How the king Pieron of Lilefort hade to wife and spouse Matabrune, for that she was riche, and endowed of great erthly goodes. The which betwene them had a sonne named Oriant.

WE rede in the auncient and autentike cronicles that sometime ther was a noble king in lilefort, otherwise named the strong yle a muche riche lande, the which kinge had to name Pieron.

And he tooke to wife and spouse Matabrunne the doughter of an other king puissaunt and riche mervailously. Bi the reason of which mariage was made and accorded peace betwene two mightye kinges, the which longe time before had ben adversaries and ennemes one a nother by mortall warre. But as than and by the treatie of mariage was pacified the said discorde. How be it neverthelesse that the said kinge Pieron him accorded to take to wife the said Macabrune for that she had great possession of lands and other infinite richesses wherby as the story saith the mariage was made be coveitise and not by love wherof many harmes grewe, and allbi the said Macabrune that wrongefully sew discorde betwen king Oriant, his wife and his children. The whiche possible came by godes wil for that the said mariage was not cordialli made as is said, or for a more meritorious welth, as sith happened to the high praise of god and his holy faithe, for finably al turned to honour by the grace of the hye god that often approveth them that he loveth sending them some advercites first. For he hath no merite towarde god to have any swetnes if first he taste no bitternes of hert, as saint Paule saith. By many triblations we must entre into the realme of god. But finally our lorde resisteth the pervers, in giving his glory to the meke as in this story appereth. For al the punicion fel on Macabrune finabli that had caused al the yll. And thei that had ben iniustly vilipended were miraculousli exalted, and it is often sene that mariage made by covetise cometh to no perfection of goodnesse. For if the coniuntions be not made bi love as god ordeined often of cometh grevous desolacion as did of her, lyke as thistory sheweth here after.

After the mariage of kinge Pieron and Matabrune as the maner is, they had betwene them a sonne noble and wise named Oriant, the which after the dyscease of his father abode with his mother as heir of the realme, whiche he succeded and governed peasiabli without to be maried.

CHAP. II.

How king Oriant chased a hart so swiftely that he lost his folke and came to a fountaine where as he spake with faire Beatrice whome he chose to be his wife.

After that the noble kinge Oriant was growen in age,

in force, and prudence, on a day he delibered him for to go to hunt. And whan al thinges were redy and he comen in the Foreste he at the playe and pursuite of his Greyhoundes reised a great harte, whereate he toke so greate pleasure that he chased him so swiftely that his folke might not folowe tyll he turned in plaine feeld where as was hedge ne bushe. And thus he left of his folke he pursued mervailously til he aproched a river wherin the said harte lepte for saufte, and so escaped the kinge and his houndes. Wherfore the king left him and retourned alone till unto a fountaine that he founde, the which was so clere and pleasaunt to his sight that he alight from his horse for to refresshe him a litle in the same place. And there he sat downe under a tree, to the which he had reined his horse the better to solace and sporte him at his owne pleasure. And thus as he was in consolacion there came to him a yonge damoysel moche grevous and of noble maintene named Beatrice accompanied of a noble knight, and two squires, with iiii damoyselles the which she held in her service and famyliarite. And there as she that in title of signorie posseded the saide grounde began to speake to the king Oriant in repreving him for that he was comen to hunte with in the boundes and limites of hir signourye and possession. And as unto him the whiche she knewe not she began to saie prudently. Faire lorde who hath moeved you to come hunte or take ony beastes within the forestes of my region, know ye not that I am lady and possesseresse of this londe, Damoysel said the king nay. And wo hath than said she given you leve or licence so to doo. I have well apperceived the harte that ye have chaced and put to flight, and hath saved him in the river, but howe be it that ye had taken him yet should he not have abiden as yours. And yet is mine intencion if it please god that ye shall recompence me or ye departe. For ye have none accion of right for to chase or take any beast wilde or tame in mi forestes, nor on mi ground. And whan king Oriant had hearde the faire Beatrice speake thus bi reason so right notably, he toke her in so great pleasure that he was sodaynly surprysed of her love in suche wise that fro than he purposed in himselfe to take her to wife and spouse. And the better to manyfest and make her have knowledge of him he began to lift up his visage in beholding her with a joifull chere and said, Know ye faire damoysel that I wolde not thinke to do you any displeasure, but me thinke that I maye well come and sporte me stil unto this region and londe as soveraine lorde therof, by reason wherof ye owe me homage. And to thende that ye pretende no cause of ygnoraunce wit ye (without that I wyl hide it) that I am Oriant kyng of Lylefort. Wherby there is neyther lorde ne damoysell in all this countrey but they ben holden to yelde me tribute and homage as my vassayll and feeal subiect. But that not withstandyng if I thought to haue endomaged you of one seile ferdynge I wolde recompence it at your desyre, for that noble prudence, curteysy, and graciosite that I perceive beynge in you, by your maintene and moderate speche. How be it that it is well in my power to make your selfe amende and repaire the iniury that ye have doone in reprevinge and chiding me for that which is mine owne. But your noble, faconde, and pleasaunt behavour causeth me somwhat to refraine mi courage, and receive your offence to marci. And whan a noble knight named Savary that long time had served the said damoysel had heard the right mighty king Oriant speake thus benignely he descended incontinent from his horse, and with his knees flexed he prostened him and did him honour and reverence in saluinge him and said. Sir king if it please you ye shall pardon my Ladie if she have ony thing offended you, for she had no cognycion of your riall mageste whan she reasoned with you. And she knowledgeth also if she hath nothinge but that it is at your pleasure and commaundement, and otherwise wold she not doo, wherfore ye shal pardon her if it please you. For she hath said nothing but bi ignoraunce, and as she that rightwisli and with good courage wil kepe yours and hers. Than answered the kinge to him and said. Know ye noble knight that I accepte ynoughe the excuse that ye have made for your noble lady. But she shall make me amendes in suche maner as shal be agreeable, for the beaute and formosite of hir noble persone moeveth me to be her husbande, and to take her to wife and spouse, as she the which is my whole desire. Than the king began for to speake in this maner and sayd. Gentill damoysell pleasaunt, vertuous, garnished of al beautie in whome I have totali set the love of my herte, is it not wel your wil that I be your husband. Pleaseth it you not to be my wife and spouse to thende that I make you to be crowned as quene and lady of Lilefort. May ye finde in your hert by suche maner to accomplishe my wil, that you and I might be assembled and conionct by mariage. Answere ye nowe and say your advise. Ha sir saide she right humblye. I am not digne ne suffisaunt that ye do to me suche honour, for the handmaiden or subgecte ought not ne marye not in any thinge compare to her prence and lorde. But sith that it pleaseth you to commaund me so to doo, in disparsinge to me of your grace I wer right simple and evil instruct if I refused your pleasure, and the excellent honour that ye so benignely and of your goodnesse unto me present. For if it shoulde please you to marye me to the least knight of your noble company yet ought I to consent of right. Wherfore to you that is my lorde, and to other incomparable: I am all redy to abey and accept your good and noble wil in the honour wherto ye require me, the which with good hert I ottroye and graunt you. And than king Oriant tooke her by the hand and said Certes lady I promise you on the faith of knighthod that as long as ye be on live never to espouse other woman than you, and I assure you even here that I shal be your husbande. And thus bi a comin accorde and by the consentement of them bothe was promised the saide mariage with one cordiall love.

CHAP. IV.

Now kinge Orient at his returninge fro the chase brought with him the faire Beatrice for to espouse and tooke her to wife.

WHAN the promesse was thus made the kinge incontinent made her to be led to Lylefort for to marye her. And in May whan the trees spryngeth and bring forthe theyr odiferaunte floures, and that the Birdes bring their armonical tunes on the smal grene twiges was made the entre of the noble quene Beatrice into the realme of Lilefort. At the which entre all the people afflued from all partes leding great joye and mirth everech in his possibilite. That is to wit, some to make fyrs and games of mirthe. Other made divers faire misteries and tourneimentes of feates of armes. And before the same came the olde queene Matrabrune mother of the prue king Oriant. The which whan he sawe her come began for to smile and have great joye of the pleasure that he had to see the noble Beatrice his love, which he loved marveilousli and with al his heart. Wherfore he sayd to his said mother which he perceived murmure a litel. I require you my right dere lady and mother that ye wyl make ioyous chere and beholde here howe I have fonde the moost faire ladi of the world, replenisshed of witte and vertues as much as ony woman livinge. And I am advised that never as longe as she liveth to have other wedded wife, for in her is all mi pleasure. Than as hevy and angrie answered his sayd mother by a maner of envye. Ah my sonne litel reioice I for presently I apperceive your ygnouraunce that ye now wil so abate your estate, as to take a simple damoysel and you being a right puissaunt and noble king might demaunde and have to wife the doughter of the moost riche and noble prince that might be found upon the earthe, and finabli you and yours possede his realme by succession. Madame said the kinge, ye, yf it please me soo. Knowe ye that I never founde none that so muche pleased me, and that was to me so agreable as she is. And ye knowe that ther is nothinge as to have his pleasure in this worlde. And also mariage ought not to be made but that yf the parties were contente and of good accorde. Wherfore I beseche you to take it in gree as well as I. For to morow in the morning if it please god I wyll that the feast and solempnite of the mariage be celebred as it behoveth. And eke I hope sith it is by the wyll of god, and of good love and assent of us bothe that there may be but al welth come therto. Certainly sonne said she sith that it please the that it be so it cannot displease me in ani maner. But I accorde totallie to thi good wil. All these wordes saide she with mouthe, but not with herte, as many doone that bi faint symulacyon make an other thought and cursed wil at hert. And so had the said Matabrune, for she ceased not to murmure in her selfe against the said mariage, and malignousli thought alwai to put therin som diversite, and seperacion. But not withstanding this the feast was not deferred. For the night before the daye of weddinge for the honour and magnificence of the good king Oriant and of his noble love Beatrice were made moriskes, comedies, daunces, interludes, and al maner of joyous sportes in the kinges palais, where as were many great princes and knightes of renowne. Pipes, taborins, doucimers, fidles, organs, psaltries, clavicordes, and mani other instrumentes there was in great nombre sowning al songes of armony. On the morow the King was had to the church accompanied of manie great princes and lordes, in so great triumphe and honour that it may not be recited. And in likewise was apparailed the noble lady Beatrice and conduited of manie noble ladies and damoysels pages with divers liveraies, as well of the kinges as the quenes. In suche wise that at the conioyninge of this noble mariage was made al singuler and inestimable solempnite in the churche. The masse done everi man returned to the palais royal, where they were received in open courte for to take theyr refection. And ther were all the assestentes served of divers delicates and venison, of wines and of al noveltees as plenteously as they could wisshe. And there presentlye for the honour of the noble king Oriant everiche of the Company efforced them to doo honour and service to the noble quene Beatrice, the which was so pleasaunt and acceptable to all the people that echone praised her. And in likewise were made the same daye many other newe games, and service to all honours. Than after with all mirthe and sowne of trumpetes and other armonious instrumentes, the mighti king Oriant and the noble quene Beatrice his wife lay to gether. And on the morrowe was yet made great ioye and exultacion of al other newe pastimes. In this estate lasted the feast and solemnite of the mariage long space in great haboundaunce of giftes, largesse of goodes, and sumptuousnesse of services in suche maner that of long time had not be sene semblable feast, to the pleasure of everi man. But the said Matabrune murmured alway in her selfe bi wicked detraccion, which she put sith in effect. And yf she made ani chere at the said feast it was bi false semblant and maner of doinge, for uniustly and wrongfully she conspired alway some evill upon the noble quene Beatrice.

CHAP. IV.

How the mighty kinge Oriant espoused the notable Beatrice, the which conceyved of him vi. sonnes and a doughter at one burthen.

THUS as the puissaunte kinge Oriant and his noble spouse Beatrice loved enterly together with as rare and true as was possible and in suche wise that there was never many man that loved their wives as he did his. It happened that right shortely after the solempnite of the marriage she conceived vi. sonnes and a doughter at one burthen. And as the king knewe that she was bigge he loved her better, and all the comins were joyfull of it. And on a daye as she was leninge in a windowe of the chambre roiall she sawe a woman in the strete that bare to christning two children that an other woman had conceived and borne at one time. And than familiarly she called the kinge of whome she was right wel beloved and saide, Sir I greatly mervaile me of a thinge that I see yonder. And wherof swete love saide the kinge. Of .ii. children saide she that a woman hath conceyved at one time, which I see yonder borne to christning, mesemeth that it is difficile for a woman to conceive two children without having the company of two men. Sweet love said the kinge, yes right wel, put away the opinion fro your minde. For by the wil of God and after nature a woman may conceive of one man to the nombre of .xii. children at ones, naturally fourmed, and parfite. The whyche wordes precedentes compared ful derely the forenamed quene, by the false and malignus Matabrune. And it is so often sene fortune, that it is better to be stil than to speake evill, whereof the sage saith. That a great speaking is seldom seen pronounced, without to have any faute, wherby he saith after that he never repented him of to little speche. But al thinges promised that king Orient and quene Beatrice loved well together. Than it happened within a while after that tidinges came unto the king that some of his enemies had destroied and slaine of his folke, and all redi had conquered of his londes bi warre. And that soone ynough and easely they had moeved to entre many princes. But what tidinges so ever he had, he made no semblaunt to resist against his contraries. For he was in suche wise enprised and taken in the love of his wife that after the tidinges he was about .vi. moneth that he coulde in no wise leave her, ne purvey anie thinge for the saide affaires, wherbi finabli his enemies came so ferforth in his landes that bi constraint he was driven to prepaire men of warre and to leve his spouse. And consequentely he made to assemble his chivalry to thende that without delaie they might be redy to accompany him in his warres against his enemies the which was doone at his commaundement. Than saw he the time that his wife approched to be delivered, wherfore beningneli he called Matabrun his mother for to be to her as recommaunde and saide, My lady mother, ye see that I am constreyned to depart for to go war upon mi enemies, Ye know also that in likewise of the grace of god my wife hath conceyved and is greate with child, wherfore I pray you if it please you of your benigne grace to have her for recommaunded in al her singular affaires, prayinge you also that in mine absence ye take and kepe her as your doughter in shewing you to be her mother. And I beleve in the pleasure of God that she wyll have you in honour and reverence as mother and obey you as your doughter. Ye se that she is meek as a dove, softe and amiable as a lambe, prudent and vertuous as is possible, wherefore I recommaunde her to you as she that knoweth the great love that is conioyned between us two, and as to mi part I wene that never man loved woman more than I love her. Ye know also the daunger that might come to a woman bigge with childe as she is, wherfore if bi your defaut any inconvenient cam to her I should not be glad ne content with you. Ye have folke of all estates at your pleasure for to commaund them to do all the service and helpe that to her shal be requisit. Therfore madame I put and leve her all in your keping and solicitude. Mi faire sonne said Matabrune thou knowest that what pleaseth the, to me is agreable, and all thi wyl is mine wherfore thou maist well knowe that I shall kepe thy wyfe the queene as my singuler doughter and better than mi selfe. Thou maist in likewise wit that I am she that wolde be most hevy and soroful if any harme came to her. And therfore doubt not but that I shal diligentli do thi pleasure, for I love her with al mi hert for gracious and noble maintene that I se in her dayli encreace, therfore take no thought. Wel madame said he, I thanke you and totally put her in your grace, wherfore in saying adewe I take my leave humblie at you. Now go said she God be thi guide. And thus the king departed from the said Matabrun his mother, whose wordes were not accordaunt to her dedes, for they were al but abuse and false simulacion, like as untruely she shewed bi her curssednes. Than after the king cam to take leave of his noble spouse and in weeping tenderly spake longe with her, and than took an amerous leave of her, in kissing her beningnely so that she fell downe in a swoune. And he tooke her up amiably making a great lamentacion and sorowe. And at her awaking in weeping bi her were made many complaintes, the which were so prudently ordeined that al the nobles knightes and barons wepte profoundly in beholding her for pitie that they had at herte. And than they kissed eche other right curtesli, taking a cardial leave without power to speake any more for sorow. Than he toke leve of her and of the other ladies and damoysells, and without any more tarieng mounted on horse backe for to go to his people against his enemies, where as he did many faire valiantines, and divers great and noble feates of armes.

CHAP. V.

How King Oriant toke leave of the noble quene Beatrice his spouse. And how the fals and pervers Matabrune composed and machined with an other matrone to commise crime and treason toward the sayd noble quene Beatrice.

WHAN the noble kinge hade thus taken his leave of his spouse and of many other of his frendes he went to the warre for to be fight his enemies the paynims and to susteine the faythe catholike of God, and to defende his lande. But of his noble feates of armes that he with his knightes and many other might doo in the sayd warre as true knightes of all mighty God, and of the victorie that they obtayned as nowe I shall leave to speake any ferther to thende that I may retourne to speake of the effecte of the mater. And also the more sooner to com without prolixite to the true cronicles and miraculous histories, of the which I pretende to make singuler mencion. And consequentli procede unto the deduccion of this present booke conteining divers noble feates and noble vertues worthi of memorie and hie recommendacions as after this declared. So it happened that after the departing of king Oriant and that he was out of the limites of Lilefort with al his army and excercite, the right cursed Matabrune considering the absence of her sonne began to compasse the treason and evil that she had conspired to do unto the noble quene Beatrice. And for to come unto her damnable and cursed wil she sent for the midwife that was chosen and deputed to receive of women the children that ben borne on erthe. The whiche midwife cam incontinent at her sending. To whome Matabrune saied. Mi freende I have sent for you for a certaine secrete that I have to tell you and declare under maner of confession. And therfore ye shal swere and promise to me your faith that never to any creature livinge ye shal discouer mi secrete, and that I intende to tell you. But if you wil consent and do it in keping to me faith and promisse I shall give to you so muche golde and silver that you nor none of yours shal never have defaute ne need of goods. And ferthermore I shal helpe you to mary your children and frendes highlie and honorably, whan the old midwife hearde the promesses that Matabrune made to her she consented to her cursed desire saying, Certainlie madame ye may alway saie and commaunde me as to your servaunt, and I promise you mi faith that any thinge what [illegible] it be never to no persone livinge shall it be discovered. Therefore saye that I shall doo as if it were a confession. And verelye said Matabrune yf ye do so in sewer I shal hold to you that I have promised, wherfore in trusting to your words I shal recite unto ye secret, and that that I pretende to do ye know and it is true how my sonne kinge Oriant hath taked the quene Beatrice that present is to his wife, the which was but a simple gentil woman as ye wel know. And ye wote wel that he might have had and may, one richer and more noble of bloude without comparison than she is, seinge and consideringe the magnifike and excellent lignage wherof he is sprunge. But his saide wife hath so enchained and bound him in her lines that he may neither eat, drinke ne rest, but if he be alwaie bi her, and to make short tale, whan his enemies were comen into his londe for to endomage him, for nothinge colde he leave her, in any wise to resist them for his defence, wherfore I wolde that you and I had advised singulerly to turne his hert fro the love of her, and set her in so great indignacion of him that he may aquaint him with some other high and noble lady and mary her. Now ye se that this quene is great with child, wherfore more easely may we cause this diversite and seperacion of his love by some maner. Madame sayde the false olde matrone, even as you please to devise of this mater I accorde me to your wil, and if you seme it good I shal make her to waste and sle the childe within her bodye, and that I shal certifie to the king that she wolde have it slaine. Frende said Matabrune I had thought another meanes more expedient and that should be of right great abominacion and horrour to the kinge as I shall shewe you the maner, ye se that she is mervailousli bigge, wherfore it is to be presupposed that she shal have two or thre children, therfore whan it cometh to the terme of her deliveraunce that shalbe shortely ye shal come to her and by faint semblaunt make maner to presente and offre you al to her service. And whan she shalbe delyvered of her chyldren ye shal give them to me secretely for to transporte them. And I shal ordeine as mani yonge whelpes that I shal make to be taken from under some bitche that hath newli whelped,and by this maner ye shall give her to understande that she hath borne them, and that they ben yssued of her body wherby after we may make her, the king, and all the other barons to beleve that she had the companie of some dogge the which hath engendred the said whelpes, bi the which we shall come to our desire without ani contradiccion. For I have my faithfull servaunte that I have nourished of youth to whome I shall secretelye give the children assone as they be borne, and at mine onlye commaundement he shall go and cast them into the river of whome shal never be mencion. And I promise you madame said the false olde matron that I shal doo even as it pleaseth you to adverte and shewe me, by so cautelus and subtill maner that the werke shal seme to be sure and notarious like as bi our entendement ye have devised.

CHAP. VI.

How the quene Beatrice childed naturallie .vi. fayre sonnes and a doughter, the whiche in theyr birth brought eche of them a chaine of silver miraculously wrought about theyr neckes.

WHAN the time limited and ordeined of almighti god approched that the noble and goodly quene Beatrice should be delivered after the cours of nature, the false matrone aforsaid went and delibered in her selfe to execute and put in effecte her malignus or moste wicked purpose and the cursed treason the which bi the exhortement and counseile of the pervers and ingrate Matabrune she had consented for to prepare and do against the said noble quene Beatrice and her poore innocent children, the whiche neverthelsse were miraculousli kept and preserved fro death bi the devine grace and proteccion of our saviour Jesu Christe, as it shalbe saide here after. And so than at the houre determined that the noble Beatrice felt her oppression with greefe of childinge incontinent the saide false olde midwife was sent for. The whiche when she was comen by false semblaunt reasoned the noble Quene of her affaires as in suche case is accustomed. And she declared to her all the trouth and how she felt her oppressed sore. Than the said matrone by fained blandisshinges gave her good courage in making semblaunt to expose her al to her service, for that she knew that the hour approched to accomplishe her cursed intente. And forthwith was sent for

Matabrune the whiche all redy had prepaired the whelpes for to perfourme the treason. But she comen made maners of great welth to the said noble quene Beatrice. And sodainly in great paine and traivable of bodye she childed .vi. sonnes and a faire doughter, at whose birthe eche of them brought a chaine of silver about their neckes issuing out of their mothers wombe. In which was vertuousli demonstred the pure and singuler dignite of the noble mother and her childe, and that God wolde upon them extend his divine grace. But the evil and detestable herts enforce them alway to pervert and totally adnichil al good werkes. And whan Matabrune saw the .vii. litle children borne having echone a chaine of silver at necke, she made them lightli and secretli to be borne a side by her chamberer of her teachinge, and than toke the vii. litle dogges that she had prepared, and all bloudy laide them under the quene in maner as they had issued of her bodye. And anone the matrone or midwife began to escrie with an high voice sayinge. Ha lady quene here is a great and mervailous mischiefe that to you is presently comen. For I have received vii. stinking dogges the which be issued of your body bi an horroure over detestable. Matabrun in likewise endevored her on the other syde to approve the said iniury (bi her commised and purpensed) saienge, Take away lightly this infamite and make to bere this foulnesse of dogges into the feeldes, and that echone holde secrete this mischiefe and enorme forfaite in suche maner that for the honour and reverence of my sonne it never be knowen ne discovered to any that liveth. Now it is not to be douted that the noble quene Beatrice to whomehad be doone this iniurious treasonne was at that houre greatly travailed and vexed of her bodi so to have childed seven children at one burthen, for a woman is often sore pained to bear one all onely. Wherfore she was as dead in her childing and apparceived nothing of the said treason that was to her done. But whan she was comen againe to her selfe having sumwhat more vigoure than she had before, the false Matabrune began to caste an eye on her by a false and cursed regarde more mortal than of a Baselike, and repreved her of the faute that herselfe had made and commised arguing her without a cause and saide. O unhappi and miserable woman full of shamful harlotri. Here is the midwife that presently hath received .vii. dogges of your body, the whiche I have made to be borne to the feldes for to hid thorrour and infection of your enorme sinne. And therfore confesse here your dede and declare to us if ye have had compani and habitacion with any dogge wherof this prosedeth and we shall kepe your counsaile. And whan the noble Queene heard these wordes she was so sorowfull that she swouned nere for anguisshe. And after that her courage was a litle renued she prayed Matabrune pitiouslye to shew her that, that she said to be issued of her bodie. And incontinent she made to shewe her the .vii. whelpes that she had ordeined for to doo the treason, whereof the noble quene wepte and sobbed profundly in bearing her culpe beholding them in axing mercy for that she had not done. But that not withstanding the false Matabrune alwai redargued her in appropriang the crime to her sayinge, unhappi woman thou ought to be brente whan thou haste willed to conceive with a dogge. Ha madame said she I thought it never, ne the case never hapened me. And therfore I pray you give me no more great mater of sorowe than I suffre presentli, but thanked be God mi creatour sith that it pleaseth him to be thus. For it is yet in his might to transmut me or anye other that him pleaseth into some dombe beast and that, that pleaseth him ought to please us. Than departed the false Matabrune, and the wicked matron bi faint simulacion made semblaunce, to recomfort her saying. Alas madame take not so much sorow that ye be not worse therefore, for if it please God we shall do in such wise that your noble spouse king Oryant in no wise shall have cognicion. And it shalbe kept so secrete that no sclaunder shall come therof. Ha swete love saide the good quene, never will the king take any consolacion with me, for he wil charge me of this offence without ever to pardon me, and wyll iudge me culpable of death. But if it pleased his grace to assigne mi poore life in sume religion for ever to serve God and do penaunce for my sinnes, alas I wolde take it in pacience and pray for him, and put paine to apease the yre of God which I so streatched on me, wherfore I praye you humblie that ye wil require mi lady that she will impetret his grace of the king mi faithful spouse. And thus suffred the good quene anguisshe on all sides. For she was betrayed of them which made maner to be sorowfull and have compassion of her mischiefe, and of thiniuries that them self had made bi their untrue courages.

CHAP. VII.

How Markes bare the vii children into a forest and left them on his mantell.

And after that the false olde woman had parfet and doone their treason that they had entreprised as said is Matabrune called a squire of hers named Markes and said, Markes my true secretarie it behoveth that presently ye doe me a service the whiche I shall declare to you. Madame said he it is wel reason that I obeye to you, for I have received mi welth and honour of your grace only, wherfore knowe that I shal accomplisshé with right good herte that that ye please to commaunde me. Now Markes said she mi freende it behoveth that to me ye be true and secret in that I have to do with you, for it must not be knowen ne reveled to no persone that liveth upon paine of your life. And also if ye hide and kepe it secrete I shal give you goodes ynough. Lady said Markes comaunde what it pleaseth you, I promise you to be true and loyal. It is of trouth sayd Matabrune that the quene of late hath childed .vi. sonnes and a doughter, the which children hath brought eche of them a chaine of silver about their neckes, which me semeth an evil signe and that in theyr age veril and discret thei mai be murderers or theves, wherfore I have advised that it is better to drowne them or make them to die in their childe hode than to have a greater sclaunder at the last and to eschewe the sorowe that he might have hadde I have given her to understande that .vii. litell dogges ben yssued of her body, that whiche I have made to slee and cast into the feildes. And I prai you on my peril and my wil to take the .vii. children and goo kyll them or caste them in some river, in suche wise that never be tidinges of them. Ladie said the Markes it shalbe done wholy as ye have pleased to ordein me, and I promise you that of these .vii. children shal never be any mencion. And than at the commaundement of Matabrune Markes mounted on his horse, and toke the .vii. childred as he was ordeined, the whiche he toke and wrapped in his mantell and in a great haste transported them out of the citie of Lilefort. And whan he was bout .x. mile out of the said citie he entred into a forest he was enspired with the grace of God for to descend of his horse, and to behold how the poore children did. And whan he was descended he laide them in the saide plaine uppon his mantel, and than began for to beholde them, And whan he sawe them so faire so pleasaunt, and so wel fourmed he had great pitie at his hert. And considered in himselfe that sith that they had brought those chaines of silver out of their mothers wombe that God hath chosen and ordened them to some perfection of welth and excellent honour. And thus as bi love and benignite he behelde these poore children they begane all to laugh and to beholde him sweetli. And than he was in suche wise moeved with pitie and compassion that he delibered in him selfe to do them no harme but by him selfe commaunded them into the holy garde proteccion and mercy of God in manere of speaking to them sayinge. Nowe I praye to God fayre children that he wil kepe and preserve you from al evil and encombraunce by his holi benigne grace and that shortly be confounded all your enemies, and the false olde witche that hath sent you hither for to purchace your death and distruction. Alas poore chyldren it greueth me sore for to leve you here in this place as desolate, wandred and habandoned of your blode. But I hope that he that hath willed to creat and fourme you to your good mothers body wil not leve you dispurveyed, and fare ye wel to God I commaunde you children, for I shall se you nevermore. And thus amyably took the said Markes leave of the vii. litle children the which at his departing took theym in his armes and pitiousli kissed them in weping tenderly with salt teres. And than he retourned to Lilefort makinge muche sorow inwardly for them.

CHAP. VIII.

How the .vii. children wer found in the forest by a devoute hermit named Helyas.

Incontinent after that he had thus taken his leave of the children he retourned to Lilefort where as the pervers Matabrune came to fore to meet him for to knowe tidinges of her cursed wyll sayinge. Now my freende Markes have ye done mi commaundement of the .vii. children as I bad you. Madam said he, know you that ye shal never have tidinges of them for I have al to hewed their membres and casted them in the river. And she said mi frende ye have done well and I shall reknoledge the pleasure or it be longe. For that ye have ben faithfull to me I shall contente you well. And whan my sonne Kinge Oriant shalbe retourned I shal do so muche towarde him that he shall make to die his espouse wherof mi herte shalbe glad, and I shalbe avenged to my gree. And with these wordes departed Matabrune and the fornamed Markes one fro the other.

Thus leave we to speake of them, and returne to speake of the children the whiche were in the forest dolorouslye wayling and as all dead for honger. But by the grace divine of God ther came into that place an holie and devout hermite named Helias, the whiche had his habitacion in the said forest. And whan he apperceived the .vii. poore litle children there abandoned and weping for honger: he had so great sorowe at his hert that he wepte for pitie and compassion to beholde them, wherfore he toke and lapped them tenderly in his mantel and with al their chaines at their neckes he bare them into the litle hous of his hermitage, and there he warmed and sustened them of his poore goodnes as well as he coulde.

CHAP. IX.

How the good and devoute hermit prayed to our Lorde for the ayde and succour of the .vii. poore children, whose praiers were exalted.

After that the good hermit had doone his possibilite to susteine and rechaufe the .vii. litle chyldren of the noble Quene Beatrice to him unknowen. He seinge the indigent puerylite of them had great feare that they should die for faute of natural foode and had none hope but only in the marcie of God. And than for them he made his praiers saying humbly Soverayne God allmighty very rectour and gobernatour of all thinges that by thy divine grace wylled to repast the children of Israel in deserte with manna of heven. And that in like wise susteined the good prophet Daniel in the pitte of Lions. And that also sithen in the new testament hast repasted fyve thousand men besyde the women and children with five barley loves and two fisshes. I supplie thee and require humbly that bi thi piti, mercy and swetnes it pleaseth thee to repast and susteine these .vii. poore litle children the whiche bi thi grace I have found naked and deinge for hunger in this forest, to thend that whan thou hast nourisshed them thei may devoutlie serve and honour the as thou knowest. And incontinent was exalted to the oraison of the devoute hermit before God, for miraculously there came into his house a faire white goat, the wiche beningnely came nere to the .vii. little children in presenting to them her milke, and ther she gave them sucke naturally as their nource. And than the good hermite knewe clerely that God had vertously sent her for the nourisshing and sustentation of the poore litle children that he had founden wherof he thanked God greatly of his divine savitude And thus this white goate gave milke sufficiently to them and than retourned to the wood. And so longe she gave them souke that they began to gro and waxe somwhat stronge and folowedher inthewoodand aboute the hermitage.

CHAP. X.

Howe the .vii. children were miraculuslie nourisshed of a white goate sent bi Goddes grace. And how Matabrune accused falsly the good quene Beatrice to king Oriant her spouse.

WHAN the forsaid children were come to age of puerilete the devoute hermite Helyas made and appropryed to eche of them a cote of leaves of the trees or of suche as he coulde get. And so they were playing within the forest where as thei gathered fruite to eate with theyr bread, for in that pointe were they nourisshed under the grace of God, and by the dilygence of the good hermete which with good herte administred the bread of the almesses geven to him. Now it happened by space of time that king Oriant their father retourned victorious outof the warre that he had agaynst his enemies whan he left his good queene bygge with the .vii. children habandoned of their bloud. And when the false olde Matabrune knew that the good kyng Oreant her sonne was comen she went agaynst him makinge the good mother and faynynge as she wolde weepe she began to saye for to accomplishe her fiers courage. A my most deare sonne ye be right hertly welcome. I am all joyful that ye be retourned in joye and health accompanied of your barons. But on the other parte my herte is so heavy and sorye for your wife and for that is to her hapened that lytle lacketh that it ne breaketh. And when the king hearde her speake so he was as abasshed and sayd, why madam is ther any harme come to my wyfe, is she dead or how. Ha my sonne said she nay: but the case is much more enorme the whiche I maye not ne dare not wel reherce for the horror and abhomynacion of the dead. And also I had lever that an other tel it you than I for it is wel knowen of all your servauntes. Forsothe said the kinge yf ony evyll be happed it is more decent and convenable that ye tel me than an other with whom I should be angry. Ha my chyld syth it pleaseth you so I shal tel you, but it greveth mi hert for the honour of you and yours. Know ye that when ye departed fro this countrey I thought that your wife had conceyved a chyld of you, but she had conceyved of a dogge the whiche is a foule sine. For here is the midwyfe that hath received .vii. litle doges of her bodi the which I have made to kyl and be casten in the feldes for to undo the sclaunder, wherfor ye ought to mak her die and cast in a fyre. And the matron was with her for to approve the lye. And whan the king heard these wordes affermed by false tongues he had so great sorow at his hert that none might have more. And bi great dispite he demaunded where that she was. And Matabrune said that she was recluse in her chambre, wherout she durst not come for shame of hir vilanous dead. And than the kinge entred into a chambre with one of his knightes and began inwardly discomforted to say. Alas what is happened to me. Alas what doloure is this, hath mi wife conceived .vii. dogges. Hath she habandoned her to brute beastes she that I thought had be the honour and beaute of al ladies. Hath she betraied me that I loved more than ever man loved woman. Am I bi her dishonoured and brought to confusion in mi realme. Why hath not God avaunced my daies where as I was upon mine enemies. I was wel borne in an unhappie houre for to se nowe this obprobre. Alas who shal counseil me Mi God almighti helpe me, for I require no more to approche her that I have so muche loved. In this sharpe anguishe reconforted him the knight in the beste wise that he might. But he was so inwardli disconforted that he laide him on a bedde where as he fell on slepe for sorow and melancoly. On the other part was the noble quene Beatrice in an other chambre where as she made no lesse sorow than her noble spouse. Than came to her a squier that long time had served her, and declared to her al the maner howe king Oriant was returned fro the warre, wherof she was greatlie abasshed, and axed the squier if in anie wise she had ben spoken of. And he answered yea: and recited to her al how the perverce Matabrune, and the false and disloyal matrone had tolde and affermed to the noble kinge Oriant of her fait. And than she began for to make her complaint to almighti God and his glorious mother sayinge. Ryght swet lady and sacred mayden mother of the savyour and redemptor Jesu Chryst what syne myght I have commysed towarde thy dere sonne Jesu Christ that .vii. dogges ben yssued out of my bodi wherbi I have lost the love of my husband the moste pleasaunt and the best that ever woman might have chosen. Alas soverayn kinge Jesus Chryst that for to washe the crimes and offences of all poore sinners hath shede wather and bloud fro your precious sid wherof your most worthi mother received so great dolour at her hert I besech you that it wil please you to clense, wasshe, and purge me of all my sines and crimes that ever I commised agaynst you. And as trulye as ye comforted your swet mother the day of your holye resurreccion, whan fyrst and before all other ye shewed you to her in body impassible and gloryfied and consequently to the other holy ladyes and to your most happy apostles I besech you humbly that ye will reconfort your servaunte inding to requir you, and to restablisshe her to the good grace and love of her true husband and spouse to whom she never thought to do wrong ne offence in any maner. And thus she abode hevi and sorrowfull in her chambre incessauntly requiringe our swet saviour Jesu Christe and the glorious Virgin Mary his right worthy mother for to impetre and get mercy.

CHAP. XI.

How kinge Oriant assembled his counseyle for to know bi what maner he ought to entreate the quene his wife the whiche wrongfully and without cause was iniuried of the parvers Matabrune mother to kynge Oriant.

THE kinge Oriant beinge reposed in melancoly as it is saide made me incontinent to assemble his counsell, that is to wit Dukes, erles, knightes and other lordes of renowne, with the bisshop and prelate of the church. And whan they were al assembled in the consistory the kinge arose and began to speake in saying. Faire lordes I have made you all to assemble in this place for to discute of a mater, the which to me is hevi and grevous to supporte. It is of trouthe notorily that sith my retourning it is shewed to me and affermed that my wife the which ye know duringe mi viage hath be delivered of .vii. litle whelpes, which she hath conceyved of a dogge, as it is presupposed, wherfore it were shame to me if ever I retourne to her by copulacion carnall. And I wil that bi your advise this maner be consulted, and howe I may acheve it. And for to answere of this mater was prefered, the bishop that said. Sir king under correccion of you and my lordes here present I shal saie as be semeth of that, that is proposed here of the quene your noble spouse the whiche is saide to have conceived .vii. dogges, me semeth that bi iustice she ought not to receive death. And here is the reason wherfore. It is possible that in her slepe be comen to here som beast that hath done her this outrage without her knowledge and consent, wherefore she is in nothing culpable. And fertermore your noble person hath touched often times to hers after the constitucion of the sacrament of mariage. Wherfore me semeth under reverence that ye ought not consent to her death, but howbeit ye mai make her dyligently to be kept in some honest place bi maner of pryson, and of the surplus let the iudgment to God that is the true iudge and only retribuer of good and evil, and the trouth shall finabli be knowen apartly. Of this counsel the king was somwhat consoled in his herte, for he had alwaye a certaine love to his wife. But after that arose another knight having a fiers Lions courage sayinge there against what sir wolde ye leave this woman thus seing the dishonour and shame that she hath doone to you? yf she be but a loneli put in prison ye mai never mari you to a nother wife and bi consequence this pusaunt realme should be left without heire of your body. Bi the which thinge considered if I were beleved she should be brent in a great fire, as it is well knowen that she hath ynough deserved it, and than ye might mari a more noble lady than she is, the which wolde appease the sorow that he have for this. Of this counsel king Oriant was not over glad, but without shewinge great semblaunt as he that desired to save the bodye of the good quene concluded this mater saying. Now lordes I shal tel you in giving you advertence, if it so were that she be culpable of death yet have I vowed and agaïne warde made promesse to God that she being dead or alive never to espouse other wife, for ony treasours or realmes that any man living may give or habandon to me and thus I certifie it you. Than al the nobles and great lords of the asistence concluded with a comune accord that it was convenable bi this maner that she helde aloneli pryson in likewise as the bishop had delibered. And at their advice the kinge ordeined two of his knightes that they shoulde put the quene his wife into some gracious prison and that she shoulde be honestly served and administred of meate and drinke as to her noble estate apperteined and that they should charge her for to praye to God for him, and to advertise her how he had preserved and defended her from death. And whan the cruel Matabrun had knowen the deliberacion of the bisshop she spake to him reverentli, and greatly iniured him for his counseile that he had given to save the quenes life. After that came the to knightes to the noble quene Beatrice and benignely at the commaundement of the kinge and his counseil put her in a faire chambre bi maner to holde prison and there they reveled to her al that had ben said and ordined bi the said counseyl. And how the kinge had defended her from peril, and yet moreover had commaunded to entreat her honistly and that she should praie to God for him, wherof greatly she thanked and praised God which seinge the case wherin she wend to be culpable had saved his life. And thus paciently in wepinges she abode in prison. But she recommaunded her oft to the kinge thanking him of his grace done to her for the offence to her imposed, wherbi she was obliged for ever to pray to God for him. And also she recommended her humbli to God and to the glorious virgin Marie in al her nedes abiding long in that place shitte, tell that one of her sonnes named Helias delivered her out of prison as it shalbe saide here after.

CHAP. XII.

How the devout hermite Helias baptized the .vii. litle children in his hermitage.

For this time we shal leave to speake of the noble kinge Oriant and of the noble quene Beatrice his true and faithfull spouse for some thing right digne and worthi of memory that I hope to saie of their .vii. litle children esclaves, nourished, and alimented in the poore hous of the good holy and devoute hermite named Helias.

After that the .vii. children were nourished and alaced of the saide white goate miraculously sene of God as before is rehersed. The above said devoute hermite to thend that they shouldbe acceptable to God bi the vertue of wasshing in the holi water sacramental made them to be baptized and christened at his good wil and pleasure. And of the said .vii. litle children there was one amonge the other the which to him was right beauteous and agreable and that pleased him muche, the whiche he named and called Helias after his owne name. And whan that they were in the age of theyr pleasaunt and fresshe grene yougth thei reane all about sporting and playinge in the said forest about the trees and floures only cladde and habitued with poore coates made of greene leaves of the trees of the said forest, and were barefeted everichone without ony covering upon their heades in colde and heat, and in this estate wente they alway together the one with the other.

CHAP. XIII.

How one of the yomen of the hunte of the pervers Matabrune founde the .vii. children in the said forest, the which tolde of them to Matabrune.

Upon a time it fortuned that a yoman of Matabrunes hunte named Savarie went for to chase and hunt in the said forest in the whiche dwelled the devoute hermite Helias. Than almighti God our Lorde willed that the sayd yoman should finde the said children of the noble king Oriant and of the good quene Beatrice his wife. The which children satte under a tree echone having a chaine of silver as it is said, under the said tree they gathered wild appelles and eat them with bread. The yoman beheld them gladlie and salued theym beningnely, and they answered nothing but ranne awaie before him. Than he sued and ranne after them unto the hermitage, the better and singulerly to knowe and consider their estate and their maner. And whan the good hermitte sawe the yoman renning after the .vii. children he salued him and said. Good frende I pray you for the love of God that ye doo no harme to these poore children. Nay for God good father said he: But I am greatly admervailed to consider theyr estate, and of the silver chaines that I see aboute their neckes. My frende saide the good hermite know ye for trouthe that even so as ye see I found them as yonge children new borne in this forest. And for to nourisshe theim miraculously came into this pleace a white goate, the which hath well susteyned and given theim her tetes to suke her milke the space of three yeres. And also to my power I have also diligently kept them winter and somer. Faire father said the yoman God yeld you good retribucion, and than he departed fro the holy hermitte, in taking leave benignely of him and of the .vii. children. And whan the yoman was retourned to Lilefort he went and salued Matabrune and to her he recounted how he had founde .vii. yonge children in the forest havinge chaines of silver about their neckes, the whiche wer sitting under a tre in gathering of wild apples. Of whose words Matabrune was greatly admervailed, wherfore she enquired of him diligently the trouthe. And whan she understode him she wist wel that thei were the .vi. sonnes and the doughter that the noble Quene Beatrice had borne and conceived of king Oriant. The which bi her wickednesse she wende to have made to die, but God our soveraine helper that alwaie saveth them that he hath chose, had kept them from all harmes under his holy proteccion for he is the iust iudge stronge and pacient the which abideth the yre of his vengeaunce unto the houre bi him ordeined. And ye ought to wite that Matabrune was ful sorye and pertourbed of these tidinges, wherfore she called secretly the said yoman and saide Come hither my freende I wold not for no treasour but that I had heard these tidinges that thou hast brought. But if thou wilt have my grace and that I gyve the great goodes it behoveth thou take suche felawes with thee as thou wilt, and forthwith go and slea the .vii. children that thou hast founde in the forest. And if thou doo it not at mi pleasure and commaundement I promise thee and be thou sure that I shall make thee dye an evil death. But if thou obey me be thou also sure that I shal rewarde thee and thi felawes in suche wyse that ye shall never have need. Madame said the yoman I shall doo your desyre, and I promyse you to slea them without doubt, so that ye shal know it expressely. Well than said she it suffiseth, go and doo your diligence. And than Matabrune full of woodnesse and furoure came to Markes that she had first ordeyned for to bere the .vii. litel children out of Lilefort and to make them die or to drowne them in a river, the which he had not done for pitie that he had to beholde them when he left them in the forest, and put out his eyen and handled him so that many wende that he had be dead.

CHAP. XIV.

How at the commaundement of Matabrune an houndes man named Savary came for to slea the .vii. litle chyldren of king Oriant unknowen in the Forest, where as they were transmued into swannes.

At the commaundement of the pervers Matabrune her

yoman or houndes man named Savary tooke .vii. felowes strong and mighti with him for to put in execucion that, that unto them was commaunded for to slea the .vii. children of the noble King Oriant and his good spouse Beatrice. And so as the sayd yoman and his felawes passed bi a village they sawe muche people assembled, wherfore thei drew nere. And whan they were approched Savarie demaunded wherfore they were so assembled. And they answered for to see a woman executed and brent by Justice. And wherfore sayd Savary, what harme hath she doone. And they sayd for that she hath murdred and slaine the childe that she bare in her owne bely. Than Savarie departed thens, and by those wordes remenbred the execucion and the murther that he went to doo on the .vii. smal children of the king and of the quene, wherby he was much esmayed and began to refraine his courage and that which he had undertaken to doo in saying to his felowes. My brethren and felawes here is a fayre glasse or spectacle for us. Howe said thei? Have ye not seen said he that these people go for to doo justice and put to death that unhappy woman for that she hath murthred and slaine that childe that she bare in her owne body. And therfore faire frendes ye wot that my lady Matabrune hath sent us hither for to go occise and put to death .vii. faire litle children the which the other daye I founde in the middes of the forest, echone of them havinge a faire chayne of sylver at his necke, but cursed be he of God and confounded may he be that any harme shall doo to them. Beholde this woman that they go to brenne and execute for one only childe that she hath murdred and was her owne. Consider we than what punicion might renne to us for to put to death the .vii. chyldren of the whiche I have spoken, the which to us ne to her that commaundeth cannot hinder ne bere any domage. Syr houndes man sayd his felowes ye spake wiseli, and we be al of the same advise. They shall have no harme sayd he: but this wee maye do for to appease and contente the intsaciable iniquite of the perverce Matabrune, we shall go to the .vii. chyldren and take al onely the chaines of silver that ben at theyr neckes, and than bere them to the cursed Matabrune and make her to beleve that we have slaine and put them to death by the tokens of the sayd chaines. To the which thinge accordid his felawes as good and true counceile. And thus delibered they entred into the forest and came unto the litle hermitage where as were dwelling the said litell chyldren with the devoute hermite Helias. But at that houre they ne founde but .vi. of the said children, for the good hermite was gone to aske meate in the villages there aboute and had led with him his godsonne one of the .vii. children for to beare the breade and suche as was given to him in the countrey for fode of him and the .vii. unknowen children. And whan the houndes man Savari and his felowes came nere the .vi. children abiden in the hermytage they set handes on them and toke them for to take away the chaines of sylver that eche of them had at their neckes, but the poore children began to crye piteously for feare that they had. Than sayd Savary. Doubt you of nothinge faire children, for we shall doo you no harme if it please God. And in this saying: thei toke the chaines of their neckes. And as soone as their chaines were of they were al transmued in an instaunt in faire white swannes by the divine grace, and began to flee in the ayre through the forest making a piteous and lamentable crye, wherof Savary and his felowes were so afrayed that they fel to the erthe as in a swonne. And whan they were risen in trimblinge all for feare they sayde one to another alas what have we founde heere? veri God comforte us, what meaneth this that those .vi. children ben transmued into swannes. Ha false, disloyall, and traytresse Matabrune by thee have we over grevously offenced God. And bi thee have we merited right greveous punicion, cursed be thou that ever sent us hither into this forest for to commyt this grevous offence and evill. Departe we hence said Savarie for all to longe have we ben here, we have founden but .vi. of the children but if the other were here present he should have no harme of us ne displeasure. Returne we lightli with out shewing to ony of this mervaylous adventure. But for to render answere of our commission to that cursed and perverce Matabrune we shal bere to her these .vi. chaines of Silver and shal give her to understande that we have lost one by the way as we retourned. And thus they ben departed out of the forest and ben retourned to Lilefort where as thei have founde Matabrune, to whome thei have certified to have slaine the .vii. children, and for a witnesse they her presented the vi. chaines that they had aboute theyr neckes. And have geven her to understand that they had lost one by the waie, wherof Matabrune nighe enraged and waxed mad for angre that they had not brought al seven and in her woodnesse repreved and thretened them sharpli. But for to have peace they promised and offred to her to yelde and restore, the value therof, wherof she somwhat contented her, and gave them some rewarde for their traveile. And whan Matabrune had the said chaines: she sent to seke for a goldesmith to whome she commaunded to make a cuppe of the chaines. And as the goldesmith had put one in the fyre to approve the silver: it multiplied in suche maner that it alone molten weyed as muche and more than all the vi. together whereof the sayd goldesmyth and all his meyny had great mervayle and were all abasshed, wherfore the sayde goldesmith gave the five other chaynes of silver unto his wife for to kepe and set aparte within her chambre or coffre. For the sayd onlye chayne the whiche he had so molten was suffycyente for to make two suche cuppes as that, that Matabrune had ordeined him to make so he forged two cuppes of the which he withheld one for himselfe with the v. other chaines of sylver that he kepte tyl a certayne time ordeyned of God as ye shal heare. And than he brought the other and presented it to Matabrune that was all admervayled how he might have forged a cuppe so great and materyall as it was of so lytle silver as she semed to have gyven, but there as God lyste to worke nothinge abydeth impossyble to his divyne wyll.

CHAP. XV.

How the good hermite Helyas retorned to his hermitage with his godsonne one of kynge Oryant sones, and founde not the other chyldren transmued into white swannes.

For to ensue the orygynall of that I have entreprysed to wrytte I shal returne to speake of the devoute Hermite Helyas and of his godsonne one of kyng Oryant sonnes, and of the paciente Quene Beatryce. It is to be knowen that anon after that the vii. children were transmued into white swannes retourned into the hermitage the abovesayde hermite and his godsonne Helias, the which founde not the v. sonnes and the doughter that they had lefte there whan they departed wherof they were mervaylously displeasaunte. And than they began to cal them with hye voyce within the forest, but none aunswered. The good Hermite sought on the one syde, and his godsonne on the other syde on all partes of the forest as longe as the day lasted, but they founde them not wherfore thei ceassed not to make great dole and sorowe all the nyght longe. And on the morowe yonge Helyas began agayne to seeke his brethern and his sister weeping and wailing dolorouslye as all discomforted through the forest. And so longe he wente hither and thyther that he arived nigh to a stagne or ponde where as he sawe vi. fayre swannes all white swimming on the water, the whiche were his bretheren and syster so transmued by the wyll of God but it was unknowen to him, how wel that naturallie he tooke pleasure to beholde them, wherfore he approched to them and they came and feested him, and he gave them bread that he had and stroked playne theyr fethers with his hande by nature that moeved him therto. And as it is notably recited in the cronycle of this present history the sayde yonge Helyas theyr brother went to visite them every daye, and did bere them to eate of the bread that was given to him for goddes sake. And whan the hermite had apperceived hym divers times so goynge to the sayde stagne he demanded him why he went so diligently theither to sporte him. And he prayed him not to be displeased, for he had founde vi. fayre white swannes the which made the greatest chere that was possible to see. Now was the sayd Helias so faire bigge, and wel fourmed of bodie and membres that his godfather the good Hermite tooke a singuler pleasure for to beholde him, for he was as parfite in his adolence that he semed almost a man viril in his force. He ne knew his pareyl in prudence of understanding. There was not a wilde beast but he tooke lightly bi renning. He was honest and well manered in all his gestes, and well attempred in his force and noble hardinesse, and all bi thinfusion of the divine grace. For he never had conversed ne haunted the worlde. And yet was he sufficientli instructe and right well learned in science and good maners in suche wise that his godfather had enterprised and was delibered for to dedie him to the service divine in office of a preste, til that the aungel of heaven came downe and reveled to the said good and devout hermite that God our soverayne Lord almightie had otherwise ordayned for as it shall be expressly reherced here after in this present History.

CHAP. XVI.

How the false and parverce Matabrune made malegnelously to afferme by an untrue knight named Makayry that the noble Quene Beatrice had forfayted with a dogge.

DURING this time was the good quene Beatrice incessably deteined of prison, the whiche paciently in her adversite alwaie praised the name of God in praying for her spouse the noble king Oriant, and that it wolde please him to succur her. But the perverce Matabrune sought incessauntly the meanes and occasions that she might for to make her die. So it happed that she had in her courte a knight disloial and wicked named Makaire the which she suborned so with money that she made him to tell and afferme to king Oriant that the good quene Beatrice his wife had be knowen and habited of a dogge, whereof she had conceyved vii. litle whelpes, of whom after is made mencion. And that she had moreover delibered to poyson and make the king to die and his mother Matabrun bi venim and other poyson: that he said that the noble quene Beatrice had ordeined to do it with all, wherto the good quene never thought, for she loved as truli her husband as ever woman loved hers, and wolde not have done ony untrouth to his body to have died therfore. But the evyll and wicked folke paine them selfe alway to noye and do accombraunce to them that ben good and loved of God. And whan the noble king Oriant had heard the fals and untrue reporte that bi this cursed knight was affermed he was merveylously sori and angry of the tidinges. Wherfore the more stedfastly to afferme this lie the said fals Makaire presented him to fight against all men that wolde say or defende the contrari of that he had reported, wherof the king was more angry than before and totalye dispited against his wife, the which was in nothing culpable of al that she was accused. So he swore God and hys othe that for these tidinges she should die, but if that there were any that wolde defende her therof in champe of bataile. Than went there a noble squire and tolde from ende to ende al these evil tidings to the good quene and how the king had sworne his oth that she shold die grevously therfore, but if there were any that wolde susteine her quarel against the forenamed Makayre, and whan the good quene heard these pitious tidinges litle lacked that she ne died for sorowe, wherfore al lamentably she began to complaine her sayinge. Alas I have anguisshe on all sides. Alas now see I well appertly that I am falsli betrayed, and yet I know no man living that for to susteine and defende mi right wolde in any maner dispose himselfe. But I shall retourne me to my sweete Lord Jesu Christ the whiche is the only piller and foundament of all verite, and I have hope that he wil helpe me. Alas mi God mi creatour that by your divine wil reised the spirite of yonge Daniell for to returne to the judiement and to save fro death the noble ladi Suzanne the which was publikeli led in justice bi to fals iudges, the which with wronge and uniustly had accused her of the vice and sinne of advoutry wherin she never thought, as afterward before al the people was notably knowen and approved the trouth by the good Daniel the which yelded the two judges al confused. Thou knowest my soveraine God in likewise that wrongfulli and without cause I am accused to mi good and faithful spousy king Oriant, wherfore I beseche and require thee humbli that it wil plaise thee to kepe and preserve me fro shamefull death and confusion of the crime and sinne that I am accused of, wherof thou knowest me innocent and nothing worthy. And than benignely recomforted her the said squire, and after in weeping for pitie he departed humbly from her companie. And the good quene abode alway dolorously reclused and shitte in prison unto the time that God the which in everi place succoureth his servauntes divineli had purveied and ordeined as afterwarde ye shall heare.

CHAP. XVII.

How the aungell of God announced to the devoute hermite Helias that the vi. sonnes and a doughter the whiche he had founde in the forest were king Oriantes children, and that he shoulde sende yonge Helias to prove the trouth.

Now hath God our soveraine lorde hearde and exalted

the devout praier of the noble Quene Beatrice, and hath sent his holy aungel fro heaven to tel and declare to the devoute hermite Helias that the six sonnes and a doughter which he had founde in the forest wher the children of king Oriant, and that his good spouse Beatrice had conceived them of him, and had childed them at on only time. But the perverse Matabrune made him to beleve bi the midwife that she had borne and conceived vii· dogges which were issued of her wombe. And also that the swannes that his godsonne Helias hent everi day to feed and susteine with bread in the ponde wher his v. brethern and his sister in such wise transmued whan Savary Matabrunes houndes man and his felowes tooke awaie the chaines the which they had about theyr neckes as he hath. And that he should sende his god sonne for to befight the false Makaire that with wronge and without cause had accused his good mother the saide quene by the enhortement of the perverce Mattabrun that wolde have made hym to dye and the other vi. children, whan she charged a servaunt of hers for to slea or make them perisshe, but for pitie that he had to beholde them he left them in the forest where as the devoute hermite found them. And sith Matabrune made to put their good mother in prison the which al redy hath ben so deceived the space of xvi. yere, wherby he would obteine victorie and justice of his enemies, and bi succession of time his brethren and his sister should returne into their owne fourme and nature humaine as they were before. And of theim should come a great fruit. For of his lignage should descende Godfrey of Boulion, that for to agment the holy faith of God shal conquere the holy lande of Jherusalem. So descended the hevenly aungel at the holy commaundement of our lorde, and came to announce unto the devoute hermit al that to him was ordeined of God as is before said. And whan he had doone his message he returned and the good hermite abode alone al ravisshed in spirit. But after as al reioiced he called beningly his godsonne Helias, the whiche came fro the stagne where as he had given bread to the swannes like as he was accustomed bi natural inclinacion, and recited to him all that the aungel had announced to him, saying: Mi godsonne, mi frende I wish not that ye were of so noble a bloud as ye be, wherof I ought highly to praise and honour you as wel for the honoure that God hath doone to you as for your noble potentes. And how said he godfather, what tidinges have ye heard? wite ye mi lorde and mi frende said the good hermite that an aungell of heaven cam to me that anounced and told to me in goddes name that ye be sonne of the right noble king Oriant and of the good quene Beatrice his faithful spouse and your mother. But it behoveth that bi the divine commaundement of God to you be declared bi me all the tidings as the aungel tolde me. So ye ought to know that your mother conceived you al vii. togither of your noble father, and sith childed of you at one only time. But the perverce Matabrun stepdame of your noble mother bi the consentment of the midwife that you your v. brethren, and your sister reseived of her bodi made her to beleve that vii. whelpes were issued of her wombe the whiche thei had unfaithfulli prepaired, and so wende your said mother. For Matabrune gave you incontinent to one of her servaunts whome she charged to sle or droune you. But the pitie that he had to beholde you moeved him to leve you al naked and nere dead for honger in the same place where as I at first founde you. Than shorte time after the said Matabrun harde some tidinges of you, and sent some folke againe for to destroy you, but thei founde as than but your v. brethern and your sister, from whome thei toke the chaines of silver that echone of them had aboute their necke as ye have, and forthwith bi the divine wil of God thei were transmued into white swannes, and ben they to whome he gave every day bread in the stagne. But in time coming they shal retourne into theyr owne nature humaine as they were afore, and shal make great fruite, but for the thinges beforesaid your father commaunded to put and hold your good mother in prison, the which hath be captive the space of xvi. whole yeres. And now againe Matabrune hath so much done bi money that an untrue knight named Makaire of your fathers courte hath affermd that she had conseived and habited with a dogge, and that she had willed to kill and enpoysen him and the said Matabrune wherfore the king hath sworne to make to die your good mother, if none be founde that against the said Makaire wil susteine her honour and hir quarell in campe of bataile. Wherfore bi me is ordeined of God that I admonest and warne you to go and upholde her good right against the forenamed Makaire and al the other that willinglie hath blamed her. And without doubt ye shal obteine victory and triumph against al her false enemies, where bi she shalbe delivered fro prison and restablisshed unto greater honour than she had before. And also there shall issue of your lignage a valiaunte and chivalrous prince that shal be named Godfrey of Boulion, the whiche in his age virill shall conquere the holy londe of Jherusalem, and other countreis of beyond the sea for ever to augment and encrease the right highe and puissaunt name of Jesus, and the holi faith catholike. And whan yonge Helias (wisely taught and enspiredof God) heardhis godfather speake in suche maner of that he had commaunded of God, he conformed him al holy to his divine wil and loving he delibered him to go see the father that had engendred him, and the good mother that had childed him, and of whose body he his v. brethern, his sister miraculously issued. And after al these thinges premised to eschue prolixite the hermit and his godsonne disposed them that he should go so clothed in leaves and barfoted as he was with a simple staffe in his hande to succour his said mother, to thend that more apertli the dyvine and vertuous miracle of God should be shewed in him and than in weping thei departed amiably. And at their departing yonge Helias ententively besought his godfather that it wolde please him diligentli to feed with bread the whit swannes his brethren and sister. And the good hermite promised him to do his best until it pleased God to dispose for them as he had ordeyned. And than yonge Helias departed and went toward the citie of Lilefort for to accomplisshe the holy commaundement of God.

CHAP. XVIII.

How king Oriant sent for the good quene Beatrice his wife for to expose to her that wherof she was accused and to condempne her to death. And how Helias his sonne arived at the palais of his father for to defende and succour his mother fro death.

In this time came the day that the noble king Oriant had decreed for to condempne and make to die his good spouse Queene Beatrice by the false accusacions that of her uniustli had ben made. So the knight sent for her to the prison for to make to expose in her presence the cryme of the whiche by the sayde Makarie she had be wrongfully accused. And whan she was led thither publykely before many noble knightes and men of councel that there were presente assembled: she began incontinent to salue the king her husbande enclining her knees in requiringe of mercy so pytiouslye that al the noble knightes had pitye to beholde her, and in lyke wise the kinge was so sory of here state that with greate payne myght he speake a worde he had such sorowe at his herte. Than he commaunded the false Makaire to declare in her presence the crime wherof he had accused her to him and forthwith he assured as a false murtherer began to say on high. Syr I have tolde you and yet wyll upholde before all here present, that I have seen her have compani and habitacion with a dogge, wherof she hath conceyved vii. whelpes, the whiche sith ben yssued of her owne bodye. And more over she wolde have gyven venim to me for to have enpoysened and made to dye you and your mother my lady Matabrune the whiche I wolde never do unto you nor to none other person. Now ladye sayde the kynge to the good Beatrice his wife, ye heare how ye ben openly accused of a shamful, horrible, and vilaineous forfaite before me and my baronny, what defence wyll ye fynde. Your faulte displeaseth me sore. But yf that ye wyll confesse the trouthe ye shall not dye, for I shall assygne your lyfe in some holy monastery of relygyon for to doo there penaunce and satisfaccion for our synne and pray to God for you and me. And yf you confesse not your dede: I promise you that shamefully I shall make you dye, if ye fynde not any that wyl susteine your quarel agaynst him that hath accused you. Alas my lorde sayde the good queene I cannot finde ony knight ne other that for to susteine my good right in ony maner wyll expose hym. But I promise you and swere heretofore all by the faith of gentylnesse that with great wronge and uniustly I am here before you accused. And how be it that it hath pleased the devine grace to so sende me this yet I never commised ne thought for to commit any vilany forfaite agaynst you ne agaynst myne honour. And

I complayne me to God Almyghty of this that I am accused in requiring him vengeaunce of all mine enemies.

And thus as this saide assemble was made for to condempne the good queene to death in the kynges palais, thither came the yonge Helyas sonne to kyng Oriant and of the quene Beatryce, the which having a staffe in his hande was delibered in courage in the confydence of God to susteyne his good mother. And whan he was comen to the gate of the palais he mette firste with a boistous churle that rigorousli axed him what he sought there? I seche (sayd he) a false and traytrous knight named Makayre. And he weeninge to mocke him sayde that it was he. And Helyas than lift up his staffe and with a free wyll hit him on the head that he felled him to the ground. And forthwith came a sergeaunt that tooke him and wenyng that he were a fole for that he was poorely clothed and barefoted and mocked him that had the stroke, saying that he should not play with a foole. Than Helyas drew him vigorously out of the sergeauntes hands and sayde to him. Let me go, for by the faith that I owe to God I shall never cease until I have vengeaunce of the fals Makaire that wrongfully hath doone great iniurye unto my mother the good queene. And amonge the other there was one in that place that whan he herde him speake so, tolde him that Makaire was in the consistory in the hall of the palays where as he accused the quene before the kinge of certayne crimes the which him semed to be falsly imposed, and said that the quene was a right notable ladi and ful of vertues, and that with great wronge the same day thei wolde make her dye. And whan Helias heard him saye so he came lightly to him and embrasing him said, Gentil frende I pray thee that it please thee to lede me to the place that thou saiest, and he led him streight. And whan Helias entred into the consistori wher as many folke weare assembled to see the demayne of the noble queene Beatryce, and yet many other that came to see what Helias wolde do that semed to be a wilde man. Than the noyse came to king Oryant which demaunded what it was. And it was tolde him that it was a yongling as al naked that axed after Makaire, and saith that he will fight against him and put him to death for to susteyne and defende the good quarell of the queene the which he sayth is his mother. Ha said the king it is than a foole, syr sayd a knight I have hearde him speake wisely. And than the king made to question him what he sought there. I seeke said he Makayre. And than one shewed him, and then he approched to him and said. Ha false traiter and untrue knight I defie thee thou shalt abie. And therwith he gave to Makaire suche a buffet with his fist that he felled him to the grounde incontinent and helde him so that he wolde have cut his throte yf he had any knife for to doo it withall. But he was lyghtly taken from his handes, and than he fled away al be bled with his owne bloud. How well that many noble knightes were right glad of that hie adventure, for thei were sore displeasaunt to see him vilaynously accuse the noble queene so pacient as was possible. And whan the king had seen him give so great a stroke to Makaire with his fist he repreved him and saide. How art thou so hardy to do this outrage in my presence. Ha syr saide he, know ye that I am come hyther at the only commaundement of God in likewyse as ye see, for to tell you the verite of the cause and of al the fait wherfore ye ben here assembled presently in this consistory. And how said the kinge. And Helias answered. Syr I shal shew you, but or I procede any ferther I wil go enbrace and kisse mine owne mother that I see yonder. And incontinent he approched the good queene and in kissinge and a colling her sayd. My right dere and faithful mother be no more sorrowfull at your herte. Cease yoor waylynges for this day I shall yelde to you all joye and consolacion bi the pleasure of God, and shall shew that falsly and with greate wronge ye have be betraied of them that should have kept you. Than of this thinge the kyng was mervaylously abasshed thinking and saying to himselfe. Here is some token of God, and in likewise were admervayled all they that were there present. Than Helyas perfurnisshed his purpose sayinge. My lorde my father I do you to understande for trouthe that whan ye left in the keeping of your mother Matabrune my mother the which was bigge of chylde with me my brethren and my sister and that ye wente to warr and fight against your ennemies, your said mother Matabrune conceyved suche an envy against my mother that she accompanied with the false olde midwife by silver suborned delibered for to do as ye shall heare. And for trouthe at the deliveraunce of her burthen she chylded vi. sonnse wherof I am one and a doughter, and also we brought from her wombe echone a faire chaine of silver at our neckes such as ye se me have one. And whan we were thus borne she made to transport us from this place. Than she tooke the sayd litle dogges and gave my good mother to understande that they were yssued of her bodi, the which she wende to be true for that she perceyved us not for the great anguisshe that she had. Consequentli she had given charge to one of her servauntes for to slea us or to drowne us in some river. But whan he was in a forest he behelde us on a plaine, and of pitie that he had to beholde us he left us there al naked and perisshing for honger without doinge us other harme. Sithen were we founden by a good and devoute hermite named Helias, the which beninegli bare us into his hermitage within the forest wher as he dwelleth yet presently. And there he warmed and susteyned us with his smal gooddes as much as to him was possible. Than he made orayson to God that he would purvey us, the which at his devoute prayer sent thither myraculously a faire white gote that susteyned and nourisshed us with milke, and the good hermite fed us with bread that was given him for goddes sake. And one day amonge all other as we were al vii. litle children under a tree gathering of wilde apples in the forest the houndes man of Matabrun founde us having eche one a chain of silver at our neckes of whome he made to her reporte. And she sent him agayne for to slea or make us to die. And an other day as the good hermite and I were gone in provision to susteyne our lives the same houndes man came with vii. other felowes the whiche tooke away the chaines fro my v. brethern and my sister, the whiche incontinent by the wyll of God were transmued in faire white swannes, and ben yet presentlie in a fayre stagne or ponde in the sayd forest, where as often times I have fed and given them bread for to eate. Sithen finably is comen the aungel of God that hath recited al to the good and devout hermite my godfather, in making him commaundement by God that this same day he should send me into the place where as I am present for to save mi faithfull mother. And for this intencion I am come hither with courage delibered in the confidence of God for to susteine and defende her from scathe by naturall inclynacion, and to be fight the traitre and untrue Makaire that bi his wickednesse wolde openly blame her. And for to make thys notabli to be verified ye may make the said Makaire and me to be kept in prison til ye please to sende for the good hermit for to witnesse the trouthe. And whan his father king Oryant hearde him speake thus he was yet more admervailed than before. So he began to speake to the noble quene his wife saying. How say ye lady, what semeth you of the words of this yonge man. Certainly my lorde I wot not how it is for I was at the houre of mi childing so sore travailed that I had not on me onie feling. How be it I know wel that mi ladi your mother never loved me, wherfore yf she have doone me yll I beleve that she shal finde it. Thus I report me to God and this yongeling that I se yonder, whiche he hath sent me for my champion and I praye you that it please you to make him be entreated as your sonne and graunt him that he requireth, desiringe above all to susteyne your noble honour and myne.

CHAP. XIX.

How the kyng Oriant commaunded to make armoures for his sonne Helias to fight agaynst Makayre and than went to the good hermite in the forest.

AFTER these wordes the noble kynge Oryant made to with draw the queene Beatrice honorably into a fayre chambre, in praysynge God his creatour as all recomforted. Than he recited to Matabrune his mother all that yonge Helias had declared wherof she blusshed all red and began to have feare, but not withstandinge she wende well assuredly to have renied al the case. How be it that the kinge made not over great semblaunt for that time: After consequentli he commaunded to enprisone and make sure the untrue knight Makaire the which was doone at his commaundement, for he doubted him of the great treason and malignite commised upon his noble spouse. Than after he gave charge to ii. noble knights to make forge armours propice and meete for yonge Helyas, the whiche by the divine wil was so pleasaunt and hardi of courage that echone loved him with good hert. And whan the king had ordeyned all these things he made maner as he wolde go hount and was mervailousli glad of these tidinges he purposed for to go to the good hermite in the forest, for to be al assured of that that his sonne had said and promised before him and his counsell. And thus is departed the noble king Oriant with divers of his secrete knightes, and is comen in to the sayd forest, and without makinge delay they have so long sought that they have found the hermitage of the hermite Helias. And whan the king sawe him he descended of his horse, and in their saluing reverentli the king demaunded his name. And the good hermite sayd, Syr I am brother Helias, and than knew the king that it was he that he sought wherof he was right joyous, and tooke him a side mekeli to be confessed of him. In the which confession he declared to him all the case as the childe had said. By the whiche the good hermite in likewise declared the houre, the day, and the time that he had founden the vii. children in the foreste and al that was happened by the selfe maner as the yonge Helias had tolde his father. And than king Oriant knew certainlie the malice doone to the good Queene Beatrice. It is not to be doubted of the sorow that he made for the paine and greavous vexacion that so longe time and uniustly he had made his wife to suffre by false and traitrous reportes. O sayde he my right faythfull lady, O my right deare and noble spouse, how may I make thee amendes how may I satisfie to thee? O false and perverce tongues much worse than deadli venim. Have ye ben so hardy to make strife betwene the husbande and the wyfe. Have ye made to lie in the bead of tribulation betwéne the sheetes of wepynges those that were wont to be in all mirth and consolation. O good Lorde God I beseche thee of merci, and pardon me mine ygnourance. Thou knowest how I have done it, for I my selfe have betraied, and maligne-lousli deceived by fals reporte. In this wise disconforted tooke the kinge leave of the devout hermite. To whome he made for to deliver a great some of golde and silver to the entente that he should founde and edifie a churche of religion for the honour and reverence of the glorious virgin our lady sainct Mary, And for the remuneracion of his vii. children the which in suche wise myraclusly there had be nourisshed and sustented by the divine providence of God. And than he retourned to his citie of Lylefort with his people for to comferme the iourney that he had ordeyned of his sonne yonge Helyas and of the fals knight Makayre, and to dispose all the mater as time semed best.

CHAP. XX.

How the noble king Oriant delivered out of prysone good queene Beatryce his wyfe. And after ordeyned all thinge to his sonne yonge Helyas for to fyght agaynste his enemyes.

WHAN the noble kinge Oriant was retourned fro the hermitage, and that he had knowen the verite of the vii.

children he made incontinent to deliver the noble queene Beatrice out of prison, and captivitie, and restored her to al libertie and fraunchyse, the better to love and honoure her without comparison more than ever he did before, so that she might go and come where as her pleased, as innocente and not culpable of that to her was imposed, wherof right humbly she yelded graces and praisynges to God. And also for her deliveraunce made joye in thanking our Lorde. After he made to take Matabrun and put her fast in pryson with iiii. sergeauntes to kepe her that she should not fle thens til her case were determined by justice. Than consequently he sent for the untrue knight Makaire for to be at the journey (ordeyned by the kinge) for to fight against hys sonne yonge Helias, that God hath sent for to susteine the iust quarell of his good mother the queene Beatrice. Helyas than was wel armed by two knightes, that the king had ordeined therto al maner of pieces of harneys right well steled. The helme of the same richeli besene as it apperteined unto a kinges sonne, with precious devises to him condesent. His sheilde on his arme, and his speare in his hande the which he couched in the reest as al enspyred of God. After they gave him a fayre armynge swearde well steeled and cuttinge. And finably they mounted him surely upon a good and mighty courser well barded and trapped as it belongeth to suche a poynte. And on the other parte was apparelled the false Makayre, the which was not over glad of that, that him behoved to doo. For he consydered well that he had no good cause ne iust quarel of that that he susteined agaynst the faithfull queene Beatrice. And moreover that he sawe her all redy delyvered of pryson at her free liberte, and the false Matabrune straitely holden in prison. But al these thinges notwithstandinge yet made he maner to have iuste cause in his fayte, but there is no wisdome agaynst the wyl of God. And whan they were both redy on the one side and other, there assembled anon many knightes the which made theim to sweare that eche of them thought to have good cause in that quarel different that the one against the other wolde susteine. The whiche Makaire like as did Helias, but or he left the feilde him selfe confessed the contrary before the kinge, the quene and many other noble knightes and damoyselles.

CHAP. XXI.

How Helyas the noble knight of the swanne vainquisshed and overcame the false Makayre in campe of battayle.

Thus hath Helyas and Makayre sworne before them that were ordeyned for to judge the champ of batayle, and of that, that should be doone. And for to se this noble adventure of armes there came so great multitude of people that they coulde not be numbred.

And also there was present kynge Oriant with his

good spouse Beatrice accompanied of great lordes the which desired mervailously that the honour of the good queene might be susteyned in the place. Than entred the ii. champions in to the place, and with yonge Helias that was apoynted as a kinges sonne came many great lordes of the court, and he was al assured as he that had the grace of God with him to whom none may noye. And on the other part was the said Makaire as all hevy and malacolious of the favour and good grace that every man bare to him. But as al fiers and proude he began to say, Come, come, drawe nere my minion ye shal see this daye if your overwening youth may resist agaynst me. And how be it that he wend to shew himselfe hardy yet he said these words but for great feare that he had. And on the other parte the noble Helias said. A trayter I am nowe right glad to see thee heare in this place, as I have desyred, for I come to thee humbly in the name of our lorde and at his commaundement for to susteine veritably the juste quarel of my good mother the which untruely thou hast over muche defamed wherfore in my good confidence I hope this daye to shew agaynst thee, the strength and hie prayse to the right arme of God. Now come, come, sayde Makayre approche. So I wil said Helyas. Than with great cours of hors and the speare couched in the reest they mette with suche raundom that Helias made Makaire and his horse to foundre to the erthe. Of the which thing Makayre was greatly admervayled and sayde. Ha yonge sonne will ye shewe the might of your pleasaunt youth agaynst me, truly ye shall fele this daye that there is strength in my arme. Wel wel said Helias, come nere, I am all assured of thee. And than with cours of horse Makaire came wening to smite him al unwars, so that by treason he made him a litle wound so that a litle bloud yssued. And whan the queene sawe that she was right sori at herte, wherfore she praied mekely unto God and his holy mother that it wolde please them to succour her poore childe, that susteyned verite, and proclamed her voyce sayinge. Soverayne God of Paradise that gave victory unto the children of Isarael against the froward Pharaon that uniustly helde them in captivitie. I praye thee if it please thee to give victory to my sonne, the whych it hath pleased thee to send hither for to deliver me out of prison, and reprove the treason and falsnesse that wickedly and with wrong was propenced against me as thou knowest the trouthe. And also all the assistentes were sory for that stroke, for echone had set theyr love on yonge Helyas but he coulde in no wise perisshe in the kepinge of God. And whan he felt himselfe so traitrously wounded he resembled the knight that taketh courage whan he seeth his bloud shedde. And in escrienge high he sayd to Makayre. A traytre, false, and disloyall haddest thou at this houre thought to betray me. Suffiseth it thee not to have wylled to betrayed mi good mother without wylling to betraye mortally her sonne. Now retourne to me, for I hope in the pleasure of God to mete thee in suche wise that upon thy bodi presently by me shall be executed the insuperable right arme of God wherin is all my trust. Well said Makayre come nere I defye thee. So shal I sayde Helyas in suche wise that it shall not nede to returne any more. And in this sayinge Helias broched his horse with his spurres and couched his speare in the reest with suche courage so that he reversed Makaires helme to the erth and uncovered his head. And whan Helias saw that, he alight of his horse and drew his swerd of armes wherwith he gave him suche a stroke that skantly he might remove. And on the other parte came his horse against Makaires horse, the which by might of flynging brake his reines behinde, and sith miraculously made him to fal from his horse, wherby yonge Helyas recovered to smite upon him vertuously smote of his arme with his swerd to the erthe. And whan the false Makaire saw himselfe sodainlye vaynquisshed he began humblye to yelde him to Helias sayinge. Ha yonge sonne, thou hast overcome me, and I yelde me wholy to thee but I adiure thee in the name of God that thou tel me what thou arte. I am said he Helyas sonne of king Oriant and of his good queene Beatrice that am comen hether at the commaundement of God for to susteine her good and iust quarel against thee and all her enemies. Ha noble kinges sonne said he I require thee take me to mercy and pardon me mine offence. A false recreaunt traytre sayd Helias thou shalt not escape so. For I will see the consumacion of thi life or I leave this feeld. Yet I pray thee said Makaire that it will please thee to save my life for this houre tyl I have tolde thee, the trouthe of the fals treason that hath be done to thi good mother and to her children without to hide any pointe before the kyng thy noble father, the mother, and the assystentes. And also I shall name and tel where the goldesmith is that hath chaines of silver that thevisshely and by violence were taken fro thi brothren and sister, wherby they were forthwith transmuted into white swannes as thou hast said. And whan Helias heard him speake so he differred to put him streight to death to the ende that by him selfe, should be confessed the treason that to his mother himselfe, with his brethren and sister had be doone. And whan he called them that were ordeined to make reporte of them two doone in the sayd feelde.

CHAP. XXII.

How Makaire confessed openly before the kyng and the queene all the people the treason doone to the sayde queene and his children. And how he was hanged as a fals traytour on the galowes.

THAN they came reverently as to him that miraculously had abtayned victory and tryumphe over his enemy. And he bad them incontinente that they should make the kynge, the Queene and the knightes to approche thither and tolde them that Makayre had promised to recite the treason that he and Matabrune had doone to his good mother and to her children. The which thinge was incontinent reported to the king, whereof he and his good quene were right joyous, and came nygh to the two champyons with all theyr noble barons and chyvalry. And than the king questioned diligentli with the sayd Makayre saying. Now Makayre be ye confused, demaunde ye mercy of your vainquissher? Alas sir said he, yea. And what sai ye more: Certainly syr I yelde me humbly unto your sonne, and nowe I know well that a good dede is never unrewarded ne an evyll unpunisshed and that none may resist agaynst the will of God. But in demaundinge you pardon I shall tell you trouthe of all the treason that afore hath ben done to your noble wife and to your children, and than doo with me what it pleaseth you, for I have well deserved the death. That is wel sayd quoth the kinge, now say on. Sir sayd Makaire it is of trouthe that Matabrune your mother counseyled her with me of all that she hath done. And fyrst she gave the good quene your wife to understand that she had conceyved, vii. dogges, but know ye that it was a lising, for she childed vii. faire children, that is to wite vi. sonnes and a doughter, the which brought at theyr byrth eche of them a chaine of sylver at theyr neckes. But Matabrune sente them to be loste or slayne by one of her servauntes named Markes, how be it he did not so, but lefte them in a foreste as your sonne hath sayd, wherof whan she was advertysed and that she had tidinges of them: her self put out both the eyene of the sayd Markes so that he is yet blind. Than she sent thither other of her servauntes for to put them to death, but they found but vi. children, to whome they did nothing but tooke away theyr chaines that was about their neckes wherby incontinent thei were mued in white swannes. And of the sayd chaines Matabrune made to make a cuppe by her goldsmith, for whom ye may sende and know the trouthe. And of this that I charged culpable the good quene to have poysoned you and your mother, I confesse here presently before you and your baronni that she never propenced it, but my selfe adiusted it to her at thynstygacion, of your mother. And here I cry her mercy, and you also of the offence that I have commised. And whan the noble kinge Oriant heard Makayre speake in this wise he began to weepe tenderly and syth benignely he came and enbraced his good spouse the noble queene Beatrice in saying. My love I have doone you great wronge, but pardon me if ye please, for I have doone it bi ygnoraunce, which displeaseth me greatly. My lord said she I forgive it you with right good herte, for I know well that ye be sorowfull of my grevous mischefe. And therwith the king and the quene went and kyssed theyr sonne Helias in blessing and thankynge him of the victory and tryumphe that he had and yelded graces unto God. And in lykewise all the knightes squires, and ladyes with all the whole comynalty that there were feasted him and made joye and solempnite for so hie and sumptuous a myracle, wherby they saw the king and the quene remised and set in good love and unite of hert togither. Than bi the commaundement of the noble kinge

Oriant the sayd fals reproved traytre Makayre was drawen to the galowes and there shamfully hanged and strangled as a recreant knight that he was.

CHAP. XXIII.

How kinge Oryant sent for the goldsmyth the which brought the other v. chaines that he had deteined and recited al the myracle doone with them.

WHAN yonge Helyas sonne of Kynge Oryant and of the good queene Beatryce had myraculously obteyned victory of his enmy Makayre as it is sayde, the kinge and the queene retorned ammerousli together into the hall of the palays with their said sonne. The which by his knightes was incontinent unarmed for to refresshe him. And after with so great joy and honour he was so nobli feasted that non hath possiblite to tell it. Every person reioyced them in theyr degree. Convives, daunces, and sports were incontinent reysed in the palays. Trompets, clerons and mani other instrumentes of musike were assembled there to reioyce his company. The bisshop and the clergy wyth al the habytauntes and burgeyses were honestly receyved. Open courte was holden to all comers, for to collaude in magnificence the sayd noble adventure. That on the morow were made devoute processions whereto all the people came in giving graces and thanks to God of all hys divine benifites, and at the retourninge was songe and celebred a masse solempnely by the sayd bisshop, in the presence of the kinge, the queene, theyr noble sonne Helyas, and al theyr chevalrye, and after masse echone were receyved better than they were before, in suche wise that bi longe space of time was made feest, game, and tourneimentes so that there was never seen such. And during this feest the goldsmith was sent for, to whome Macabrune had gyven the chaynes of silver to make a cuppe, for to know the trouth of him. The which came incontinent and brought v. of the sayde chaynes and a cuppe of sylver that he had over whan he made the other, as it pleased God for to recover the vi. children. And so freely he came to the kynge and sayde. Syr here ben vi. chaynes of sylver and a cuppe, the which myraculously I have had of the surplus of the cup that your mother, Matabrune gave me to make, and how was this doone sayd the king: wyte ye sir sayd the goldsmyth that your mother brought me vi. chaynes of sylver for to make a cuppe, suche as she devised. But whan I began to melte the first of the sayd chaynes it multiplied so by the grace of God that it weyed twise as muche as all the vi. chaynes together, wherfore I reserved one for payment of the facion. And sith I have kept reverentlye the other v. chaynes in my coffre as precious and ful of vertue, the whych I present you here. And if in this doing I have offended or mysse doone agaynst your riall maiestie: I offre me to make amendes. Certainli sayd the kyng ye speake wisyly and like a good man, and if ye have commised oni wrong in this I forgeve you hertely. Than the king, and the queene tooke those precious chaynes and kissed them reverentlie in weeping and bewayling naturally theyr poore children that by so great treason were mued and converted into swannes. And soone upon that came Markes that was blinde by Matabrune, and by the furour of her rage had both his eyne put out whan the king saw him he demaunded him who hath doone it. Alas syr sayd he, your mother hath done this evill. And wherfore sayde the kinge: Alas syr sayde he, whan your vii. children were borne she gave me them for to drowne or make them die to the ende to make the queene beleve that she had whelped vii. dogges. But whan I was in a forest I layde them all in a playne upon my mantell for to se them. And as I began to behold them they began all to laugh upon me so lovinglye that for to have lost my life I cold not have doone them any harme but yet it greved me sore to be constreyned to leve them in that place all dispourveyed. And whan she wist that they were yet alive, and that I had not fulfilled her wicked wil she herselfe by her madnesse put oute bothe mine eyene. And whan Helyas heard him speke thus he had greate pitte on him, wherfore humbly he turned hym to God sayinge. Soverayne God of paradise that by thy divine goodnesse and insaciable mercye enlumined and gave syght to the poore blinde man the whiche satte in the hie way begginge for his life. I thee supplie and requyer humbly by the benignite that it wil please thee to enlumyne and geve sight to this poore blinde creature, the which hath ben cause of the salvacion of my life, by the which he hath loste hys eeyen. And whan he had made his prayers he made the signe of the crosse upon the eyen of the sayd Markes, the which incontinent after bi the grace of Almighti God saw as clerely as ever he dyd, wherfore the kinge and the queene with all the whole assistentes were greatli admervayled. And incontinent they gave laudes and thankynges unto our Lord, with him the which was newly enlumined of his sight. In reknowledgyng the graces and vertus of our Saviour, and redemptour Jesu Christ the which he had myraculousli shewed at the praier and supplycacion of his good knight Helyas.

CHAP. XXIV.

How the false Matabrune made the kepers of the prison so dronkin that they slept whiles she fled away. And how the Swannes, retourned to theyr fourme humayne.

Noow ye ought to wit or we procede any ferther that the same day that the justes were made betwene Helias and Makaire that Matabrune beinge in prison made in suche wyse to drinke them that king Oriant had commysed to keep her that she made them to slepe all dronken. And sith founde maner to escape, and with certayne of her folke she withdrew her in a castel of hers named Maubruiant to thend to kepe and preserve her from harme which she thought should come to her, for the perverce treason and untrouth that she had commised agaynst the kinge and his good spouse the noble queene Beatrice. Wherfore the kyng made grevously to punysshe them that had her in keping.

But for to returne to the subgect of the cronykill of the noble Helias knight of the swanne. It is to be noted that the said Helias knight of the swanne demaunded of kyng Oriant his father that it wolde please him to give him the chaines of silver of his brethern and sister that the goldesmith had brought. The which he delivered him with good herte for to dispose them at his pleasure. Than he made an othe and sware that he wolde never rest tyll he had so longe sought by pondes and stagnes that he had founde his v. brethren and his sister, which were transmued in to swannes. But our lorde that consoleth his freendes in exaltinge their good will shewed greatly his vertue. For in the river that ranne about the kinges palays appered visibly the swannes before all the people. And whan Helias had seen them: he called diligentli the king and the queene his father and mother saiing. I pray you my lord and my lady that ye will lightly come and se your other notable children mi v. brethren and my sister. The which ben now presently arived upon the river that is about this palays. And incontinent the kynge and the queene descended wyth many lordes, knightes, and gentilmen, and came with great diligence upon the water syde, for to see the above sayde Swannes. The king and the queene behelde them piteousli in weeping for sorow that they had to se theyr poore children so transmued into swannes. And whan they saw the good Helias come nere them they began to make a mervaylous feast and reioyced them in the water. So he approched upon the brinke, and whan they sawe him nere them: they came lightli fawning and flikering about him making him chere, and he playned lovingli theyr fethers. After he shewed them the chaynes of silver, where by they set them in good ordre before him. And to five of them he remised the chaynes about theyr neckes, and sodeynlye they began to retourne in theyr propre humayne forme as they were before, and before al miraculsly they shewed them iiii. fayr sonnes and a doughter. To whome diligentlie the king and the queene ranne, and naturalli kissed them as their children, wherof everye man had mervaile, and ioyed of the divine miracle of God so notably shewed. And whan the other swanne (whose chaine was molten for to make the cuppes as afore is sayd) saw his brethren and his sister retourned into theyr humaine fourmes he lept agayn all sorowfully into the river, and for dole that he had he plucked almost al his fethers to the bare flesshe. And whan the good Helias saw him so dolorously demeane himselfe; he tooke him to weepe for sorow, and recomforted him sayinge. My dere brother my freende, have somwhat pacience, and discomforte you not. For I shall make so meeke and humble praiers unto God almighti for you, that yet I shall se you ones a noble knight. And than the swanne began to enclyne and bowe downe his head as in thanking him and syth plunged hymselfe all togyther in the water. And for him in likewise the kinge and the queene made moche lamentacion. But Helyas conforted them sweetly, and sayde to them that he wolde in suche wyse pray unto our lorde for him that in shorte time he should retourne into his owne naturall fourme. And thus they ceased somwhat of theyr sorowe by the consolacion and goodly wordes of the said Helias for theyr other sonne, wherfore than they toke benignely the other v. children and ledde them to the churche where they made them to be baptised. And the mayden was named Rose, of whome after warde descended a noble lignage and worthy of praising. And the other sonnes were named and called at the fonte after the good discrecion of the kinge and the queene. The whiche sonnes also in lykewise were ryght noble and vertuous knyghtes and beloved of God. Than after their baptising thei were solempnely conduited and ledde into the palays, and there feasted in all joye as it apperteyned well. And thither cam many for to see them in laudinge and magnifienge the name of our almighty saviour, that so miraculously shewed his great vertue.

CHAP. XXV.

How kinge Oriant gave his realme to his sonne Helias, whereof he made to crowne him kynge honourably and than gave him leve to go take his mother Matabrun in the castell of Maubruyant, and there he brente her in a great fyre.

After all these thinges afore sayd king Oryant knowledged the grace of God that was sowen in his sonne the noble Helyas: he made to call afore him dyvers great barons and knyghtes with his peers which were alwai with him. And they comen he made to call in present the noble Helias and said to him. My right dere and welbeloved sonne. I have knowledged and also my lords here present have sene that ye be fulfilled of Gods grace, as notabli apereth by the miracles and digne faites that by your holi praier have here be shewed, wherfore I depose me presently of al my realme constituing you king and lorde of all my landes and countreys and wil that fro hens forwarde ye be honoured and served and obeyed without any gaynsayinge. And in the witnesse of this thinge, and for to shewe that it so pleaseth me, heare is the crowne of the realme, the which in the presence of the queene your mother and all the noble assistentes I set upon your head and give it to you as king. My lorde sayd Helias I thanke you humbly, how well that I am not worthy ne suffisaunt to rule and governe one so noble and puissaunt realme as yours is. But sith that it pleaseth you so to doo, and that it is the wyll of God, in nothing wyl I gainesay you. For sothe sayd king Oriant I give it you with all my hert. Moreover my sonne noble kinge I doo you to wit that Matabrune my mother the which I had made to enpryson for the treason and iniury that she dyd to your mother and her children wherof ye be one, hath found maner to escape, and is flede for warrandise into a castell of hers called Maubruant. So I tel you that I put her case towarde you for to do right and justice, suche as by you and your counceyll shall be founde and ordeyned, but I wyl not be present, wel my lorde sayd Helyas syth it pleaseth you so, I promise you my faith that I shall never cease tyl I have wonne and taken the sayd castel named Maubruant and done right justice upon her that in suche maner with wronge hath wylled to betray my mother and us her chyldren. And after that the noble Helias was crowned and constituted king and lorde of the realme of Lilefort with all honour and tryumph as afore is saide in the presence of his mother Queene Beatrice and of al the noble prynces and knyghtes of the realme, the whiche were ryght ioyous. He made to prepaire a lytle hoste of men of warre to go with him to Maubrayant, that is to wite aboute foure thousand Crosbowe men, two M. men of armes, al chosen folke beside fotemen that were about vi. C. And than accompanyed with an C. noble knightes he departed fro Lylefort, with his people he went and besyeged the castell of Maubruyant, and to make short he gave so stronge and mervaylous assaute to al them that were within that they might nothing resist wherfore he and his men wel armed entred their in valyauntlye without any gaynsaying. And in entringe in to the sayd castell escried kinge Helias with an hie voyce to his people saying. Upon your lives kepe ye that the false Matabrune yssue not out of this place. The which untruelye wolde have betrayed and caused to dye my good mother and all her children. And whan Matabrune had hearde the noyse, and that she sawe the Castel taken, she fortified her within a tour with certayne of her gentylmen and damoyselles wening to holde her there in saufte. But when kynge Helyas knew it he came to the dore of the sayde toure with certayne of his folke and brake it open, and founde her therin. And as soone as the kinge apperceyved her he came to her with great courage and kest her to the earth saying. Ha false olde witche thou hast betrayed my mother and made us to suffre so muche evyll. Yf it were not for the honour of God, and the bloud wherof I am comen my selfe should slea thee. And than she wist not what to saye but that they should lede her to king Oriant her sonne. But Helias told her that she should never se him, and made to lede her downe to the base courte, wher as a great place was made with a stake and wood and coles for to brenne her as she had deserved, wherto echone besied. And whan she was so bounde at the stake, and that ther was no more remedi of her life she was somwhat moved with contricion, and cryed unto kynge Helyas in saying, Ha my sonne I cry you mercy. I knowledge and it is true that I have wel deserved the deathe for I have falsly betrayed your mother, and made her to understande that of her body were yssued vii. whelpes, and she of trouthe childed vii. fayre children, the which at their birth brought eche of them a chaine of silver at theyr necke but by mine untrouthe I sent them by on of my servauntes for to droune or slea them, but God preserved them from yll, and yet by my wickednesse I thought to make to die the good queene Beatryce your mother, in imposynge to her crime that she wold have betraied her spouse king Oriant and me, wherin she never thought, so is it good ryght that I die, for towarde God I have deserved it. To whom I beseche that he pardon me, and that the paine that I shal suffre in dienge may be tourned if it please him to the satisfaccion of all my sinnes. And also I require you to pardon me for I die willingly and I forgive you mi death. Truly sayd kinge Helias I pardon you as to my parte, but yet shall ye die by justice, and I pray God forgyve you. Than was wood and dry thornes layde about her and fyre set therin and so she was brent for her demirites before al the people. And whan the execucion was doone, the kinge with his people retourned diligently to Lilefort wher as he was honourabli received, and than he went and tolde his mother what he had doone sayinge. Mother reioyce you, for ye be revenged now of the perverce Matabrune, for I have made her to be brente for her demerites. And the queene answered, My right dere sonne I thanke you, Jesus forgeve her soule. And thus they abode amiable in good peace wherof all the people reioyced.

CHAP. XXVI.

How Helyas tooke leave of the kyng his father and of his mother for to folow the adventure of his brother the swanne that appered on the river before a ship.

After certayne tyme that the victoryous kynge Helyas had posseded the Realme of Lyleforte in good peace and tranquilite of justice it happened on a day as he was in his palais loking towarde the river that he apperceived the swanne one of his brethren that was not yet tourned into his fourme humayne, for that his chaine was molten for to make Matabrune a cup as it is sayd. And the sayd swanne was in the water before a ship the which he had led to the wharfe as abiding king Helias. And whan Helias saw him : he saide in himselfe. Here is a signification that God sendeth to me for to shew to me that I ought to go by the guyding of this swanne into some countrey for to have honour and consolacion, under the bounte and magneficence of his holy and excellent name. And in this good purpose inspired of the Holi Goste he assembled his brethren and his syster, and came to kynge Oryant bis father and queene Beatrice his mother, and in the presence of all his parentes he sayd. My right deare and honoured father, and you also my sweet mother with all my brethren and sister and freendes here present. It is now needful and convenient that I take leve at you. For here bi within the river is mi brother the swanne that commeth to fetche me in a shippe that he ledeth and gideth to the wharfe in abiding me, wherfore know ye my lorde my father that I render to you the crowne riall the which it pleased you to gyve me. And I remitte whole into your handes the Realme of Lilefort. And thus humbly I take leve of you in leving this noble countrey for to go at the commaundement of our Lord bi the condutinge of my brother. For I have stedfast hope in me that our Lord hath doone all for the best, and that he wyl leve him yet in the fourme of a swanne for to guyde and leade me surely to some good porte where as I maye to his digne wyll doo some vertuous fruyte. And thus wil I go with him, and to Jesu Christ I commaunde you. And in this saying: he went and kissed the kyng and the queene his father and mother, his brethren and his syster. The which wepte so tenderly that it was pitie for to se them.

CHAP. XXVII.

How the swanne brother of kyng Helyas conduted the sayde shyppe wherin Helyas was tyll they came to the Citye of Nymaie.

AND whan Helyas had thus mekelye taken his leave of all his parentes and freendes he made to bere his armures and armes of honoure into the shyppe, with hys target and his bright sheelde, of whiche as it is writen the felde was of sylver and there on a double crosse of golde. Than after the noble kinge Oriant came and presented to his sonne an horne, and said. My right dere and welbeloved sonne, here is an horne that I gyve you, the which ye shal keep if it please you, for my sake. And be ye sure that it hath suche vertue that what man soever bloweth it loude may not have anoy ne domage at the pleasure of God. And I beseche God humbly that he give you joyful going and honour at your retourning, and saufte in your viage. And thus as Helias was yet in the palays with the kyng the swane kest three or four mervaylous cryes as by maner to call his brother, wherof the king and the queene with all them that were there were greatly abasshed. So descended anon the sayd Helyas with his parentes and frendes, the which came to convey him unto the brinke of the water. And whan the swanne sawe hem he flickered and regoysed as in making maner to mete the saide Helyas. And there every man blessed the sayd swanne saying. It is domage of this poore child that hath lost his fourme humain the which God sende him. But yet was not the time comen ordeined of God that he should turne in his humanitie, for a more greater welth that should ensue after. And there was the kinge and the quene with their children weping profoundeli for pitie that they had to beholde their noble bloude so transfigured into a swane. Than entred Helias into a shyp taking general leave of all his freendes. The which retourned weping and sorowing for the good Helias the noble knight of the swanne, that went at his adventures in strange countries at the good commaundement of God, and the guiding of the swanne. So the swanne put him afore the shippe, the which he made to scoure upon the water in suche wise that they were anon ferre fro Lyleforte. And thus conduited the swanne from ryver to ryver the noble Helyas tyl unto the place ordeyned of God for to give him a wyfe, of whome should yssue a fayre doughter that should bere three sonnes, by whome should be gretli exalted the fayth of our lorde Jesu Christ. Of the which the first was Godfrey of Boulyon, the which sithen conquered and posseded the realme of the holy lande of Jerusalem. The seconde was his brother Baudwyne the which succeded him in the sayde realme. And the thyrde was theyr brother Eustace the which was a right noble knight. But that not withstanding yet was he not a kinge as the two first were for that he sucked another nourice than his mother bicause the child cried. And the mother was marvalous angry, as hereafter shalbe shewed in folowinge by ordre the true cronycle.

CHAP. XXVIII.

How the erle of Frankbourke made to come and appere by justice Clarysse duchesse of Boulyon at Nimaye wyllynge to usurpe her of her duchy, in gyvinge false understandynge to Otton emperour of Almayne, the whiche helde the courte of his parlyament at the sayde cytie of Nymaie.

To come alwaye to the effecte of the noble cronycle the which I have begon to treate to the verite of that which is wryten in many other notable hystoryes. I shall leve a lytle to speake of the noble Helyas knyght of the swanne that is fletinge on the water comynge to the cytye of Nimaye before the emperour and by divine provydence to susteyne the right of the good duchesse of Boulyon, as after it is sayde.

It is so that the ryght noble emperour of almayne named Otton first of that name, that had under him the land of Dardaine, of Lyege, and of Nammur, helde his syege of justice and the court of his parliament in the citie of Nimay. And thither al they that were oppressed, or domaged came to axe right of themperour, that was a verie iust iudge and good justicier. So than the erle of Frankebourke made to apere the duchesse of Boulyon before him, uniustlye to usurpe the duchy bi false giving to understande. And at a day set appered the erle demaundaunt in mater of novelte on the on parte, and the duchesse of Boulyon defendresse on the other parte. The whiche had brought her doughter with her that was a faire damoisel. And whan the counsel was comen and assembled afore the emperour, the erle made to plede his cause. In the which plea he made iniuriously to pose and put in faite that the said duchesse had made to enpoysen her husband, the which was his brother. And that her said husband about the space of iii. yeres was in straunge countreys without retourning home. During the whiche time and in his abscence she had conceyved and borne a doughter, the which for the sayde cause he wolde say that she was not of legitime mariage. And moreover that the londe and duchi of Boulias was comen of his father. By the which he wolde say and promise by his pleding that the duchesse might not of right possede ne holde the said duchy as dowayresse of her husbande, ne her doughter in lykewise as heire of the said duke, for she was not ligitime as he said before, and that he offred to prove it, tendaunt to the ende to take and holde in his hande the said duchy of Boulion as a successour and seul heritier of his brother (in his life husband to the said duchesse) and duke of Boulion. Than after the pledynge of the sayd demaundaunt, the duchesse defended her cause to the best she might, denienge al that he had proposed agaynst her and her doughter, whose honour he had hurte in protesting of theniuries. Certes ladi said themperour, here is an iniurious mater and that wil cause your death if ye pourvei not, seing that he offreth him to prove it, if ye be not let by your opposites. Sir sayd the erle to thende that ye seme it not to be true here is my guage for to susteyne it to the utteraunce, and be fight it to the death that it is as I have said. Wherfore she is culpable to die and not to possede the said duchy. Now ladi said themperour ye have heard the offer that he maketh you, which semeth me way of right, wherbi I cannot refuse him his demaund. And therfore make diligence to seeke a knight for to fighte and susteyne your quarell, by the which ye may denye that which hath be now proposed by your adverse party. And yf ye thinke that ye may finde ony that will take thys charge for you: I shall gladly give you space and delaye to pourvey you. Than the good lady as al abasshed loked aboute her if there were ony present that in her need wolde helpe her. But none wolde medle seynge the case to her imposed. Wherfore she committed her to God prayinge him humbly to succour her, and reprove thiniury that wickedly to her was imposed by the sayd erle.

CHAP. XXIX.

How Helias the noble knight of the swanne aryved at Nymaie for to defende the duchesse of Boulon, who themperour receyved gladly.

For to retourne to the myraculous hystory of the ryght noble and valiant Helyas knyght of the swanne, the which hath be somwhat interrupt for to recite this that afore is sayde servinge to the matter followinge. It is to be noted that so as the erle of Franckebourcke and the duchesse of Boulyon were so pledynge before the emperour of Almayne in his parliament at the towne and cytie of Nymaie for the matter aforesayd, approched thyther the good Helyas guided by the swanne the which began to blowe hyghly his horne that his father kyng Oriant had gyven him, in suche maner that they that were in the parlyment with the Emperour were all admervailed to here a sowne so lowde. Than in continent they looked out at the windowes and sawe the swanne come ledinge a shyppe, within the which was the noble Helias knight of the swanne, well garnysshed of spere, swerde and armures as belongeth to a knight. And whan the emperoure sawe him arive he had great mervayle. For he apperceived the swanne that retourned with the shyp incontinent that the noble Helias was out with his armoures, wherfore he sent for him. And in this wise behelde him the noble Clarysse duchesse of Boulion. The which to this purpose tolde a dreame to her doughter, wherof she hadde visyon the night before saiynge. Truly, doughter I wene that our lorde this daye wyll helpe and succoure me by his divine grace. For this nighte me thought in my dreame that I pleaded agaynste the erle of Frankenbourke that by his treason accused me of crime of death wherbi I was condempned to be brente in a fyre. But there came a swanne fleynge that broughte me water that put out the sayde fyre. And of this water yssued a byg fishe the which fructified in suche wyse that echone lyved therwith til into Jerusalem and all the countrey. Wherby I beleve at the pleasure of God that the swanne whiche hath guyded this noble knight hither shalbe cause to delyver me of the crime wherof I am falsely accused. And thus as the duchesse of Boulyon devised with her doughter thyther came the good knight Helias, which at the commaundement of the emperour aryved in the hall where as he helde his parliament. And there reverently he salued the saide emperour. And the emperour againwarde received him muche honestly, in demaunding him of his tidinges and how he was theithercomen. Syr said Helias I am a poore knyght adventurous for to serve you trulye whan ye shall have any need of my simplesarvice. Than sayd the emperour. My freend I thanke you, and ye be welcome. And sith you seke adventures in feates of armes and chyvalry ye maye finde them here without goinge ferther. And for to declare you al the case. Here is this noble ladi duchesse of Boulyon with her doughter, the which the erle of Frankebourke her present hath accused her of a cryme ynough to make her die, and also to disheryte her doughter of the sayde Duchy of Boulion, yf she finde not some champion or noble knight that wolde defende her ryght a gaynst the sayde Erle afore named, the which hath casten his guage for to susteyne publikely against any defendaunte that which he hath proposed. And now ye have hearde the case, the which should be a fayre adventure, yf ye would susteyne it. And I shall save her in restablysshynge unto her her heritage, and also ye shall have her doughter in mariage, which ye se so gracious and a right fayre mayden. And whan the good Helyas had hearde themperour he behelde the duchesse the whiche semed him moche beninge and of noble mayntene. Also he considered the beaute and gracious countenaunce of her doughter, the which to him was mervaylously pleasaunt and agreable to beholde. Than he demaunded of themperour that it wolde please him to give him leave to speake a litle secretly with the duchesseof Boulion, which he graunted gladly, wherfore he thanked him. And than Helias tooke her by the hande and drew her somwhat a parte, and sayd to her. Fayre ladye it behoveth yf it please you that ye tell to me and swere the trouth of this I shal demaunde of you. And this same dai bi the pleasure of God I shall be your faithfull servaunt. Alas noble knyght said she. I promyse you by the livinge God and on the faith of gentilnesse that I shall tel you al the trouthe of that ye shal axe me. Now madame said he by the othe that he have here made, be ye not in any thinge culpable of this cryme whereof ye be presentlye accused? Bi mi trouth my freend said she, naye. And I beseche God that he never doo me anye grace to my body and soule if I ever thought of that wherof I am falsly and without cause accused. And truly madame sayde he than have ye founde a champion of me for to susteyne and defende your ryght in suche wyse that by the pleasure of God that in veray verite this daye your enemy shalbe overcome.

CHAP. XXX.

How Helyas the vertuous knight of the swanne dyd fight agaynst the erle of Francbourcke, the which he conquered and slew.

WHAN the noble knight of the swanne had interrougued and questioned the duchesse of Boulyon he came streyght to the emperoure and sayde. Syr make him to come hyther that iniustly accuseth thys noble ladye, for to disherite or make her dye, for I am redye to defende her. And with these wordes yssued the erle saying My freende what demaunde ye? Ye shew you muche over wenynge to medle you of a thinge that toucheth you not. Vassall sayd Helias here is my glove that I deliver you, in suchewise that the honour of God and for this ladyes sake ye shal se what an adventurous knight can do. And the erle receyved his guage. So was the bataile accorded incontinent by the emperour, the which receyved theyr othes, demaunded whan they wolde fight.

Than Helias required themperour that it wolde please him to ordeyne it presently, the which he graunte. And the erle for shame durst not refuse him. Than forthwith the feeld was prepayred, the listes dressed, and the champions surely armed as behoved in such a case. Incontinent the noble Helias tooke his speare, his swearde, and his sheelde of sylver with a double crosse of golde, the which he set upon his left arme. And on the other parte the erle was mounted on his hors. And syth they came into the feelde arayed for them. And there was present the emperour with his counseyl and the duchesse of Boulion with her doughter, accompayned of many lordes and ladyes. And whan the duchesse and her doughter saw cominge Helias their noble champion, they praied God that he wolde kepe him fro harme, and give him victory over his enemy after the ryght of that he iustly defended. So incontinent was ordeyned the batayle of the two knightes, the which with cours of horse came rinning one agaynst the other the speres in the reste, and encountred so rudely that both theyr speres shivered all in peeces. And than they drewe theyr swerdes wherwith they smote together so longe that the erle might scarce doo any more. But the noble Helias had alwaye good courage as he that had set all his truste in God, and that with iust title susteined charitabli the right of the noble duchesse of Boulion. Than the erle demaunded of the noble Helyas that it wolde please him to gyve him trewes for to speak with him, the which he graunted. Certes free knight sayd the erle yf it wolde please you to apease this batayle and that I may winne that that I demaunde I shall give you my doughter in mariage, and ye shal have my londe of Dardayne that is a noble and fruitfull countrey. And than answered Helias. Traytre wenest thou to make me of thy consorce, wyt thou that I wolde soner let me to be hewen in all my membres than I wolde commit treason as thou hast doone, and therfore speake no more of it. For of me getest thou no merci for this dede. And I promise thee that this dai bi the pleasure of God which hath sent me hither I shall deliver the noble duchesse of thy treason, and I shall espouse her doughter maugre thy wicked wyll. Now defende the against me. Than Helias approched the said erle and smote him so courageousli with his swerde that he frushed al his helme wherwith the erle fel backewarde upon his horse. Than the erle thought to revete him selfe and came to Helias, the which he smote so hard upon his right arme that he made the swerde flee out of his hande. And whan Helias sawe that he was dystytute of his swerde, he descended lightli from his horse, and came and seased the erle by the bodye and valiauntly by force kest him to the erthe. And wolde he or not he arached his shield fro his necke. And sith by strength of his handes he deseased him of his swearde maugre his tethe. And whan the erle felte him so dispourveyed he began to yelde him to Helyas saying. A knight save my life and I shal give thee my landes. Ha false traytour sayd Helyas thou shalt not escape so. For I wil have whol victori of the for to venge the noble duchesse and her doughter that thou hast sclaundred. And therwith he lift up the swerde that he had taken frō the erle, and gave him suche a stroke that his helme went of and than he cut of his head and so he dyed mischevousli. And than the duchesse and her doughter gave laudes and graces to God of the victorye of theyr enemy which they saw vainquysshed by the grace of God, which had sent the noble knyght to be their helper.

CHAP. XXXI.

How the good Helias wedded the doughter of the Duchesse of Boulyon.

THAN after that the noble Helias had victoriouslye conquered the erle of Frankebourke his enemi: he came benigneli and salued the emperour Otton which received him benignely as a prue and noble knight. After he salued Clarysse the noble duchesse of Boulyon, the which thanked hym reverently of that he had doone for her, for he had saved her life, and the heritage of her noble douchy. Than Helias tooke the duchesses doughter bi the hand and enbraced and kissed her benignely in saying. Mi love ye ought wel to be mi wife, for I have frelie bought you, and saved your honour in champ of batayle. And the mayden answered humbly. Certaynly noble knyght my mother and I ben beholden to God and you of the right happy iurney that this daye we have by you receyved, wherfore at the good pleasure of mi mother I yelde me totalli to you, as it hath ben promised. And forthwith the emperour came to the duchesse saying. Ladi I yelde to you your londe and duchy of Boulyon playnle and peasybly, and restablysshe you in honour without any culpe of cryme as the trouthe is seen. Certes sayde the duchesse I thanke you highly. But as to the regarde of my londe and duchi of Boulion I give it freely to this valiaunt knight that notabli hath conquered it. And also I gyve him my doughter in mariage the which from hensforth with him shalbe sayd and called lady. For I wyll shortly go and yelde me a nune or religiouse in some nonery, as I have avowed to God the which this day hath succoured me by so noble a knight. And whan the Emperour called to him Helias the noble knight of the swane, unto whome he declared publikely and openly before all that he was duke of Boulyon, and that him behoved to wedde the doughter of the noble dame Clarisse lyke as he had promised, wherto benignely consented the said Helias. And thus by consentement of both parties was in continent made apparaile for the morow to make the feast and solempnite of the spousayles.

And al that night til on the morow echone were delibered to sporte and joy. Knights and gentilmen reioyced them of this marvaylous adventure. Ladies and demoyselles daunced with them in al games and merye cheres, and in suche wise that it should be to longe for to tel al the games, daunces, and turneymentes that were doone at the sayd feast. And on the morow was reverently celebred the mariage in the churche where as came many great Lordes, ladies, and other estates. And after was the feaste made in themperours halle, where as every man to his poore reioyced with al his hert. Trumpetes, clerons, tabourins and other minstralsi was there in that place assembled to make mirth melodiously. And to make shorte there was the greatest triumphe that ever was seen. Than at nyght the good Helias duke of Boulion lai with his spouse the which night she conceyved of him a daughter that at her baptisme was named Ydian, of whome yssued the prue and worthy prince Godfrey of Boulion, and sith his two brethren Baudwin and Eustace. The which were two noble and valiaunt knightes as theyr dedes shewed afterward. And thus appereth that the noble Helyas knyght of the Swanne conquered and wanne victoriousli the duchi of Boulion with the swearde. And after that the feaste and solempnite of the weddinge had lasted about xv. dayes, the sayd Helias duke of Boulion and his noble wife dysposed them to go into their countrei with their estate. So the said new duke tooke leave of themperour in sweringe and promisinge to him homage of the sayd duchi as it was of right, and in thankinge him honourablye he departed from him and fro al his noble barons and knyghtes for to go to Boulyon. But in goinge he founde many of the parentes and frendes of the foresayd erle of Frankebourke, the which assayled him on the way weening to avenge his death. But he shewed him so valiaunt and knightli that they were not the most strongest, for he and his folke had passage at their owne pleasure whither his enemies wolde or not. And triumphantli he came unto the said place of Boulion wher as he was honourabli received with great ioye and exultation. After he helde on a dai open court to al comers. In which were received honourably al the noble barons and lordes of the countrey, and this time hanging waxed great with childe the noble duchesse his wife in suche maner that at the ende of ix. moneths she childed of a faire doughter. The which was honestlye baptysed in greate company of divers noble lordes and damoyselles. And she was named Ydain at the fonte, the which sithe was mother of the prue and valiaunt prince Godfrey of Boulyon, and of his brethren Baudwin and Eustace. And during the childebed of the noble duchesse were made many notable convives and mery pastimes. Then afterwarde grew and sprainge the saide mayden by the wyll of God that she was in pleasaunt age of flouringe youthe. And upon a day as the duchesse wente in sportynge with her husbande the good Helyas, she demanded of him pryvelie of what countrey he was, and what freendes he had. But he sayd nothing, and defended her never to speake therof, or he wolde go his way and never dwel with her any more. So she helde her stil for that time, and they abode the space of vii. yere living in love and cordialite one with the other.

And in this time durynge the auncient duchesse mother of the good Helias wife was yelded in religion, lyke as she had promised and vowed to God.

CHAP. XXXII.

How Helias the noble duke of Boulion left his lande for that his wife disobeyed his commaundement, and after the swanne his brother brought him to Nymaye to the emperour Otton.

On a daye as the Duchesse of Boulion laye in bed with her husband Helyas there toke her a mervaylous wyll to aske agayne of hym of what folke he was comen. The which notably he had defended her, or that he wolde go his way. But as a woman that is lyght herte and wyll sooner doo the contrary to that her husbande commaundeth her than otherwise. It hapened on a night as they were to gether she was not at her ease because she durst not say and fulfil her wil. But at the last she was hardi ynough, so that she sayd. Certainly my lorde I wolde fayne knowe of what place ye be come, and who ben your parentes and freendes, as other whyle I have asked? wherfore I wolde fayne that it wolde please you to tell me. And whan the noble Helias heard her sai so he was greatli angri at his hert. And in anger sayd. Certes ye shall know nothing. And I swere and promise you by my faith that to morow erlye I shall departe fro this countrey. And at Boulion shal ye se me never more. And I shall go streyght to Nimaie and take leave at themperour and of you in the presence of all his barons.

And whan the duchesse understode him: she began to wepe tenderli, and sith arose from her bed and came and complained to her folke saying. Alas, alas my lordes and ladies now have I loste the company of my good and faythfull frende, by mine overmuche speaking, and could not hyde my courage. And anon after she came to the bedde of her doughter Ydain that her father loved derely, and tolde her therof. And than she adressed her to her fathers bedd weeping pitiously saying. Alas mi lorde my father have pitie on my good mother and me. Alas wyll ye leve us: Virgin Mary helpe, shall I abide orpheline in mi yonge dais. Alas father leve us not for Gods sake regarde your bloud, and take pitie theron. And than the noble duke that was mervaylously sorye recomforted her sayinge. Fayre doughter make not suche sorow, for I shal wel pourvey your mother and you yf God wyl, or that I departe. Than in the morning Helias arose and tenderly weping he went and harde masse devoutly as he was accustomed. And after masse he sayd to his knights and familiers. Lords I require and pray you charitably that ye wil guide my wife your lady and my doughter unto the citie of Nimaie wheras themperour is, to the ende that I may take leave of hym honourably as apperteineth, and that I may commaunde also to him mine affaire in these parties, for I shal never retorne. The noble knightes accorded gladly his demaund. And yet he said agayne. My frendes I you recommaunde that ye be alway redy to kepe and defende this noble countrey of Boulyon and the honour of my wife your duchesse and of my doughter. And so they promised him to do at his good wyl. Now my lordes sayd he I thanke you al, prayinge you that ye holde me faith as ye have promised. More over my lordes and frendes the houre is comen that I must departe fro this place, for anon ye shal se come nere the swanne, the which by the wyl of God shallede his shyppe for toguidemeto Nimaie. And as they spake thus together the swanne arived myraculously as he had sayd, and kest a mervaylous crye in callyng his brother Helias. And than he tooke leave mẹkeli of al his knightes, gentilmen and damoyselles that wept tenderly the departing of theyr good lord with the noble duchesse and her doughter that it was piti to se them. And semblably al the citezins wept and wailed the abscence and departing of theyr noble duke, that so swetlie had susteined them in good peace and liberte without to vex or trouble them with oni subsides or tailies, but for to take them from grefe had anulled al false usages and set good customes and fredomes wherfore they wende never to recover such a nother. Than entred Helyas into the shippe, where as he and the swanne feasted them ioyusle as brethren, for the houre approched that he should returne to his fourme humayne. And so they left Bulion and drewe toward Nimaie to go to themperour as the noble Helias had proposed to do for to put his wife and his doughter in his saufgarde with theyr noble countree of Boulion.

CHAP. XXXIII.

How the duchesse of Boulion complayned to the emperour for the departing of Helyas.

Incontinent after that the noble Helyas was departed fro Boulyon, the duchesse his wyfe and her doughter Ydain companyed of many noble knightes and damoyselles prepared them for to go to Nymaie before the emperour. And whan they were comen into his palais she fell downe before him wepynge and complaynynge her of her good husbande that wolde leve her, saying: Alas noble emperour I pray you yf it please you have pitie on me and on my poore doughter, for if it be not by your meane and benignite I shal lese this day the noble knight that here in your presence toke me to wife and spouse. How lady sayd the emperour is your husband dead? Alas syr said she, nay, but he will retourne into the countrey fro thens he came whan he aryved here in this place for to succour me, as echone saw clerely. For the swanne that ye saw is retourned with his shyppe to fetche him, and he is gone with him. It must be than said the emperoure that ye have doone him some offence, wherof he is angre with you. Than the sayd duchesse tolde and recyted to hym howe and what maner she had trespassed his commaundement, wherfore he repreved hyr, sayinge that she had not well doone.

And thus as they spake together: came Helias that by the guiding of his brother the swanne arived nigh to the palays of themperour. Wherfore he began to sowne hys vertuous horne, as he had doone whan he arived first. And whan the emperour had heard him he mervailed and sayd to the duchesse that he had heard her husband. Alas said she I know well that he wolde come hither. But it is to take leave at you, without ever to retorne but if ye moeve him by your high sapience.

CHAP. XXXIV.

How Helias arived at Nimaie wher as he was goodly receyved of the emperour.

Att these wordes arived Helias before themperour, the which he salued humbly. And the emperour receyved him benignely in saïenge noble duke ye be right welcom. Sir said he pardon me, for I have forsaken my duchi, and never wyll I possede any thinge of it, for it behoveth me singulerly to retourne to the countre fro whens I fyrst departed by the wyll of God. But this not wythstandyng and all stryfe premysed right affectuously I recommaund you my wife. And semblably my noble doughter the which presentli I give you as your doughter. And I pray you that it please you of your benignite to be her good father and frende and to mary her whan time shall come at your good discrecion. Al redy of your grace and bounte ye have be meane of the cause of our mariage, so againe I require you to kepe theyr honour, and maintene them under your safgarde in the fraunchise of your countrei, and noble duchy of Bolion for I wyl never retourne. A noble duke mi dere freend, yf ye have made any othe therof as ye say, it is not of necessite to holde vowes against charite. For ye shal soner have pardon to breake your othe that is not lawful than to accomplisshe it. If ought be misdoone, and so shortly to leave your wife is against God and charite, ye have also your faire doughter Ydain that ye se wepe so piteousli before you of whome ye should have pitie. Certis sir said Helias me behoveth to go lightli into an other region by the commaundement of God that calleth me for an other welth, wherfore I pray you pardon me for I may abide no longer, yonder is the swanne that abideth. My freende said the emperour, sith it is the wyll of God I wyll not gaynsay it. And than he came nere to his wyfe and his daughter the which he kissed tenderly weeping, so that he left them as al in a swoune before themperour, of whome he toke humbli leave in recommaunding them againe to his good grace. And he promised so to do, and to mary his doughter nobly with out fayle. And so departed the noble Helias, and went towarde the river where as his brother abode him in likenesse of a swanne. For he kepe the shyppe al way tyl that his brother were returned. And whan he was comen the swanne reioyced for to see him. So she departed with greate dilygence fleting alway fro river to river tyl they came into the countrei of Lilefort that was the londe of theyr nativite.

CHAP. XXXV.

How Helias the noble knight of the swanne retourned into the Citie of Lylefort within the shyppe of his brother the swanne. The whiche myraculously and by the will of our lorde retourned before his parentes and freendes in his fyrst fourme humayne.

UPON a day as the noble kynge Oryant sat at the table, and his noble spouse the good quene Beatrice with their iiii. sonnes and their doughter, there arived theyr two other noble sonnes Helyas and his brother the swanne that had guided him in his viage as it is said. And whan Helias knewe the place of Lilefort he began ioyously to blow his horne upon the river, in suche maner that the voice therof came to his father. The which incontinent arose fro the table as all reioyced saying. My wife and ye al mi children have ye joye and mirthe at harte, for here is mi sone Helias. Than diligently they arose and went to the windowes of the palays. And in beholding to the river they apparceyved the noble Helyas the which al redy yssued out of the shyppe. And anon there ran to mete him his foure brethren with theyr sister for to welcome him. And there they enbraced and kissed him for joy that they had to se him, and after ioyously he went with them into the palais before his father and his mother, wher as was made so goodly meting that it is not possible to tel. For incontinent his father and his mother kissed and enbraced him wepinge for joy that they had to receive him for the noble vertues and miraculous dedes that God had shewed in him. The one feasted him, the other reioyced him. They were all ravisshed to se him and whan thei had wel received him, his mother axed him benignely. Swet sone where have ye be? It is now wel nere viii. yeres that we have not sene you. Mother sayde he ye shal knowe it a nother time if it please God. And wher is sayd she my sonne the swanne that led you in a shyp. Certes madame sayd he, he is retourned into the water. Certaynly said the noble queene, me semed this night in my slepe that the swanne shoulde be turned to his owne fourme humayne, yf that we had the two cuppes that the goldsmith forged of his chaine, and make to be made of them, ii. chalices. And than set the chalyces upon two aulters in the church. And betwene the aulters make a bedde and lay the swanne therin, and after make to say two masses by two good and devoute preestes upon the sayd aulters and consacre in the chalyces. Than that eche of us dispose our conscience wel and devoutly so that we were worthy to pray our Saviour Jesu Christ. And I beleve that he will streche his vertues over him, and he shall retourne to his fourme humayne. Than kyng Oriant and Helias helde her counseyll good.

CHAP. XXXVI.

How queene Beatryce made greate joye of her sonne that was retourned to his right fourme.

THAN incontinent thei sent for the goldesmith that had

forged the two cuppes of the chayne of silver. And he comen to the kinge made to deliver to him the two cuppes for to make two chalices, as it had ben ordeined. And for to make it short were wel and duli ordeined two aulters and a bedde as it was sayd. Than came the noble Helias to the water side where he found his brother the swann and made maner to call him. And famelierly he came to him, and folowed him as his good and faythful brother. And in likewise as afore time he had conduited the sayde Helias, so Helyas conduted him to the churche before the crucifixe. And in the presence of the kynge, the queene, theyr chyldren and other lordes he was layde in the bedde betwene the two aulters, where as were devoutly sayd two masses, which al they above sayd heard wel and devoutly being mekely prosterned on both their knees prayinge Almighty God that by his divine bounte it wolde please him to show his vertue. So it happened that the time ordayned of God was accomplysshed that the swanne should retourne in his fourme humayne. Ryght so as the preestes consacred the body of our Lorde at the masse the swanne retourned into his propre fourme and was a man. And thus transmued he arose fro the bedde joyning his handes, and escried saying, Lordes I thanke you humblye. Jesu by his grace yelde you the devoute prayers that ye have made for me, for bi his mercy I am delivered and put fro great payne. And than wente he and mekely kissed the king his father, his mother, and after al his brethren and his sister. Than after the masse were the belles solempnely rongen and Te Deum songe for joye in thanking God of his devine vertues. After that wer made processyons and praysinges to God. And at the retournynge was baptized the sayd childe, and named Emery. The whiche sith was a noble knight. And at the comyng fro the chyrche the tables were arayed in the kings palaice where as echone were honourabli received with greate joye for love of that devine adventure so clerely shewed tofore all. And thus the noble kinge Oriant and the good queene Beatrice finabli recovered all their children bi the grace of God, wherfore fro than forthon they lived holyly and devoutly in our lorde.

CHAP. XXXVII.

How the noble Helyas tooke leave of his parantes and freendes, and made him selfe religious there as he was nouryśshed with the good hermite, where he made to buylde a castell like to that of Boulyon.

WHAN the good and worthy knight of the swanne named Helyas had sith his retourninge abiden a space of tyme in Lylefort with his father and mother in the company of his fyve brethren and his sister the which he loved of a synguler, fylyall, and fraternall love, he disposed him selfe to go into the hermitage where he had be nourisshed with his godfather the good devoute hermit Helyas, the which was disceased in our lorde.

And in that place his father king Oriant had doo

make a religion for the honour of God and memorye of his vii. children, as it is sayd before. So the sayd noble knight Helias assembled his parentes and freendes, and to them recounted al the adventures that to him were hapned sith his departinge. And howhe hadespousedthe noble duchesse of Boulyon, the which had conceyved of hym a fayre doughter named Ydain. And whan he had tolde to them as it is sayde, he shewedthem his courage and that he had intencion to doo saying. My lorde mi father and you mi lady my mother, my brethren my sister, and al my freendes. I wyll here in generall recommaunde you to God, and say farewell, for to go amende my lyfe and yelde me religyous. For seyinge the graces and devine benefyces that God hath pleased to shew for us, it behoveth to his divine wyll that I take payne to save my soule and pray for al my freendes. Wherfore humbly I recommaund you your subiects that ye treate them amyably without to oppresse them with ony grevousnesse. And my brethren and frendes I pray and require you all that knightly ye kepe and defende alway your countrey as good and valiaunt knightes. And in these wordes sayinge there was none that durst gayn say him for the love of God the whiche in all theyr anguysshes had succoured them, but began all to weepe dorolorusly for the departing of the good Helias. The which all thinge promised tooke his leave of them benignely, and kyssed them al at his parting lovyngly in weepynge, and thus he departed from them with a simple staffe in his hande. Syth as a good and devoute knight he came to the place of the sayd hermitage that he had chosen for to save his soule. And there he was mekli received of the other religious men that his father the kynge Oriant had there founded. After that he made to edyfye and buylde in that place a castel semblable and like to that of Boulyon. The which whan it was ended he made in lyke wyse to name Boulion, and the forest that was about it Dirdayne. Than in the sayd castell of Boulyon he ordeyned certaine markettes and fayres, the which he made free and quite of all customes and imposicions to all marchauntes goynge, cominge, and soiournyng at the sayd fayres in that place of Boulion, for the augmentacion and profyte of the said relygyon. In suche wise that he ordeyned xxx. religious men for to singe and ministre the devine service in the sayd religyon. And there he abode relygyous observinge the rule that there was constituted, and used his dayes in our lorde Jesu Christe.

CHAP. XXXVIII.

How the puyssaunt and vertuous emperour Otton espoused the erle of Boulyon to the fayre Ydain doughter of the noble knight of the swanne Helyas. And how after the dreame that she had the aungell of God announced to her that she shoulde conceyve and have thre noble knyghtes.

WHAN fayre Ydain doughter of Helyas the noble knight of the swanne was at the wyll of God comen to the age of xiii. yeres. Otton the puissunte Emperour, of Almayne maryed her to the noble Erle of Bouleyn named Eustace. And the feast was made in the emperours palays at Nymaie. And theyther came manye great lordes and noble knightes, gentilmen, and damoiselles, the whiche were well receyved. And amonge the other laydyes was the noble duchesse of Boulion mother of Ydain. The which in weepe piteously bewayled her good spouse the noble Helyas. Than was the feast greate, and the wedding honourably solempnised as themperour wolde for the love of Helyas. And the night comen the sayd erle of Boleyn lay with his spouse fayre Ydaine. The which conceyved of him the prue knight Godfrey of Boulyon. And the same night in her slepe she thought that she found in her bed three fayre children. The which she elacted and gave to souke of her owne milke in so great habundaunce that they were well and substauncially nourysshed. And than her semed that the two fyrst had eche of them a crowne of fine golde upon theyr heades, but the crowne of the thyrde was broken by cause another woman than his mother had geven him souke of her milke. And at this point the noble Ydain a waked of her dreame. Than harde she the voyce of an aungell that God had sent her sayinge. Ydayn God sendeth the greeting. Know thou for trouth that thou shalt conceyve of thy husbande three male children which thou shalt nourisshe with thine owne milke. And God shall give them his blessid benediction. For they shall conquere the realme of the holy lande of Jerusalem, and shall delyver the holy sepulcre of our lorde Jesu Christ out of the puissaunce and captivite of the unbelevinge Sarazins. And therfore governe them well. And whan the good Ydaine had hearde these tidinges she thanked and praysed our soverayne lorde God of his good advertisinge, and of the grace that he did to her. And thus by three yeres folowing she conceyved and childed three fayre sonnes. That is to wit the fyrst Godfrey of Boulion, the seconde Baudwin and the thirde Eustace. The whiche she loved and nourisshed diligently. But in a solempnite of penthecost arived at Boulion the bysshop of Liege, the duke of Brabant, the duke of Fryse, the erle of Flaundres, the erle of Nammer and many other great prynces and mighti barons. The whiche were there assembled for to make a certayne parlyament touching the provysyon of some affayres that was to do in the countre. So that the countesse was at the masse that right solempnely was songen before the sayd princes. Bi the whiche she left yonge Eustace somwhat to longe fro the breste, wherfore he began to weepe so fast that a woman beinge one of the nourices ranne diligently for to apease him, and gave him her pappe for to souke. And whan his mother the countesse retourned to visite him she founde the sayd nourice the whiche gave him to souke of her milke. Wherfore she was so greatly angred and displeased that she sayd. Ha woman evyll advysed what have ye presently doone. Now shall my sonne Eustace lese his noble dignite for to have taken of your mylke, wherfore I oughte well to hate you. Alas madame sayd the nourice for Goddes love pardon me, for certaynli I wende to have doone well because he wept so fast to thende to have stylled him. So the sayd countesse abode all the day by her three children without ani meate or drink for the displeasure that she had of that another woman than she had given souke to her chylde. And after dyner the erle of Boulyon led all the princes, lordes, and barons afore named into his secrete chambre for to shewe unto them his three faire sonnes, Godfrey Baudwin, and Eustace. And whan that they saw the noble countesse besyde her three children they salued her and them right benignely. And in lykewyse on her sede she receyved and fested them with her speche as muche as to her was possible, and to them shewed her iii. chyldren, but for to make them any welcoming she wolde not ons arise. Wherfore her husbande the erle was sor displeased, but he conveyed eche of them to his loging without makyng ony semblaunt therof. Than he returned agayne to her al angry for to blame her therof and sayde. Wyt ye lady that ye have greatly angred me, whan ye dayned not ones to aryse before so high and notable princes, before whome a quene of ony realme should wel have rysen for to salue them. A my lorde sayde she be not discontent with me yf ye please. For by the honour of your thre sonnes I may preaise my selfe as muche as any queene how noble that she be. How so said the erle. Certaynlye my lorde sayd she all the worlde ought well to honour and praise me for theyr dignitees. For they shal yet venge ones more the death of our Saviour Jesu Christ. And shall conquere the realme of the holy lande of Jerusalem, wherby they shall delyver the holy sepulcre of our lorde fro the handes of the misbelevinge Sarazyns, the whiche there is no kynge that dare undertake. What sayd the erle I trowe that ye dreme: and of trouthe who that should here you say and preferre suche wordes wold saye that ye had not good mynde. Ha my lorde sayd she, holde not for a vayne thing this that I tell you. For this hath tolde me and announced the aungell of our Lorde God by holy prophecy.

And at these wordes her husbande the erle of Boulein regarded her no more. But that he sayd, God give that it be so as ye have sayde.

CHAP. XXXIX.

How the noble duchesse of Boulion sent many squyers and messengers over all countreys and regyons for to fynde her noble husbande the good Helias knight of the swanne.

By the holy wyll and commaundement of God the good countesse of Boleyne Ydaine was nourisshing diligently of her three children Godfrei, Baudwyn, and Eustace. And in thys doynge helde her compani her good mother the noble duchesse of Boulyon, the whiche of times devysed with her of her good husbande Helias. For whom she had sent many messagers squyres and other in divers countreys and regyons to the ende that they myght finde him, or in ony maner heare tydinges of him as she right for desired. And amonge the messagers that sought him one her squyre named Ponce arived in Jerusalem, for to knowe and diligently enquyred if the sayd Helias had enterprysed the viage of the holi sepulcre for his remissyon. And in suche wyse that he was the space of xv. dayes within Jerusalem and in the pylgrymages and devoute places cyrcumiacentes accustomed to be doone in the said holy vyage. So he came into a church, at the entrynge wherof he founde an abbot of a churche, clothed after the Frenche facion of his religion. Whome he demaunded of whens he was. And he sayd. My frende I am of the countrey of Gaule not ferre fro Boulyon, and am abbot of Saincteron named Girarde. And than in likewise the abbot demaunded of whens he was. My lorde sayde Ponce the noble squire I am of Boulyon proprely. My frende said the abbot, you be right wel founde. Glad am I of your coming, and sith it pleaseth God thus we two together shall retourne into our countrey. Than the good abbot Gyrarde of Saincteron ledde the squyre Ponce to his lodging where as he feasted him greatlie. And there they devised one with another of theyr affaires.

And it is to be noted that at that same time wer assembled in Jerusalem many princes and great lordes, Sarazins and Painims of Turkie. As the sowdan of Perse. The kynge Dorbrye, Abraham of Damas. The king of Dortaine. Dodekin of Thabarie. The king of

Anthyoche. Solyment of Nikes. The king Feliston. The kynge of Scabon. Dodequin of Damas. King Mabrun of Oliferne, and Corborant his sonne, the which were comen al thither at the commaundement of king Corbadas, that in theyr presence and during his life wolde give his realme of Jerusalem to Cornumaraunt his sonne and crowne him king therof. The which was xv. yere olde. And the sayd new kynge was crowned by the consentment of the sayd princes resygned fro the father to the sonne in great feast and solempnite within Jerusalem like as thei were accustomed to do after theyr gestes and ceremonies. And it is for to be knowen that the sayd Cornumeraunt the new kyng of Jerusalem founde maner and space for to speake to the abbot of Saincteron the whiche for that time was in the cite of Jerusalem of whome he enquired diligentli of the state of the princes of Gaule and of theyr maner of doing. The which abbot told and cited to him trouthe, wherefore greatlye he praysed and loved him. Than all wisely the sayd abbot of Saincteron demaunded of him familiarly the saufconduyt and acquite for the countreys and landes of beyonde the sea for him and the sayd squire Ponce the more sureli to retourne into theyr countries. The which the king Cornumeraunt him graunted benignly, in presentinge to him larglye of his goodes for the wisedome and the honour of spekinge that he had founde in him. And after theyr sauf conduyte made they tooke reverently leave of the king, and on the next day in the morning they departed fro the holy citye of Jerusalem, and sith came unto the port of Jaffe otherwise named Joppen. And fro thens mounted upon the sea and after by valeis and mountaynes they wente tyl thei arived within Rome.

CHAP. XL.

How the abbot of Saincteron and the squyre Ponce departed fro Rome at theyr retournyng fro the holye sepulcre. And sith by the wil of God they ariued at the new castell of Boulyon.

AFTER that Gyrarde the abbot of Saincteron, and the squyre Ponce had doone theyr devocions within the cite of Jerusalem they departed diligently for to retourne into theyr countrey. And even as they were in the feeldes Almighti God (that alwai doth for the best) wolde that they should be wandred of theyr way. And in such wise they were fro their way in a place inhabitable that thei wist not what to thinke. So it happened that after mani travailes paines, and labours they arived nigh to the sayd castell of Boulyon that the good Helyas had newly made to edifie after the fourme and construccion of the other Boulion towarde Dardayne. Wherfore Ponce sayd to the abbot, Certes my lorde heare is Boulyon, we ben in our countrey. In our countrey sayd the abbot I trow that it lacketh a great dele. Certainly my lorde sayd Ponce, yet is this castel like and of the same fourme of it named Boulyon, and I beleve that he that made it had intencion so to doo. And after al these wordes bi cause the night came on, they went and lodged them in a vyllage nigh ynough to the said castell. And in theyr lodgis they sent for the curat of the vyllage for to wit of him in what place and in what country they were arived. Truly lordes sayd the curat, you have passed the greatest forest of Dardeyne and ben presently arived nigh to the castell of Boulyon. Now sayd the abbot we ben of the countrey that ye name, and it is well CC. leges fro hens. It is trouth my lorde said the curate, I have be in the countrey that he speake of. But for to declare you the trouth the Castell that ye have seen is called Boulyon le restaure, that is to sai restored, for that a noble and vertuous knight named Helias sonne to the mighty king Oryant and of the quene Beatryce his spouse went in a ship upon the guyding of a swanne, that so led him bi adventure to Nymaie, were as he wanne a champ of batayle agaynste the erle of Frankebourke, wherbi the emperour made to give him in maryage the duchesse of Boulyon wherof ye speake. In suche wyse that he was about viii. yere there and than after he retourned into his realme of Lilefort by the leding of the swanne aforesayd. And at his commyng he did doo make this castel and named it Boulyon as the other and the forest about it Dardayne. And whan Ponce heard him speake so he wist wel that he should have certaine tidings of that he desired, whereof he thanked our lord, and than without making semblaunt he said to the curate, Good syr the king and the queen that ye say to be father and mother of that knyght ben they now abydyng in the castel: Certes syr sayd he ye. For thei loved so muche the said Helyas theyr sonne that they have lefte Lilefort and ben comen to dwell here for the love of him. And the noble knight sayd Ponce that ye speake of is he dead: Nay forsoth sayd thee curate, and it is not vi. dayes sith I saw him. But for to declare you the verite, he hath ben during his youth of so good lyfe that Almyghtye God had doone and shewed mani fayre vertues and divine miracles at his holy prayer and orayson wherby he hath mad him religious. And is now in a devote religion that his father hath edified for the honour of God, and in the commemoracion of him and his brethren, where as he prayeth God and doth penaunce for to save his soule. Veryly sayd the squire I am all reioyced in this that ye say. Wherfore sayd the curat? For I was sayd he servaunt to the sayd Helias that was duke of Boulion, and am yet servaunt to the duchesse hys wife, the whiche hath sent me into many countries for to seche him and thanked be God I have heard of him. And so Ponce abode mery there al night. And on the morne the abbot and he went to the sayde castell, wherin at comyng fro the masse they met king Oriant, the queene, theyr v. sonnes and theyr doughter. And whan Emeri the last transmued sonne of the king saw them and had knowen theyr habite he came to them and made them chere asking them of whens thei were. And Ponce said, My lord we ben of Boulion in the lond of Dardein. And what do you in these parties said Emery. Syr said Ponce, it is longe syth I cesed not to go in many countreys and regions, as wel on this side as beyonde the se for to finde a noble knight that a swanne guided and ledde out of Boulyon, whan he left his wife the noble duchesse of Boulyon, whose servaunt I am. And whan Emery hearde him he began to laugh, Certes my frende it is my brother Helias. My lorde sayd Ponce, lyveth he yet: Yea truly my frende sayd Emery, and ye shall see him if God wyl or ye passe this country. I pray you therof sayd Ponce. Than Emery called the king, the quene, his brethren, and his sister and sayd. Certaynly if ye wil heare any tidinges of the duchesse of Boulyon my brothers wife, and of Ydain his noble doughter, here ben to notable lordes, that ben the same countrei. And forthwith thei came to Ponce, the which recyted to them the contency of the noble duchesse of Boulion that was mervailously soroful for that her good husband Helias had left her. And of her noble doughter Ydaine, of whome he tolde them to have receyved certayne tidinges that she was maried to the mighti erle of Boulein. Than sayd the king and the queene, wolde God that they were here. And therwith they enbraced and kissed the abbot and Ponce. And than he led them into the castel, wher they were feasted and served of the kings sonnes and other barons. In the whichechere they soiourned a whole day in visiting all the places of the castell. And on the morow the noble Emery led the abbot of Saincteron and the good squire Ponce to the place where as his brother Helias was relygious

And there his brother Emery founde him kneeling on his knees before the high aulter in the churche. So he salued him humbli. And reverentli he yelded him his salute in saying Fayre brother Emeri, what is ther of new : Brother said Emery, here ben two notable lordes that I bring you. The which wil tell you tidinges of your wife the duchesse of Boulyon and of your doughter Ydain, that is maryed to the erle of Boleyn. Than Helias knew Ponce for he had afore seen him. Wherfore humbly he came and enbraced and kissed him sayinge. My freende ye be welcome, tell me yf it please you some tidinges of my wyfe, and of my doughter Ydain. And than he tolde him how she had sent him into many countrees, and of his adventures syth his departing. And than he asked him if he wold retourne into his countree of Boulion. Certes sayd Helias, nay. For never by the will of God shall I departe fro this regyon where as I pretende to save my soule be his holy and worthy grace. Certes my lorde said he, I am right glade to see you, and also mi ladi shall be greatli reioysed to here of you. My frend sayde Helyas ye shall recommaunde me singulerli to her good grace, and also to my doughter Ydain. Of whom I am right ioyous that she is honourabli maried with the noble erle of Boulion. And than in weeping he tooke the abbot of Sainteron bi the hande and with Ponce ledde him to se al the places of his religion. Than with his brother Emery he made them good chere and fested them greatly and after all these thinges the squire Ponce prayed him humbli of his good plesure to geve him some true token, wherby the duchesse myght notably knowe that he had doone his devoyre to fynde him. And Helias sayd. My frend ye speake wysely. And for a token of me ye shall bere her this rynge. The which or now she gave me ryght amerously. Than after the good Helyas gave greate gyftes to the abbot and to Ponce. And with them he sent to his wife and his doughter Ydain greate treasoures and mani fayre giftes. Than tooke they leve humbly of the sayd Helias and with his brother Emery thei retourned to the castel of Boulion restaure, where they were agayne honourably receyved. And than kyng Oryant and the quene his wife prepared riche and sumtuous giftes. The whiche they sent to theyr doughter the noble duchesse of Boulyon, and also to her doughter the noble countesse of Boleon, in recommaunding them singulerly to theyr good grace. Than the abbot of Saincteron and the squyre Ponce tooke reverently theyr leve of the noble king Oriant, and of the queene his wife and of al theyr courte, and departed fro them for to retourn into theyr countrey, in the place of Boulyon in Dardayn.

CHAP. XLI.

How the squyre Ponce arived at Boulyon for to bere tydinges to the duchesse of the noble Helias knight of the swanne, the whiche was at that time yolden a religyous.

Upon a daye of the feast of the ascencyon of our lorde

Jesu Chryst as the erle of Boulyon, his wife Ydain, and the noble Duchesse her mother with many other lordes and damoyselles were sytting at the table and helde court plenayre by maner of consolacion, arived Ponce the noble squyre at the castell of Boulyon, the whiche led a mule charged with dyvers giftes and riche presentes and came into the halle wher as was the feast aforesayd. And incontinent that the noble duchesse apperceyved him she arose fro the table, and came tenderly enbracing him and sayde. My freende Ponce ye be right welcome. Have ye founde my husbande or can ye ony tidinges of him. Cyrtes madame sayde Ponce. Yea? By the same tooken that here is his rynge that he gave me to beare to you. And whan she saw the rynge she was al reioyced, and kisse it mo than an C. times, in weeping and bewayling piteously the abscence of her good and faythfull husbande Helyas, and than sayde. Truley Ponce my freende this is a good tooken that ye have founde him. Madame said he highli I have also brought a mule charged with many notable giftes and riche presentes that he and his mighty parentes have sent to you, and to my ladi the countesse Ydain your noble doughter. For I doo you notabli to wit that he is sonne of the ryght puyssant and redoubted king of Lylefort named Oriant, and of the illustred and noble quene Beatrice his wife. And eke he hath five noble brethren and all valyaunt knightes. And he hath also a fayre sister, and shortly he is of right great kine. Of these wordes was greatly inioyed the duchesse his wife his doughter and the noble erle, in suchwyse that they wept for ioye that they had at theyr hertes to here suche good tidinges. Than the sayd Ponce recited to them that he was religious in a fayre abbai that his father and he had made to constytue and edifie for the honour of God. And how he had sene al with the abbot of Saincteron, in retourning fro the holy cite of Jerusalem, where upon saythe the cronicle and gest of this myraculous history that whan the noble duchesse of Boulyon knew and understoode that her good husbande Helias was yolden religious, she made incontinent to prepare her estate. And with her doughter Ydayn she set her on the way with the sayd Ponce which they tooke for to guyde them to the religion where he had found the good Helias. Than tooke thei leave of the noble erle of Bolyon in recommaunding him his three sonnes Godfrey, Baudwin, and Eustace. The which were all redy in age adolescent. And after they departed fro Boulyon and travayled so longe by mountaynes and valees that they came to the place of religion where as the noble Helias was yolden religious. Than the noble duchesse his wife with her doughter Ydain demaunded so muche after him that they came and found him lieng in a bedde ryght sore sicke. And God knoweth than in what ioye they behelde eche other. The wife be wept her husbande, the doughter bewayled her father. And he on the other side wept tenderly to se there his wife and his doughter, so that all they that behelde them wepte for sorow and pitie. And after that they had ben there a space of time, the good Helias was so sike and weyke of paynes and travayles that he had susteyned in his yough that holili and devoutli he desceased in our lorde Jesu Chryst, the which called hym to be with hym for to rewarde him for the paynes and grevous vexaccions, that he had suffred and wyllyngli borne at his holi and dyvine commaundement and to geve him space in the glory pardurable with the happi sainctes of the realme of paradise. And whan the duchesse saw her husbande dead, she was so sorowfull at her herte that she disceased with him in our lorde, wherfore her noble doughter, Ydain and all the lordes and damoysellės that were comen with her made suche sorow that pitie was to see. And after al thinges all the religions of the sayd abbay assembled them and honestly with great reverence they buried the noble Helias and his wife in one tombe before the high aulter of the churche. And theyr service was well and devoutly doone as it apperteined to theyr estate. Than the noble Ydain departed and gave muche of her goodes to the sayd abbay for the honour of God and for the love of her father and mother the which there were engraved. And so departed fro the place with her folke, and retourned into her countrey and duchy of Boulion where as she founde Eustace her noble husbande. To whom she recited in weeping how her good father and mother were discesed in our lorde, and bothe buried togither bi the divine wyll. And whan the sayd Eustace her husband heard these tidinges he was muche sorowfull and dolen at his herte. And he wyth his wyfe and all hys housholde did beare the doole as long as it was expedient for such a noble prince.

CHAP. XLII.

How Ydain the noble duchesse of Boulyon endoctryned her three sonnes, Godfrey, Baudwyn, and Eustace in all maner of good operacyons, vertues, and maners.

After that the noble Ydain duchesse of Boulyon was retourned into her countrei she kept syngulerly her three sonnes, Godfrey, Baudwin and Eustace, whiche she made instructe by a wyse master. And she herselfe endoctryned them in all good maners and honeste of life sayinge, Alwai above all thinges give laude and glorye to God in all your workes, and sayd. My children ye ought to knowe that ye be extract and issued of a lignage as noble and vertuous as is possible to be, That is to wete of the noble knight of the swanne sonne of the puyssaunt king Oryant and of the good queene Beatryce his spouse. And ye have v. kinges and a quene of your excellent and illustryous parent. The whyche all myraculously and by the announcement of an aungel have ben producte in valoure and you also in lykewyse. And therefore than my fayre children abide alway in the feare and love of God our soveraigne protectour in giving him laud and honour. Be swet, soft and curteys to your subiectes without oppressyng or domaging them in ani wyse yf ye be able and possible to reedifie the churches of God, and offre willingly your owne bodies in sacrifice in susteyning the holy faythe catholyke. Keepe and defende iustly your countre. Bere and sustayne the right of poore widowes and orphelins. Distribute and deele of your goddes to the nedy, conforte the sorowfull and thinke for to save your soule for to have the grace of God. And I promyse you my chyldren that yf ye governe you that ye shal prospere in this worlde and have heaven at your ende. And in this maner where bi theyr good mother Ydain devoutly introduct and taught these three yong sonnes Godfrey, Baudwyn and Eustace, the whiche were al way together in theyr youthe, often times to remembre the good and helthfull doctrine that she had given them. And semblably also they were bi theyr notable scole maister suffyciently enstructe in scyence and in all good maners.

CHAP. XLIII.

How the three noble brethren Godfrey, Baudwyn, and Eustace appropried and used them in all maner of noble games and assayes of worthinesse.

And whan in the adolescence they were somwhat comen to the age of strengthe, they began to practyse them in shotinge with theyr bow and arbelstre, to playe with the swerde and buckeler, to runne, to just, to play with a poll axe, and to wrastle. And began to bere harneys, to roune horses and to approve them as desyringe to be good and faythful knightes to susteyne the faith of God. And thus thei grew al three in strength and height mervailously and in suchwyse that of theyr age was none found like to them they were fayre and well fourmed of bodye, wyse, courteys and well taught. They served God gladli, they made them to be beloved of great and small. And echone honoured them echone gave them benediccion, and also they gate grace of great princes and noble lordes. And whan Godfrey the fyrste borne was comen to the age of xv. yeres accomplisshed his good mother Ydain made to dispose and put them in poynt as to him well apperteined for to go to Nimaie to themperour for to receyve the ordre of knighthode, and sayd to him. My fayre sonne Godfrey ye be the eldest of your brethren and are of age competent for to be knight. Wherfore here is a robe of honour the which I have diligently prepaired for you to receyve the noble degree and vertuous title. Your squires and pages ben well appointed of liverayes to you apperteining, and all they of yours also. Wherfore ye shall go into the citie of Nimaie to themperour the which hath good knowledge of you bycause of your grauntfather the noble and vertuous knyght of the swanne, and my good mother his wyfe, whose soules God pardon. And so of him you shalbe made knight in giving you the swearde of honour. And your two brethren shall go with you for to beare you company. And than answered Godfrey My right lady and mother I hertelye thanke you whan you procure me suche honour. And I am al redy to departe and go towarde themperour at your good commaundement. Now go than my sonne your case is al redy. And than departed Godfrey of Boulyon mounted upon a horse of price accompanied of his two brethren, and of many noble and gentill knightes, squires, and pages. The which have riden so longe that they came to Nimaye. And incontinent the good Godfrey came and presented hem to fore the emperour, in saluinge him debonayrlye. And he received him gladly and al his company with good hert saying. Right noble chylde and my deare frende, ye be right hertli welcome. I know you to be extract and issued of the moste noble and illustrious Helias Knyght of the Swanne. Therfore for the love of him and of your mother his doughter, the which I have maried and conioyned in my noble palays bi theyr good consentement, wherfore bi the pleasure of God I shal adube you knight or ye departe fro me. Syr sayd Godfrey, I thanke you humbly. And than the noble emperour made to prepare and ordeyne a solempne feast for the love of Godfrey of Boulyon. Than incontinent after the feast were ordeyned justes, tournementes and mani other games and noble feates of armes. In the whiche the noble Godfrei shewed him right prue and valiaunt, in such wise that by the sayde emperour he was made and ordeyned knight with ryght great honour and joye. And whan the feast was passed Godfrey retourned honourabli to Boulion with his brethren Baudwin and Eustace. The which sith in theyr age were made noble knightes as theyr brother Godfrey. And thus they aryved at Boulyon with theyr company, where they were received with great joye and honour. Than certayne tyme after theyr noble father Eustace duke of

Boulion and erle of Boleyn disceased in our Lorde. The whiche by his grace and mercy have him into his infinite glory with the holy saynctes and blessed company of heven. And thus abode the saide Godfrey duke of Bulion, as the first borne of his brethern. And he was so good and so prue to right and governe the welth publyke, and so polytike in keping his countrey that he was beloved of every person. Than began soone after to approche the time that our Lorde God had ordeyned for to put and reduce the realme of the holy lande of Jerusalem into the handes of prue and noble Godfrey of Boulyon. In the which time chosen of God and by his good enhortement should be unyed and congregeed the princes of christendom for to passe over the sea and susteyne the fayth of God Jesu Christe agaynst the misbelevinge paynims. As it is writen and recited in the cronicles and faytes of the sayd Godfrey and his brethren. And al by the wil of God the whiche exalteth his freendes in this worlde and after theyr bodely death bringeth them to the life everlastinge of heaven. To the whiche bring us, the Father, the Sonne, and the Holy Gost. Amen.

Thus endeth the life and myraculous hystory of the most noble and illustryous Helyas knight of the swanne with the birth of the excellent knyght Godfrey of Boulyon, one of the nyne worthiest, and the last of the three chrysten.

Imprinted at London by me — Wyllyam Copland.

DOCTOR FAUSTUS.

DOCTOR FAUSTUS.

THE fame of Doctor Faustus, the renowned magician of Germany, has been so long established in this country, that it has obtained for him a very exalted station among the heroes of English romance. Scarcely had his countrymen invested him with the magical attributes now so liberally afforded to him, before his name, history, and adventures, were introduced into England, there to obtain for him a popularity equalling, if not excelling, that which had been awarded to him in his native land.

In that native land the Story of Faust has been produced again and again in an endless variety of forms; its last and noblest being that mighty work to which perhaps more than any other Goethe owes the world-wide reputation which he now enjoys. To the special interest given to this romance by Goethe's having selected it as the ground work of his great dramatic Epos, we are indebted for the fact that the literary history of the Faust Legend has been investigated by Goethe's admiring countrymen, not only with German learning but with German fulness; so that he who wishes to ascertain when, where, and how, the Legend arose, and what have been its various developments, must wade through thousands of pages, some critical, some bibliographical, and many very speculative.

Acknowledging therefore generally our obligations to Von der Hagen, Rosenkrantz, Görres, Streglitz, and a host of other writers on the subject, we avow ourselves more particularly indebted for the materials of the present Introduction to Duntzer's very excellent Essay *Die Sage von Doctor Johannes Faust*, and to the yet deeper and more searching work by Baron Reichlin-Meldegg, entitled *Die Deutschen Volksbucher von Johann Faust dem Schwarz-Kunstler und Christoph Wagner seinem Famulus, nach Ursprung Verbreitung, Inhalt, Bedentung, und Bearbeitung, mit steter Beziehung auf Goethe's Faust.* *

The latter of these, who is we believe the most recent writer upon the subject, attributes the origin of the story to the Reformers, who regarded the Church of Rome as the especial seat and dominion of Satan; and the first complete edition of the Faustus Legend, which appeared in 1587, is characterized throughout by a strong Protestant and anti-Romish feeling.

* These two works, and indeed almost every thing that has been written on the subject of Faust, have been reprinted by Scheible in *Das Kloster*; four volumes of that curious series being entirely occupied with Faust and his Legends and their literary history.

The following is the title of it, *Historia von D. Johann Fausten, dem weitbeschreiten Zauberer und Schwazkunstler, wie er sich gegen dem Teufel auf eine benandte Zeit verschreiben, was er hierzwischen für seltzame Abenthewer gesehen selbs angerichtet und getrieben, bis er endlich seinen wohlverdienten Lohn empfangen. Mehrentheils aus seinen eigenen Schriften, allen hochtragenden fürwitzigen und gottlosen Menschen zum schrecklichen Beispiel, abschewlichen Exempel und trewhertzigen Warnung zusammengezogen und in Druck verfertigt.* Jacobi III. *Seyd Gott unterthanig, widerstehet dem Teufel so fleuchtet er von euch.* Cum Gratia et Privilegio, *gedruckt zu Frankfurt am Main durch Johann Speig.* 1587.

This work consists of a collection of traditions current in the Middle Ages and in the sixteenth century, in all of which Faust is made to figure as the Hero. In short, Faust is the personification of all the conjurors who preceded him; and his story is a *Faustiad* of all the legends of magicians which had ever been circulated. The reader who desires to see the evidence of this will do well to consult Reichlin-Meldegg's very learned work, in which he will find as it were side by side, in a manner which leaves no doubt as to their identity, the Faust Legend and the original story from Wierus, Lercheimer, &c. of some other Arch-Magus, which the Historian of Dr. Faustus has not scrupled to appropriate to his own hero.

That this hero was no imaginary one is clearly proved by the testimony of contemporary writers. Among the most important of these is the famous Trithemius, who in a letter to Johann Wedunger dated 20th August, 1507, speaks of the subject of this notice as one "qui se principem necromanticorum ausus est nominare, gyrovagus, battologus et circumcellio est," and as having formed for himself this fitting title, "Magister Georgius Sabellicus, Faustus Junior, Fons Necromanticorum, Astrologus, Magus Secundus, Chiromanticus Agromanticus, Pyromanticus, in hydra arte secundus." In 1539 he is mentioned by Begardo in his *Index Sanitatis.* Gastius also alludes to him in his *Sermones Convivales*, and he is also alluded to by Manilius in his *Collectanea*, on the authority of Melancthon.

"In truth," says Gorres,* "although there is a good deal of conflicting evidence in regard to the particular spot where he was born and flourished, there is little doubt of his being an historical personage, and one who had wit to take advantage of the times in which he lived; whose superior intellects and

* In his Volksbucher—as quoted by Roscoe, *German Novelists*, vol. i. p. 260.

adroitness outstripped the superstitious fear and prejudices of his countrymen, to whom he was indebted for so much of his notoriety. The Reformation had newly awakened religious zeal, to which Faustus, long familiar with the quietism and insipidity of the northern character, was so far from giving the rein, and entering into all the fervours of pious transcendentalism, that he rather turned polemic, and by venturing to dissent and to oppose, drew down upon himself the anger and abhorrence of the saints. Shortly Faustus appeared conspicuous in history, as the common representative of mischievous magicians, guilty of all kinds of diablerie. Their sins, throughout centuries, were all laid at his door; and when the general faith, falling as it were to pieces, divided into ferocious schisms, it found a common point of approach in a man, who, during his frequent tours, and his intercourse with all ranks of people, had boasted of his infernal connections and influence in the *nether* lands."[1]

The first Popular History of Faustus was, as has been shown, published in 1587. In the following year there was another issue of this edition, bearing the date 1588, agreeing generally with the former, both in the title and in its contents, and with the preface bearing as in the first edition the date of 4th September, 1587.

In the next year, 1589, there appeared an edition with decided although not very important alterations. It is described in the title page as being "newly revised and enlarged by the addition of several pieces," (newe übersehen und mit vielen Stücken gemehret.)

Twelve years after the first History of Faust had been given to the public, there appeared an entirely new work upon the subject, written by Georg Rudolf Widman, and published at Hamburgh in 1599, by Herman Moller. This was long supposed to have been the original of the English Story Book. But on comparing the English version with the German editions of 1587 and 1588, it is obvious that the latter was the one from which the author of our Life and Death of Dr. John Faustus translated. For although a comparison between the editions of 1587 and 1588 show that the latter was not greatly altered, the number of chapters in it was reduced from 76 to 68, while some changes were made in the order of their arrangement. In the old English version this latter arrangement is followed, and the chapters are again reduced by compression from 68 to 61.

How soon this Translation was made is uncertain; but that it must have been within two years of the first publication of the *Faust-sage* in 1587, is shown by the fact that Marlowe's Tragical *History of Doctor*

Faustus, which is palpably founded on the German Story Book, appeared in 1589. My friend, Mr. Payne Collier, has kindly furnished me with the following proof that a revised edition of it appeared as early as 1592. The following is a copy of the title. "The Historie of the damnable life and deserved death of Doctor John Faustus, Newly imprinted and in convenient places imperfect matter amended: according to the true Copie printed at Franckfort, and translated into English by P. F. Gent. Seene and allowed. Imprinted at London by Thomas Orwin, &c. 1592."

It is impossible, in the limits of this Introduction, to attempt to give a List of the various Editions of this Romance which have been issued from Marlowe's time to the present day, in order to satisfy the popular curiosity respecting this Prince of Conjurors. It has been frequently printed as a Chap-book since the commencement of the present century.

As we shall have to speak of the Second Part of his History in the Introduction to that rare Romance, we may now bring this notice to a close, with the statement, that by an entry in the Register of the Stationers' Company, it appears that in the year 1588, "A Ballad of the Life and Death of Doctor Faustus, *the great Congerer*," was licensed to be printed by the learned Aylmer, Bishop of London, which was probably an

English version of the German Metrical Volksbuch, entitled, "*Ein warhaffte und eischrokliche Geschickt: von D. Johann Fausten dem weitbeschreiten Zauberer und Schwarzkunstler, &c. Getruckt zu Tubingen, bey Alexander Hock im Jar* MDLXXXVIII."

The following Ballad which is preserved in the Roxburghe Collection (v. iii. p. 280) in the British Museum, may possibly be a modernized version of that licensed by Aylmer.

THE JUST JUDGMENT OF GOD SHEW'D UPON DR. FAUSTUS.

To the tune of "Fortune my Foe," &c.

All Christian men give ear a while to me,
How I am plung'd in pain, but cannot see:
I liv'd a life the like did none before,
Forsaking Christ, and I am damn'd therefore.

At Wertemburgh, a town in Germany,
There was I born and bred of good degree,
Of honest stock, which afterwards I sham'd,
Accurst therefore, for *Faustus* was I nam'd.

In learning high my uncle brought up me,
And made me Doctor of Divinity:
And when he dy'd he left me all his wealth,
Which cursed gold did hinder my soul's health.

Then did I shun the Holy Bible book,
Nor on God's word would never after look;
But studied the accursed conjuration,
Which was the cause of my utter damnation.

The Devil in Fryar's weeds appeared to me,
And straight to my request he did agree,
That I might have all things at my desire,
I gave him soul and body for his hire.

Twice did I make my tender flesh to bleed,
Twice with my blood I wrote the Devil's deed,
Twice wretchedly I soul and body sold,
To live in pleasure, and do what things I would.

For four and twenty years this Bond was made,
And then at length my soul for it was paid;
Time ran away, and yet I never thought,
How dear my soul our Saviour Christ had bought.

Would I at first been made a beast by kind,
Then had not I so vainly set my mind;
Or would not when Reason began to bloom,
Some darksome den had been my deadly tomb.

Wo to the day of my nativity!
Wo to the time that once did foster me!
And wo unto the hand that sealed the Bill!
Wo to myself the cause of all my ill!

The time I pass'd away with much delight,
'Mongst princes, peers, and many a worthy knight,
I wrought such wonders by my magick skill,
That all the world may talk of *Faustus* still.

The Devil carried me up in the skie,
Where I did see how all the world did lie:
I went about the world in eight days space,
And then return'd into my native place.

What pleasure I did wish to please my mind,
He did perform, as bond and seal did bind:
The secrets of the stars and planets told,
Of earth and sea, with wonders manifold.

When four and twenty years was almost run,
I thought on things that then was past and done;
How that the Devil will soon claim his right,
And carry me to everlasting night.

Then all too late I curst my wicked deed,
The dread thereof does make my heart to bleed:
All days and hours I mourned wond'rous sore,
Repenting then of all things done before.

I then did wish both sun and moon to stay,
All times and seasons never to decay;
Then had my time ne'er come to dated end,
Nor soul and body down to hell descend.

At last when I had but one hour to come,
I turn'd the glass for my last hour to run:
And called in learned men to comfort me,
But Faith was gone, and none could succour me.

By twelve o'clock my glass was almost out,
My grieved conscience then began to doubt:
I pray'd the studious to stay in chambers by,
But as they staid they heard a doleful cry.

Then presently they came into the hall,
Whereas my brains were cast against the wall;
Both arms and legs in pieces they did see,
My bowels gone, there was an end of me.

You conjurors and damned witches all,
Example take by my unhappy fall:
Give not your souls and bodies unto hell,
See that the smallest hair you do not sell.

But hope in Christ his kingdom you may gain,
Where you shall never fear such mortal pain;
Forsake the Devil, and all his crafty ways,
Embrace true Faith that never more decays.

FINIS.

THE
HISTORY
OF THE
Damnable Life and Deserved Death
OF
DR. JOHN FAUSTUS.

NEWLY PRINTED, AND IN CONVENIENT PLACES, IMPERTINENT MATTER AMENDED, ACCORDING TO THE TRUE COPY, PRINTED AT FRANKFORD; AND TRANSLATED INTO ENGLISH, BY P. R. GENT.

LONDON:

PRINTED BY C. BROWN; FOR M. HOTHAM, AT THE BLACK BOY ON LONDON BRIDGE, AND SOLD BY THE BOOKSELLERS.

A DISCOURSE OF THE MOST FAMOUS DR. JOHN FAUSTUS, OF WITTENBURG, IN GERMANY, CONJURER AND NECROMANCER; WHEREIN IS DECLARED MANY STRANGE THINGS THAT HIMSELF HAD SEEN AND DONE IN THE EARTH AND AIR, WITH HIS BRINGING UP, HIS TRAVELS, STUDIES, AND LAST END.

CHAP. I.

OF HIS PARENTAGE AND BIRTH.

John Faustus, born in the town of Rhodes, being in the province of Weimer, in Germany, his father a poor husbandman, and not able well to bring him up, yet having an uncle at Wittenburg, a rich man, and without issue, took this Faustus from his father, and made him his heir, insomuch that his father was no more troubled with him, for he remained with his uncle at Wittenburg, where he was kept at the university in the same city, to study Divinity; but Faustus being of a naughty mind, and otherwise addicted, plyed not his studies, but betook himself to other exercises, which his uncle oftentimes hearing, rebuked him for it; as Eli oftentimes rebuked his children for sinning against the Lord, even so, this good old man laboured to have Faustus apply his study to Divinity, that he might come to the knowledge of God and his law. But it is manifest that many vertuous parents have wicked children, as Cain, Reuben, Absolom, and such like, have been to their parents. So Faustus having godly parents, who seeing him to be of a toward wit, were desirous to bring him up in those vertuous studies, namely, of Divinity; but he gave himself secretly to necromancy, and conjuration, insomuch that few or none could perceive his profession.

But to the purpose, Faustus continued at study in the university, and was by the rectors, and sixteen masters afterwards, examined how he had profited in his studies, and being found by them, that none of his time were able to argue with him in divinity, or for the excellency of his wisdom to compare with him, with one consent, they made him Doctor of Divinity: But Doctor Faustus, within short time after he had obtained his degree, fell into such fantasies, and deep cogitations, that he was mocked of many, and of the most part of the students was called the Speculator, and sometimes he would throw the scriptures from him, as though he had no care of his former profession, so that he began a most ungodly life, as hereafter more at large may appear, for the old proverb saith, Who can hold what will away? So, who can hold Faustus from the devil, that seeks after him with all his endeavours; for he accompanied himself with divers that were seen in those devilish arts, and that had the Chaldean, Persian, Hebrew, Arabian, and Greek Tongues, using figures, characters, conjurations, incantations, with many other ceremonies belonging to those infernal arts, as necromancy, charms, soothsaying, witchcraft, enchantment, being delighted with their books, words, and names so well, that he studied day and night therein, insomuch that he could not abide to be called Doctor of Divinity, but waxed a worldly man, and named himself an astrologian, and a mathematician, and for a shadow sometimes a physician, and did great cures, namely with herbs, roots, waters, drinks, receits and glysters; and without doubt he was passing wise and excellent perfect in Holy Scriptures: But he that knoweth his master's will, and doth it not, is worthy to be beaten with many stripes. It is written, No man can serve two masters, and thou shalt not tempt the Lord thy God. But Faustus threw all this in the wind, and made his soul of no estimation, regarding more his worldly pleasures than the joys to come; therefore at the day of judgment, there is no hope of his redemption.

CHAP. II.

How Dr. Faustus began to practise his devilish art, and how he conjured the devil, making him to appear, and meet him on the morrow-morning at his own house.

You have heard before that all Faustus's mind was to study the arts of necromancy and conjuration, the which exercise he followed day and night, and taking to him the wings of an eagle thought to fly over the whole world, and to know the secrets of heaven and earth, for his speculation was so wonderful, being expert in using his vocabula, figures, characters, conjuration, and other ceremonial actions, that in all haste he put in practice to bring the devil before him, and taking his way to a thick wood near to Wittenburg, called in the German tongue, Spisser Holt, that is in English, the Spisser's Wood, as Faustus would oftentimes boast of it among the crew, being in jollity, he came into the wood one evening into the cross-way, where he made with a wand a circle in the dust, and within that many more circles and characters; and thus he past away the time until it was nine or ten of the clock in the night, then began Dr. Faustus to call on Mephistophiles the Spirit, and to charge him in the name of Belzebub, to appear there presently, without any long stay; then presently the devil began so great a rumour in the wood, as if heaven and earth would have come together, with wind, and the trees bowed their tops to the ground, then fell the devil to roar, as if the whole wood had been full of lyons, and suddenly about the circle run the devil, as if a thousand waggons had been running together on paved-stones: After this, at the four corners of the wood it thunder'd horribly, with such lightning, as the whole world to his seeming had been on fire. Faustus all this while, half amazed at the devil's so long tarrying, and doubting whether he were best to abide any more such horrible conjurings, thought to leave his circle, and depart, whereupon the devil made him such musick of all sorts, as if the nymphs themselves had been in place: whereat Faustus revived, and stood stoutly in his circle, expecting his purpose, and began again to conjure the spirit Mephistophiles in the name of the Prince of Devils, to appear in his likeness: whereat suddenly, over his head hung hovering in the air a mighty dragon; then calls Faustus again after his devilish manner, at which there was a monstrous cry in the wood, as if hell had been open, and all the tormented souls cursing their condition. Presently, not three fathom above his head, fell a flame in manner of lightning, and changed itself into a globe; yet Faustus feared it not, but did persuade himself that the devil should give him his request before he would leave. Oftentimes after to his companions he would boast that he had the stoutest head under the cope of heaven at command. Whereat they answered, They knew no stouter than the Pope or Emperor. But Dr. Faustus said, The head that is my servant, is above all upon earth; and repeated certain words out of St. Paul to the Ephesians, to make his argument good, The Prince of the World is upon earth and under heaven. Well, let us come again to his conjuration, where we left him at the fiery globe; Faustus vexed at his spirit's so long tarrying, used his charms, with full purpose not to depart before he had his intent; and crying on Mephistophiles the spirit, suddenly the globe opened, and sprung up in the height of a man, so burning a time, in the end it converted to the shape of a fiery man. This pleasant beast ran about the circle a great while, and lastly, appeared in the manner of a Gray Fryar, asking Faustus, what was his request? Faustus commanded, that the next morning at twelve of the clock, he should appear to him at his house; but the devil would in no wise grant it. Faustus began to conjure him again, in the name of Belzebub, that he should fulfil his request; whereupon the spirit agreed, and so they departed each on his way.

CHAP. III.

The conference of Dr. Faustus, with his spirit Mephistophiles, the morning following at his own house.

Dr. Faustus, having commanded the spirit to be with him, at his hour appointed, he came and appeared in his chamber, demanding of Faustus what his desire was:

Then began Dr. Faustus anew with him, to conjure him, That he would be obedient unto him, and to answer him certain articles, to fulfil them in all points:

1. That the spirit would serve him, and be obedient unto him in all things that he asked of him, from that hour until the hour of his death.

2. Further, any thing that he desired of him, he should bring him.

3. Also that in all Faustus's demands and interrogations, the spirit should tell him nothing but that which was true.

Hereupon the spirit answered, and laid his case forth, that he had no such power of himself, until he had first given his prince (that was ruler over him) to understand thereof, and to know if he could obtain so much of his lord: Therefore speak farther, that I may do thy whole desire to my prince; for it is not in my power to fulfil without his leave: Shew me the cause why? said Faustus. The spirit answer'd Faustus, Thou shalt understand, that with us it is even as well a kingdom, as with you on earth; yea, we have our rulers and servants, as I myself am one; and we have our whole number the legion, for although that Lucifer is thrust and fallen out of heaven, through his pride and high mind, yet he hath notwithstanding a legion of devils at his command, that we call the Oriental Princes, for his power is infinite, also there is a power in meridie, in septentrio, in occidente, and for that Lucifer hath his kingdom under heaven; we must change and give ourselves to men, to serve them at their pleasure. It is also certain, we have not as yet opened to any man the truth of our dwelling, neither of our ruling, neither what our power is, neither have we given any man any gift, or learned him any thing, except he promise to be ours.

Dr. Faustus upon this, arose where he sat, and said, I will have my request, and yet I will not be damned. The spirit answered, Then shalt thou want thy desire, and yet art thou mine notwithstanding, if any man would detain thee, it is but in vain, for thy infidelity hath confounded thee. Hereupon spake Faustus, Get thee hence from me, and take St. Valentine's farewel, and Crisman with thee; yet I conjure thee, that thou be here at evening, and bethink thyself of what I have asked thee, ask thy prince's counsel therein. Mephistophiles, the spirit thus answer'd, vanished away, leaving Faustus in his study, where he sat pondering with himself how he might obtain his request of the devil, without the loss of his soul, yet he was fully resolved in himself, rather than to want his pleasure, to do what the spirit and his lord should condition upon.

CHAP. IV.

The second Time of the Spirit's appearing to Faustus at his House, and their Parley.

Faustus continued in his devilish cogitations, never moving out of the place where the spirit left him, such was his fervent love to the devil; the night approaching, this swift-flying spirit appeared to Faustus, offering himself with all submission to his service, with full authority from his prince, to do whatsoever he would request; if so be Faustus would promise to be his. This answer I bring thee, an answer must thou make by me again: yet I will hear what is thy desire, because thou hast sworn to me to be here at this time. Dr. Faustus gave him this answer, though faintly for his soul's sake, that his request was none other, but to become a devil, or at the least a limb of him, and that the spirit should agree to these articles following:

1. That he might be a spirit in shape and quality.

2. That Mephistophiles should be his servant at his command.

3. That Mephistophiles should bring him any thing, and do for him whatsoever he desired.

4. That all times he would be in the house invisible to all men, except only to himself, and at his command, to shew himself.

5. That Mephistophiles should at all times appear at his command, in what form or shape soever he would.

Upon these points the spirit answered Dr. Faustus. That all this should be granted him, and fulfilled, and more if he would agree unto him upon certain articles as followeth:

1. That Dr. Faustus should give himself to the lord Lucifer, body and soul.

2. For confirmation of the same, he should make him a writing written in his own blood.

3. That he would be an enemy to all Christian people.

4. That he would deny the Christian belief.

5. That he let not any man change his opinion, if so be, any man should go about to dissuade or withdraw him from it.

Farther the spirit promised Faustus to give him certain years to live in health and pleasure, and when such years were expired, that then Faustus would be fetched away; and if he would hold these articles and conditions, that then he should have whatsoever his heart would wish or desire; and that Faustus should quickly perceive himself to be a spirit in all manner of actions whatsoever. Hereupon Dr. Faustus's mind was inflamed, that he forgot his soul, and promises Mephistophiles to hold all things as he mentioned them: he thought the devil was not so black as they use to paint him, nor hell so hot as the people say.

CHAP. V.

The third Parley between Dr. Faustus and Mephistophiles, about a Conclusion.

AFTER Dr. Faustus had made his promise to the devil, in the morning betimes, he called the spirit before him, and commanded him, that he should always come to him like a friar, after the order of St. Francis, with a bell in his hand like St. Anthony, and to ring it once or twice before he appeared, that he might know of his certain coming: then Faustus demanded of his spirit what was his name? The spirit answer'd, My name is as thou sayest, Mephistophiles, and I am a prince, but a servant to Lucifer, and all the circuit from septrenttio to the meridian, I rule under him. Even at these words was this wicked wretch Faustus inflamed, to hear himself to have gotten so great a potentate to serve him,forgetting the Lord his Maker, and Christ his Redeemer, he became an enemy to all mankind; yea, worse than the gyants, whom the poets said to climb the hills to make war with the gods, not unlike the enemy of God and Christ, that for his pride was cast into hell; so likewise Faustus forgot, that high climbers catch the greatest falls, and sweet meats have oft sowrest sauce.

After a while Faustus promised Mephistophiles to write and make his obligation with all assurance of the articles in the chapter before rehearsed: a pitiful case, Christian reader, for certainly this letter or obligation was found in his house, after his most lamentable end, with all the rest of his damnable practices us'd in his whole life.

Wherefore I wish all Christians to take example by this wicked doctor, and to be comforted in Christ, concerning themselves with that vocation, whereunto it hath pleased God to call them, and not so esteem the vain delights of this life as did this unhappy Faustus in giving his soul to the devil: and to confirm it the more assuredly, he took a small penknife, and prickt a vein in his left hand, and for certainty thereupon were seen on his hand these words written, as if they had been written in his own blood, O homo fuge; whereat the spirit vanished, but Faustus continued in his damnable mind.

CHAP. VI.

How Dr. Faustus set his Blood in a Saucer on warm Ashes, and writ as followeth:

I JOHN FAUSTUS, doctor, do openly acknowledge with mine own hand, to the great force and strengthening of this letter, that since I began to study, and speculate the course and nature of the elements, I have not found, through the gift that is given me from above, any such learning and wisdom that can bring me to my desire, and for that I find that men are unable to instruct me any farther in the matter; now have I Dr. Faustus, to the hellish prince of Orient, and his messenger Mephistophiles, given both body and soul, upon such conditions, that they shall learn me, and fulfill my desires in all things, as they have promised and vowed unto me, with due obedience unto me, according to the articles mentioned between us.

Farther, I do covenant and grant with them by these presents, that at the end of twenty four years next ensuing, the date of this present letter, they being expired, and I in the mean time, during the said years, be served of them at my will, they accomplishing my desires to the full in all points as we are agreed: that

heard a rushing of armed men, and trampling of horses, this ceasing, came a kennel of hounds, and they chased a great hart in the hall, and there the hart was slain: Faustus took heart, came forth and looked upon the hart, but presently before him there was a lion and a dragon together, fighting so fiercely, that Faustus thought they would have thrown down the house; but the dragon overcame the lion, and so they vanished. After this came in a peacock and peahen, the cock bruising of his tail, turning to the female, beat her, and so vanished. Afterward followed a furious bull, that with a full fierceness ran upon Faustus, but coming near him vanished away. Afterward followed a great old ape, this ape offered Faustus the hand, but he refused; so the ape ran out of the hall again. Hereupon fell a mist in the hall, that Faustus saw no light, but it lasted not; and so soon as it was gone, there lay before Faustus two great sacks, one full of gold, another of silver.

Lastly, was heard by Faustus all manner of instruments of musick, as organs, clarigolds, lutes, viols, citterns, waits, hornpipes, flutes, anomes, harps, and all manner of other instruments, which so ravished his mind, that he thought he had been in another world, forgot both body and soul, insomuch, that he was minded never to change his opinion concerning that which he had done. Hereat came Mephistophiles into the hall to Faustus, in apparel like unto a fryar, to whom Faustus spake, thou hast done me a wonderful pleasure in shewing me this pastime; if thou continue as thou hast begun, thou shalt win my heart and soul, yea, and have it. Mephistophiles answered, This is nothing, I will please thee better; yea, that thou may'st know my power on all, ask what request thou wilt of me, that shalt thou have, conditionally hold thy promise, and give me thy hand-writing. At which words the wretch thrust forth his hand, saying, Hold thee, there hast thou my promise. Mephistophiles took the writing and willed Faustus to take a copy of it; with that the perverse Faustus being resolute in his damnation, wrote a copy thereof, and gave the devil the one, and kept in store the other. Thus the spirit and Faustus were agreed, and dwelt together: no doubt there was a vertuous house keeping.

CHAP. VIII.

The manner how Faustus proceeded in this damnable Life and of the deligent Service that Mephistophiles used towards him.

DR. FAUSTUS having given his soul to the devil, renouncing all the powers of heaven, confirming all his lamentable action with his own blood, and having already delivered his writing now into the devil's hand, the which so puffed up his heart, that he forgot the mind of a man, and thought himself to be a spirit. Thus Faustus dwelt at his uncle's house at Whittenburg, who dyed, and bequeathed it in his testament to his cosen Faustus. Faustus kept a boy with him, that was his scholar, an unhappy wag, called Christopher Wagner, to whom this sport and life that he saw his master followed, seemed pleasant. Faustus loved the boy well, hoping to make him as good or better seen in his hellish exercises than himself, and he was fellow with Mephistophiles: otherwise Faustus had no company in his house but himself and boy, and spirit that ever was deligent at Faustus's command, going about the house, cloathed like a fryar, with a little bell in his hand, seen of none but Faustus. For victuals and other necessaries, Mephistophiles brought him at his pleasure, from the Duke of Saxony, the Duke of Bavaria, and the Bishop of Salisburgh: and they had many times their best wine stolen out of their cellars by Mephistophiles, likewise their provisions for their own table: such meat as Faustus wished for, his spirit brought him in. Besides that, Faustus himself was become so cunning, that when he opened his window, what fowl soever he wished for, it came presently flying into the house, were it never so dainty. Moreover, Faustus and his boy went in sumptuous apparel, the which Mephistophiles stole from the mercers at Norenburg, Aspurg, Franckford and Tipzig; for it was hard for them to find a lock to keep out such a thief; all their maintainance was but stolen and borrowed ware: and thus they lived an odious life in the sight of God, though as yet the World were unacquainted with their wickedness; it must be so, for their fruits be none other, as Christ saith in John, where he calls the devil a thief and murtherer; and that found Faustus, for he stole him away both body and soul.

CHAP. IX.

How Dr. Faustus would have married, and how the Devil had almost killed him for it.

Dr. Faustus continued thus in this epicurish life day and night, believed not that there was a God, hell, or devil; he thought that soul and body dy'd together, and had quite forgot divinity, or the immortality of the soul, but stood in that damnable heresie day and night, and bethinking himself of a wife, called Mephistophiles to council: which would in no case agree, demanding of him if he would break the covenant made with him, or if he had forgot it: hast thou (quoth Mephistophiles) sworn thy self an enemy to God and to all creatures? To this I answer thee, Thou canst not marry, thou canst not serve two masters, God and my prince: for wedlock is a chief institution ordained of God, and that thou hast promised to defie as we do all, and that hast thou not only done: but moreover, thou hast confirmed it with thy blood, persuade thyself that what thou dost in contempt of wedlock, it is all to thy own delight. Therefore Faustus look well about thee, and bethink thyself better, and I wish thee to change thy mind; for if thou keep not what thou has promised in thy writing, we will tear thee in pieces like the dust under thy feet: Therefore, sweet Faustus, think with what unquiet life, anger, strife, and debate thou shalt live in, when thou takest a wife, therefore change thy mind.

Dr. Faustus was with these speeches in despair: and as all that have forsaken the Lord can build upon no good foundation, so this wretched Doctor having forsook the rock, fell into despair with himself; fearing, if he should motion matrimony any more, that the devil should tear him in pieces. For this time (quoth he to Mephistophiles) I am not minded to marry: Then dost thou well, answered his spirit. But within two hours after, Faustus called again to his spirit, who came in his old manner like a fryar. Then Faustus said unto him, I am not able to resist or bridle my fancy, I must and will have a wife, and I pray thee give thy consent to it. Suddenly upon these words came such a whirlwind about the Place, that Faustus thought the whole house would have come down, all the doors of the house flew off the hooks: after all this his house was full of smoak, and the floor covered with ashes; which when Dr. Faustus perceived, he would have gone up stairs, and flying up he was taken and thrown down into the hall, that he was not able to stir hand nor foot, then round about him ran a monstrous circle of fire, never standing still, that Faustus cry'd as he lay, and thought there to have been burned. Then cryed he out to his Spirit Mephistophiles for help, promising him he would live, for all this, as he had vowed by his hand writing. Hereupon appeared unto him an ugly devil, so dreadful and monstrous to behold, that Faustus durst not look on him. The devil said, What wouldst thou have, Faustus? How likest thou thy wedding? What mind art thou in now? Faustus answered, he had forgot his promise, desiring of him pardon, and he would talk no more of such things. Thou art best so to do; and so vanished from him. After appeared unto him his friar Mephistophiles, with a bell in his hand, and spake to Faustus, It is no jesting with us, hold thou that which thou hast vowed, and we will perform that which we have promised, and more than that, thou shalt have thy heart's desire of what woman soever thou wilt, be she alive or dead, and so long as thou wilt thou shalt keep her by thee. These words pleased Faustus wonderful well, and repented himself that he was so foolish to wish himself married, that might have any woman in the whole city brought him at his command, the which he practised and persevered in a long time.

CHAP. X.

Questions put forth by Dr. Faustus unto his Spirit Mephistophiles.

Dr. Faustus living in all manner of pleasure that his heart could desire, continuing of his amorous drifts, his delicate fare, and costly apparel, called on a time his Mephistophiles to him, who being come, brought him a book in his hand of all manner of devilish and enchanting arts, the which he gave Faustus, saying, Hold, my Faustus, work now thy heart's desire: the copy of this enchanting book was afterwards found by his servant Christopher Wagner: Well, (quoth Faustus to his spirit) I have called thee to know what thou canst do, if I have need of thy help. Then answered Mephistophiles, and said, My lord Faustus, I am a flying spirit, yea, so swift as thought can think, to do whatsoever. Here Faustus said, But how came lord and master Lucifer to have so great a fall from heaven? Mephistophiles answered, My lord Lucifer was a fair angel, created of God as immortal, and being placed in the Seraphims, which are above the Cherubims, he would have presumed upon the Throne of God, with intent to thrust God out of his seat; upon this presumption the Lord cast him down headlong, and where before he was an angel of light, now dwells in darkness, not able to come near his first place, without God send for him to appear before him; as Raphael, unto the lower degree of angels, that have their conversation with men, he may come, but not unto the second degree of the heavens, that is kept by the arch-angels, namely Michael and Gabriel, for these are called Angels of God's wonders, these are far inferiour places to that from whence my lord and master Lucifer fell: and thus far Faustus, because thou art one of the beloved children of the lord Lucifer, following thy mind in manner as he did his, I have shortly resolved thy request, and more I will do for thee at thy pleasure.

I thank thee Mephistophiles (quoth Faustus) come, let us now go to rest, for it is night; upon this they left their communication.

CHAP. XI.

How Dr. Faustus dreamed that he had seen Hell in his Sleep, and how he questioned with the Spirit of matters concerning Hell, with the Spirit's answer.

THE night following after Faustus's communication with Mephistophiles, as concerning the fall of Lucifer, Dr. Faustus dreamed that he had seen a part of hell, but in what manner it was, or in what place he knew not, whereby he was much troubled in mind, and called unto him Mephistophiles his spirit, saying unto him, I pray thee resolve me in this doubt: What is hell? What substance is it of? In what place stands it? And when was it made? Mephistophiles answered, Faustus, thou shalt know, that before the fall of my Lord Lucifer there was no hell, but even then was hell ordained; it is no substance, but a confused thing; for I tell thee, that before all elements were made, or the earth seen, the spirit of God moved upon the waters, and darkness was over all; but when God said, Let there be light it was at his word, and the light was on God's right hand, and he praised the light. Judge thou farther, God stood in the middle, the darkness was on his left hand, in the which my lord was bound in chains until the day of Judgment: in this confused hell is nought to find but a sulphurish fire, and stinking mist or fog: farther, we devils know not what substance it is of, but a confused thing; for as the bubble of water flyeth before the wind, so doth hell before the breath of God: moreover, the devils know not how God hath laid the foundation of our hell, nor where it is: but to be short, Faustus, we know that hell hath neither bottom nor end.

CHAP. XII.

The second question put forth by Dr. Faustus to his spirit, what kingdoms were in hell, how many, and what were the rulers names.

Faustus spake again to his spirit, saying, Thou speakest of wonderful things; I pray thee now tell me what kingdoms are there in your hell? How many are there? What they are called? And who rules them? The spirit answered him, My Faustus, know that hell is, as thou wouldest think with thyself, another world, in the which we have our being under the earth, even to the heavens; within the circumference whereof are contained ten kingdoms, namely, 1. Lacus Mortis. 2. Stagnum Ignis. 3. Terra Tenebrosa. 4. Tartarus. 5. Terra Oblivionis. 6. Gehenna. 7. Erebus. 8. Barathrum. 9. Styx. 10. Acheron.

The which kingdoms are governed by five kings; that is, Lucifer in the Orient, Belzebub in Septentrio,

Belial in Meredie, Ascheroth in the Occident, and Phlegeton in the midst of them all: whose rules and dominions have no end until the day of doom; and thus far, Faustus, hast thou heard of our rule and kingdom.

CHAP. XIII.

Another question put forth by Dr. Faustus to his spirit, concerning his lord Lucifer, with the sorrow that Faustus fell afterwards into.

Dr. Faustus began again to reason with Mephistophiles, requiring him to tell in what form and shape, and in what estimation his lord Lucifer was, when he was in favour with God: Whereupon his spirit required of him three days respite, which Faustus granted. The three days being expired, Mephistophiles gave him this answer: Faustus, my lord Lucifer, (so called now for that he was banished out of the clear light of heaven) was at the first an angel of God, yea he was so of God ordained for shape, pomp, authority, worthiness, and dwelling, that he far exceeded all the other creatures of God, yea, or gold and precious stones; and so illuminated that he far surpassed the brightness of the sun, and all other stars where God placed him on the cherubims; he had a kingly office, and was always before God's seat, to the end he might be the more perfect in all his being; but when he began to be high minded, proud, and so presumptuous, that he would usurp the seat of God's Majesty, then was he banished out from amongst the heavenly powers, separated from their abiding, into the manner of a fiery stone, that no water is able to quench, but continually burneth until the end of the world. Dr. Faustus, when he had heard the words of his spirit, began to ponder with himself having divers and sundry opinions in his head, and very pensively, saying nothing to his spirit, he went into his chamber, and laid him on his bed, recording the words of Mephistophiles, which so pierced his heart that he fell into sighing and great lamentation, crying out, Alas! Ah, woe is me! What have I done? Even so shall it come to pass with me: am I not also a creature of God's making, bearing his own image and similitude, into whom he hath breathed the spirit of life and immortality, unto whom he hath made all things living subject: but woe is me! My haughty mind, proud aspiring stomach, and filthy flesh, hath brought my soul into perpetual damnation, yea, pride hath abused my understanding, insomuch that I have forgot my Maker, the Spirit of God is departed from me; I have promised the devil my soul, and therefore it is but a folly for me to hope for grace, but it must be even with me as with Lucifer, thrown into perpetual burning fire, ah! woe is me, that ever I was born. In this perplexity lay this miserable Dr. Faustus, having quite forgot his faith in Christ, never falling to repentance truly, thereby to attain the grace aud holy spirit of God again, the which would have been able to have resisted the strong assaults of Satan; for although he had made him a promise, yet he might have remembred, through true repentance sinners may once come again into the favour of God, which faith the faithful firmly hold, knowing they that kill the body are not able to hurt the soul: but he was in all his opinions doubtful, without faith or hope, and so he continued.

CHAP. XIV.

Another disputation betwixt Dr. Faustus and his Spirit, of the Power of the Devil, and his Envy to Mankind.

AFTER Faustus had a while pondered and sorrowed with himself on his wretched estate, he called again Mephistophiles unto him, commanding him to tell him the judgment, rule, power, attempts, tyranny and temptation of the devil; and why he was moved to such kind of living? Whereupon the spirit answered to this question, that thou demandest of me will turn thee to no small discontentment, therefore thou shouldst not have desired of me such matters, for it toucheth the secrets of our kingdom, although I cannot deny to resolve thy request: therefore know Faustus, that so soon as my lord Lucifer fell from Heaven, he became mortal enemy both to God and man, and hath used (as now he doth) all manner of tyranny to the destruction of man, as is manifested by divers examples: one falling suddenly dead, another hangs himself, another drowns himself, others stab themselves, others unlawfully despair, and so come to utter confusion: the first Adam, that was made perfect to the similitude of God, was by my lord's policy, the whole decay of man; yea, Faustus, in him was the beginning and first tyranny of my lord Lucifer to man; the like did he with Cain, the same with the children of Israel when they worshipped strange gods, and fell to whoredom with strange women; the like with Saul, so did he by the seven husbands of her that after was the wife of Tobias; likewise Dagon our fellow brought to destruction fifty thousand men, whereupon the ark of God was stoln, and Belial made David to number his men, whereupon were slain sixty thousand. Also he deceived King Solomon, that worshipped the gods of the heathen: and there are such spirits innumerable, that can come by men, and tempt them, and drive them to sin, and weaken their belief; for we rule the hearts of kings and princes, stirring them up to war and bloodshed, and to this intent do we spread ourselves through all the world, as the utter enemies of God and his son Christ, yea, and all that worship them, and that thou knowest by thyself Faustus. How have we dealt by thee? To this said Faustus, Then thou didst also beguile me? I did what I could to help thee forward, for as soon as I saw how thy heart did despise thy degree taken in divinity, and didst study to search and know the secrets of our kingdom, then did I enter into thee, giving thee divers foul and filthy cogitations, pricking thee forward in thy intent, persuading thee thou couldst never attain to thy desire, till thou hadst the help of some devil; and when thou wast delighted in this, then took I root in thee, and so firmly, that thou gavest thyself to us both body and soul, which thou canst not deny. Hereat answered Faustus, thou sayest true, I cannot deny it. Ah, woe is me, most miserable Faustus! How have I been deceived? Had I not had a desire to know too much, I had not been in this case; for having studied the lives of the holy saints and prophets, and thereby thought to understand sufficient heavenly matters, I thought my self not worthy to be called Dr. Faustus, if I should not also know the secrets of hell, and be associated with the furious fiends thereof; now therefore must I be rewarded accordingly. Which speeches being uttered, Faustus went very sorrowful away from his spirit.

CHAP. XV.

How Dr. Faustus desired again of his Spirit, to know the Secrets and Pains of Hell; and whether those damned Devils, and their Company, might ever come to the Favour and Love of God again.

Dr. Faustus was pondering with himself how he might get loose from so damnable an end as he had given himself unto, both soul and body: but his repenting was like that of Cain and Judas, he thought his sin greater than God could forgive; hereupon resting his mind, he lookt up to heaven, but saw nothing therein, for his heart was so possessed of the devil, that he could think of nought else but of hell, and the pains thereof. Wherefore in all haste he called unto him his spirit Mephistophiles, desiring him to tell him some more of the secrets of hell; what pain the damned are in? And how they were tormented? And whether the damned souls might get again the favour of God, and so be released out of their torments or not. Whereupon the spirit answered, My Faustus, thou may'st well leave to question any more of such matters, for they will but disquiet thy mind; I pray thee, what meanest thou, thinkest thou through these thy fantasies to escape us? No, for if thou shouldest climb up to heaven, there to hide thyself, yet would I thrust thee down again; for thou art mine, and thou belongest to our society: Therefore, sweet Faustus, thou wilt repent this thy foolish demand, except thou be content that I shall tell thee nothing. Quoth Faustus, ragingly, I will know, or I will not live, wherefore dispatch and tell me; to whom Mephistophiles answered, Faustus, it is no trouble unto me at all to tell thee; and therefore since thou forcest me thereto, I will tell thee things to the terror of thy soul, if thou wilt abide the hearing: thou wilt have me to tell thee of the secrets of hell, and of the pains thereof: know, Faustus, that hell hath many figures, semblances and names; but it cannot be named or figured in such sort to the living that are damned, as it is to those that are dead, and do both see and feel the torments thereof: for hell is said to be deadly, out of which came never any to life again but one, but he is nothing for thee to reckon upon; hell is blood-thirsty, and is never satisfied; hell is a valley into which the damned souls fall; for so soon as the soul is out of

man's body, it would gladly go to the place from whence it came, and climbeth up above the highest hills, even to the heavens, where being by the angels of the first model denied entertainment, (in consideration of their evil life spent on earth) they fall into the deepest pit or valley, that hath no bottom, into a perpetual fire which shall never be quenched; for like as the flint thrown in the water loseth not vertue, neither is the fire extinguished; even so the hellish fire is unquenchable: and even as the flint-stone in the fire burns red hot, and consumeth not, so likewise the damn'd souls in our hellish fire are ever burning, but their pain never diminishing: therefore is hell called the everlasting pain, in which is never hope for mercy: so it is called utter darkness, in which we see neither the light, the sun, moon, nor stars; and were our darkness like the darkness of night, yet were there hope of mercy: but ours is perpetual darkness, clean exempt from the face of God. Hell hath also a place within it, called Chasma, out of which issueth all manner of thunders and lightnings, with such shriekings and wailings, that oftentimes the very devils themselves stand in fear thereof. For one while it sendeth forth wind, with exceeding snow, hail and rain, congealing the water into ice: with the which the damned are frozen, gnash their teeth, howl and cry, yet cannot die.

Other whiles, it sendeth forth most horrible hot mists, or fogs, with flashing of flames of fire and brimstone; wherein the sorrowful souls of the damned lie broiling in their reiterated torments: yea, Faustus, hell is called a prison, wherein the damned lie continually bound; it is called Pernicies and Exitium, death, destruction, hurtfulness, mischief, a mischance, a pitiful and evil thing, world without end. We have also with us in hell a ladder, reaching of exceeding highth, as though the top of the same would touch the heaven, to which the damned ascend to seek the blessing of God, but through their infidelity, when they are at very highest degree, they fall down again into their former miseries, complaining of the heat of that unquenchable fire: yea, sweet Faustus, so much understand thou of hell, the while thou art desirous to know the secrets of our kingdom. And mark, Faustus, hell is the nurse of death, the heat of fire, the shadow of heaven and earth, the oblivion of all goodness; the pains unspeakable, the griefs unremovable, the dwelling of the devils. Dragons, serpents, adders, toades, crocodiles, and all manner of venemous and noisome creatures; the puddle of sin, the stinking far ascending from the Stygian lake, brimstone, pitch, and all manner of unclean metals, the perpetual and unquenchable fire, the end of whose miseries was never purposed by God: yea, yea, Faustus thou sayest I shall, I must, nay, I will tell thee the secrets of our kingdom, for thou buyest it dearly, and thou must and shalt be partaker of our torments, that (as the Lord said) shall never cease, for hell, the woman's belly, and the earth, are never satisfied, there shalt thou abide horrible torments, howling, crying, burning, freezing, melting, swimming in a labyrinth of miseries, scolding, smoaking in thine eyes, stinking in thy nose, hoarseness in thy speech, deafness in thy ears, trembling in thy hands, biting thine own tongue with pain, thy heart crushed as with a press, thy bones broken, the devils tossing fire-brands unto thee: yea, thy whole carkase tossed upon muck-forks from one devil to another; yea, Faustus, then wilt thou wish for death, and he will fly from thee, thine unspeakable torments shall be every day augmented more and more, for the greater the sin, the greater is the punishment; how likest thou this, my Faustus? A resolution answerable to thy request.

Lastly, Thou wilt have me tell thee that which only belongeth to God, which is, if it be possible for the damned to come again into the favour of God, or not; why, Faustus, thou knowest that this is against thy promise; for why shouldest thou desire to know that having already given thy soul to the devil, to have the pleasure of the world, and to know the secrets of hell; therefore thou art damned, and how canst thou then come again to the favour of God; wherefore I discreetly answer, no; for whomsoever God hath forsaken and thrown into hell, must there abide his wrath and indignation, in that unquenchable fire, where is no hope of mercy to be looked for, but abiding his perpetual pains, world without end: for even as much it availeth thee, Faustus, to hope for the favour of God again, as Lucifer himself; who indeed, although he and we have a hope, yet it is to small avail, and taketh none effect, for out of that place God will neither hear crying nor singing; if he do, thou shalt have a little remorse, as Dives, Cain, and Judas had. What helpeth the emperor, king, prince, duke, earl, baron, lord, knight, esquire, or gentlemen, to cry for mercy being there? Nothing, for if on earth they would not be tyrants and self-willed, rich with covetousness, proud with pomp, gluttons, drunkards, whoremongers, backbiters, robbers, murtherers, blasphemers, and such like, then were there some hope to be looked for; therefore my Faustus, as thou comest to hell with these qualities, thou mayst say with Cain my sins are greater than can be forgiven, go hang thy self with Judas: and lastly, be contented to suffer torments with Dives. Therefore know Faustus, that the damned have neither end nor time appointed, in the which they may hope to be released; for if there were any such hope that they by throwing one drop of water out of the sea in a day, until it were dry, or there were one heap of sand, as high as from the earth to the heavens, that a bird carrying away but one corn in a day, at the end of this so long labour, that yet they might hope at the last God would have mercy on them, they would be comforted; but now there is no hope, that God once thinks upon them, or that their howling shall ever be heard; yea, so impossible it is for thee to hide thy self from God, as it is impossible for thee to remove the mountains, or to empty the sea, or to tell the drops of rain that have fallen from heaven until this day, or to tell what there is most of in the world : yea, and as for a camel to go through the eye of a needle, even so impossible it is for thee, Faustus, and the rest of the damned, to come again into the favour of God? and thus Faustus hast thou heard my last sentence, and I pray thee, how dost thou like it? but know this, that I counsel thee to let me be unmolested hereafter with such disputations, or else will I vex thee every limb to thy small contentment. Doctor Faustus parted from his spirit very pensive and sorrowful, laying him on his bed, altogether doubtful of the grace and favour of God, wherefore he fell into fantastical cogitations: fain he would have had his soul at liberty again, but the devil had so blinded him, and had taken such deep root in his heart, that he could never think to crave God's mercy; or if by chance he had any good motion, streightways the devil would thrust in a fair lady into his chamber, which fell to kissing and dalliance with him; through which means he threw the godly motions in the wind, going forward still in his wicked practice, to the utter ruin both of body and soul.

CHAP. XVI.

Another Question put forth by Dr. Faustus to his Spirit Mephistophiles of his own Estate.

Dr. Faustus being yet desirous to hear more strange things, called his spirit unto him, saying, my Mephistophiles, I have yet another suit unto thee, which I pray thee deny me not to resolve me of. Faustus (quoth the spirit) I am loath to reason with thee any further, for thou art never satisfied in thy mind, but always bringest me a new: yet I pray thee this once (quoth Faustus) do me so much favour as to tell me the truth in this matter, and hereafter I will be no more so earnest with thee. The spirit was altogether against it: but yet once more he would abide him. Well (said the spirit to Faustus) what demandest thou of me. Faustus said, I would gladly know of thee if thou wert a man in manner and form as I am, what wouldest thou do to please both God and man? Whereat the spirit smiled, saying, my Faustus, if I was a man as thou art, and that God had adorned me with those gifts of nature which thou once hadst, even so long as the breath of God were by and within me, would I humble my self unto his majesty, endeavouring all that I could to keep his commandments, praise him and glorifie him, that I might continue in his favour, so were I sure to enjoy the eternal joy, and felicity of his kingdom. Faustus said, but that I have not done. No, thou sayest truth, quoth Mephistophiles, thou hast not done it; but thou hast denyed the Lord thy Maker, which gave thee the breath of life, speech, hearing, sight, and all other thy reasonable senses, that thou mightest understand his will and pleasure, to live to the glory and honour of his name, and to the advancement of thy body and soul: him, I say, being thy Maker, hast thou denyed and defied, yea, wickedly hast thou applied that excellent gift of understanding, and given thy soul to the devil, therefore give none the blame but thine own self-will, thy proud and aspiring mind, which hath brought thee unto the wrath of God and utter damnation. This is most true (quoth Faustus) but tell me Mephistophiles, wouldst thou be in my case as I am now ? yea, saith the spirit (and with that fetch'd a great sigh) for yet I would so humble my self, that I would win the favour of God. Then, said Dr. Faustus, it were time enough for me, if I amended. True, said Mephistophiles, if it were not for thy great sins, which are so odious and detestable in the sight of God, that it is too late for thee, for the wrath of God resteth upon thee. Leave off (quoth Faustus) and tell me my question to my greater comfort.

CHAP. XVII.

Here followeth the Second Part of Dr. Faustus, his Life and Practices, until his End.

Dr. Faustus having received denial of his spirit to be resolved any more in such questions propounded, forgot all good works, and fell to be a kalender-maker by the help of his spirit, and also in short time to be a good astronomer or astrologian: he had learned so perfectly of his spirit the course of the sun, moon, and stars, that he had the most famous name of all the mathematicians that lived in his time, as may well appear by his works dedicated unto sundry dukes and lords, for he did nothing without the advice of his spirit, which learned him to presage of matters to come, which have come to pass since his death. The like praise won he with his kalenders and almanacks-making; for when he presaged of any thing, operations, and alterations of the weather or elements, as wind, rain, fogs, snow, hail, moist, dry, warm, cold, thunder, lightning, it fell so duly out, as if an angel of heaven had forewarned it. He did not, like the unskilful astronomers in our time, that set in winter, cold moist air, frosty, and in the dog days, hot, dry, thunder, fire, and such like; but he set in all his works, the day and hour, when, where, and how it should happen. If any wonderful thing were at hand, as mortality, famine, plague, wars, he would set the time and place, in true and just order, when it would come to pass.

CHAP. XVIII.

A Question put forth by Dr. Faustus to his Spirit, concerning Astronomy.

Now Faustus falling to practice, and making his prognostications, he was doubtful in many points; wherefore he called unto him Mephistophiles his spirit, saying, I find the ground of the science very difficult to attain unto; for when that I confer Astronomia and Astrologia, as the mathematicians and ancient writers have left in memory, I find them vary, and very much to disagree: wherefore I pray thee to teach me the truth of this matter. To whom his spirit answered, Faustus, thou shalt know, that the practitioners or speculators, or at least the first inventors of these arts, have done nothing of themselves certain, whereupon thou mayest attain to the true prognosticating or presaging of things concerning the heavens, or of the influence of the planets; for if by chance some one mathematician or astronomer have left behind him any thing worthy of memory, they have so blinded it with ænigmatical words, blind characters, and such obscure figures, that it is impossible for any earthly man to attain the knowledge thereof, without the aid of some spirits, or else the special gift of God, for such as are the hidden works of God from men, yet do we spirits, that fly and fleet all elements, know such; and there is nothing to be done, or by the heavens portended, but we know it, except only the day of doom. Wherefore, Faustus learn of me, I will teach thee the course and re-course of the planets, the cause of winter and summer, the exaltation and declination of the sun, and eclipse of the moon, the distance and highth of the poles and every fixed star, the nature and opposition of the elements, fire, air, water, and earth, and all that is contained in them, yea, herein there is nothing hidden from me, but only the filthy essence which once thou hadst, Faustus, at liberty, but now thou hast lost it past recovery; therefore leaving that which will not be again had, learn now of me to make thunder, lightning, hail, snow, and rain, the clouds to rend the earth, and craggy rocks to shake and split in sunder, the seas to swell and roar, and over-run their marks; knowest thou not that the deeper the sun shines, the hotter it pierces; so the more thy art is famous whilst thou art here, the greater shall be thy name when thou art gone. Knowest thou not that the earth is frozen, cold, and dry; the water running, cold and moist, the air flying, hot and moist; the fire consuming hot and dry: yea, Faustus, so must thy heart be inflamed like the fire to mount on high: learn, Faustus, to fly like my self, as swift as thought from one kingdom to another, to sit at princes' tables, to eat their dainty-fare, to have thy pleasure of their ladies, wives and concubines; to use all their jewels and costly robes, as things belonging unto thee, and not unto them: learn of me, Faustus, to run through walls, doors, and gates of stone and iron, to creep into the earth like a worm, or swim in the water like a fish; to fly in the air like a bird, and to live and nourish thyself in the fire like a salamander; so shalt thou be famous, renowned, far spoken of, and extolled for thy skill, going on knives not hurting thy feet, carrying fire in thy bosom and not burning thy shirt: seeing through the heavens, as through a crystal, wherein is placed the planets, with all the rest of the presaging comets, the whole circuit of the world from east to west, north and south: there shalt thou know, Faustus, whereof the fiery sphere above, and the signs of the Zodiack doth not burn and consume the whole face of the earth, being hindred by placing the two moist elements between them, the airy clouds and wavering waves of water: yea, Faustus, I will learn thee the secrets of nature, what the cause is, that the sun in summer, being at the highest, giveth all his heat downwards on the earth; and being winter at the lowest, giveth all his heat upwards into the heavens, that the snow should be of so great vertue as the honey, and the Lady Saturnia in Occulto, more hot than the sun in manifesto. Come on, my Faustus, I will make thee as perfect in these ways as my self, I will learn thee to go invisible, to find out the mines both of gold and silver, the fodines of precious stones, as the carbuncle, the diamond, saphire, emerald, ruby, topas, jacinth, granat, jaspies, amethyst; use all these at thy pleasure, take thy heart's desire: thy time Faustus weareth away, then why wilt thou not take thy pleasure of the world? Come up, we will go unto kings at their own courts, and at their most sumptuous banquets be their guests; if willingly they invite us not, then by force we will serve our own turn with their best meat and daintiest wine. Agreed, quoth Faustus, but let me pause a while upon this thou hast even now declared unto me.

CHAP. XIX.

How Dr. Faustus fell into despair with himself, for having put a Question unto his Spirit, they fell at Variance, whereupon the Rout of Devils appeared unto him, threatning him sharply.

Dr. Faustus resolved with himself the speeches of his spirit, and became so woful and sorrowful in his cogitations, that he thought himself already frying in the hottest flame of hell; and lying in this muse, suddenly there appeared unto him his spirit, demanding what thing so grieved and troubled his conscience? Whereat

Dr. Faustus gave no answer; yet the spirit lay very earnestly upon him to know the cause, and if it were possible he would find a remedy for his grief, and ease him of his sorrows. To whom Faustus answered, I have taken thee unto me as a servant to do my service and thy service will be very dear unto me; yet I cannot have any diligence of thee farther than thou list thyself, neither dost thou in any thing as it becometh thee. The spirit replyed, My Faustus, thou knowest that I was never against thy commandment as yet, but ready to serve and resolve thy questions, although I am not bound unto thee in such respects as concern the hurt of our kingdom; yet was I always willing to answer thee, and so am I still: therefore my Faustus, say on boldly, what is thy will and pleasure? At which words the spirit stole away the heart of Faustus, who spake in this sort: Mephistophiles, tell me how and after what sort God made the world, and all the creatures in it? And why man was made after the image of God? The spirit hearing this, answered Faustus, Thou knowest that all this is in vain for thee to ask: I know that thou art sorry for what thou hast done, but it availeth thee not; for I will tear thee in a thousand pieces if thou change not thy opinions, and hereat he vanished away. Whereat Faustus, all sorrowful that he had put forth such a question, fell to weeping and to howling bitterly, not for his sins towards God, but that the devil was departed from him so suddenly in such a rage. And being in this perplexity, he was suddenly taken with such extream cold, as if he would have frozen in the place where he sate, in which the greatest devil in hell appeared unto him, with certain of his hideous and infernal company, in most ugly shapes, that it was impossible to think upon; and traversing the chamber round about where Faustus sate, Faustus thought to himself, Now are they come for me, though my time be not come, and that, because I have asked such questions of my servant Mephistophiles: at whose cogitations the chiefest devil, which was the lord unto whom he gave his soul, that was Lucifer, spake in this sort: Faustus, I have seen thy thoughts, which are not as thou hast vowed unto me, by the virtue of this letter; and shewed him the obligation, which he had written with his own blood; wherefore I am come to visit thee, and to shew thee some of our hellish pastimes, in hope that will draw and confirm thy mind a little more stedfast unto us. Content (quoth Faustus) go to, let me see what pastime you can make. At which words the great devil in his likeness, sate him down by Faustus, commanding the rest of his devils to appear in the form as if they were in hell. First entered Belial in form of a bear, with curled black hair to the ground, his ears standing upright; within his ears were as red as blood, out of which issued flames of fire, his teeth were at least a foot long, and as white as snow, with a tail three ells long, at the least, having two wings, one behind each arm; and thus one after another they appeared to Faustus in form as they were in hell. Lucifer himself sate in a manner of a man all hairy, but of brown colour like a squirrel, curled, and his tail turning upwards on his back as the squirrels use, I think he could crack nuts too like a squirrel. After him came Belzebub in curled hair of a horse-flesh colour, his head like the head of a bull, with a mighty pair of horns, and two long ears down to the ground, and two wings on his back, with two pricking things like horns; out of his wings issued flames of fire, his tail was like a cow's. Then came Astaroth in the form of a worm, going upright on his tail, and had no feet, but a tail like a glow-worm, under his chops grew two short hands, and his back was cole-black, his belly thick in the middle, yellow, like gold, having many bristles on his back like a hedge-hog. After him came Cannagosta, being white and grey mixed, exceeding curled and hairy, he had a head like the head of an ass, and a tail like a cat, and claws like an ox, lacking nothing of an ell broad. Then came Anobis; this devil had a head like a dog, white and black hair, in shape like a hog, saving that he had but two feet, one under his throat, the other at his tail; he was four ells long, with hanging ears like a blood-hound. After him came Dithican: he was a short thief, in form of a large bird, with shining feathers, and four feet; his neck was green, and body red, and his feet black. The last was called Brachus, with very short feet, like a hedgehog, yellow and green, the upper side of his body was brown, and the belly like blue flames of fire, the tail red like the tail of a monkey. The rest of the devils were in form of unreasonable beasts, as swine, harts, bears, wolfs, apes, buffes, goats, antelopes, elephants, dragons, horses, asses, lions, cats, snakes, toads, and all manner of ugly odious serpents and worms; yet came in such sort that every one at his entry into the hall, made their reverence unto Lucifer, and so took their places, standing in order as they came until they had fill'd the whole hall, wherewith suddenly fell a most horrible thunder-clap, that the house shook as if it would have fall'n unto the ground; upon which every monster had a muck-fork in his hand, holding them towards Faustus, as tho' they would have run a tilt at him: which when Faustus perceived, he thought upon the words of Mephistophiles, when he told him how the souls in hell were tormented, being cast from devil to devil upon muck-forks, he thought verily to have been tormented there by them in like sort: but Lucifer perceiving his thought, spake to him, My Faustus, how likest thou this crew of mine? Quoth Faustus, Why came you not in another manner of shape? Lucifer reply'd, We cannot change our hellish form, we have shewed ourselves here as we are there; yet can we blind men's eyes in such sort, that when we will, we appear unto them as if we were men or angels of light, although our dwelling be in darkness. Then said Faustus, I like not so many of you together. Whereupon Lucifer commanded them to depart, except seven of the principal, forthwith they presently vanished, which Faustus perceiving, he was somewhat better comforted, and spake to Lucifer, where is my servant Mephistophiles, let me see if he can do the like. Whereupon came a fierce dragon flying, and spitting fire round about the house, and coming towards Lucifer, made reverence, and then changed himself to the form of a friar, saying, Faustus, what wilt thou? Faustus said, I will that thou teach me to transform myself in like sort, as thou and the rest have done. Then Lucifer put forth his paw and gave Faustus a book, saying, Hold, do what thou wilt, which he looking upon, straightways changed himself into a hog, then into a worm, then into a dragon, and finding thus for his purpose it liked him well. Quoth he to Lucifer, And how cometh it that so many filthy forms are in the world? Lucifer answered, they are ordained of God, as plagues unto men, and so shalt thou be plagued, quoth he; whereupon came scorpions, wasps, emets, bees, and gnats, which fell to stinging and biting him, and all the whole house was filled with a most horrible stinking fogg, insomuch that Faustus, saw nothing, but still was tormented; wherefore he cryed for help, saying, Mephistophiles, my faithful servant, where art thou? Help, help, I pray thee. Hereat the spirit answered nothing, but Lucifer himself said, Ho, ho, ho, Faustus, how likest thou the creation of the world? And incontinent it was clear again, and the devils and all the filthy cattel were vanished, only Faustus was left alone seeing nothing, but hearing the sweetest musick that ever he heard before, at which he was so ravished with delight, that he forgot his fears he was in before, and it repented him that he had seen no more of their pastime.

CHAP. XX.

How Dr. Faustus desired to see Hell, and of the Manner how he was used therein.

Dr. Faustus bethinking how his time went away, and how he had spent eight years thereof, he meant to spend the rest to his better contentment, intending quite to forget any such motions as might offend the devil any more: wherefore on a time he called his spirit Mephistophiles, and said unto him, Bring thou hither unto me thy Lord Lucifer or Belial; he brought him (notwithstanding) one that was called Belzebub, the which asked Faustus, his pleasure? Quoth Faustus, I will know of thee if I might see hell, and take a view thereof? That thou shalt said the Devil, and at midnight I will fetch thee. Well, night being come, Dr. Faustus waited very diligently for the coming of the devil to fetch him, and thinking that he tarried too long, he went to the window, where he pulled open a casement, and looking into the element, he saw a cloud in the north more black, and darker, and obscurer than all the rest of the skie, from whence the wind blew most horribly right into Faustus's chamber, and filled the whole house with smoak, that Faustus was almost smothered; hereat fell an exceeding thunder-clap, and withal came a great rugged black Bear all curled, and upon his back a chair of beaten gold, and spake to Faustus, saying, Sir, up and away with me: and Dr. Faustus that had so long abode the smoak, wished rather to be in hell than there, got on the devil, and so they went on together. Mark how the devil blinded him, and made him believe he carried him into hell, for he carried him into the lake, where Faustus fell into a sound sleep, as if he had sate into a warm water or bath: at last they came to a place which burneth continually with flashing flames of fire and brimstone, wherout issued an exceeding mighty clap of thunder; with so horrible a noise that Faustus awaked; but the devil went forth on his way, and carried Faustus therein, yea, notwithstanding however it burnt, Dr. Faustus felt no more heat then as it were the glimps of the sun in May, there heard he all manner of music to overcome him, but saw none playing on them; it pleased him well, but he durst not ask for he was forbidden it before. To meet the devil and the guest that came with him came three other ugly devils, the which ran back again before the bear, to make the way; against whom there came running an exceeding great hart, which would have thrust Faustus out of the chair; but being defended by the other three devils, the hart was put to the repulse: thence going on the way, Faustus looked, and behold there was nothing but snakes, and all manner of venomous beasts about him, which were exceeding great: unto the which snakes came many storks, and swallowed up the whole multitude of snakes, that they left not one: which when Faustus saw, he marvelled greatly; but proceeding farther on their hellish voyage, there came forth out of an hollow clift an exceeding great flying bull, the which with such a force hit Faustus's chair with his head and horns, that he turned Faustus and his bear over and over, so that the bear vanished away: whereat Faustus began to cry, Oh! woe to me that ever I came here! For he thought there to have been beguiled of the devil; and to make an end before his time appointed or conditioned of the devil: but shortly after came to him a monstrous ape, bidding Faustus to be of good chear, and said, Get upon me. All the fire in hell seemed to Faustus to have been put out, whereupon followed a monstrous thick fog, that he saw nothing, but shortly after it seemed to him to wax clear, where he saw two great dragons fastned unto a waggon, in the which the ape ascended and set Faustus therein; forth flew the dragons into an exceeding dark cloud, where Faustus saw neither dragons nor chariot wherein he sate, and such were the cries of tormented souls, with mighty thunder-claps, and flashing lightnings about his ears, that poor Faustus shook for fear; upon this they came to a water, stinking and filthy, thick like mud, into the which ran the dragons, sinking under with waggon and all, but Faustus felt no water but as it were a small mist, saving that the waves beat so sore upon him, that he saw nothing under or over him but only water, in the which he lost his dragons, ape and waggon; and sinking yet deeper and deeper, he came at last as it were upon a high rock, where the waters parted and left him thereon: but when the water was gone, it seemed to him he should there have ended his life, for he saw no way but death : the rock was so high from the bottom as heaven is from the earth : there sate he, seeing nor hearing any man, and looked ever upon the rock : at length he saw a little hole out of which issued fire ; thought he, how shall I now do? I must either fall to the bottom or burn in the fire, or sit in despair. With that in his madness he gave a skip into the fire hole, saying, Hold, you infernal hags, take here this sacrifice as my last end, that which I have justly deserved. Upon this he was entred, and finding himself as yet unburned or touched of that fire, he was the better appayed. But there was so great a noise that he never heard the like before, it passed all the thunder that ever he had heard. And coming down farther to the bottom of the rock, he saw a fire wherein were many worthy and noble personages, as emperors, kings, dukes, and lords, and many thousand more tormented souls, at the edge of which fire, ran a most pleasant, clear, and cold water to behold; into the which many tormented souls sprang out of the fire to cool themselves, but being so freezing cold, they were constrained to return again into the fire, and thus wearied themselves and spent their endless torments out of one labyrinth into another, one while in heat, another while in cold: but Faustus, standing here all this while gazing on them that were thus tormented, he saw one leaping out of the fire, shrieking horribly, whom he thought to have known, wherefore he would fain have spoken unto him, but remembring he was forbidden, he refrained speaking. Then this devil that brought him in, came to him again in likeness of a bear, with the chair on his back, and bid him set up, for it was time to depart: so Faustus got up, and the devil carried him out into the air, where he had so sweet musick, that he fell asleep by the way. His boy Christopher, being all this while at home, and missing his master so long, thought his master would have tarried and dwelt with the devil for ever: but whilst the boy was in these cogitations, his master came home: for the devil brought him home fast asleep as he sate in his chair, and threw him on his bed, where (being thus left of the devil) he lay until day. When he awaked, he was amazed, like a man that had been in a dark dungeon; musing with himself, if it were true or false that he had seen hell, or whether he was blinded or not; but he rather perswaded himself he had been there than otherwise, because he had seen such wonderful things; wherefore he most carefully took pen and ink, and wrote those things in order as he had seen; which writing was afterwards found by his boy in his study; which afterwards was published to the whole city of Wittenburg in print, for example to all christians.

CHAP. XXI.

How Dr. Faustus was carried through the Air, up to the Heavens to see the whole World, and how the Skie and Planets ruled; after the which he wrote a Letter to his Friend of the same to Liptzig, and how he went about the World in eight Days.

THIS letter was found by a freeman and citizen of Wittenburg, written with his own hand, and sent to his friend at Liptzig a physician, named Love Victori, the contents of which were as followeth: Amongst other things (my beloved friend and brother) I remember yet the former friendship we had together when we were school-fellows, and students in the university at Wittenburg, whereas you first studied physick, astronomy, astrology, geometry, and cosmography, I to the contrary, you know, studied divinity, notwithstanding now in any of your own studies, I am sure I have proceeded farther than your self; for since I began I have never erred, for might I speak it without affecting mine own praise, my kalenders and other practices have not only the commendations of the common sort, but also the chiefest lords and nobles of this our Dutch nation, because (which is chiefly to be noted) I write and presage of matters to come, which all accord and fall out so right, as if they had already been before. And for thee (my beloved Victori) you write to know my voyage which I made unto the heavens, the which (as you certifie me) you have had some suspicion of, although you partly perswade your self that it is a thing impossible; no matter for that, it is as it is, and let it be as it will, once it is done in such a manner as now according unto your request, I will give you here to understand: I being once laid in my bed, and I could not sleep for thinking on my kalender and practice, I marvell'd with my self how it were possible that the firmament should be known, and so largely written of by men, or whether they write true or false, by their own opinions and suppositions, or by due observation and true course of the heavens: behold, I thought my house would have been blown down, so that all my doors and chests flew open, whereat I was not a little astonished, for withal I heard a groaning voice, which said, Get up, the desire of thy heart, mind, and thought thou shalt see. At the which I answered, What my heart desireth that would I fain see, and to make proof if I shall see, I will away with thee. Why then, quoth he, look out the window, there cometh a messenger for thee. That did I, and behold there stood a waggon with two dragons before it to draw the same, and all the waggon was of a light burning fire, and for that the moon shone I was the willinger at that time to depart; but the voice spoke again, sit up, and let us away. I will (said I) go with thee, but upon condition, that I may ask after all things that I see, hear, or think on. The voice answered, I am content for this time,

Hereupon I got me into the waggon, so that the dragons carried me up right into the air.

The waggon had four wheels, the which rattled so, and made such a noise, as if it had been all this while running on the stones, and round about us flew flames of fire; and the higher that I came, the more the earth seemed to be darken'd, so that methought I came out of a dungeon; and looking down from heaven, behold Mephistophiles my spirit and servant was behind me, and when he perceived that I saw him, he came and sate by me, to whom I said, I pray thee Mephistophiles, whither shall I go now? Let not that trouble thy mind, (said he) and yet they carried us higher up. And now I will tell thee(good friend and school-fellow) what things I have seen and proved; for on the Tuesday I went out, and on Tuesday seven nights following I came home again, that's eight days, in which time I slept not, no not one wink came within my eyes: and we went invisible of any man; and as the day began to appear, after the first night's journey, I said to my spirit Mephistophiles, I pray thee how far have we now ridden? I am sure thou knowest, for methinks we have ridden exceeding far, the world seemeth so little. Mephistophiles, answered me, My Faustus believe me, that from the place from whence thou camest unto this place where we now are, is already forty-seven leagues right in heighth. And as the day increased, I looked down into the world, Asia, Europe, and Africa I had a sight of:

and being so high, quoth I to my spirit, tell me how these kingdoms lie, and what they are called? The which he denied not, saying, See this on our left hand is Hungaria, this is also Prussia on our left hand, and Poland, Muscovia, Tartary, Silesia, Bohemia, Saxony; and here on our right hand, Spain, Portugal, France, England, and Scotland; then right on before us lie the kingdoms of Persia, India, Arabia, the king of Althar, and the great Cham: now we are come to Wittenburg, and are right over the town of Weim, in Austria, and ere long we will be at Constantinople, Tripoli, and Jerusalem, and after will we pierce the frozen Zone, and shortly touch the horizon and the zenith of Wittenburg. There looked I on the ocean sea, and beheld a great many ships and galleys ready to battle one against another: and thus I spent my journey, and I cast my eyes here, now there, towards south, north, east, and west; I have been in one place where it rained and hailed, and in another where the sun shone excellent fair, and so I think that I saw most things in and about the world, with great admiration, that in one place it rained, and in another hail and snow: on this side the sun shone bright, some hills cover'd with snow never consuming, others were so hot that grass and trees were burned, and consumed therewith. Then looked I up to the heavens, and behold they went so swift, that I thought they would have sprung into thousands: likewise it was so clear and so hot, that I could not gaze upon it, it so dimned my sight; and had not my spirit

Mephistophiles covered me, as it were with a shadowing cloud, I had been burnt with the extream heat thereof: for the skie which we behold here, when we look up from the earth, is so fast and thick as a wall, clear and shining bright as chrystal, in which is placed the sun, which casteth forth his rays and beams over the whole world, to the uttermost confines of the earth. But we think that the sun is very little, no, it is altogether as big as the world: indeed the body substantial is but little in compass, but the rays or streams that it casteth forth by reason of the thing wherein it is placed, maketh him to extend and shew himself all over the whole world, and we think that the sun runneth his course, and that the heavens stand still; no, it is the heavens that moves his course, and the sun abideth perpetually in his place, he is permanent and fixed in his place, and although we see him beginning to ascend in the orient or east, at the highest in the meridian or south, setting in occident or west, yet is he in the lowest in septentrio or north, and yet he moveth not, it is the axle of the heavens that moveth, the whole firmament, being a chaos or confused thing, and for that proof I will shew this example: like as thou seest a bubble made of water and soap blown out of a quill, it is in form of a confused mass or chaos, and being in this form is moved at pleasure of the wind which runneth round about that chaos, and moveth him also round, even so the whole firmament or chaos, wherein are placed the sun, and the rest of the planets, is turned and carried at the pleasure of the spirit of God, which is wind: yea, Christian reader, to the glory of God, and to the profit of my soul, I will open unto thee a divine opinion touching the rule of this confounded chaos, far more than my rude German author, being possessed with the devil, was able to utter, and prove some of my sentences before to be true, look into Genesis, into the works of God, at the creation of the world, there shalt thou find that the spirit of God moved upon the water, before heaven and earth were made. Mark how he made it, and how by his word every element took his place; these were not his works but his words, for all the words he used before, concluded afterwards in one work, which was in making man: mark reader with patience, for thy soul's health, see into all that was done by the word and work of God; light and darkness was, the firmament stood, and the great and little light in it: the moist waters were in one place, the earth was dry, and every element brought forth according to the word of God. Now follow his works: he made man after his own image. How? Out of the earth. The earth will shape no image without water; there was one of the elements; but all this while there was wind: all elements were at the word of God; man was made, and in a form by the work of God, yet moved not that work before God had breathed the spirit of life into his nostrils, and made him a living soul: here was the first wind and spirit of God, out of his own mouth: which we have likewise from the same seed which was only planted by God in Adam: which wind, breath, or spirit, when he had received, he was living and moved on earth; for it was ordain'd of God for his habitation, but the heavens are the habitation of the Lord: and like as I shewed before of the bubble or confused chaos made of water and soap, thro' the wind and breath of man is turned round, and carried with the wind; even so the firmaments wherein the sun and the rest of the planets are fixed, be moved, turned, and carried with the wind, breath, and spirit of God; for the heavens and firmaments are moveable as the chaos, but the sun is fixed in the firmament. And farther, (my good school-fellow) I was thus nigh the heavens, where methought every planet was but as half the earth, and under the firmament ruled the spirits in the air: as I came down, I looked upon the world and heavens, and methought that the earth was inclosed (in comparison) within the firmament as the yolk of an egg within the white, methought that the whole length of the earth was not a span long, and the water was as it had been twice as broad and as long as the earth: even thus at eight days end I came home again, and fell asleep, and so I continued sleeping three days and three nights together, and the first hour I waked, fell fresh again to my kalender, and have made them in right ample manner as you know: and to satisfie your request for that you write unto me, I have (in consideration of our old friendship had at the university of Wittenburg) declared unto you my heavenly voyage, wishing no worse unto you than unto myself, that is, that your mind were as mine in all respects: dixi, Dr. Faustus the astrologian.

CHAP. XXII.

How Dr. Faustus made his Journey through the principal and most famous Lands in the World.

DR. FAUSTUS having over run fifteen years of his appointed time, he took upon him a journey, with full intent to see the whole world, and calling his spirit Mephistophiles unto him, he said, Thou knowest that thou art bound unto me upon conditions, to form and fulfil my desire in all things, wherefore my intent is to visit the whole face of the earth visible and invisible, when it pleaseth me; therefore I command and injoyn thee to the same. Whereupon Mephistophiles answered, I am ready, my lord, at thy command: and forthwith the spirit changed himself into the likeness of a flying horse, saying, Faustus, sit up, I am ready. Dr. Faustus softly sate upon him, and forwards they went: Faustus came through many a land and province, as Pannonia, Austria, Germany, Bohemia, Silesia, Saxony, Messene, During, Frankland, Swaalband, Byerland, Sayrir, Corinthia, Poland, Litaw, Lesland, Prussia, Denmark, Muscovia, Tartaria, Turky, Persia, Cathai, Alexandria, Barbaria, Ginny, Porut, the Streights Maghellane, India, all about the frozen zone, and Terra-incognita, Nova Hispaniola, the Isles of Tereza, Madera, St. Michaels, the Canaries, and the Trenorirolcio into Spain, and Mainland, Portugal, Italy, Campania, the Kingdom of Naples, the Isles of Sicilia, Malta, Majorca, Minorca, to the Knights of the Rhodes, Candy or Crete, Cypress, Corinth, Switzerland, France, Freezeland, Westphalia, Zeland, Holland, Brabant, and all the seventeen provinces in Netherland, England, Scotland, Ireland, and America, and Island, the Gut-Isles of Scotland, the Orcades, Norway, the Bishoprick of Bream; and so home again. All these kingdoms, and provinces, and countries he passed in twenty-five days, in which time he saw nothing that delighted his mind, wherefore he took little rest at home, and burning in desire to see more at large, and to behold the secrets of each kingdom, he set forward again, on his journey on his swift horse Mephistophiles, and came to Trent, for that he chiefly desired to see this town, and the monuments thereof, but there he saw not any wonders, except two fair palaces that belonged unto the bishop, and also a mighty large castle that was built with brick, with three walls, and three great trenches, so strong that it was impossible for any prince's power to win it; then he saw a church wherein was buried Simon and the bishop of Popo, their tombs are of most sumptuous stone-marble, closed and joyned together with great bars of iron; from thence he departed to Paris, where he liked well the academy; and what place or kingdom so ever fell in his mind, the same he visited. He came from Paris to Mentz, where the river of Maine falls into the Rhine, notwithstanding he tarried not long there, but went into Campania, in the kingdom of Neapoly, in which he saw an innumerable sort of cloysters, nunneries, and churches, and great houses of stone, the streets fair and large, and streight forth from one end of the town to the other all alike, and all the pavement of the city was of brick, and the more it rained in the town, the fairer the streets were: there saw he the tomb of Virgil, and the highway that he cut through the mighty hill of stone in one night, the whole length of an English mile: where he saw the number of gallies, and argezies that lay there at the city head, the wind-mill that stood in the water, the castle in the water, and the houses above the water, where many gallies might ride most safely from rain or wind: then he saw the castle on the hill over the town, and many monuments therein, also the hill called Vesuvius, wheron groweth all the Greekish wine, and most pleasant sweet olives. From thence he came to Venice, whereat he wonder'd not a little, to see a city so famously built, standing in the sea, where through every street the water came in such largeness, that great ships and barks might pass from one street to another, having yet a way on both sides the water whereon men and horses might pass: he marvelled also how it was possible so much victuals to be found in the town, and so good and cheap, considering that for a whole league nothing grew near the same. He wonder'd not a little at the fairness of St. Mark's Place, and the sumptuous church standing thereon, called St. Mark, how all the pavement was set with coloured stones, and all the rood or loft of the church double gilded over. Leaving this, he came to Padua, beholding the manner of their academy, which is called the mother or nurse of christendom, there heard he the doctors, and saw most of the monuments of the town, entred his name in the university of the German nation, and wrote himself Dr. Faustus, the insatiable speculator: Then saw he the worthiest monument in the world for a church, named St. Anthony's cloyster, which for the pinacles thereof, and the contrivement of the church, hath not the like in christendom. The town is fenced about with three mighty walls of stone and earth, betwixt the which runneth goodly ditches of water; betwixt every four and twenty hours passeth boats betwixt Padua and Venice with passengers, as they do here betwixt London and Gravesend, and even so far they differ in distance: Faustus beheld likewise the counsel-house and castle, with no small wonder. Well, forward he went to Rome, which lay, and doth yet lie on the river Tybris, the which divideth the city into two parts; over the river are four great stone bridges, and upon the one bridge, called Ponte St. Angelo, is the Castle of St. Angelo, wherein are so many great cast pieces as there are days in the year, and such pieces as will shoot seven bullets off with one fire: To this castle cometh a privy vault from the church and the Palace of St. Peter, through the which the pope (if any danger be) passeth from his palace to the castle for safeguard. The city hath eleven gates, and a hill called

Vaticinium, whereupon St. Peter's church is built: in that church the holy fathers will hear no confessions, without the penitent bring money in his hand. Adjoining to the church is the Campo Santo, the which Carolus Magnus built, where every day thirteen pilgrims, have their dinners served of the best; that is to say, Christ and his twelve apostles. Hard by this he visited the churchyard of St. Peter, where he saw that pyramid that Julius Cæsar brought forth of Africa; it stood in Faustus's time leaning against the church-wall of St. Peter's; but Pope Sixtus hath erected it in the middle of St. Peter's churchyard; it is fourteen fathom long, and at the lower end five fathom four square, and so forth smaller upwards; on the top is a crucifix of beaten gold, the stone standing on four lions of brass. Then he visited the seven churches of Rome, that were St. Peter, St. Paul, St. Sebastian, St. John Lateran, St. Laurence, St. Mary Magdalen, and St. Mary Majora. Then went he without the town, where he saw the conduits of waters that run level through hill and dale, bringing water into the town fifteen Italian miles off. Other mountains he saw, too many to recite. But amongst the rest he was desirous to see the pope's court, and his manner of service at his table, wherefore he and his spirit made themselves invisible, and came to the pope's court and privy chamber, where he was; there saw he many servants attending on his holiness, with many a flattering sycophant carrying his meat; and there he marked the pope, and the manner of his service, which he seeing to be so unmeasurable and sumptuous : Fie (quoth Faustus) why had not the devil made a pope of me ? Faustus saw there notwithstanding, such as were like to himself, proud, stout, wilful gluttons, drunkards, whoremongers, breakers of wedlock, and followers of all manner of ungodly excess; wherefore he said to his spirit, I thought that I had been alone a hog or pork of the devil's, but he must bear with me a little longer; for these hogs of Rome are ready fatted, and fitted to make him roast meat, the devil might do well to spit them all, and have them to the fire, and let him summon the nuns to turn the spits; for as none must confess the nun but the frier, so none should turn the roasting frier but the nun. Thus continued Faustus three days in the pope's palace, and yet had no lust to his meat, but stood still in the pope's chamber, and saw every thing whatsoever it was. On a time the pope would have a feast prepared for the Cardinal of Pavia, and for his first welcome the cardinal was bidden to dinner, and as he sate at meat the pope would ever be blessing and crossing over his mouth: Faustus would suffer it no longer, but up with his fist and smote the pope on his face, and withal he laughed that the whole house might hear him, yet none of them saw him, or knew where he was. The pope perswaded his company that it was a damned soul, commanding mass presently to be said for his delivery out of purgatory, which was done; the pope sat still at meat, but when the latter mess came to the pope's board, Dr.

Faustus laid hands thereon, saying This is mine, and so he took both dish and meat, and flew into the Capitol or Campadolia, calling his spirit unto him, and said, Come let us be merry, for thou must fetch me some wine, and the cup that the pope drinks out of; and hereupon morte caval, we will make good cheer in spight of the pope and all his fat abbey lubbers. His spirit hearing this, departed towards the pope's chamber, where he found them yet sitting, quaking; wherefore he took from before the pope the fairest piece of plate, or drinking goblet, and a flagon of wine, and brought it to Faustus: but when the pope and the rest of his crew perceived they were robbed, and knew not after what sort, they perswaded themselves that it was a damned soul that before had vexed the pope so, and that smote him on the face; wherefore he sent commandment through the whole city of Rome, that they should say a mass in every church, and ring all the bells, for to lay the walking spirit, and to curse him with bell, book, and candle, that so invisibly had misused the pope's holiness, with the Cardinal of Pavia, and the rest of their company: but Faustus notwithstanding made good cheer with that which he had beguiled the pope of, and in the midst of the order of St. Bernards, barefooted friars, as they were going on procession through the market place, call'd Campo de fiore, he let fall his plate, dish, and cup, and withal for a farewel, he made such a thunder-clap and storm of rain, as though heaven and earth would have met together, and left

Rome, and came to Millain in Italy, near the Alps or borders of Switzerland where he praised much to his spirit the pleasures of the place, the city being founded in so brave a plain, by the which ran most pleasant rivers on every side of the same, having besides within the compass of a circuit of seven miles, seven small seas: he saw also therein many fair places, and goodly buildings, the duke's palace, and the mighty strong castle, which is in a manner half the bigness of the town. Moreover, it liked him well to see the hospital of St. Mary, with divers other things: he did there nothing worthy of memory, but he departed back again towards Bologina, and from thence to Florence, where he was well pleased to see the pleasant walk of merchants, the goodly vaults of the city, for that almost the whole city is vaulted, and the houses themselves are built outwardly in such sort, that the people go under them as under a vault: then he perused the sumptuous church in the duke's castle, called Nostra Dama, our lady's church, in which he saw many monuments, as a marble door most huge to look upon, the gates of the castle are bell-mettal, wherein are graven the holy patriarchs, with Christ and his twelve apostles, and divers other histories out of the Old and New Testament: then went he to Senia, where he highly praised the church and hospital of Sancta Maria Formosa, with the goodly buildings, and especially the fairness and greatness of the city, and beautiful women: then came he to Lions in France, where he marked the situation of the city, which lay between two hills, invironed with two waters; one worthy monument pleased him well, that was the great church, with the image therein; he commended the city highly for the great resort that it had unto it of strangers: from thence he went to Cullen, which lyeth upon the river of Rhine, wherein he saw one of the antientest monuments in the world, the which was the tomb of the three kings that came by the angel of God, and their knowledge they had in the stars, to worship Christ, which when Faustus saw, he spake in this manner: ah! alas, good men! How have you erred, and lost your way? You should have gone to Palestina, and Bethlehem in Judea; how came you hither? Or belike after your death you were thrown into Mare Mediterraneum, about Tripolis in Syria, and so you steered out of the Straights of Gibralterra, in the ocean seas, and so into the Bay of Portugal. And not finding any rest, you are driven along the coast of Gallicia, Bisky and France, and into the narrow seas: then from thence into Mare Germanicum, and taken up I think about the town of Dort in Holland: you were brought to Cullen to be buried, or else (I think) you came most easily with a whirl-wind over the Alps, and being thrown into the river of Rhine, it conveyed you to this place where you are kept a monument: then saw he the church of St. Ursula, where remains a monument of the thousand virgins; it pleased him also to see the beauty of the women. Not far from Cullen lieth the town of Ach, where he saw the gorgous temple that the emperour Carolus Quartus built of marble-stone for a remembrance of him, to the end that all his successors should there be crowned. From Cullen in Ach, he went to Geneva, a city in Savoy, lying near Switzerland, it is a town of great traffick, the lord thereof is a bishop, whose wine-seller Faustus and his spirit visited for the love of his good wine: from thence he went to Strasburg, where he beheld the fairest temple that ever he had seen in his life before, for on every side thereof he might see through, even from the covering of the minster, to the top of the pinacle, and it is named one of the wonders of the world; wherefore he demanded why it is call'd Strasburg? His spirit answer'd, because it hath so many high-ways common to it on every side, for Stros in Dutch is a High-way, and hereof came the name: yea, said Mephistophiles, the church that thou so wondrest at, hath more revenues belonging to it, than the twelve dukes of Silesia, are worth, for there pertain unto this church fifty five towns, and four hundred and sixty three villages, besides many houses in the town. From thence went Faustus to Basil, in Switzerland, where the river of Rhine runneth through the town, parting the same as the river of Thames doth London: in the town of Basil he saw many rich monuments, the town wall'd with brick round about, without it goeth a great trench: no church pleased him but the jesuits church, which was sumptuously builded, and set full of alabaster pillers, where the spirit told Faustus that before the city was founded, there used a Basiliscus, a kind of serpent; this serpent killed as many men, women and children, as he took a sight of, but there was a knight that made himself a cover of chrystial, to come over his head, and down to the ground, and being first covered with a black cloth, over that he put the chrystial, and so boldly went to see the Basiliscus, and finding the place where she haunted, he expected her coming even before the mouth of the cave, where standing a while, the Basiliscus came forth, where when she saw her own venemous shadow in the chrystial, she split in a thousand pieces, wherefore the knight was richly rewarded of the emperor, after the which the knight founded this town upon the place where he had slain the serpent, and gave it the name Basil, in remembrance of his deed.

From Basil, Faustus went to Costnitz in Sweitz, at the head of the Rhine, where is a most sumptuous bridge that goeth over the Rhine, even from the gates of the town, to the other side of the stream; at the head of the river of Rhine, is a small sea, called of the Switzers, the Black Sea, twenty thousand paces long, and fifty hundred paces broad. The town Costnitz took the name of this; the emperor gave it a clown for expounding of his riddle; wherefore the clown named the town Costnitz, that is in English, Cost me nothing. From Costnitz he came to Ulm, where he saw the sumptuous town-house built by two and fifty of the ancient senators of the city: it took the name Ulm, because the whole land thereabouts is full of Elms: but Faustus minding to depart from thence, his spirit said unto him,

Faustus, think of the town as you will; it hath three dukedoms belonging to it, the which they have bought with ready money. From Ulm he came unto Watzberg, the chiefest town in Frankland, wherein the bishop altogether keepeth his court, through the which town passeth the river Mayne, that runs into the Rhine: thereabouts groweth strong and pleasant wine, the which Faustus well proved: the castle standeth on a hill on the north-side of the town, at the foot thereof runneth the river; this town is full of beggarly friers, nuns, priests, and jesuits; for there are five sorts of begging friers, besides three cloysters of nuns; at the foot of the castle stands a church, in the which there is an altar, where are engraven all the four elements, and all the orders and degrees in heaven, that any man of understanding whosoever, that hath a light thereof, may say, that it is the artificialest thing that ever he beheld. From thence he went to Norenberg, whither as he went by the way, his spirit informed him that the town was named of Claudius Tiberius, the son of Nero the Tyrant: in the town are two famous cathedral churches, one called St. Sabelt, the other St. Laurence; in which church stands all the relicks of Carolus Magnus, that is to say, his cloak, his hose, his doublet, his sword and crown, the scepter and apple: it hath a very glorious gilded conduit in the market-place of St. Laurence; in which conduit is the spear that thrust our Saviour into the side, and a piece of the holy cross; the wall is called the fair wall of Norenberg, and five hundred and twenty eight streets, a hundred and sixty wells, four great and two small clocks, six great gates, two small doors, eight stone-bridges, twelve small hills, ten fair market-places, thirteen common hot houses, ten churches, within the town are twenty wheels of water-mills, it hath a hundred and thirty eight tall ships, two mighty town-walls of hew'd stone and earth, with very deep trenches: the walls have a hundred and eighty towers about them, and four fair platforms, ten apothecaries, ten doctors of the common-law, fourteen doctors of physic. From Norenberg he went to Auspurg, where at the break of the day he demanded of his spirit, whereupon the town took his name: This town (quoth he) hath had many names; when it was first built, it was called Vindelica; secondly, it was called Zizaria, the iron-bridge: lastly, by the Emperour Octavus Augustus, it was called Augusta, and by the corruption of language, the Germans had named it Auspurg. Now for because that Faustus had been there before, he departed (without seeing their monuments) to Ravensberg, where his spirit certified him that the city had seven names: the first Diperia, the second Quadratis, the third Heaspolis, the fourth Reginipolis, the fifth Imbripolis, the sixth Ratisbona, the last is Ravensburg. The situation of this city pleas'd Faustus well, also the strong and sumptuous building; by the walls thereof runneth the river Danubius, in Dutch called Danow, into which not far from the compass of the city falleth near hand threescore other small rivers and fresh waters: Faustus also liked the sumptuous stone-bridge over the same water, with the church standing thereon, the which was founded Anno 1115, the name whereof is called St. Remedian; in the town Faustus went into the cellar of an inn-holder, and let out all the beer and wine that was in the cellar. After which feat, he returned into Mentz in Bavaria, a right princely town: the town appeared as if it were new, with great streets therein, both of breadth and length from Mentz to Salisburg, where the bishop is always resident: here saw he all the commodities that were possible to be seen, for at the hill he saw the form of a bell made in Chrystial, a huge thing to look upon, that every year groweth bigger and bigger, by reason of the freezing cold. From thence he went to Vienna in Austria, the town is of great antiquity, that it is not possible to find the like; in this town, said the spirit, is more wine than water, for all under the town are wells, which are filled every year with wine, and all the water, that they have, runneth by this town; this is the river Danubius. From thence he went into Prage, the chief city of Bohemia; this is divided into three parts, that is old Prage, little Prage, and new Prage: little Prage is the place where the emperour's court is placed; upon an exceeding high mountain there is a castle, where are two fair churches; in the one he found a monument which might well have been a mirrour for himself, and that was the sepulchre of a notable conjurer, which by his magick had so inchanted his sepulchre, that whosoever set foot thereon, should be sure never to die in their beds. From this castle he came and went down over the bridge; this bridge hath twenty four arches, and in the middle of the bridge stands a very fair monument, being a cross builded of stone, and most artificially carved. From thence he went into the old Prage, the which is separated from the new Prage, with an exceeding deep ditch, and round about inclosed with a wall of brick; unto this is adjoyning the Jews town, wherein are thirteen thousand men, women, and children, all jews; there he viewed the colledge and the gardens, where all manner of savage beasts are kept; and from thence he fetched a compass round about the three towns, whereat he wonder'd greatly to see so mighty a city stand all within the walls. From Prage he flew into the air, and bethought himself what he might do, or which way to take; so looked round about, and behold he espied a passing fair city, which lay not far from Prage, about some four and twenty miles, and that was Bressaw in Silesia, in which when he was entred, it seemed to him that he had been in Paradise so neat and clean were the streets, and so sumptuous were their buildings. In the city he saw not many wonders, except the brazen virgin that standeth on a bridge over the water, and under which standeth a mill like a paper mill, which virgin is made to do execution upon those disobedient town-born children, that be so wild that their parents cannot bridle them; which when any such are found with some hainous offence, turning to the shame of their parents and kindred, they are brought to kiss the virgin, which openeth her arms: the person then to be executed kisseth her, then doth she close her arms together with such violence, that she crusheth out the breath of the party, breaketh his bulk, and so he dieth; but being dead she openeth her arms again, and letteth the party fall into the mill, where he is stamped into small morsels, which the water carrieth away, so that no part is found again. From Bressaw he went toward Cracovia in the kingdom of Bolionia, where he beheld the academy, the which pleased him wonderful well: in the city the king most commonly holdeth his court at a castle, in which castle are many famous monuments; there is a most sumptuous church in the same, in which standeth a silver altar guilded, and set with rich stones, and over it is a covenance full of all manner of silver ornaments belonging to mass. In the church hangeth the jaw-bones of a huge dragon, that kept the rock before the castle was edified thereon: it is full of all manner of munition, and hath always victuals for three years to serve three thousand men; through the town runneth a river, called the Vessnal or Wessel, where over is a fair wooden-bridge; this water divideth the town and Gasmere, in this Gasmere dwell the Jews, being a small walled town by themselves, to the number of twenty-five thousand men, women and children; within one mile of the town there is a salt mine where they found stones of pure salt, one thousand pound, two thousand pound, or more in weight, and that in great quantity: this salt is as black as the New-castle coals when it comes out of the mines, but being beaten to powder, it is as white as snow. The like they have four miles from thence at a town called Buckma. From thence Faustus went to Sandentz, the Captain thereof was called Don Spicket Jordan, in this town are many monuments, as the tomb and sepulchre of Christ, in as ample a manner as that is at Jerusalem, at the proper costs of a gentleman, that went thrice a year to Jerusalem, from that place and returned again; not far from that town is a new town wherein is a nunnery of the order of St. Dioclesian, into which order may none come except they be gentlewomen, and well formed, and fair to look upon, which pleased Faustus well; but having a will to travel further, and to see more wonders, mounting up towards the east over many lands and provinces, as in Hungaria, Transilvania, Shede, Ingatz, Sardinia, and so into Constantinople, where the Turkish emperor kept his court: this city was surnamed by Constantine the founder thereof, being builded of very fair stone: In the same the Great Turk hath three fair palaces, the walls are strong, the pinacles are very huge, and the streets very large: but this liked not Faustus, that one man should have as many wives as he would; the sea runneth hard by the city; the wall hath eleven gates: Faustus abode there a certain time to see the manner of the Turkish emperour's service at his table, where he saw his royal service to be such, that he thought if all the christian princes should banquet together, and every one adorn the feast to the utmost, that they were not able to compare with the Turk and his table, and the rest of his country service. Wherefore it so affrighted Faustus, that he vowed to be revenged on him; for his pomp he thought was more fit for himself; wherefore as the Turks sate at meat, Faustus shewed them a little apish play, for round about the privy chamber he sent forth flashing flames of fire, insomuch that the whole company forsook their meat and fled, except only the Great Turk himself; him Faustus charmed in such sort that he could neither rise nor fall, neither could any man pull him up: With this was the hall so light, as if the sun had shined in the house; then came Faustus in form of a pope to the Great Turk, saying, All hail, emperor, now art thou honoured, that I so worthily appear unto thee, as thy Mahomet was wont to do. Hereupon he vanished, and forthwith it thundred that the whole palace shook: the Turk greatly marvelled what this should be that so vexed him, and was perswaded by the chiefest counsellours, that it was Mahomet his prophet, which had so appeared unto them, whereupon the Turk commanded them to fall down on their knees, and to give him thanks for doing them so great honour, as to shew himself unto them; but the next day Faustus went into the castle where he kept his wives and concubines, in which castle might no man upon the pain of death come, except those that were appointed by the Great Turk to do him service and they were all gelded, which when Faustus perceived, he said to his spirit Mephistophiles, How likest thou this sport? Are not these fair ladies greatly to be pitied, that thus consume their youth at the pleasure of one only man?

Why, quoth the spirit, mayest not thou instead of the emperour embrace his fair ladies? Do what thy heart desireth herein, and I will aid thee, and what thou wishest thou shalt have it performed. Wherefore Faustus (being before this counsel apt enough to put such matters in practice) caused a great fog to be round about the castle, both within and without, and he himself appeared amongst the ladies in all points as they used to paint Mahomet; at which sight the ladies fell on their knees and worshipped him. Then Faustus took the fairest by the hand, and led her into a chamber, where after this manner he fell to dalliance, and thus he continued a whole day and a night; and when he had delighted himself sufficiently with her, he put her away, and made his spirit bring him another; so likewise he kept with her twenty-four hours play, causing his spirit to fetch him most dainty fare, and so he passed away six days, having each day his pleasure of a sundry lady, and that of the fairest; all which time the fog was so thick and so stinking, that they within the house thought that they had been in hell for the time, and they without wondred thereat, in such sort that they went to their prayers, calling on their God Mahomet, and worshipping of the image; where the sixth day Faustus exalted himself into the air like a pope, in the sight of the Great Turk and all his people, and he had no sooner departed the castle, but the fog vanished away: Whence presently the Turk went to his wives and concubines, demanding of them if they knew the cause why the castle was beset with a mist so long: They said it was the God Mahomet himself that had caused it, and how he was in the castle personally six days, and more for certainty he hath lain with six of us six nights one after another. The Turk hearing this fell down upon his knees, and gave Mahomet thanks, desiring him to forgive him for being offended with his visiting his castle and wives these six days; but the Turk commanded that those whom Mahomet had lain by should be most carefully look'd to, perswading himself (and so did all the whole people who knew of it) that out of them to Mahomet should be raised a mighty generation: But first he demanded of his ladies, if Mahomet had not actual copulation with them according as earthly men have? Yea my lord (quoth one) as if you had been there yourself, you could not have mended it; for he lay with me stark naked, kissed, and culled me, and so delighted me, that for my part I would he came two or three times a week to serve me in such sort again. From thence Faustus went to Alker, the which before times was called Chairam, or Memphis; in this city the Egyptian Soldian holdeth his court; from thence the river Nilus hath his head and spring, it is the greatest fresh water river that is in the whole world, and always when the sun is in Cancer, it overfloweth the whole land of Ægypt. Then he returned again towards the north-east, and to the town of Osen and Sebasa in Hungaria; this Osen is the closest city in Hungaria, and standing in a fertile soil, wherein groweth most excellent wine, and not far from the tower there is a well called Zipzan; the water whereof changeth iron into copper: There are mines of gold and silver, and all manner of metal: we Germans call this town Osen, but in the Hungarian speech it is Start; in the town standeth a very fair castle, and very well fortified. From thence he went to Austria, and so through Silesia into Saxony, unto the towns of Magdeburg, and Lipzig and Lubeck, Magdeburg is a bishoprick: In this city is one of the pitchers wherein Christ changed the water into wine in Cana in Galilee. At Lipzig nothing pleased Faustus so well as the great vessel in the castle made of wood, the which is bound about with twenty-four iron hoops, and every hoop weigh'd two hundred pound weight; you must go upon a ladder thirty steps high before you can look into it; he saw also the new church-yard where it was wall'd, and standeth upon a fair plain; the yard is two hundred paces long, and round about the side of the wall are good places, separated one from each other to see sepulchres in, which in the middle of the yard standeth very sumptuous; therein standeth a pulpit of white work and gold. From thence he went to Lubeck and Jamberg, where he made no abode, but away again to Erford in Duriten, where he visited the Frescold; and from Erford he went home to Wittenburg, when he had seen and visited many a strange place. Being from home one year and a half, in which time he wrought more wonders than are here declared.

CHAP. XXIII.

How Dr. Faustus had sight of Paradise.

After this Dr. Faustus set forth again to visit the countries of Spain, Portugal, France, England, Scotland, Denmark, Sweden, Poland, Muscovy, India, Cataia, Africa, Persia, and lastly into Barbaria amongst the Black-Moors; and in all his wandring he was desirous to visit the ancient monuments and mighty hills, amongst the rest, beholding the high hill called Theno Reise, was desirous to rest upon it. From thence he went into the Isle of Britain, wherein he was greatly delighted to see the fair water, and warm baths, the divers sorts of metal, with many precious stones, and divers other commodities, the which Faustus brought thence with him. He was also at the Orcades behind Scotland, where he saw the tree that bringeth forth fruit, that when it is ripe, openeth and falleth in the water, wherein ingendreth a certain kind of fowl and birds; these islands are in number twenty three, but ten of them are not habitable, the other thirteen were inhabited. From thence he went to the hill Caucasus, which is the highest in all that tropick, it lyeth near the borders of Scythia; hereon Faustus stood and beheld many lands and kingdoms: Faustus being on such an high hill, thought to look over all the world, and beyond; for he went to Paradise, but he durst not commune with his spirit thereof; and being on the hill Caucasus, he saw the whole land of India and Scythia, and as he looked towards the east, he saw a mighty clear streak of fire coming from heaven upon earth, even as if it had been one of the beams of the sun. He saw in the water four mighty waters springing, one had his course towards India, the second towards Ægypt, the third and fourth towards Armenia; when he saw these he would needs know of his spirit what waters they were, and from whence they came; his spirit gave him gently an answer, saying, it is Paradise that lyeth so far in the east, the garden that God himself hath planted with all manner of pleasure: and the fiery streams which thou seest is the wall or fence of the garden: but the clear light which thou seest afar off, that is the angel that hath the custody thereof with a fiery sword: and although thou thinkest thy self to be hard by, thou art yet further thither from hence, than thou hast ever been: the water that thou seest divided in four parts, is the water that issueth out of the well in the middle of Paradise. The first is called Ganges or Pison, the second Gihon, the third Tygris, and the fourth Euphrates, also thou seest that he standeth under Libra and Aries right towards the Zenith; and upon this fiery wall standeth the angel Michael, with his flaming sword, to keep the tree of life, which he hath in charge. But the spirit said to Faustus, neither thou, nor I, nor any after us, yea, all men whatsoever, are denyed to visit, or come any nearer than we be.

CHAP. XXIV.

Of a certain Comet that appeared in Germany, and how Dr. Faustus was desired by certain Friends of his to know the meaning thereof.

In Germany, over the town of St. Elzeben, was seen a mighty great comet, whereat the people wonder'd, but Dr. Faustus being there, was asked of certain of his friends his judgment or opinion in the matter: whereupon he answered, it falleth out often by the course and change of the sun and moon, that the sun is under the earth, and the moon above; but when the moon draweth near the change, then is the sun so strong, that it taketh away the light of the moon, in such sort as she is red as blood, and on the contrary side, after they have been together, she soon taketh her light from him, and so increasing in light to the full, she will be as red as the sun was before, and change herself into divers and sundry colours, of which springeth the prodigal monster, or as you call it a comet, which is a figure or token appointed of God as a forewarning of his displeasure: as at one time he sendeth hunger, plague, sword, or such like, being all tokens of his judgements, which comet cometh through the conjunction of the sun and moon, and begetteth a monster, whose father is the sun, and whose mother is the moon: moon and sun.

CHAP. XXV.

Another Question put forth to Dr. Faustus concerning the Stars.

THERE was a learned man of the town of Halberstat, named N. W. who invited Dr. Faustus to his table, but falling into communication before supper was ready, they looked out of the window, and seeing many stars in the firmament, this man being a Dr. of physick, and a good astrologian, said, Dr. Faustus, I have invited you as my guest, hoping you will take in good part with me, and withal, I request you to impart some of your experience in the stars and planets; and seeing a star fall, he said, I pray you, Faustus, what is the condition, quality or greatness of the stars in the firmament? Faustus answered him, my friend and brother, you see that the stars that fall from heaven, when they come to the earth, they be very small to our thinking as candles, but being fixed in the firmament, they are many as great as a city, some as great as a province or dukedom, others as great as the whole earth, other some far greater than the earth twelve times, and from the height of the heavens there is scarce any earth to be seen, yea, the planets in the heavens are some so great as this land, some so great as the whole empire of Rome, some as Turky, yea, some as great as the whole world.

CHAP. XXVI,

How Faustus was asked a Question concerning the Spirits that vexed Men.

THAT is most true (said he to Faustus) concerning the stars and planets; but I pray you in what kind or manner do the spirits use to vex men so little by day, and so greatly by night? Dr. Faustus answered, Because the spirits are of God forbidden the light, their dwelling is in darkness, and the clearer the sun shineth, the farther the spirits have their abiding from it, but in the night when it is dark, they have their familiarity and abiding near unto us men. For although in the night we see not the sun yet the brightness thereof so lighted the first moving of the firmament, as it doth here on earth in the day, by which reason we are able to see the stars and planets in the night, even so the rays of the sun piercing upwards into the firmament, the spirits abandon the place, and so come near us on earth, the darkness filling our heads with heavy dreams and fond fancies, with shrieking and crying in many deformed shapes: and sometimes when men go forth without light, there falleth to them a fear, that their hairs standeth up an end, so many start in their sleep, thinking there is a spirit by them, groping or feeling for him, going round about the house in their sleep, and many such like fancies, and all this is, because in the night the spirits are more familiarly by us, than we are desirous of their company, and so they carry us, blinding us, and plaguing us more than we are able to perceive.

CHAP. XXVII.

How Dr. Faustus was asked a Question concerning the Stars that fell from Heaven.

Dr. Faustus being demanded the cause, why the stars fall from heaven? he answered, That it is but our opinion; for if one star fall, it is the great judgment of God upon us, as a forewarning of some great thing to come: for when we think that a star falleth, it is but as a spark that issueth from a candle, or flame of fire; for if it were a substantial thing, we should not so soon lose the sight of them as we do. And likewise if so be that we see as it were a stream of fire fall from the firmament, as it oft happeneth, yet are they not stars, but as it were a flame of fire vanishing, but the stars are substantial; therefore are they firm and not failing; if there fall any, it is a sign of some great matter to come, as a scourge to a people or country: and then such stars falling, and the gates of heaven are opened, and the clouds send forth floods, and other plagues, to the damage of the whole land and people.

CHAP. XXVIII.

How Faustus was asked a Question concerning Thunder.

In the month of August, there was over Wittenburg a mighty great lightning and thunder; and as Dr. Faustus was jesting merrily in the market-place with certain of his friends and companions, being physicians, they desired him to tell them the cause of that weather: Faustus answered, It hath been commonly seen heretofore, that before a thunder-clap fell a shower of rain, or a gale of wind; for commonly after a wind falleth rain, and after rain a thunder-clap, such thickness come to pass when the four winds meet together in the heavens, the airy clouds are by force beaten against the fixed chrystial firmament, but when the airy clouds meet with the firmament, they are congealed, and so strike, and rush against the firmament, as great pieces of ice when they meet on the water: then each other sounded in our ears, and that we call thunder, which indeed was none other than you have heard.

The Third and Last of Dr. Faustus his merry Conceits, shewing after what Sort he practised Necromancy in the Courts of great Princes: and lastly of his fearful and pitiful End.

CHAP. XXIX.

How the Emperour Carolus Quintus requested of Faustus to see some of his Cunning, whereunto he agreed.

The Emperor Charles the fifth of that name, was personally with the rest of the nobles and gentlemen, at the town of Intzbrack, where he kept his court, unto the which also Dr. Faustus resorted, and being there well known of divers nobles and gentlemen, he was invited in the court to meat, even in the presence of the emperor, whom when the emperor saw, he looked earnestly upon him, thinking by his looks he was some wonderful fellow: wherefore he asked one of his nobles, whom he should be? He answered, that he was called Dr. Faustus: whereupon the emperor held his peace until he had taken his repast: after which he called unto him Faustus into his privy-chamber; where being come, he said unto him, Faustus, I have heard much of thee, that thou art excellent in the black art, and none like thee in my empire; for men say that thou hast a familiar spirit with thee, and that thou canst do what thou list: it is therefore (said the emperor) my request of thee, that thou let me see proof of thy experience, and I vow unto thee by the honour of my imperial crown, none evil shall happen unto thee for so doing. Hereupon Dr. Faustus answered his majesty, that upon those conditions he was ready in any thing that he could to do his highness's command in what service he could appoint him. Well, hear then what I say, (quoth the emperor;) being once solitary in my house, I called to mind my elders and ancestors, how it was possible for them to attain to so great a degree and authority, yea, so high, that we, the successors of that line, are not able to come near. As for example: the great and mighty monarch of the world, Alexander Magnus, was such a pattern and spectacle to all his successors, as the chronicles make mention of, having so great riches, conquering and subduing so many kingdoms, the which I and those that follow me (I fear) shall never be able to attain unto: wherefore Faustus my hearty desire is, that thou wouldst vouchsafe to let me see that Alexander and his Paramour, the which was praised to be so fair; and I pray thee shew me them in such sort, that I may see their personages, shapes, gesture and apparel, as they used in their lifetime, and that here before my face, to that end that I may say, I have my long desire fulfilled, and to praise thee to be a famous man in thy art and experience. Dr. Faustus answered, my most excellent Lord, I am ready to accomplish your request in all things, so far forth as I and my spirit are able to perform: yet your majesty shall know, that their dead bodies are not able substantially to be brought before you; but such spirits as have seen Alexander and his Paramour alive, shall appear unto you in manner and form as they both lived in their most flourishing time; and herewith I hope to please your Imperial Majesty. Then Faustus went a little aside and spoke to his spirit, but he returned again presently, saying, Now if it please your Majesty you shall see them, yet upon this condition, that you demand no question of them, nor speak unto them; which the emperor agreed unto. Whereupon Dr. Faustus opened the privy-chamber door, where presently entred the great and mighty emperour, Alexander Magnus, in all things to look upon as if he had been alive; in proportion, a strong set thick man, of a middle stature, black hair, and that both thick and curled, head and beard, red cheeks, and a broad face, with eyes like a Basilisk, he had a compleat harness furnished and engraven, exceeding rich to look upon: and so passing towards the Emperor Carolus, he made a low and reverend courtesie: whereat the Emperor Carolus would have stood up to receive and greet him with the like reverence: Faustus took hold on him, and would not permit him to do it. Shortly after Alexander made humble reverence, and went out again; and coming to the door, his paramour met him. She coming in made the emperor likewise reverence, she was cloathed in blue velvet, wrought and embroidered with pearls and gold; she was also excellent fair, like blood and milk mixed, tall and slender, with a face as round as an apple, and thus passed they certain times up and down the house, which the emperor marking, said to himself, Now I have seen two persons which my heart hath long wished to behold; and sure it cannot otherwise be (said he to himself) but that the spirits have changed themselves into these forms, and have but deceived me, calling to mind the woman that raised the Prophet Samuel: and for that the emperor should be more satisfied in the matter, he said I have often heard that behind in her neck, she had a great wart or wen; wherefore he took Faustus by the hand without any words and went to see if it were able to be seen on her or not: but she perceiving that he came to her, bowed down her neck, where he saw a great wart, and hereupon she vanished, leaving the emperor and the rest well contented.

CHAP. XXX.

How Dr. Faustus, in the sight of the Emperor, conjured a Pair of Harts horns upon a Knight's Head, that slept out at a casement.

When Dr. Faustus had accomplished the emperor's desire in all things, as he was requested, he went forth into the gallery, and leaning over a rail, to look into the privy-garden, he saw many of the emperor's courtiers walking and talking together, and casting his eyes now this way, now that way, he espied a knight leaning out of the window of the great hall, who was fast asleep, (for in those days it was hot) but the person shall be nameless that slept, for that he was a knight, though it was all done to no little disgrace of the gentleman: It pleased Dr. Faustus, through the help of his spirit Mephistophiles, to fix on his head, as he slept, a huge pair of hart's horns: And as the knight awaked, thinking to pull in his head, he hit his horns against the glass, that the panes thereof flew about his ears. Think here how this good gentleman was vexed, for he could neither get backward nor forward; which when the emperor heard, all the courtiers laught, and came for to see what had happened: The emperor also, when he beheld the knight with so fair a head, laughed heartily thereat, and was therewith well pleased. At last Faustus made him quit of his horns again, but the knight perceived not how they came.

CHAP. XXXI.

How the above mentioned Knight went about to be revenged of Dr. Faustus.

Dr. Faustus took his leave of the emperor and the rest of the courtiers, at whose departure they were sorry, giving him many rewards and gifts ; but being a league and a half out of the city, he came into a wood, where he beheld the knight that he had jested with at the court with others in harness, mounted upon fair palfreys, and running with full charge towards Faustus ; but he seeing their intent ran towards the bushes, and before he came among the bushes he returned again, running as it were to meet them that chased him: whereupon suddenly all the bushes were turned into horsemen, which also ran to encounter with the knight and his company, and coming to them, they inclosed the knight and the rest, and told them they must pay their ransom before they departed, whereupon the knight seeing himself in such distress, besought Faustus to be good to them, which he denyed not but let them loose ; yet he so charmed them, that every one, knight and other, for the space of a whole month, did wear a pair of goat's horns on their brows, and every palfrey a pair of ox' horns on his head ; and this was their penance appointed by Faustus.

CHAP. XXXII.

How three young Dukes being together at Wittenburg, to behold the University, requested Faustus to help them at a Wish to the Town of Muncheon in Bavaria, there to see the Duke of Bavaria's Son's Wedding.

THREE worthy young dukes, the which are not here to be named, but being students altogether, at the university of Wittenburg, met on a time altogether, where they fell in reasoning concerning the pomp and bravery that should be in the city of Muncheon in Bavaria, at the wedding of the duke's son, wishing themselves there but one half hour to see the manner of their jollity; to whom one replyed, saying to the two other gentlemen, If it please you to give me the hearing, I will give you good counsel, that you may see the wedding, and be here again to-night, and this is my meaning: Let us send to Dr. Faustus, make him a present of some rare thing, and open our minds unto him, desiring him to assist us in our enterprize, and assure ye he will not deny to fulfil our request: Hereupon they all concluded: sent for Faustus, told him their minds, and gave him a gift, and invited him to a sumptuous banquet, wherewith Faustus was well contented, and promised to further their journey to the uttermost: And when the time was come that the three young gentlemen came into his house, commanding them that they would put on their best apparel, and adorn themselves as rich as they could: he took off his great large cloak, went into the garden that was adjoyning unto his house, and set the three young dukes upon his cloak, and he himself in the midst: but he gave them in charge, that in any wise they should not at once open their mouths to speak, or make answer to any man so soon as they went out, not so much as if the Duke of Bavaria or his son, should speak to them, or offer them courtesie, they should give no word or answer again; to which they all agreed. These conditions being made, Dr. Faustus began to conjure, and on a sudden arose a mighty wind, heaving up the cloak, and so carried them away in the air, and in due time they came unto Muncheon to the duke's court; where being entred into the utmost court, the marshal had espyed them, who presently went to the duke, shewing his grace that all the lords and gentlemen were ready set at the table, notwithstanding there were newly come three goodly gentlemen with one servant, the which stood without in the court, wherefore the good old duke came out unto them, welcoming them, requiring what they were, and whence? But they made no answer at all; whereat the duke wonder'd, thinking they had been all dumb: notwithstanding for his honour's sake he took them into the court, and feasted them. Faustus notwithstanding spake to them, if any thing happen otherwise than well, when I say, Sit up, then fall you all on the cloak, and good enough. Well, the water being brought, and that they must wash, one of the three had some manners, as to desire his friend to wash first, which when Faustus heard, he said, Sit up; and all at once they got on the cloak, but he that spoke fell off again, the other two with Dr. Faustus, were again presently at Wittenburg: but he that remained was taken and laid in prison: wherefore the other two gentlemen were very sorrowful for their friend, but Faustus comforted them promising that on the morrow he should also be at Wittenburg. Now all this while was the duke taken in great fear, and strucken into an exceeding dumps, wond'ring with himself that his hap was so hard to be left behind, and not the rest: and now being locked and watched with so many keepers: there was also certain of the guests that fell to reasoning with him to know what he was, and also what the other were that were vanish'd away? but the poor prisoner, thought with himself, if I open what they are, then it will be evil also with me. Wherefore all this while he gave no man any answer, so that he was there a whole day, and gave no man a word: wherefore the old duke gave charge that the next morning they should rack him until he had confessed; which when the young duke heard, he began to sorrow, and to say with himself, It may be, that to morrow (if Dr. Faustus come not to aid me) I shall be racked and grievously tormented, insomuch that I shall be constrained by force to more than willingly I would do. But he comforted himself with hope that his friends would entreat Dr. Faustus about his deliverance, as also it came to pass: for that before it was day, Dr. Faustus was by him, and he conjured them that watched him into such a heavy sleep, that he with his charms made open all the locks in the prison, and therewithal brought the young duke again in safety to the rest of his fellows and friends, where they presented Faustus with a sumptuous gift, and so departed one from another.

CHAP. XXXIII.

How Dr. Faustus borrowed Money of a Jew, and laid his own Leg in Pawn for it.

IT is a common proverb in Germany, that although a conjurer have all things at command, the day will come that he shall not be worth a penny; so it is like to fall out with Dr. Faustus, in promising the devil so largely; but as the devil is the author of all lies, even so he led Faustus his mind in practising things to deceive the people, and blinding them, wherein he took his whole delight, thereby to bring himself to riches; notwithstanding in the end he was never the richer; and although during twenty four years of his time that the devil set him, he wanted nothing; yet was he best pleased when he might deceive any body. For out of the mightiest potentates courts in all these countries, he would send his spirit to fetch away their best cheer. And on a time, being in his merriment, where he was banquetting with other students in an inn, thereunto resorted many Jews: which when Dr. Faustus perceived, he was minded to play a merry jest to deceive a Jew, desiring one of them to lend him some money for a time; the jew was content, and lent Faustus three score dollers for a month, which time being expired, the Jew came for his money and interest: but Dr. Faustus was never minded to pay the Jew again; at length the Jew coming home to his house, and calling importunately for his money, Dr. Faustus made him this answer; Jew, I have no money, nor know I how to pay thee; but notwithstanding, to the end thou mayest be contented, I will cut off a limb of my body, be it arm or leg, and the same thou shalt have in pawn for thy money; yet with this condition, that when I shall pay thee thy money again, then thou shalt give me my limb. The Jew that was never a friend to a Christian, thought with himself this fellow is right for my purpose, that will lay his limbs in pawn for money, and was therewith very well content: wherefore Dr. Faustus took a saw, and therewith seemed to cut off his leg, being notwithstanding nothing so. Well, he gave it to the Jew, yet upon this condition, when he got money to pay, the Jew should deliver him his leg, to the end he might set it on again. The Jew was with this matter very well pleased, took his leg, and departed; and having to go far home, he was somewhat weary, and by the way he thus bethought him; what helpeth me a knave's leg? if I should carry it home, it would stink and infect my house; besides, it is too hard a piece of work to set it on again: wherefore what an ass was Faustus, to lay so great a pawn for so small a sum of money? and for my part, quoth the Jew to himself, this will never profit me any thing; and with these words he cast the leg away from him into a ditch. All this Dr. Faustus knew right well, therefore, within three days after sent for the Jew, to make him payment of his sixty dollers: the Jew came, and Dr. Faustus demanded his pawn, there was his money ready for him: the Jew answered, The pawn was not profitable nor necessary for any thing, so I cast it away: But Faustus threatning, replyed, I will have my leg again, or else one of thine for it. The Jew fell to intreat, promising him to give him what money he would ask if he would not deal strictly with him; wherefore the Jew was constrained to give him sixty dollers more to be rid of him, and yet Faustus had his leg on, for he had but blinded the Jew.

CHAP. XXXIV.

How Dr. Faustus deceived the Horse-courser.

AFTER this manner he deceived a horse-courser, at a fair, called Pheifering: for Faustus, through his conjuring, had gotten an excellent fair horse, whereupon he rid to the fair, where he had many chapmen that offered him money; lastly, he sold him for forty dollers, and willing him that bought him, that in any wise he should not ride him over the water; but the horse-courser marvelled with himself that Faustus bade him ride over no water. But (quoth he) I will prove, and forthwith he rid him into the river, presently the horse vanished from under him, and he was left on a bottle of straw, insomuch that the man was almost drowned; the horse-courser knew well where he lay that had sold him his horse: whereupon he went angerly to his inn, where he found Dr. Faustus fast asleep, and snorting on a bed; but the horse-courser could no longer forbear him, but took him by the leg, and began to pull him off the bed; but he pulled him so that he pulled his leg from his body, insomuch that the horse-courser fell backwards in the place, then began Dr. Faustus to cry with open throat, he hath murthered me. Hereat the horse-courser was afraid, and gave the flight, thinking no other with himself, but that he had pulled his leg from his body: by this means Dr. Faustus kept his money.

CHAP. XXXV.

How Dr. Faustus eat a Load of Hay.

DR. FAUSTUS being at a town in Germany called Zwickow, where he was accompanied with many doctors and masters, and going forth to walk after supper, they met with a clown that drew a load of hay. Good even, good fellow, said Faustus to the clown, what shall I give thee, to let me eat my belly-full of hay? The clown thought with himself, what a mad man is this to eat hay? Thought he with himself, thou wilt not eat much: they agreed for three farthings he should eat as much as he could; wherefore Dr. Faustus began to eat, and so ravenously, that all the rest of the company fell a laughing; blinding so the poor clown, that he was sorry at his heart, for he seemed to have eaten more than half of the hay; wherefore the clown began to speak him fair, for fear he should have eaten the other half also: Faustus made as though he had pity on the clown, and went away: when the clown came in the place where he would be, he had his hay again, as he had before, a full load.

CHAP. XXXVI.

How Dr. Faustus served the twelve Students.

At Wittenberg, before Faustus's house, there was a quarrel between seven students, and five that came to part the rest, one part stronger than the other. Wherefore Dr. Faustus seeing them to be over-matcht, conjured them all blind, insomuch that the one could not see the other, and he dealt so with them, that they fought and smote at one another still; whereat all the beholders fell a laughing; and thus they continued blind, beating one another until the people parted them and led each one to his own house, where being enter'd into their houses, they received their sight presently again.

CHAP. XXXVII.

How Dr. Faustus served the drunken Clowns.

Dr. Faustus went into an inn wherein was many tables full of clowns, the which was tippling kan after kan of excellent wine; and to be short, they were all drunken; and as they sate, they so sang and hollowed, that one could not hear a man speak for them, this angred Dr. Faustus: wherefore he said to them that called him in, mark, my masters, I will shew a merry jest: the clowns continued still hollowing and singing; he conjured them that their mouths stood as wide open as it was possible for them to hold them, and never a one of them was able to close his mouth again; by and by the noise was gone; the clowns notwithstanding looked earnest one upon another, and knew not what was hapned: one by one they went out, and so soon as they came without, they were all as well as ever they were, but none of them desired to go in any more.

CHAP. XXXVIII.

How Dr. Faustus sold five Swine for six Dollars apiece.

Dr. Faustus began another jest; he made ready five fat swine the which he sold to one for six dollars apiece, upon this condition, that the swine-driver should not drive them into the water. Dr. Faustus went home again, and as the swine had fouled themselves in the mud, the swine-driver drove them into the water, where presently they were changed into so many bundles of straw, swimming upright in the water; the buyer looked wishfully upon them, and was sorry in his heart; but he knew not where to find Faustus; so he was content to let all go, and lose both mony and hogs.

CHAP. XXXIX.

How Dr. Faustus played a merry Jest with the Duke of Anhalt in his Court.

Dr. Faustus on a time went to the Duke of Anhalt, who welcomed him very courteously; this was in the month of January; where sitting at table, he perceived the dutchess to be with child; and forbearing himself until the meat was taken from the table, and that they brought in the banqueting dishes, Dr. Faustus said to the dutchess, Gracious Lady, I have always heard that great bellied women do always long for some dainties; I beseech therefore your grace, hide not your mind from me, but tell me what you desire to eat: She answered him, Dr. Faustus, now truly I will not hide from you what my heart doth much desire; namely, that if it were now harvest, I would eat my belly full of grapes and other dainty fruit. Dr. Faustus answered hereupon, Gracious lady this is a small thing for me to do, for I can do more than this; wherefore he took a plate and set it upon one of the casements of the window, holding it forth, where incontinent he had his dish full of all manner of fruit, as red and white grapes, pears, and apples, the which came from out of strange countries; all these he presented to the dutchess, saying, Madam, I pray you vouchsafe to taste of this dainty fruit, the which came from a far country, for there the summer is not yet ended. The dutchess thanked Faustus highly, and she fell to her fruit with full appetite. The Duke of Anhalt notwithstanding could not withhold to ask Faustus with what reason there were such young fruits to be had at that time of the year? Dr. Faustus told him, May it please your grace to understand, that the year is divided into two circles of the whole world, that when with us it is winter, in the contrary circle it is notwithstanding summer; for in India and Saba, there falleth or setteth a sun, so that it is so warm, that they have twice a year fruit; and, gracious lord, I have a swift spirit, the which can in a twinkling of an eye fulfil my desire in any thing: wherefore I sent him into those countries, who hath brought this fruit as you see, whereat the duke greatly admired.

CHAP. XL.

How Dr. Faustus, through his Charms, made a great Castle in the presence of the Duke of Anhalt.

Dr. Faustus desired the Duke of Anhalt to walk a little forth of the court with him; wherefore they went together in the field, where Dr. Faustus (through his skill) had placed a mighty castle, which when the duke saw he wonder'd thereat, so did the dutchess and all the beholders, that on that hill which is called Rohumbuel, should on the sudden be so fair a castle. At length Dr. Faustus desired the duke and dutchess to walk with him into the castle, which they denied not: this castle was so wonderful strong, having about it a great deep trench of water, the which was full of fish, and all manner of water-fowl, as swans, ducks, geese, bitterns, and such like: about the wall was five stone doors, and two other doors also; within was a great open court, wherein was inchanted all manner of wild beasts, especially such as was not to be found in Germany, as apes, bears, buffs, antelopes, and many more strange beasts; also there were harts, hinds, roe-bucks, and does, and wild swine: all manner of land-fowl that any man could think on, which flew from one tree to another. After all this he set his guests to the table, being the duke and dutchess, with all their train, for he had provided them a most sumptuous feast both of meat, and also of drink; for he set nine messes of meat upon the board at once, and all this must his Wagner do, to place all things on the board, the which was brought unto him by the spirit invisibly, of all things their hearts could desire, as wild-fowl, venison, and all manner of dainty fish that could be thought on; of wine also great plenty, and of divers sorts, French wine, Cullen wine, Crabashir wine, Renish wine, Spanish wine, Hungarian wine, Waszburg wine, Malmsey and Sack; in the whole there was one hundred cans standing round about the house. This sumptuous banquet the duke took thankfully, and afterwards he departed homeward, and but to their thinking, they had neither eat nor drank, so were they blinded while they were in the castle. But as they were in their palace, they looked towards the castle, and beheld it all on a flame of fire, and all those that saw it wonder'd to hear so strange a noise, as if a great ordinance had been shot off; and thus the castle burned and consumed clean away, which done, Dr. Faustus return'd to the duke, who gave him great thanks for shewing of him so great a courtesie, and gave him a hundred dollars, and liberty to depart, or stay there, at his own discretion.

CHAP. XLI.

How Dr. Faustus, with his Company, visited the Bishop of Salisburg's Wine-cellar.

Dr. Faustus having taken leave of the duke, he went to Wittenburg, near about Shrove-tide, and being in company with certain students, Dr. Faustus was himself the God of Bacchus, who having well feasted the students before with dainty fare, after the manner of Germany, where it is counted no feast, unless all the bidden guests be drunk, which Dr. Faustus intending, said, Gentlemen, and my guests, will it please you take a cup of wine with me in a place or celler whereunto I will bring you? they all said willingly, We will, which, when Dr. Faustus heard, he took them forth, set each of them upon a holly-wand, and so was conjured into the Bishop of Salisburg's Cellar, for thereabouts grew excellent pleasant wine; there fell Faustus and his company a drinking and swilling, not of the worst, but of the best. And as they were merry in the cellar, came to draw drink the bishop's butler; which when he perceived so many persons there, he cry'd with a loud voice, Thieves, thieves. This spighted Dr. Faustus wonderfully, wherefore he made every one of his company to sit on their holly-wand, and so vanished away; and in parting, Dr. Faustus took the butler by the hair of the head, and carried him away with them, until they came to a mighty high lopped tree; and on the top of that huge tree he set the butler, where he remained in a most fearful perplexity. Dr. Faustus departed to his house, where they took their valete one after another, drinking the wine that they had stolen in their bottles out of the bishop's cellar. The butler that had held himself by the hands upon the lopped tree all the night, was almost frozen with the cold, espying the day, and seeing the tree of huge great highness, thought with himself, it is impossible to come off this tree without peril of death; at length, espying certain clowns passing by, he cry'd, For the love of God help me down! The clowns seeing him so high, wonder'd what mad man would climb up so huge a tree; wherefore as a thing most miraculous, they carried tydings to the Bishop of Salisburg: then was there great running on every side to see him on the tree, and many devices they practised to get him down with ropes: and being demanded of the bishop how he came there? he said, that he was brought thither by the hair of the head, by certain thieves that were robbing of the wine-cellar, but what they were he knew not, for (said he) they had faces like men, but they wrought like devils.

CHAP. XLII.

How Dr. Faustus kept his Shrove-tide.

There were seven students and masters that studied divinity, jurisprudentiæ, and medicinæ; all these having consented, were agreed to visit Dr. Faustus, and to celebrate Shrove-tide with him; who being come to his house, he gave them their welcome, for they were his dear friends, desiring them to sit down, where he served them with a very good supper of hens, fish, and other roast, yet were they but slightly cheared; wherefore Dr. Faustus comforted his guests, excusing himself that they had stolen upon him so suddenly, that he had not leisure to provide for them so well as they were worthy; but my good friends (quoth he) according to the use of our country, we must drink all this night; and so a draught of the best wine bedwards is commendable. For you know that in great potentates' courts they use at this night great feasting, the like will I do for you; for I have three great flaggons of wine, the first is full of Hungarian wine, containing eight gallons; the second of Italian wine, containing seven gallons: the third containing six gallons of Spanish wine, all the which we will tipple up before it be day; besides we have fifteen dishes of meat, the which my spirit Mephistophiles hath fetcht so far, that it was cold before he brought it, and they are all full of the daintiest things that one's heart can devise; but saith Faustus, I must make them hot again; and you may believe me, gentlemen, that this is no blinding of you; whereas you think that this is no natural food, verily it is as good and as pleasant as ever you eat. And having ended his tale, he commanded his boy to lay his cloth, which done, he served them with fifteen messes of meat, having three dishes in a mess; in the which were all manner of venison, and dainty wild-fowl; and for wine there was no lack, as Italian wine, Hungarian wine, and Spanish wine; and when they were all made drunk, and that they had eaten their good cheer, they began to sing and dance until it was day, and so they departed every one to his own habitation: at whose departing, Dr. Faustus desired them to be his guests again the next day following.

CHAP. XLIII.

How Dr. Faustus feasted his Guests on Ash-wednesday.

Upon Ash-wednesday came unto Dr. Faustus, his bidden guests, the students, whom he feasted very royally; insomuch that they were all full and lusty, dancing and singing as the night before: and when the high glasses and goblets were caroused one to another, Dr. Faustus began to play them some pretty feats, insomuch that round about the hall was heard most pleasant musick, and that in sundry places; in this corner a lute, in another a cornet, in another a cittern, clarigolds, harp, horn-pipe, in fine, all manner of musick was heard there in that instant, whereat all the glasses and goblets, cups, and pots, dishes, and all that stood upon the board began to dance; then Dr. Faustus took ten stone pots, and set them down on the floor, where presently they began to dance, and to smite one against another, that the shivers flew round about the whole house, whereat the whole company fell a-laughing: then began he another jest, he set an instrument upon the table, and caused a mighty great ape to come among them, which ape began to dance and skip, shewing them merry conceits. In this and such pastime they passed away the whole day; when night being come Dr. Faustus bid them all to supper, which they lightly agreed unto, for students in these cases are easily intreated; wherefore he promised to feast them with a banquet of fowl, and afterwards they would go all about with a mask; then Dr. Faustus put forth a long pole out of the window, whereupon presently there came innumerable numbers of birds, and wild fowl, and so many as came had not the power to fly away again, but he took them, and flung them to the students, who lightly pulled off the necks of them, and being roasted, they made their supper; which being ended, they made themselves ready for the mask; Dr. Faustus commanded every one to put on a clean shirt over the other cloaths: which being done, they looked one upon another; it seemed to each one of them that they had no heads; and so they went forth unto certain of their neighbours, at which sight the people were most wonderfully afraid, and as the use of Germany is, that wheresoever a mask entreth, the good man of the house must feast them; so as these maskers were set to their banquet, they seemed again in their former shape with heads, insomuch, that they were all known who they were; and having sat, and well eat and drank, Dr. Faustus made that every one had an ass's head on, with great and long ears, so they fell to dancing and to drive away the time until it was midnight, and then every one departed home, and as soon as they were out of the house, each one was in his natural shape, and so they ended, and went to sleep.

CHAP. XLIV.

How Dr. Faustus the Day following was feasted by the Students, and of his merry Jests with them while he was in their Company.

THE last bacchanalia was held on Thursday, where ensued a great snow, and Dr. Faustus was invited unto the students that were with him the day before, where they had prepared an excellent banquet for him, which banquet being ended, Dr. Faustus began to play his old projects. And forthwith was in the place thirteen apes, that took hands, and danced round in a ring together, then they fell to tumbling and vaulting one after another, that it was most pleasant to behold; then they leaped out of the window and vanished away: then they set before Dr. Faustus a roasted calve's-head, which one of the students cut a piece off, and laid it on Dr. Faustus his trencher, which piece was no sooner laid down, but the calve's-head began to cry mainly out like a man, murther, murther: but, alas! what dost thou to me? whereat they were all amazed, but after a while considering of Faustus's jesting tricks, they began to laugh, and they pulled asunder the calve's-head, and eat it up. Whereupon Dr. Faustus asked leave to depart, but they would in no wise agree to let him go, except that he would promise to come again presently. Then Faustus, through his cunning made a sledge, the which was drawn about the house with four fiery dragons, this was fearful for the students to behold, for they saw Faustus ride up and down, as though he would have fired and slain all them that were in the house: this sport continued until mid-night, with such a noise that they could not hear one another, the heads of the students were so light, that they thought themselves to be in the air all that time.

CHAP. XLV.

How Dr. Faustus shewed the fair Helena unto the Students upon the Sunday following.

THE Sunday following came the students home to Dr. Faustus his own house, and brought their meat and drink with them; those men were right welcome guests unto Faustus, wherefore they all fell to drinking of wine smoothly; and being merry, they began some of them to talk of beauty of women, and every one gave forth his verdict what he had seen, and what he had heard; so one amongst the rest said, I was never so desirous of any thing in this world as to have a sight (if it were possible) of fair Helena of Greece, for whom the worthy town of Troy was destroyed and razed down to the ground; therefore, saith he, that in all men's judgements she was more than commonly fair, because that when she was stol'n away from her husband, there was for her recovery so great blood-shed. Dr. Faustus answered, for that you are all my friends, and are so desirous to see that stately pearl of Greece, fair

Helena, the wife to King Menelaus, and daughter of Tyndarus and Leda, sister to Castor and Pollux, who was the fairest lady of all Greece, I will therefore bring her into your presence personally, and in the same form and attire as she used to go when she was in her chiefest flower and choicest prime of youth. The like have I done for the emperor Carolus Magnus; at his desire, I shewed him Alexander the Great, and his paramour; but (said Dr. Faustus) I charge you all that upon your perils you speak not a word, nor rise up from the table so long as she is in your presence; and so he went out of the hall, returning presently again, after whom immediately followed the fair and beautiful Helena, whose beauty was such, that the students were all amazed to see her, esteeming her rather to be an heavenly than an earthly creature: This lady appeared before them, in a most rich gown of purple velvet, costly imbroidered: her hair hanging down loose, as fair as the beaten gold, and of such length, that it reach'd down to her hams, having most amorous cole-black eyes; a sweet and pleasant round face, with lips as red as any cherry; her cheeks of a rose colour, her mouth small, her neck white like a swan; tall and slender of personage; in sum, there was no imperfect place in her, she looked round about her with a roling hawk's eye, a smiling and wanton countenance, which near-hand inflamed the hearts of all the students, but that they persuaded themselves she was a spirit, which made them lightly pass away such fancies:

and thus fair Helena and Faustus went out again one with another. But the students, at Faustus entring in the hall again, requested him to let them see her again the next day, for that they will bring with them a painter to take a counterfeit, which he denyed, affirming that he could not always raise up his spirit, but only at certain times; yet, said he, I will give unto you her counterfeit, which shall be as good to you, as if yourself should see the drawing thereof; which they received according to his promise, but soon after lost it again. The students departed from Faustus to their several lodgings, but none of them could sleep that night for thinking of the beauty of fair Helena; therefore a man may see how the devil blindeth and enflameth the heart oftentimes with lust, that men fall in love with harlots from which their minds can afterwards be hardly removed.

CHAP. XLVI.

How Dr. Faustus conjured the four Wheels from the Clown's Waggon.

Dr. Faustus was sent for to come to the Marshal of Brunswick, who was marvellously troubled with the falling sickness, now Faustus had this quality, he seldom rid, but commonly walkt a-foot, to ease himself when he list, and as he came near unto the town of Brunswick, there overtook him a clown with four horses, and an empty waggon; to whom Dr. Faustus (jestingly to try him) said, I pray thee good fellow, let me ride a little to ease my weary legs; which the buzzardly ass denied, saying, That his horse was weary, and he would not let him get up: Dr. Faustus did this but to prove this clown if there were any courtesie to be found in him, if need were; but such churlishness is usually found among clowns, but he was well requited by Faustus, even with the like payment: for he said to him, Thou dotish clown, void of all humanity, seeing thou art of so churlish a disposition, I will pay thee as thou hast deserved, for the four wheels of thy waggon thou shalt have taken from thee; let me see then how thou canst shift? Whereupon his wheels were gone, his horses fell also down to the ground as though they had been dead: Whereat the clown was sore affrighted, measuring it as a just scourge of God for his sins and churlishness: wherefore with a trembling and wailing, he humbly besought Dr. Faustus to be good unto him, confessing he was worthy of it; notwithstanding if it pleased him to forgive him, he would hereafter do better; which submission made Faustus his heart to relent, answering him on this manner: Well, do so no more, but when a poor man desireth thee, see that thou let him ride; but yet thou shalt not go altogether clear, for although thou have again thy four wheels, yet thou shalt fetch them at the four gates of the city, so he threw dust on the horses, and revived them again: and the clown for his churlishness, was fain to fetch his wheels, spending his time with weariness, whereas if before he had shewed a little kindness, he might quietly have gone about his business.

CHAP. XLVII.

How four Jugglers cut one anothers Heads off, and set them on again, and Faustus deceived them.

Dr. Faustus came in Lent unto Frankland fair, where his spirit Mephistophiles gave him to understand that in an inn were four jugglers that cut one anothers heads off: and after their cutting off sent them to the barber to be trimmed, which many people saw. This angred Faustus, for he meant to have himself the only cook in the devil's banquet, and went to the place where they were, to beguile them, and as the jugglers were together, ready one to cut off another's head, there stood also the barber ready to trim them, and by them upon the table stood likewise a glass full of stilled waters, and he that was the chiefest among them, stood by it. Thus they began, they smote off the head of the first, and presently there was a lilly in the glass of distilled water, where Faustus perceived this lilly as it was springing, and the chief juggler named it the tree of life: thus dealt he with the first, making the barber wash and comb his head, and then he set it on again, presently the lilly vanished away out of the water, hereat the man had his head whole and sound again: the like did he with the other two: and as the turn and lot came to the chief juggler, that he also should be beheaded, and that this lilly was most pleasant, fair, and flourishing green, they smote his head off, and when it came to be barbed, it troubled Faustus his conscience, insomuch that he could not abide to see another do any thing, for he thought himself to be the principal conjurer in the world: wherefore Dr. Faustus went to the table, whereat the other jugglers kept that lilly, and so he took a small knife and cut off the stalk of the lilly, saying, to himself, None of them shall blind Faustus. Yet no man saw Faustus to cut the lilly: but when the rest of the jugglers thought to have set on their master's head, they could not: wherefore they looked on the lilly, and found it bleeding: by this means the juggler was beguiled, and so dyed in his wickedness: yet no one thought that Dr. Faustus had done it.

CHAP. XLVIII.

How an old Man, the Neighbour of Faustus, sought to perswade him to mend his Life, and to fall unto Repentance.

A GOOD Christian, an honest and vertuous old man, a lover of the Holy Scriptures, who was neighbour to Dr. Faustus, when he perceived that many students had their recourse in and out unto Dr. Faustus, he suspected his evil life, wherefore like a friend he invited Dr. Faustus to supper unto his house, to which he agreed, and having entred their banquet, the old man began with these words: My loving friend and neighbour Dr. Faustus, I am to desire of you a friendly and Christian request, beseeching you would vouchsafe not to be angry with me, but friendly resolve me in my doubt, and take my poor inviting in good part. To whom Dr. Faustus answered, My good neighbour, I pray you say your mind Then began the old patron to say, My good neighbour, you know in the beginning how that you have defied God and all the host of heaven, and given your soul to the devil, wherewith you have incurred God's high displeasure, and are become from a christian far worse than a heathen person; oh! consider what you have done, it is not only the pleasure of the body, but the safety of the soul that you must have respect unto; of which if you be careless, then are you cast away, and shall remain in the anger of the Almighty God. But yet it is time enough, O Faustus! If you repent, and call upon the Lord for mercy, as we have example in the acts of the Apostles, the Eighth Chapter, of Simon in Samaria, who was led out of the way, affirming that he was Simon homo sanctus. This man notwithstanding in the end, was converted, after he had heard the Sermon of Philip, for he was baptized and saw his sin and repented. Likewise I beseech you, good brother Dr. Faustus, let my rude sermon be unto you a conversion, and forget thy filthy life that thou hast led, repent, ask mercy, and live: for Christ saith, come unto me all ye that are weary and heavy laden, and I will refresh you. And in Ezekiel, I desire not the death of a sinner, but rather that he will convert and live. Let my words, good brother Faustus, pierce into your adamant heart, and desire God for his Son Christ his sake to forgive you. Wherefore have you lived so long in your devilish practices, knowing that in the Old and New Testament you are forbidden, and men should not suffer any such to live, neither have any conversation with them, for it is an abomination unto the Lord, and that such persons have no part in the kingdom of God. All this while Dr. Faustus heard him very attentively, and reply'd: Father, your persuasions like me wondrous well, and I thank you with all my heart for your good will and counsel, promising you, as far as I may, to allow your discipline: whereupon he took his leave, and being come home, he laid him very pensive on his bed, bethinking himself of the words of this old man, and in a manner began to repent that he had given his soul to the devil, intending to deny all that he had promised to Lucifer. Continuing in these cogitations, suddenly his spirit appeared unto him, clapping him upon the head, and wrung it as though he would have pulled his head from his shoulders, saying unto him, Thou knowest Faustus, that thou hast given thyself body and soul, to my Lord Lucifer, and thou hast vowed thyself an enemy to God and to all men; and now thou beginnest to hearken to an old doting fool, which perswadeth thee as it were to good, when indeed it is too late, for thou art the devil's, and he hath great power presently to fetch thee. Wherefore he hath sent me unto thee to tell thee, That seeing thou hast sorrowed for that which thou hast done; begin again, and write another writing with thine own blood; if not, then will I tear thee in pieces. Hereat Dr. Faustus was sore afraid, and said, My Mephistophiles, I will write again what thou wilt: Then presently he sat him down, and with his own blood wrote as followeth: which writing was afterwards sent to a dear friend of Faustus, being his kinsman.

CHAP. XLIX.

How Dr. Faustus wrote the second time with his own Blood, and gave it to the Devil.

I Dr. John Faustus, do acknowledge by this my deed and hand-writing, that since my first writing, which is seventeen years past, I have right willingly held, and have been an utter enemy to God and all men; the which I once again confirm, and give fully and wholly myself unto the devil, both body and soul, even unto great Lucifer, and that at the end of seven years ensuing after the date hereof, he shall have to do with me according as it pleaseth him, either to lengthen or shorten my life as it pleaseth him; and hereupon I renounce all persuaders, that seek to withdraw me from my purpose by the word of God, either ghostly or bodily; and farther I will never give ear to any man, be he spiritual or temporal, that moveth any matter for the salvation of my soul. Of all this writing, and that therein contained, be witness my blood, which with mine own hands I have begun and ended. Dated at Wittenburg the 25th of July.

And presently upon the making of this writing, he became so great an enemy to the poor old man, that he sought his life by all means possible; but this good old man was strong in the Holy Ghost, that he could not be vanquished by any means; for about two days after that he had exhorted Faustus, as the poor old man lay in his bed, suddenly there was a mighty rumbling in the chamber, which he was never wont to hear, and he heard as it had been the groaning of a sow, which lasted long: whereupon the good old man began to jest and mock, and said, Oh! what barbarian cry is this? Oh fair bird! what foul musick is this? A fair angel, that could not tarry two days in his place? Beginnest thou now to turn into a poor man's house, where thou hast no power, and wert not able to keep thine own two days? With these and such like words the spirit departed; and when he came home, Faustus asked him how he had sped with the old man, to whom the spirit answered: The old man was harnessed so, that he could not once lay hold upon him, but he would not tell how the old man had mocked him, for the devils can never abide to hear of their fall. Thus doth God defend the hearts of all honest Christians that betake themselves to his tuition.

CHAP. L.

How Dr. Faustus made a Marriage between two Lovers.

In the city of Wittenburg was a student, a gallant gentleman, named N. N. This gentleman was far in love with a gentlewoman, fair and proper of personage: this gentlewoman had a knight that was a suiter unto her, and many other gentlemen, which desired her in marriage, but none could obtain her. So it was that in despair with himself, that he pined away to skin and bones. But when he opened the matter to Dr. Faustus, he asked counsel of his spirit Mephistophiles, the which told him what to do. Hereupon Dr. Faustus went home to the gentleman, who bad him be of good cheer, for he should have his desire, for he would help him to that he wished for, and that this gentlewoman should love none other but him only: wherefore Dr. Faustus so changed the mind of the damosel by the practice he wrought, that she could do no other thing but think on him whom before she had hated, neither cared she for any man but him alone. The device was thus: Faustus commanded the gentleman that he should cloath himself in all the best apparel that he had, and that he should go unto the gentlewoman and shew himself, giving him a ring, commanding him in any wise that he should dance with her before he departed; who following his counsel, went to her, and when they began to dance, they that were suitors, began to take every one his lady by the hand; this gentleman took her who before had so disdained him, and in the dance he put the ring into her hand that Faustus had given him, which she no sooner toucht, but she fell presently in love with him, smiling at him in the dance, and many times winking at him, rolling her eyes, and in the end she asked him if he could love her, and make her his wife. He gladly answered that he was content; whereuponthey concluded, and were married by the means and help of Faustus, for which the gentleman well rewarded him.

CHAP. LI.

How Dr. Faustus led his Friends into his Garden at Christmas, and shewed them many strange sights, in the nineteenth Year.

In December, about Christmas, in the city of Wittenburg, were many young gentlemen, which were come out of the country to be merry with their friends, amongst whom there were certain well acquainted with Dr. Faustus, who often invited them home unto his house; they being there on a certain time; after dinner he had them into his garden, where they beheld all manner of flowers and fresh herbs, and trees bearing fruit, and blossoms of all sorts; who wonder'd to see that his garden should so flourish at that time, as in the midst of the summer, when abroad in the streets, and all the country lay full of snow and ice; wherefore this was noted of them as a thing miraculous, every one gathering and carrying away all such things as they best liked, and so departed, delighted with their sweet smelling flowers.

CHAP. LII.

How Dr. Faustus gathered together a great Army of Men in his extremity, against a Knight that would have Conjured him on his own Journey.

Dr. Faustus travelled towards Evzéleben, and when he

was nigh half the way, he espied seven horsemen, and the chief of them he knew to be the knight with whom he had jested in the emperor's court, for he had left a great pair of hart's-horns upon his head; and when the knight now saw that he had a fit opportunity to be revenged of Faustus, he ran upon him, and those that were with him, to mischief himself, intending privily to slay him: which when Faustus espied, he vanished away into a wood that was hard by them, but when the knight perceived that he was vanished away, he caused his men to stand still; but where they remained, they heard all manner of warlike instruments of musick, as drums, flutes, trumpets, and such like, and a certain troop of horsemen running towards them; then they turned another way, and were also met on that side; then another way, and yet were freshly assaulted, so that which way soever they turned themselves, they were encountred, insomuch that when the knight perceived that he could escape no way, but that his enemies lay on him which way soever he offered to fly, he took good heart, and ran amongst the thickest, and thought with himself better to dye than to live with so great infamy: therefore being at handy blows with them he demanded the cause, why they should so use them? But none of them would give him answer, until Dr. Faustus shewed himself unto the knight; whereupon they enclosed him round, and Dr. Faustus said unto him, sir, yield your weapon and your self, otherwise it will go hard with you. The knight knew no other, but that he was conjured with an host of men, whereas indeed they were none other but devils, yielded: then Faustus took away his sword, his piece, and horse, with all the rest of his companions. And farther he said unto him, sir, the chiefest general of our army hath commanded me to deal with you, according to the law of arms, you shall depart in peace, whither you please; and then he gave the knight an horse, after the manner, and set him thereon, so he rode, the rest went on foot, until they came to their inn, where he being alighted, his page rode on his horse to the water, and presently the horse vanished away, the page being almost sunk and drowned, but he escaped, and coming home, the knight perceiving the page to be bemired, and on foot, asked where his horse was: who answered, that he was vanished away. Which when the knight heard, he said, of a truth this is Faustus his doing, for he serveth me now, as he did before at the court, only to make me a scorn and laughing stock.

CHAP. LIII.

How Dr. Faustus used Mephistophiles, to bring him seven of the fairest Women he could find in all the Countries he had travelled the twenty Years.

When Dr. Faustus called to mind that his time from day to day drew nigh, he began to live a swinish and epicurish life: wherefore he commanded his spirit Mephistophiles to bring him seven of the fairest women that he had seen in all the times of his travel: which being brought, first one, then another, he lay with them all, insomuch that he liked them so well, that he continued with them in all manner of love, and made them to travel with him all his journies: these women were two Netherland, one Hungarian, one Scottish, two Walloon, one Franklander. And with these sweet personages he continued long, yea, even to his last end.

CHAP. LIV.

How Dr. Faustus found a Mass of Money, when he had consumed twenty two of his Years.

To the end that the devil would make Faustus his only heir, he shewed unto him where he should go and find a mighty huge mass of money, and that he should find it in an old chapel that was fallen down, half a mile distance from Wittenburg: there he bad him to dig, and he should find it, which he did: and having digged reasonable deep, he saw a mighty huge serpent, which lay on the treasure it self: the treasure it self lay like a huge light burning; but Dr. Faustus charmed the serpent, that he crept into an hole, and when he digged deeper to get up the treasure, he found nothing but coals of fire: there he also saw and heard many that were tormented, yet notwithstanding he brought away the coals, and when he was come home, it was turned into silver and gold, and after his death it was found by his servant which was almost, by estimation, one thousand gilders.

CHAP. LV.

How Dr. Faustus made the Spirit of fair Helena of Greece his own Paramour, and Bed-fellow in his twenty-third year.

To the End that this miserable Faustus might fill the lust of his flesh, and live in all manner of voluptuous pleasure it came in his mind, after he had slept his first sleep, and in the twenty third year past of his time, that he had a great desire to lie with fair Helena of Greece, especially her whom he had seen, and shewed unto the students at Wittenburg; wherefore he called his spirit Mephistophiles, commanding him to bring to him the fair Helena, which he also did: Whereupon he fell in love with her, and made her his common concubine and bed-fellow; for she was so beautiful and delightful a piece, that he could not be an hour from her, if he should therefore have suffer'd death, she had stolen away his heart; and to his seeming, in time she was with child, whom Faustus named Justus Faustus. The child told Dr. Faustus many things which were done in foreign countries; but in the end, when Faustus lost his life, the mother and the child vanished away both together.

CHAP. LVI.

How Dr. Faustus made his Will, in which he named his Servant Wagner, to be his Heir.

Dr. Faustus was now in his twenty-fourth, and last year, and he had a pretty stripling to his servant, which had studied also at the university of Wittenburg: This youth was very well acquainted with his knaveries and sorceries, so that he was hated as well for his own knavery, as also for his master's; for no man would give him entertainment into his service, because of his unhappiness, but Faustus. This Wagner was so well belov'd of Faustus, that he used him as his son, for do what he would, his master was always therewith contented. And then when the time drew nigh, that Faustus should end, he called unto him a notary, and certain masters, the which were his friends, and often conversant with him, in whose presence he gave this Wagner his house and garden. Item, He gave him in ready money sixteen thousand gilders. Item, One farm. Item, a gold chain, much plate, and other household stuff, that gave he to his servant, and the rest of his time he meant to spend in inns and students company, drinking and eating, with other jollity: And thus he finished his will at that time.

CHAP. LVII.

How Dr. Faustus fell in talk with his Servant, touching his Testament, and the Covenants thereof.

Now when this will was made, Dr. Faustus called unto his servant saying, I have thought upon thee in my testament, for that thou hast been a trusty servant unto me, and faithful, and hast not opened my secrets: And yet farther (said he) ask of me before I dye, what thou wilt, and I will give it unto thee. His servant rashly answered, I pray you let me have your cunning. To which Dr. Faustus answered, I have given thee all my books, upon this condition, that thou wouldest not let them be common, but use them for thy own pleasure, and study carefully in them; and dost thou also desire my cunning? That thou mayest peradventure have, if thou love and peruse my books well. Farther said Dr. Faustus, seeing that thou desirest of me this request, I will resolve thee: My spirit Mephistophiles his time is out with me, and I have nought to command him, as touching thee: Yet I will help thee to another, if thou like well thereof. And within three days after, he called his servant unto him, saying, Art thou resolved, wouldst thou verily have a spirit? Then tell me in what manner or form thou wouldst have him? To whom his servant answered, That he would have him in the form of an ape: Whereupon appeared presently a spirit unto him in manner and form of an ape, the which leaped about the house. Then, said Faustus, See, there thou hast thy request, but yet he will not obey thee until I be dead; for when my spirit Mephistophiles shall fetch me away, then shall thy spirit be bound unto thee, if thou agree; and thy spirit shalt thou name Aberecock, for so he is called: But all this upon a condition that you publish my cunning, and my merry conceits, with all that I have done (when I am dead) in an history, and if thou canst not remember all, the spirit Aberecock will help thee: so shall the acts that I have done be made manifest unto the world.

CHAP. LVIII.

How Dr. Faustus having but one Month of his appointed Time to come, fell to Mourning and Sorrowing with himself for his devilish Exercise.

TIME ran away with Faustus, as the hour-glass; for he had but one month to come of his twenty-four years, at the end whereof he had given himself to the devil, body and soul, as is before specified. Here was the first token, for he was like a taken murtherer, or a thief, the which finding himself guilty in conscience before the judge have given sentence, fears every hour to die; for he was grieved, and in wailing spent the time, went talking to himself, wringing of his hands, sobbing and sighing; his flesh fell away, and he was very lean, and kept himself close, neither could he abide, see, or hear of his Mephistophiles any more.

CHAP. LIX.

How Dr. Faustus complained that he should in his lusty Time, and youthful Years, die so Miserably.

THE sorrowful time drawing near, so troubled Dr. Faustus, that he began to write his mind, to the end he might peruse it often and not forget it, which was in manner as followeth: Ah! Faustus, thou sorrowful and woful man, now must thou go to the damnable company in unquenchable fire, whereas thou mightest have had the joyful immortality of thy soul, the which now thou hast lost! Ah! gross understanding, and wilful will! What seizeth upon thy limbs; other than robbing of my life? Bewail with me, my sound and healthful body, will, and soul; bewail with me my senses, for you have had your part and pleasure as well as I. Oh! envy and disdain! How have you crept both at once upon me, and now for your sakes I must suffer all these torments? Ah! whither is pity and mercy fled? Upon what occasion hath heaven repayed me with this reward, by sufferance, to suffer me to perish? Wherefore was I created a man? The punishment I see prepared for me of myself, now must I suffer. Ah! miserable wretch! There is nothing in this world to shew me comfort! Then woe is me! What helpeth my wailing?

CHAP. LX.

How Dr. Faustus bewailed to think on Hell, and the miserable Pains therein provided for him.

Now thou Faustus, damned wretch! how happy wert thou, if, as an unreasonable beast, thou mightest die withasoul? so shouldest thou not feel any more doubts; but now the devil will take thee away both body and soul, and set thee in an unspeakable place of darkness; for although other souls have rest and peace, yet I, poor damned wretch must suffer all manner of filthy stench, pains, cold, hunger, thirst, heat, freezing, burning, hissing, gnashing, and all the wrath and curse of God; yea, all the creatures God nath created are enemies to me. And too late I remember that my spirit Mephistophiles did once tell me, there was great difference amongst the damned, for the greater the sin, the greater the torment; as the twigs of a tree make greater flames than the trunk thereof, and yet the trunk continueth longer in burning, even so the more that a man is rooted in sin, the greater is his punishment. Ah! thou perpetual damned wretch! how art thou thrown into the everlasting fiery lake, that shall never be quenched, there must I dwell in all manner of wailing, sorrow, misery, pain, torment, grief, howling, sighing, sobbing, running at the eyes, stinking at the nose, gnashing of teeth, snare to the ears, horror to the conscience, and shaking both of hand and foot? Ah! that I could carry the heavens upon my shoulders, so that there were time at last to quit me of this everlasting damnation. Oh! what can deliver me out of the fearful tormenting flame, the which I see prepar'd for me? Oh! there is no help, nor can any man deliver me; nor my wailing of sins can help me; neither is there rest for me to be found day or night. Ah! woe is me! for there is no help for me, no shield, no defence, no comfort; where is my help? Knowledge dare I not trust; and for a soul to Godwards, that have I not, for I ashame to speak unto him; if I do, no answer shall be made me; but he will hide his face from me, to the end, that I should not behold the joys of the chosen. What mean I then to complain, where no help is? No, I know no hope resteth in my groanings; I had desired it would be so, and God hath said, Amen, to my misdoings; for now I must have shame to comfort me in my calamities.

CHAP. LXI.

Here followeth the Miserable and Lamentable End of Doctor Faustus, by which all Christians may take an Example and Warning.

THE full time of Dr. Faustus, his four and twenty years being come, his spirit appeared unto him, giving him his writing again, and commanding him to make preparation, for that the devil would fetch him against a certain time appointed. Dr. Faustus mourned and sighed wonderfully, and never went to bed, nor slept a wink for sorrow. Wherefore his spirit appeared again, comforting him, and saying, My Faustus, be not thou so cowardly minded; for although thou lovest thy body, it is long unto the day of judgment, and thou must die at the last, although thou live many thousand years: the Turks, the Jews, and many an unchristian emperor are in the same condemnation; therefore, my Faustus, be of good courage, and be not discomforted, for the devil hath promised that thou shalt not be in pains, as the rest of the damned are. This and such like comfort he gave him, for he told him false, and against the saying of the Holy Scriptures: yet Dr. Faustus that had no other expectation but to pay his debt, with his own skin, went (on the same day that his spirit said the devil would fetch him) unto his trusty and dearly beloved brethren and companions, as masters and batchelors of art, and other students more, the which did often visit him at his house in merriment; these he intreated, that they would walk into the village called Rimlich, half a mile from Wittenburg, and that they would there take with him for their repast, a small banquet, the which they agreed unto; so they went together, and there held their dinner in a most sumptuous manner. Dr. Faustus with them, dissemblingly was merry, but not from the heart; wherefore he requested them, that they would also take part of his rude supper, the which they agreed unto: for (quoth he) I must tell you what is the victualler's due: and when they slept (for drink was in their heads) then Dr. Faustus paid the shot, and bound the students and masters, to go with him into another room, for he had many wonderful matters to tell them, and when they were entered the room, as he requested, Dr. Faustus said unto them as followeth:

CHAP. LXII.

An Oration of Dr. Faustus to the Students:

My trusty and well-beloved friends, the cause why I have invited you in this place is this: forasmuch as you have known me these many years, what manner of life I have lived; Practising all manner of conjurations, and wicked exercises, the which I obtained through the help of the devil, into whose devilish fellowship they have brought me; the which use, the art, and practice, urged by the detestable provocation of my flesh, and my stiff-necked and rebellious will, with my filthy infernal thoughts, the which were ever before me, pricking me forward so earnestly that I must perforce have the consent of the devll to aid me in my devices. And to the end I might the better bring my purpose to pass, to have the devil's aid and furtherance, which I never have wanted in my actions, I have promised unto him at the end, and accomplishment of twenty four years, both body and soul, to do therewith at his pleasure; this dismal day, these twenty four years are fully expired; for night beginning, my hour-glass is at an end, the direful finishing whereof I carefully expect; for out of all doubt, this night he will fetch me to whom I have given myself in recompence of his service, body and soul, and twice confirmed writings with my proper blood. Now have I called you, my well-beloved lords, friends and brethren, before that fatal hour, to take my friendly farewel, to the end that my departure may not hereafter be hidden from you, beseeching you herewith (courteous loving lords and brethren) not to take in evil part, any thing done by me, but with friendly commendations to salute all my friends and companions wheresoever, desiring both you and them, if ever I have trespassed against your minds in any thing, that you would heartily forgive me; and as for those lewd practices, the which these full twenty four years I have followed, you shall hereafter find them in writing: and I beseech you let this my lamentable end, to the residue of your lives, be a sufficient warning, that you have God always before your eyes, praying unto him, that he will defend you from the temptation of the devil, and all his false deceits, not falling altogether from God, as I wretched and ungodly damned creature have done; having denied and defied baptism, the sacrament of Christ's body, God himself, and heavenly powers, and earthly men: yea, I have denied such a God, that desireth not to have one lost. Neither let the evil fellowship of wicked companions mislead you, as it hath done me: visit earnestly and often the church; war and strive continually against the devil, with a good and stedfast belief in God and Jesus Christ, and use your vocation and holiness. Lastly, to knit my troubled oration, this is my friendly request, That you would go to rest, and let nothing trouble you: also if you chance to hear any noise or rumbling about the house, be not therewith afraid, for there shall no evil happen unto you; also I pray you rise not out of your beds: but above all things, I intreat you, if hereafter you find my dead carcase, convey it unto the earth, for I die both a good and bad christian, though I know the devil will have my body, and that would I willingly give him, so that he would leave my soul to quiet; wherefore I pray you, that you would depart to bed, and so I wish you a quiet night, which unto me, notwithstanding, shall be horrible and fearful.

This oration was made by Dr. Faustus, and that with a hearty and resolute mind, to the end he might not discomfort them; but the students wonder'd greatly thereat, that he was so blinded, for knavery, conjuration, and such foolish things, to give his body and soul unto the devil, for they loved him entirely, and never suspected any such thing, before he had opened his mind unto them; wherefore one of them said unto him, ah! friend Faustus, what have you done to conceal this matter so long from us? We would by the help of good divines, and the grace of God, have brought you out of this net, and have torn you out of the bondage and chains of Satan, whereas we fear now it is too late, to the utter ruin both of body and soul. Dr. Faustus answered, I durst never do it, although often minded to settle myself to godly people, to desire counsel and help; and once my old neighbour counselled me, That I should follow his learning, and leave all my conjurations: yet when I was minded to amend, and to follow that good counsel, then came the Devil, and would have had me away, as this night he is like to do: and said, so soon as I turned again to God, he would dispatch me altogether. Thus, even thus (good gentlemen, and dear friends) was I inthralled in that fanatical bond, all good desires drowned, all piety vanished, all purposes of amendment truly exiled, by the tyrannous oppression of my deadly enemy. But when the students heard his words, they gave him counsel to do nothing else but call upon God, desiring him, for the love of his sweet son Jesus Christ his sake, to have mercy upon him: teaching him this form of prayer: O God! Be merciful unto me, poor and miserable sinner; and enter not into judgment with me, for no flesh is able to stand before thee; although, O Lord! I must leave my sinful body unto the devil, being by him deluded, yet thou in mercy, may preserve my soul.

This they repeated to him, yet he could take no hold: but even as Cain, he also said, that his sins were greater than God was able to forgive: for all his thought was on the writing, he meant he had made it too filthy in writing with his own blood. The students and the other that were there, when they had prayed for him, they wept, and so went forth; but Faustus tarried in the hall, and when the gentlemen were laid in bed, none of them could sleep, for that they attended to hear if they might be privy of his end. It happened that between twelve and one o'clock at midnight, there blew a mighty storm of wind against the house, as though it would have blown the foundation thereof out of its place. Hereupon the students began to fear, and go out of their beds, but they would not stir out of the chamber, and the host of the house ran out of doors, thinking the house would fall. The students lay near unto the hall, wherein Dr. Faustus lay, and they heard a mighty noise and hissing, as if the hall had been full of snakes and adders, with that the hall-door flew open: wherein Dr. Faustus was, then he began to cry for help, saying, murther, murther; but it was with a half voice, and very hollow; shortly after they heard him no more. But when it was day, the students, that had taken no rest that night, arose and went into the hall, in the which they left Dr. Faustus, where notwithstanding, they found not Faustus, but all the hall sprinkled with blood, the brains cleaving to the wall, for the devil had beaten him from one wall, against an other: in one corner lay his eyes, in another his teeth; a fearful and pitiful sight to behold. Then began the students to wail and weep for him, and sought for his body in many places. Lastly, they came into the yard, where they found his body lying on the horse-dung, most monstrously torn, and fearful to behold, for his head, and all his joints were dashed to pieces : the forenamed students and masters that were at his death, obtained so much, that they buried him in the village, where he was so grievously tormented. After the which they turned to Wittenburg, and coming into the house of Faustus, they found the servant of Faustus very sad, unto whom they opened all the matter, who took it exceedingly heavy. There they found this history of Dr. Faustus noted, and of him written, as is before declared, all save only his end, the which was after, by the students, thereunto annexed : farther, what his servant noted thereof, was made in another book. And you have heard he held by him in his life, the spirit of fair Helena, who had by him one son, the which he named Justus Faustus, even the same day of this death, they vanished away, both mother and son. The house before was so dark, that scarce any body could abide therein : the same night Dr. Faustus appeared unto his servant lively, and shewed unto him many secret things which he had done and hidden in his life-time. Likewise there were certain which saw Dr. Faustus look out of the window by night, as they passed by the house.

And thus ended the whole history of Dr. Faustus his conjuration, and other acts, that he did in his life; out of which example every Christian may learn, but chiefly the stiff-necked, and high-minded, may thereby learn to fear God, and to be careful of their vocation, and to be at defiance with all devilish works, as God hath most precisely forbidden; to the end we should not invite the devil as a guest, nor give him place, as that wicked Faustus hath done: for here we have a wicked example of his writing, promise, and end, that we may remember him, that we go not astray, but take God always before our eyes, to call alone upon him, and to honour him all the days of our life, with heart, and hearty prayer, and with all our strength and soul, to glorifie his holy name, defying the devil and all his works; to the end we may remain with Christ in all endless joy, amen, amen: that wish I to every Christian heart, and God's name be glorified. Amen.

FINIS.

DOCTOR FAUSTUS.

SECOND REPORT.

THE SECOND REPORT

OF

DOCTOR FAUSTUS.

THE '*Second Report of Dr. Faustus*' is a production at once so rare and so curious, and withal so necessary to complete the History of that renowned Magician, as to render it quite unnecessary to explain the reason for its appearance in the present series of Romances.

It is, like the First Part, of German origin, being in a great measure derived from the *Wagner Buch* as it is generally called, which appeared in octavo as early as 1593 under the following title, "*Ander Theil D. Johann Fausti Historien darinn beschreiben ist; Christophori Wagners aufgerichter pact mit dem Teufel, so sich genannt Auerhahn und ihm in eines affen Gestalt erschienen, auch seine aventeuerliche Zoten und Possen, so er durch Beforderung des Teufels geübt, und was es mit ihm zulezt fur ein schrecklich Ende genommen. Neben einer feinen beschreiburg der neuen Inseln, was für Leute darinn wohnen, was für Früchte darinn wachsen, was sie für Religion und Gotzendienst haben, und wie sie von den Spaniern eingenommen worden. Alles aus seinen verlassenen Schriften, und weil es ganz Kurzweilig zu lesen in Druck verfertigt durch* Fridericum Schotum Tolet. *Jetzt zu P.*" The preface occupies the first eleven pages, and concludes, "Datum den 10ten. Mai, Anno 1593 Fredericus Scholus Tolet, zetzt zu P." Another edition appeared in the following year 1594, and it has been frequently reprinted. That which is least rare being the edition of 1714 which is taken from that of 1594, with some few modifications.

Like the earlier book of which Faustus was the hero, this *Wagnerbuch* was soon spread abroad in France, England, and of course in the Low Countries. In the last it has enjoyed considerable popularity. A literal translation of it appeared at Delft certainly as early as 1607. There is also a modified version of it which has been frequently reprinted.

It is from this Second Part of Faustus, or History of his Servant Wagner that the following Romance has been compiled. It is not a translation, but the chief materials are derived from the German. The many allusions to English customs which are scattered through various part of the work afford the clearest proof that the compiler, whether or not he was really an English gentleman student in Wittenberg, as on the title he professes to be, was an Englishman and that the book itself was intended for English readers. He had probably been induced to undertake it by the popularity which had attended the publication of the first Story, the Ballad of Dr. Faustus the Great Congerer, and Marlowe's Play upon the same subject.

Of the present work there appears to have been only two editions; viz. "*The Second Report of Doctor John Faustus, containing his appearances, and the deeds of Wagner. Written by an English gentleman Student in Wittenberg an University of Germany in Saxony. Published for the delight of all those which desire novelties, by a friend of the same gentleman. London, Printed by Abell Jeffes, for Cuthbert Burby, and are to be sold at the Middle Shop at Saint Mildred's Church by the Stockes*, 1594." 4to. and

"*The Second Report of Doctor John Faustus, declaring how he was amongst the infernal spirits, and how he used to appear again upon the earth, and what strange things he did: also very wonderful apparitions of the infernal king and his followers. And likewise strange exploits of Wagner and his three familiars. London. Printed for Ralph Smith, at the Bible, in the Piazza, under the Royal Exchange, in Cornhill*, 1680," 4to. which only differs from the former in some few orthographical particulars, and in not containing the writer's prefatory address "*Unto them which would know the trueth.*"

The present edition is chiefly taken from that of 1680, but the Editor was enabled by the kindness of the late Francis Douce, Esq. to give the title and preface from the edition of 1594.

The following extract from the Epistles of Trithemius, (20 August, 1507) already referred to, and wherein he describes the Charlatan, who has been identified by recent writers as the hero of the romance, may form a fitting conclusion to this notice.

'HOMO ille de quo mihi scripsisti, Georgius Sabellicus, qui se principem necromanticorum ausus est nominare, gyrovagus, battologus et circumcellio est; dignus, qui verberibus castigetur, ne temere deinceps tam nefanda, et Ecclesiæ sanctæ contraria publice audeat profiteri. Quid enim sunt aliud tituli, quos sibi assumit, nisi stultissimæ ac vesanæ mentis indicia, qui se fatuum, non philosophum ostendit? Sic enim titulum sibi convenientem formavit; magister Georgius Sabellicus, Faustus junior, fons necromanticorum, astrologus, magus secundus, chiromanticus, agromanticus, pyromanticus, in hydra arte secundus. Vide stultam hominis temeritatem, quanta feratur insania, ut se fontem necromanticæ profiteri præsumat, qui vere omnium bonarum literarum ignarus, fatuum se potius appellare debuisset, quam magistrum. Sed me non latet ejus nequitia. Cum anno priore de marchia Brandenburgensi redirem, hunc ipsum hominem apud Geilenhusen oppidum inveni; de quo mihi plura dicebantur in hospitio frivola, non sine magna ejus temeritate ab eo promissa. Qui mox, ut me adesse audivit, fugit de hospitio, et a nullo poterat persuaderi, quod se meis præsentaret aspectibus. Titulum stultitiæ suæ, qualem dedit ad te, quem memoravimus, per quendam civem ad me quoque destinavit. Referebant quidam in oppido sacerdotes, quod in multorum præsentia dixerit, tantam se omnis sapientiæ consecutum scientiam atque memoriam, ut si volumina Platonis et Aristotelis omnia cum tota eorum philosophia in toto periissent ab hominum memoria, ipse suo ingenio, velut Ezras alter Hebraeus, restituere universa cum præstantiore valeret præstantia. Postea me Neometi existente Herbipolim venit, eademque vanitate actus in plurimorum fertur dixisse præsentia, quod Christi salvatoris miracula non sint miranda, se quoque omnia facere posse, quæ Christus fecit, quoties et quandocunque velit. In ultima quoque hujus anni quadragesima venit Stauronesum, et simili stultitia gloriosus de se pollicebatur ingentia, dicens se in Alchemia omnium, qui fuerint unquam esse perfectissimum, et scire atque posse, quicquid homines optaverint. Vacabat interea munus docendi scholasticum in oppido memorato, ad quod Francisci ab Sickingen Balivi principis tui, hominis mysticarum rerum percupidi, promotione fuit assumptus: qui mox nefandissimo fornicationis genere, cum pueris videlicet, voluptari cœpit: quo statim deducto in lucem fuga pænam declinavit paratam. Hæc sunt quæ mihi certissimo constant testimonio de homine illo, quem tanto venturum esse desiderio præstolaris. Cum venerit ad te, non philosophum, sed hominem fatuum et nimia temeritate agitatum invenies.'

THE SECOND REPORT OF Doctor John Faustus,

CONTAINING

HIS APPEARANCES, AND THE DEEDS OF WAGNER.

WRITTEN BY AN ENGLISH GENTLEMAN, STUDENT IN WITTENBERG, AN UNIVERSITY OF GERMANY, IN SAXONY.

PUBLISHED FOR THE DELIGHT OF ALL THOSE WHICH DESIRE NOVELTIES BY A FREND OF THE SAME GENTLEMAN.

LONDON:

PRINTED BY ABELL JEFFES FOR CUTHBERT BURBY, AND ARE TO BE SOLD AT THE MIDDLE SHOP, AT ST. MILDRED'S CHURCH, BY THE STOCKES. 1594.

THE

SECOND REPORT

OF

Doctor John Faustus,

CONTAINING

HIS APPEARANCES, AND THE DEEDS OF WAGNER.

WRITTEN BY AN ENGLISH GENTLEMAN, STUDENT IN WITTENBERG, AN UNIVERSITY OF GERMANY, IN SAXONY.

PUBLISHED FOR THE DELIGHT OF ALL THOSE WHICH DESIRE NOVELTIES BY A FREND OF THE SAME GENTLEMAN.

LONDON:

PRINTED BY ABELL JEFFES FOR CUTHBERT BURBY, AND ARE TO BE SOLD AT THE MIDDLE SHOP, AT ST. MILDRED'S CHURCH, BY THE STOCKES. 1594.

UNTO THEM WHICH WOULD KNOW THE TRUETH.

I.

It is plaine that many thinges in the first book are meere lies, for proofe marke this, it is said that it is translated, so it is, and where it is word for word. But I have talked with the man that first wrote them, having them from Wagner's very friend, wherein he saith many thinges are corrupted, some added de novo, some canceld and taken awaie and many were augmented. As for addition to the Coppy is there were Mephostophiles disputeth of the number of Hels, and some other disputations: And let a man marke them duely, they shall find them I will not say childish, but certainly superficiall, not like the talk of Divels, where with foldings of words, they doe use to dilate at large, and more subtell by farre. But as for his obligation and the most part, it is certain they are most credible andout of all question.

II.

For to take away a doubt, whether there was such a man, which is generally a thing not beleeved, I assure them this, that there was, and it is prooved thus: nor is Germany so unknowen but that the trueth of these thinges following may be founde if any suspect.

III.

First there is yet remainingthe ruins of his house,not farrefrom Melanchton's house as they call atthe townes end of Wittenberg, right opposite to the Schooles.

IV.

Secondly there is yet to be seene his tree, a greate hollowe trunke, wherein he used to reade Nigromancy to his Scholers, not farre from the towne in a very remote place, which I think is sufficient testimony to any reasonable eare. And enquire of them which have been there, see if they will not affirme it. Notwithstanding I doe not goe by these meanes, I to entreate men to beleeve, for I care not whether they do or no, but onelyto certifie you of the truethas I myselfewould bee.

V.

Next his tombe is at Mars Temple, a three miles beyond the Citty, uppon which is written on a marble stone by his own hand, this Epitaph, which is somewhat old by reason of his small skill in graving.

"HIC JACEO JOHANNES FAUSTUS, DOCTOR DIVINI JURIS INDIGNISSIMUS,QUI PRO AMORE MAGLÆ DIABOLICÆ SCIENTLÆ VANISSIME CECIDI AB AMORE DEI : O LECTOR PRO ME MISERRIMO DAMNATO HOMINE NE PRECERIS, NAM PRECES NON JUVANT QUEM DEUS CONDEMNAVIT : O PIE CHRISTIANE MEMENTO MEI ET SALTEM UNAM PRO INFIDUCIA MEA LACHRYMULAM EXPRIME ET CUI NON POTES MEDERI, EJUS MISERERE ET IPSE CAVE."

The Stone was found in his study, and his wil was fulfilled, and he lieth betwixt a heap of three and thirty fir trees in the fort of the Hill in a great hole where this is erected.

VI.

If these will not serve, then shall you heare the testimonie of a learned man John Wierus, cap. 4. libro 1. de magis infamibus. Which I have translated.

John Faustus borne at Kundling, a little village, learning Magicke at Graconia, where he was openly taught and exercised it.

In sundry places of Germany with the admiration of many and with manifold lies frauds and illusions, with vain vaunting and promises but could doe nothing: one example I will shew to the reader, uppon this condition that he will passe his faith to me that he will not imitate him: Then reherseth he one of his knaveries, how he tooke upon him to make no haire grow upon a man's face, and tooke away with a powder which I will not name, both the beard that he had and all the skinne, causing such inflammations in his face that it burned it all over cruelly. This he committed being taken at Battoburg, uppon the bankes of the river Mosa, hard upon the boundes of Gelderland: Another (saith this learned Physition) not unknowen to me, having a blacke bearde, the rest of his face somewhat dark and swarte, witnessing melancholy (for hee was splenaticke) when he came to Faustus who readily saide: Truely I thought you had been my familiar, straightwaie marking your feete, whether long and crooked nailes stood out of them. So likening this man to the divell which he thought had come unto him, which Divell he was wont to call Sorarius.

VI.

For his death in the same place, thus saith he. At length hee was found in a village of the Dutchy of Wittenberg by his bed side starke dead, and his face turned backwards, and the midnight before, the house was shaken as it is reported. Thus farre he, an authour not to be doubted of and approved through Christendome of singular and exact judgement, as appeareth by his writings of the like argument confutation.

VII.

More in the same place he saith: That a schoolmaster amongst the Goslaryens, instructed of Faustus the magician, or rather Infaustus his evill doctrine, learned a way how the Divell might be bound by spell on a glasse, who as you may ther reade was so affrighted that lying one whole year speechless at thend he spoke of his feare and divels appearance, and then having received his christian rites died.

As for the Author this Doctor Wier, doubt you not of his credite, for he is alledged of the very singularest schollers as the best that ever wrote in that argument. We have a Gentleman of our owne countrey, Maister

Reginold Scot, Esquier, that doth universally quote him as his chiefe and especiall helpe in his discovery of Witchcraft, yea and he testifieth of him not without good desart, saying: I Bode in his lawyerly Phisicke reasoneth contrarily, as though Melancholye were farthest of from these old women whom we call witches. And the most famous and noble physician, John Wier for his opinion in that behalfe: loe where he calleth him the most famous Phisitian as he was then certainly, in Discovery of Witchcraft, lib. 3. cap. 7.

IX.

Thus farre I have set downe that you may know and perswade your selves so farre as you see just cause by the reasons. Vale.

THE SECOND REPORT

OF

DR. JOHN FAUSTUS.

In nomine æternæ & sempervivæ majestatis. Amen.

Spectatum admissi risum teneatis amici?

CHAP. I.

DOCTOR JOHN FAUSTUS whose parentage howsoever hitherto informed, is known to be base, his father when he was at the best, but the son of a poor farmer, his mother the daughter of one of the same condition, born in a small village called Kundling in Silesia, brought up in literature at Gracovia, after at Wittenberg, whose life made him famous, and death notorious: being thus tormented and torn in pieces, at the time appointed betwixt the Divels and him, moved by this example woful and lamentable enough, the hearts of the students and scholars which were witnesses of his distraughture, with an inward terror of conscience vexed and tormented, they departed and declared the whole volumes of his detestable life, which afore his tragedy was thus acted, were not known. Christopher Wagner his familiar servant, unto whom he had committed the secrets of his bosom, and had intimated unto him what ever his twenty-four years familiarity with the black art, and more black devils had taught him: he after the death of his thus slain master musing at every thing thus done, every thing thus done being wonderful: (as men do whom fear makes passionate, and meditation of former loss, urgeth a latter augment of fresh sorrows:) in a distraughtful fury (the company of students being departed which were eye-witnesses of the Doctors lamentable end) conveyed himself unto his master's library, viewing with sorrowful eyes the only monuments of his life, the disputations betwixt him and Mephostophiles, his answers and demands, and else whatsoever questions moved or disputed of betwixt the devils and him; the memorials of his heavens and hells voyages, his conveyance with many the like comical journies. The boy of a sodain fell into a deep considering of his former merriments, sports and delights, in so much that in this conceit he flung out of his study, as if he meant to bury the remembrance of these matters by contempt and negligence: coming into the same hall wherein his masters latest tragedy was perform'd, sighing for his want, he remembered (for as then he lately read it) how that one article to the which his master had bound Mephostophiles was, that after his death he should be a spirit in nature and essences as others were. The wag at this began to smile (oh how such things seeming pleasant make fools hearts merry) conceiving with himself how to make his own master become his man: And to have the number of his spiritual followers doubled, scorning the alonely attendance of one servant. To this therefore he determined a time for the raising of his master's spirit: and therewith he fell to read earnestly of other matters, so long that he began to leave as wearied, and wearied began to muse. Sodainly the air began to receive an alteration and change with a thick foggy mist, as if it would have shut up the desired day from man's view, the winds raged, the thunder lifted up his voyce above the common strain, hail and rain immediately following, and all these but the ordinary presages of an appearing spirit. At this Kit began to tremble, not as afraid of that which came, but strucken with inward horror of conscience, thinking that no other time had been appointed to be his dooms day. Sodainly (for alwayes such haps are sodain) the doors flew open as if they would have fled from flying, and in all pomp entered as it were the prologue of a comedy, a fellow so short and little, as if he should be of one year, and yet not so briefe as ill favoured, in his hands a club, on his head a crown of laurel, riding upon a low mule, his name was Gomory, a strong and mighty duke, the ruler of six and twenty legions, and next in bravery appeared Volac a great governour, in the shape like a boy with wings like an Angel of Hell seeming to be of old rusty iron, riding upon a dragon with four heads, in his hands he held a flaming torch to give light to the after commers and beholders: next after him appeared Asmody a king mighty and puissaunt, raggod and bristled like a bore on foot, bearing a banner or lance. After him issued Lucifer the king of the Orient, with the four monarchs of his dominions, betwixt them were two mighty spaniels which drew in a fiery cart, Doctor John Faustus, whom if reason had not better ruled Wagner would have saluted, for so natural was his semblance, so lively his countenance as if it had either been a new Faustus, or not the old murthered Faustus, but the fear which his masters harm put him in cast him besides the renewing of his old acquaintance, after these came diverse others with trumpets and excellent melody. This right marvelous triumph thus presented each one did his humble obeysance the last beginning (though good there were none) and in the end with huge tumult and echoing of trumpets they crowned him a king, which when they had done, with the like ceremonies they conveyed out again the doctor whom his wretchedness made a king, and his new kingship nothing. Wagner started as if he had now begun to marvail, amazed at this merry interlude; having recovered his memory again, he began softly to speak to himself in such like manner. Is this (quoth he) the honour my master hath in hell? is this the reverence with which the fiends infernal used to entertain such guests? O ye spirits of hell, and ye even now revived emperors of great Limbus, from whence have you drawn this extraordinary humanity, is it to scorn poor Faustus, or to mock Wagner, that you shew such reverence to a vile object, what then would they do to Wagner who is worthy to have a fitter servant than their king? At these words he blusht exceedingly, and began to rage very grievously with his consciences terror, and with some few tears repenting his irreligious conclusion, rose up from the ground, and supposing it to be but an illusion, dream, or a temptation, or else some conceit proceeding from his moist and melancholick fantasie overprest with too many vapors, raised up by continual thought into his pores: wherefore he went forthwith into the streets, (so much he distrusted himself) and demanded whether it rain'd, hail'd, or thundred, and it was answered, that it neither rain'd, hail'd, nor thundred. Wagner, albeit he was newly revived from a fear, and scarcely throughly wakened from this his great terror, yet with this comical jest his decayed spirits began to recover their old strength and power, turning these great braveries of devils into a merriment and his conceived fear into a meer fansy. This was the first time that ever Faustus appeared unto his servant Wagner, who recited this unto his companions as a matter of great truth and little moment.

CHAP. II.

How certain drunken Dutchmen were abused by their own conceit and self imagination, of seeing the grand Doctor, Doctor Faustus.

It shall not be impertinent (my very good friends) to declare as I am bound by a Translatours duty, to shew what these my Dutch friends and students have imparted unto me, not for that I will be a king of your hearts to command you to believe, but that you may with the rest of the history conceive the common opinion of him in the vulgars belief here in Germany, as concerning such the like illusions before pretended. About the same time, the next year wherein Faustus was thus handled, betwixt 6. and 7. a clock in the morning, the five and twentieth day of June, 1539, there chanced certain Scholars to the number of nine, and five other Merchants (called of them Copshmen) two being English, to walk abroad to a little village within 4 English mile (which is about one of theirs) of Wittenburg, called Shaftsburg, to the intent to make merry: whither being come they were exceeding pleasant, as Dutchmen are, especially when they be at their good beer, for they are men very impatient of thirst wherewith the Italian mocks them saying:

> Germani multos possunt tolerare labores,
> O utinam possent tam bene ferre sitim.

Unto which they merrily answer,

> Ut nos dura sitis, sic vos Venus improba vexat,
> Lex lata est Veneri Julia, nulla mero.

So long they drunk, that at last they came to be within a little of drunk, fetching over the Green nine Muses so often at sundry draughts till they began to be exceeding merry and pleasant, till it being time to depart, so they set out for Wittenburg, and being within a mile or such a matter of the city, they came to a thick grove called of them the Phogelwald, which is Birds-

wood in English, a place somewhat delightsome above any thereabouts, situated upon the top of a very high hill, but the armes of it spread themselves somewhat lower into the neighbour vallies and medows, full of very fine crystalline brooks and springs, which running through the large ranks of trees empty themselves into the Elve, a river which keeps his current by Wittenberg; in this place in a fair summer sun shine day, gather together a great number of country maids, servants, and other of the female sex, which they call Phogels (birds) unto them there resort on such like dayes, a great number of scholars to meet with these birds, which exercise venery either for pleasure, but indeed seldome but for gain, with whom when they have danced a great while (after some odd tune as after that which they call Robinsons delight, but more truly a jest, though somewhat tolerable) some 20. or 30. or 40. couple together, then here steps out one couple, and here another, and get them to such odd corners, as their continual practice doth make known: on the same day wherein this merry company were wandring, who if I should not much err, I durst say they were most deeply drunk, being a sun-shining day, having no other way to pass to Wittenberg, but only by this Phogelwald, where they determined to be lusty with some of the Phogels, they came at length to these forenamed places, whereas to them it seemed sundry women dancing, and amongst them divers scholars, and verily they deemed Master Doctor Faustus likewise, and seeing divers maids standing idle, so many as would fit their many, they went to take them by the hands, and as their order is saluting them, to hop a bout or two (for all the High Dutchmens dances stand upon hopping, turning, winding, and such odd gestures) and as they seemed, they danced at great leisure till this said Faustus came to them, requesting them not to be amazed, for that it was reported he was dead, assuring them in very deed he was not in this world, but had changed it for a better, which if it did please them he would shew unto them, where betwixt their delights and his were no comparison; at his request they were all contented, and he leading the foremost, brought them down into a fair pleasant green, whereon instead of certain flowers grew pots full of the best beer, which they tasting on found them as good as any that ever they drunk in their whole lives, and farther unto a most rich and sumptuous palace, wherein as they seemed, they dwelt many dayes with great mirth and pleasure, till at length one more full of courtesie than the rest thanked Master Faustus for his good entertainment, at which words sodainly was heard so great a noyse and howling especially of the poor Doctor, who was immediately reared up into the air, accompanyed with such a sort of black clouds and mists, as therewith not only the sky, but also their eyes were mightily darkened, and they brought into a deep cavern, wherein besides most soft beds they had nothing to comfort themselves, in which they wallowed and slept till they snorted, some of the scholars that were present at their departure being in a soberer conceit than the rest, desirous to see whither they would go, followed them fast after, till they espied them in this dirty case, for instead of beds they were all bewrapped, and some more than half sunk in deep and yielding mire by the rivers banks. Whom when they saw in this more than miserable case moved with pity, conveyed them in waggons home: and being demanded in the morning (for then they were a little wiser) the occasion of their so great and seldom seen disorder, they declared it from the beginning to the ending, which they were so far from believing that they counted it as canonical, which when some students reported unto me, I could not abstain from hearty laughter not only to see how they had abused themselves, but also others by so fond belief. For I said that in drunkenness so thick a vapor as riseth from so thick a matter as their beer, clambering up and spreading it self so universally in the fantasie, maketh it to conceive no other impression, but that which the mind afore it came to be oppressed was conversant about, and it was evident that in all the talk they had, there was nothing mentioned but only Faustus, and Faustus merriments, and where a thing is amongst so many so agreeingly talked of, it is likely it should take effect as well in all as in one. Well I was content to subscribe to their folly rather to satisfie their self-willed conceits than my own thought. Many odd pranks Faustus is made father of, which are either so frivolous as no body can credit but like frivolous people, are so meerly smelling of the cask, that a man may easily know the child by the father.

CHAP. III.

Wagners conference with Doctor Faustus, and how miserably they broke up their disputations.

WAGNER one morning arose betimes and departed to Wittenberg, but a small mile from the house, and having purveyed himself of all necessaries, was admitted for a scholar (immediately after his master was departed out of this world) into the University. Where, for that he was Faustus true and familiar servant, he was both well and manifoldly acquainted, wherein he remained in all solace amongst a great number of his companions, who then rather frequented his company, not only for that he was Faustus his servant whose memory was very freshly continued among them, but that they were verily assured that he had a great part of his masters skill and science, which they honoured with more than lawful reverence. Upon a day Christopher Wagner (as many times he did) separated himself from his other companions and friends, to ruminate upon his melancholick conceits, erring far in a place full of trees, and the fulness of trees gave it the name of the Grove, sodainly like as all such chances hap, Faustus or Faustus spirit clapt him up on the shoulder, saying: Wagner good morrow. Wagner vailed his scholers bonnet, thinking verily he was some other student: but beholding his

Master Faustus, he was most terribly affrighted, and stepping aside he began to mumble to himself a Benedicite, and crossing himself, rehearsing and saying, Conjuro te in nomine Patris et Filii et Spiritus Sancti, &c. making a circle, &c. Faustus rowling his eyes, and for meere fury and anger stamping, bound (for so he seemed) with the vehemency of the exorcism, ran about most terribly the brims thereof, that therewith the neighbour ground did seem to tremble, casting out a blackish slomy sulphury smoak out of his mouth, wherewith the bright air was much darkened: at length appeased, either forced with necessity or knavery, he spake and that very distinctly. Wagner (qd he) art thou afeard of me as of a spirit, or infernal Ghost, am not I (ungrateful rascal) Faustus, am not I thy Master Faustus? Quoth Wagner very confidently, what thou wert I know, what also thou art who knows not? though once my master, now thou shalt be my servant, though once my friend and familiar, now I may justly term thee neither: the laws of Devils hath not made me secure from thy tyranny, and how may thy friendship availme? For how can that help which is not? affections are not amongst fiends, nor passions amongst spirits. Wherefore Faustus if thou wilt that I be thy master, as whether thou wilt or no, I will conjure thee, &c. to answer directly and truly to all my questions. Ah Wagner (quoth Faustus) is this the duty of a servant? dost thou mistrust that in me, which neither I mean, nor thou of thy duty oughtest to imagine? And as for affections in Spirits, certainly there is none, but I am none, feel me my good Wagner, behold flesh, blood, and bones; and Spirits have neither flesh, blood nor bones. Believe me I shall teach thee the nature and essence of Devils, I will teach thee that which neither thou canst desire of me or think, Extra captum humanum. Then my good boy Wagner come to me, and use me not as a spirit, whose body is nothing but a spirit, and as logicians say substantia incorporea, and I will open unto thee the secrets of the world, and hell, and else whatsoever in the works of nature. Come my Wagner, my son, my darling, my sweet delight, and rejoicing, the only hope of my labours, boldly, lovingly, courteously, above all, which am the very same matter and substance I once was, and if thou doubtest, as well thou mayest, reach thy hand to me, for I cannot mine to thee, and feel whether I am not as I say I am, flesh, blood, and bones: Wagner half astonished at this his fervent speech, yet rather hearing it than believing it: Why Faustus, let me speak to you somewhat considerately, thou sayst thou art substance, and all substance is heavy, and no heavy thing can ascend upwards, and as thy conference with Mephistophiles doth plainly declare, the place of spirits is in the air, in which nothing that is heavy can remain, and therefore thou art not substance or not Faustus. Quoth Faustus, that no heavy thing is in the air is plainly false, for thou seest that material bodies are in the air, as hail, snow, and other meteors: Whereto Wagner answered, Faustus, they truly are in the air, and not of the air, and you know the causes of them are terrestrial vapors drawn from the earth by the attractive vertue of the sun, and therefore they fall down because they are heavy, for were they of the air as are spirits, then should they still remain in it: but briefly no violent motion may be called natural, as that heavy material dew is carried from the earth by a violent and contrary motion: the sun therefore leaving the Zenith of any horizon and coming to the Nadir oppositely, the material bodies of Dew, (as the causes alwayes fail with the effects) and nextly the concretion of snow and hail, because they are substance, cannot remain in the light and unheavy air: Wherefore I have answered thee that thou art either a spirit or not substance. I wondred when I read this discourse, with what patience the doctor could indure so long an argument, but it proved otherwise, for the Doctor brake forth into these speeches, unable to contain himself any longer.

Wagner, thou seemest to gather natural arguments of metaphysical effects, I say unto thee Wagner, sith thou art thus far entred into a philosophical discourse, that I being as I am Faustus, may be, for so I am, a dweller in the profound Abysse of the Air, whose compass is measurable in this, that it is not measurable: for let us speak according to men naturally, the rather to fit thy capacity, we see that in the regiment of mans body, the man is of quality like to the predominant complexion and element, as if Choler abound, the man is light, nimble, and for a while furious, seldome strong, ready to meddle, and carried away with phanatick illusions: if blood abound, he is ruddy, fair, gentle, &c. Et sic de reliquis. If therefore the predominant element is able so much to change the nature of men, as to make it above the rest capable or incapable, the same reason maketh that this body of mine which thou seest, being governed and predomineered by that quick and ready spirit and soul which makes a man immortal is no hindrance why this corporal reality of me should accompany my spirit, not as a body, but as a part of the same spirit: and otherwise Wagner, the whole world is in the air, and as it were the centre of the heavens, and what substance soever is made, fishes which dwell in the deep seas except (and yet not always) are moved in the air. Kit believe me, I am as thou seest Faustus and the same very same.

Wagner almost at the last cast, said, we dispute not what you are Faustus, but what by reason you may be. Well, answered Faustus, seeing thou wilt not believe, nor give any credit to my sayings and which I prove by arguments, I hope thou wilt believe thine own eyes, and if thou seest what I say unto thee, thou wilt neither be obstinate nor incredulous, and rather than Wagner (whom I do love as myself) should be carried away with so palpable an heresie, behold Wagner, and believe, and straightways he drew his knife the prologue of his knavery, and looking first upon Wagner, and next on the weapon which he had in his hand, as if with his eyes he would have moved him to some pity, and moved them to be witnesses of the truth, he strook himself into his thigh twice or thrice, and after his stroaks followed blood so hastily, as if it would have overtaken the injurious worker of his effusion: which blood Faustus received in a silver boule and stanching his wound, but not until the blood might be seen over the cup-brims, then Faustus lifted the blood on high saying, see here the witness of the truth; Wagner take it, look how fresh it is, it is not that which comes from a spirit, it is blood both in nature and colour, and if this be not enough to make thee believe that which I do tell thee, it boots not, there is not any truth at all.

I thought it enough for an extemporal dis and controversie, I thought the scholar had heard as well and as long as the doctor had taught, but yet he had not ended. Wagner receiving the cup and looking on the blood beheld him without saying any thing, shewing by his silence his meaning. Faustus minding to revenge and recompense Wagner his unbelief, nay further (quoth he) feel my hand, tell me whether it hath not the natural heat and essential solidity, then immediately he stretched forth his arm. Wagner with sodain extasie of joy carried away, ran to embrace his old master as his new friend, whom when Faustus had encircled he fell to beating the poor scholar most miserably, that Wagners pitiful roaring seemed to be an eccho to the doctors blows: now (quoth Faustus) hereafter be learned either to be more wary or less mistrustful, and therewith laughing effusedly vanished away, leaving Wagner to be a witness (yet almost half dead with his buffeting) of their conference, and that he was a good substantial burgess of hell: Wagner, poor boy, for the space of seven hours not able scarce of himself to stir or take breath, and without much stirring either of hand or foot, whereby any able life might be conjectured: at length lifting up his head and sighing a little (for a little was as much as he could do at that time) he reared himself up and laying his head upon his hand, and his hand upon the ground, he after sighs, sent out most sorrowful groans, and after groans some feeble words, as he afterwards reported it to his companions and familiar acquaintance: to accuse either his masters vigor or his own folly, he thought as meerly vain as little prevailing: wherefore comforting himself with his misery, because he was comfortless, rose up, and looked for the cup of blood: in place whereof he found his cup full of piss, and all beraied: sore ashamed and sore withal, so well as he might, which was sorely enough, he rose up, and what by creeping and going he got home to his chamber, where he abode till he recovered his health again.

Thus was his philosophical incredulity recompenced with rustical cruelty, such was the good love of the spirit, that for a long space after he was not able to walk out of his chamber. This did he affirm for most certain truth, and to his saying added his beaten skin, as a testimonial and witness to his familiarly beloved acquaintance, one of the whic hrecounted it all summarily in a letter from Wittenberg to me, where I was at Lipzig, knowing that I intended to certifie my friends in England of a matter so notable and strange, and worthy of memory, and augmented by fame more than of very deed, for idle headed fellows having gotten such a notable fellow as Faustus to father their lies upon, ceased not dayly and hourly to beget new children, but they cost very little nursing and bringing up : they had the wide world, a very good grandam, where they might feed their fill : as for the disputations betwixt those two in this place, and those which you shall find in other places likewise abundantly, consider from whose brains they proceed, for you must give the German leave to shew his art ; for wit for the most part they have very little, but that which they toil for like cart-horses. But in all their doings you shall easily perceive if any thing be in them excellent, either with how much liking and urging they bring it forth, or how it is wetted over with dropping of the tap exceedingly.

CHAP. IV.

Wagners cosenage committed upon the sellers of his masters goods.

According to the law of the country, the goods of Faustus were to be confiscated and applyed to the treasury, by an edict published against conjurers by Sigismond Duke of Saxony. According to the tenor thereof Faustus goods were to be alienated, but Wagner so handled the matter that the spear being stuck up, and his goods set to be sold, Wagner had provided bidders and money of his own, the one were such as were never seen more, and the other but round counters.

The messengers being thus cosened by Wagner, durst not for shame report it, nor he for fear of further punishment vaunt of it: the one content to put up the loss quietly, and the other to enjoy them without further contradiction.

CHAP. V.

The Description of Vienna.

FAME had so far carried the report of Faustus death, as it had the memory of his life, and for that by continual motion rumors encrease, as saith the heroical fountain of Latin verse, Virgil,

Mobilitate viget viresque acquirit eundo.

In Austrich these news were very frequent, being a province mightily replenished with people, and marching upon the hems of the Hungarian, is a neer neighbour to the most cruel dog and tyrant, the Turk. In Vienna, a city of the same, by which as the Thames by London, the great and often but never enough praised, river of great Danuby keeps his current (the city itself being every way bigger than the fair city of London) within the walls, the head of the city resteth upon the mountain of Orstkirken, the front displayeth the wild plains upon the descendent of the same hill, but she washes her feet in the river: her body and her brest covering the large valley lying betwixt hill and hill: not far into the city, Danuby is derived in two arms, which by running about a certain hill, of some half a mile and more, meet at length again in the same channel; in this island is the dukes court, out of which are two and thirty marvellous good stone bridges, intending to either side of the city: at the very promontories ends, stand two no less fair than high and strong castles, in this place did the duke keep his court, with very great royalty, unto whom when this was reported, hearing of a certain that Wagner had great store of his masters skill, and whatsoever, he caused one that in such matters is commonly commanded, to ride to Wittenberg, to the intent to hear the truth, for many things more than the truth were certified unto him: the messenger without delay (because the journey was long) departed and left the court, and we him a while.

CHAP. VI.

A long discourse betwixt the Devil and Wagner, and ended with a good Philosophical repast.

WAGNER solitary musing in his chamber and conversing with many multitudes of thoughts, suddenly appeared Mephistophiles his masters familiar, after him Akercocke, which was Wagners, and after all, Faustus: quoth Mephistophiles, what chear? Sirrah such as you see, we are as we were, and never the better: and welcome Akercocke; but my very good Faustus, that you come at this time I rejoyce. So then they all sat down, and sat right against him. Then entred in divers delicate viands, and there not then to be ended, with unseen symphonies of musick. Then spake Wagner and said, Claud te jam rivos, now we have satisfied our appetite with meat, I pray you hear me with patience, for I have a thing in my mind, of which I would fain be resolved, but because you so foully, and so often foully entreated my master, for demanding some questions, you shall ratifie this article with me again: first, that in my demands you shall answer truely and patiently, for what hurt can redound to you by answering of a question, seeing if you are sure of any thing you may hold fast, a question cannot take it away: without delay these good fellows confirmed the article with a great oath: but he would take their simple word without surety, he knew their honesty so well. Then Wagner pulling down his cap over his eyes, and leaning upon his elbow a while, and throwing up his eyes to heaven, and then sighing, at length folding his arms within themselves, sat still a little time, then spitting a little and fetching a hearty hem with a good courage spake unto them thus:

Sirs, it is not unknown to you how dear I have always accounted of my Master, whose condition is as far from that it was, as mine from yours, for which I have more often lamented his departure than mine own misery, being once every way a man, so thoroughly instructed with the weapons of all sciences, that in all the world hardly his par could be found, so that your victory over such a man is more to be wailed than over many a thousand such as I am. To be short, that you may understand whither I will go without further oration. Wherefore I desire you, I pray you, nay I by your article command you, that you declare unto me truly without collusion, whether that Faustus here present in that state wherein he now is, may come again to be a living man amongst us, either his old shape renewed, or be in a new: for some philosophers say, and some divines, as Origenes and Tertullian, and whether they say truly or no I know not, that no sooner the soul of man departeth from one, but that it doth enter into another. Wherefore I considering with my self thus much, and often for his cause that he may not onely be Faustus, but also a living man and dweller upon the earth, to enjoy not only those graces which through his great deserts he had lost, but also according to his infinite knowledge, multiply them through God's favors again and again abundantly. And though you shall perhaps deny that the same individual cannot be againe resuscitated, yet that Numero it may in spite of you all, I know it may: for we do not doubt that the same individual may Numero be again regotten, because that after seven and thirty thousand years, the heavenly constellation shall be in every point per totum the same then that now it is, according to Plato and the astronomers. And therefore we shall be the same in Numero, and shall sit in this or that schole or place as now we do, that is in that Magno anno, in that great year: Whereupon Plato said, that after the great year he should return to Athens, and should there read;

Because the constellations shall happen so; therefore, that returning, the same effects shall with them likewise return. Now having heard my resolution, answer me to my first proposition in full and amply, as that I may be satisfied. At the conclusion of this speech Faustus turned his head aside laying it betwixt his hands hiding it, so sat a great while. Ak. he friskt up and down for he had neither clog nor chain because he was in number of the wild ones, and over the table and back again. Ak. was the familiar which F. gave to W. who asked him in the fashion of an ape. Such cranks, such lifts, careers and gambalds, as he plaid there, would have made a horse laugh. Me. who as it seemed was the speaker of the parliament in Hell, rose and walked about very hastily, at length he came to the table and striking his fist on it (the print was seen two years after, and was carried to S. Margaret's Church for a relique, to shew what a fellow the Devil is in his anger) and again beating said, thou, then left them and came and went, and came and went again, here he takes me one book and hurles it against a cupboord, and then he takes the cupboord, and hurles it against the wall, and then he takes the wall and throws it against the house, and the house out at the window. Pacifying his rage at the length, rowling his eyes and seeming to beat his teeth together, he sat down further off, and thus quietly spake with a loud voyce. Were it not Wagner that our solemn vow forbiddeth to disturb or torment thee for any demands, this thy fond pride should be rewarded with most intolerable punishments: as for the question I will answer thee more substantially than such a foolish doltish one doth require. And for that we have day enough before us, I will travel further in it than the gravity of the argument can require, if it be but that thou mayest see how great an ass thou art, which canst imagine so gross a matter in thy more gross head: as for thy great yeer be it as you will, expect in you, in the mean time we will enjoy him and thee at our pleasure in despight of God and heaven, and his imperial armies of saints. Thy question is this: whether the spirit of a damned man can return into the body of another man. To which I answer negatively, it cannot.

1. If this were to them granted, they should observe and keep the embryons in the womb of the mother, that they might constitutively unite themselves to it, to have at the least wise, sensuall consolation and delectation.

2. Then secondly, because it is common to reasonable creatures to fashion and informate the body, and to perfect it with some natural delightment, not to vex it.

3. Then thirdly, because of the law and order of nature, the souls from the places in their departure to them allotted, assigned and deputed of God, neither do nor can depart at any time: for it is written, For the soul is a spirit going and returning. And they which do otherwise hold opinion, are to be accused nay condemned in this with Pythagoras, who did abstain from all living animals and creatures, believing that in some the souls of some men did dwell and abide. Thus far

the Arrogonian named Bartholomew Sibylla a Monopolitane, who writ upon this question being at Wittenberg, at the request of him that did set forth the Dutch coppy shews himself to be a good philosopher and no worse divine. But mark what follows, this is written according to men in faith : the Devil was out of the first streete of Coany when he was past this last period. For that Pythagorical opinion; if that were, this absurdity would follow: (I will speak plainly the rather to fit thy capacity) and if the soul should pass out of the dead into the living, then should mortality be the cause of the souls immortality, (this is prettily spoken) and by that means make it corruptible, which cannot be. And seest thou Wagner? for I will teach thee by demonstrations, and therewith he took a coal of fire and held it to him so long that it came to be but a coal: now thou seest Wagner, that so long as fire was in this subject it had life, but the quality being removed from the quantity, neither is the quality found or seen or known whither it vanisheth, nor can the same fire, though fire, return into another body or subject, albeit the quantity remaineth. Thus may the soul of man be compared to a fire in the soul, as concerning his entrance and departure, but not reentrance, for that coal may take life again, that is fire, but so cannot humane body : because one spirit can be united but to one body, and not two to one, nor one spirit to two bodies: wherefore that spirit being departed it is irrevocable, because of the unity, and the impossibility of returning in the one, in the other of receiving any other. As for other reasons directly by circumstance, if the soul goeth either to joy or pain immediately, then I am certain that that hope which thou hast is meerly vain, as any thing which may hap under that title; for proof behold. And so then through the wainscot door of Wagner's study entred in two kings, which drawing their swords did there in presence combate together fiercely and courageously, one of them shortly after fainting under the adversaries strokes fell down, the other victorious, yet wounded, very canonically as a man may say, staggered immediately, as if he would fain have not fallen, yet for all that he fell: then entred two men carrying torches with the snuffs downwards, with great solemnity (more than is here needful to be recapitulated, for I see nothing but that this might have been very well left out for any thing worthy the gravity of the matter) which when they had carried out the first slain combatant, with armed men, and a dying stroke of the drum, clothed all in the colour which best notes by his external hue the internal sorrow. Then next there entred two pages all in silver white crowned with bayes, carrying their torches aloft, declaring the height of their glory by the height of their flames: next to them divers trumpeters and all in white, urging forth into the wast air their victorious flourishes; next a great standard-bearer, and I cannot tell what, but the conclusion was, that the triumph was exceeding great and pompous, adorned with as many ceremonies as such a victory might or could be. The spirit when they were all gone began to speak and said,

This was the battle which was fought for the great realm of Asia, by Hercules and Orontides, where Orontides was slain, and Hercules sore wounded, but yet recovered, after which he atchieved his twelve labors, and the thirteenth of which the poet speaketh, the hardest of all.

> Tertius hinc decimus labor est durissimus, una
> Quinquaginta simul stupravit nocte puellas.

This history is as I do think in the chronicle of hell, for I did never hear of it before, nor any body else, I appeal to all the histories. Marry it may be this was when Hercules was a little boy, and then peradventure indeed the records make no mention of it, but yet we have that recorded which he did when he was less than a little boy, as his killing of a serpent in his cradle, and such a history as I do remember is enroll'd in the golden book of the seven wise masters of Rome, an authentical author. But let that pass, and let us draw more near unto the cause; for as the Devil was afore our dayes, so by authority he may alledge experience, and we must of necessity believe that it is either true or a lie. Mephostophiles continued his speech for all this parenthesis, declaring to Wagner his meaning in this point: for (quoth he) as you see these two champions contending for the title of victory, one of them must needs, if they try the extreamest as they did, receive the dishonour, the other the glory, so in the combat wherein the dying body battaileth with the lively soul, the soul if grace hath made it acceptable, shall enjoy those everlasting pleasures of Paradise, and dwell in heaven blessed and glorious amongst the beautiful angels, but if it be counted as reprobate and outcast of God, then according to that punishment which his great sins did deserve, he can have no other place but the continual horror of hell, wherein the miserable dwel, and the ugly company of black devils and frightful angels. There is no other mean but honour and dishonour in this cause, no other mean but joy or pain, no other mean but heaven or hell perpetually: there is no place left for a third. I could more copiously dispute of this matter, but that I will not be too tedious in so exile a question. For where it is said in an author to which I am witness, for I stood by his elbow when he writ the lines, "Animæ sunt in loco certo et expectant judicium, neq; se inde possunt commovere." Which place as appeareth in the precedent chapter is heaven or hell: again it is said, "Anima quæ peccaverit ipsa morietur." Of necessity then the soul to whom the Lord imputeth not his sin shall live, for they are immediate oppositions, for the soul that is in joy will not come to these troubles, nor that which is in torment cannot: therefore it is said: "Et revertatur pulvis in terram quem admodum erat, et spiritus revertatur ad Dominum, qui dedit illum," so there is no mention in any scripture of the souls returning, but to a certain place deputed of God to him. But before I go any further in the declaring of that which is here to be set down, I know they that have their consciences more of the precise cut, will say, that here was a learned devil: true it is, he is learned, strong, and above all human conceit, subtil and crafty, and if they say it is blasphemously done, to have the word spoken to the world by so vile a mouth, first they know how mightily the Devil is conversant in holy writ, in any thing to overthrow a christian thought, knowing that the word of God is a word of power to attain salvation to whom grace is given and to work eternal damnation where that gift is wanting, knowing it is the only means to debel and conquer the christian thought, for as a man is governed by a law and by it lives, so if any thing be evidently directed against him in it, it stays his heart, it overthrows him, it takes away his power for ever: nor is it more blasphemous to be spoken to us men, than to God himself, as it is in St. Alatherio, where the Devil was not afraid to assail his creator with most terrible arguments of the divine letter. They which have right minds can persuade themselves accordingly: but otherwise they may cavil as long as they will, which they may do to their small profit, assuring them this, that in coveting by fault-finding to seem learned, they make themselves the notes and reproach, not only of the learned, but even of the absurd and barbarous rude fools, and that they are the only spirits of errour and contention, and the chief causes of unbelief by vain reasonings and questions to the unresolved christian. But as for this speech which is but humile dicendi genus, in very truth, let them thus think, that if there were any such controversy betwixt Wagner and his spirit, as is here mentioned, that those are not the words which were spoken, but that they do proceed from a young scholar who gave me this copy, and not of a Devil, of whose familiarity and frequency and of other circumstantive causes, I will God willing in the catastrophe and conclusion of this book deliver unto you my poor opinion. In the mean while I will follow the matter into which we are fallen my good friends, and without further ado I pray, without any more excusive phrase, patiently expect the good hour wherein the death of this volum is prepared. Mephostophiles taking breath a little, presented his speech saying: it is said likewise, "Factum est autem ut moreretur mendicus, &c." And it came to pass that the beggar dyed, and was carried away of Angels into Abrahams bosome, and that rich man died, and was buried, and he being in hell lifted up his eyes, when he was in torments, and saw Abraham afar off, and Lazarus in his bosome. Nor nothing doth that impugn which is said of the Papist that he cannot come into Gods presence, nor be one of the elect, unless he be purified from his sins, for which purification they ordained a place so terribly stuck with pins, needles, daggers, swords, nails, &c. soultring with hot burning furnaces, and so every way formidable with material sulphury fires, that no tongue can express, nor any heart imagine, wherein the sinful soul must be many times and often cleansed, but I hope if this were true then Lazarus should have been likewise so drest in their terrible imagined terrors, which he was not unless they will be impudent to say that he had no sin. I shall not need to dispute how absurd it is to say, that the sin of the soul in the body committed, must be extirpated and purified by a material substance and *rigor*, not of the matter of the like argument. And hereupon he seemed to sigh as if some sodain thought had overprest his stomach. I can quoth he largely discourse of all divine and humane propositions, but as the unlearned parat who speaketh oft and much, and understandeth never any thing to profit himself. Ah that unto us spirits no secrets are secret, no doings of man unhid, and yet we Devils cursed of God, are incapable of any of Gods mercies, though through them we were created. We know repentance is the way to attain the celestial favour: we know Gods mercies how great they are, and that we ought to despair of nothing (such is our seeing blindness) so it appertain to God and godliness, of which we do not despair. No Wagner we are so far from living again, as we are from certainty to be saved. But instead of that, we are crossed with all kind of vexations, for since the first time that I with my master and fellows fell down from heaven being of the most royal order of angels, potestates, cherubins, and seraphins, riding upon the wings of the wind in all bright shining majesty, and enjoying the most glorious and divine presence of our Creator, till for our hearts swelling pride, and haughty insolency within as little space of time as we were created in, with his dreadful lightning he threw us down headlong into the bottomless abysses of the air, wherein we indure these tortures and alike wicked souls with us, as our manifold deserts have brought upon us:

and for that we know that the way to mercy is utterly denied, and that we are as much hated of our selves as of God, we think it the sweetest remedy in these manifold miseries to have partakers of our common wo with us. Wherefore it is most expedient for us to be thus enviously malicious against all mankind, making them as far in Gods dreadful curse as our selves.

Wagner melting at these words, his eyes undid the great burthen of his sorrow, straining himself so long that he wept and yet could say nothing, but only a small volley of sobs hastily following; Mephostophiles seeing how Wagner was drowned in so deep a melancholy, told him pulling him by the sleeve that he would be still demanding of such foolish questions which will profit him so little as mought be. Knowest thou not (quoth he) that all the rhetoricks are the servants of my tongue or that we can move pity or hatred when we please? fool as thou art, forget these vain conferences, perswade thy self that they are but the effect of speech, long canst thou not live, and yet dost thou live as if thou didst not long, youthly should be thy thoughts and fraught with the rank lustiness of conceit and amorous delight, if thou wilt ask questions, let them be such as appertain to love and wealth, to pleasure, to pastime, and to merriment. How sayest thou to such a one, naming a gentlewoman, the most beautiful lady under the cope of heaven? thou shalt enjoy her, nay, any one so she be one whom thou list to call beautiful, whosoever thy eyes shall lay their delight upon. And presently musick was heard so sweet, so plenteous, and so ravishing, as if on musick depended all sweet, all plenty, all ravishment. The doors conveying themselves aside, as giving place to so divine a fairness, entring in a blue velvet gown rased, and thickly beset in the gards with most pure oches of gold, not altogether ignorant of precious stones fur'd with royal ermines, loose about her: her heads ornament (though greater ornament to her head than her head there could not be) was a kind of attired caul (such as I have seen none in England according to their description) raised up at corners with stiff square wyres of beaten gold, on that a chaplet or frontire of roses, on the chaplet a vaile of lawn, which covered all her fair body, denying the sight of such an angel, but only through a shadow. In brief she was such a one as would have roused the basest desire in the whole world, to attempt wonderous enterprises; in her silken soft hand she held a lute, discoursing sweetly upon the solemn strings with her nimble fingers: a maid carrying a blue waxen taper in a silver white candlestick made in the fashion of a censer, but it was derived into two several branches, in whose ends were curiously wrought two most beautiful places to pight tapers on. The maid bi'r lady would have well contented a reasonable proper squire, it was a pretty rank lass, round about as plump as a bladder, which being yet smoking new is blown up with wind; well I will not trouble you with these rude descriptions any longer, but desire you to conceive the excellency of this fair lady, for it is far more copious in the Dutch copy than is here necessary to be recapitulated. Wagners heart leaping at this sight, looked about him, as if he would have no body privy to himself but himself, and so it was indeed, for Faustus, Mephostophiles, and Akercock were gone, and thereupon with a boon courage advancing himself upon his toes and weeding himself in the best German fashion, as he could very well, began to travail unto her, but remembring his bad apparel stept back and blusht, and hid his face, but sodainly returning again as if he had known now how rather to become his weeds, began to fewter himself, but O wonder, his habit was changed with his thought, and he was now no more Wagner but Armisuerio the ladies lord. And to be short this new Armisuerio and old Wagner, met with the lady, and saluting her in the best kind of Bon noche, used her as he would do his lady and she him as her lord. So passing over their weary night in such pleasure as I could find in my heart to enjoy, or any man, unless an eunuch beside.

CHAP. VII.

The arrival of the Messenger at Wittenberg, and the description of Wagner.

It is time to winde about another furrow with our sweating teem and bring our speech to another matter, entring out of one into another, for change is sweet. Not forgetting by the way the pursevant or as we may better call him, a messenger who lately departed from Vienna in Austria, and I think by that time this disputation was finished, had almost overtaken all the way 'twixt him and home, which was some fifteen dayes travail, after five German miles to the dayes labor, and arrived at Wittenberg, by enquiry came to Wagners chamber, which was in the way as you go to the publick school, as ye go from Melancthons house, a pretty house and of a reasonable large size, built of hewn stone, and environed with a good thick wall, of some three foot and a half thick, and twenty high, at the bottom guarded about with a good broad mount of seven yards over, and round about very large and secret walks, far from all company and resort, and there he might talk without fear with the Devil and his dam too, thither this fellow coming, knocked peremtorily at the door. Wagner was even now gone to his study, and rising up in a pedlers chafe, that he should go to his book, and especially if it were goodness not once in a month, yet then to be troubled, he swore a little thing would make him never study more, it should not, but putting on his cloak and his hat, came down and unbolted the door: unto whom the messenger seeing such a pretty jolly fellow did some little reverence. Wagner as yet scarce having let down his choler, stept back, and perceiving him wear such a weed as serjeants there do use to wear, thinking within himself that some had come from the prince for cozening of his servants, shut the door upon him, and went powting and swearing and pittifully chafing, that if the knave offered to sue him he would surely kill him at the least, down he fetcht a good bastinado and set it behind the door and opened it again, and demanded some what mildly what he had to say to him; to whom the messenger said, that he came from the Arch-duke of Austria from Vienna, who willing to hear some certainty of his master, did send for him, assuring himself that not only he could satisfie his desire in that matter, but also shew him as much skill as ever his master had. Wagner hearing the purpose of his message with good effectual words, thankt him again, and rendered most serviceable reverence to his good lord and master for remembring so gently his poor servant, &c. desiring him to tarry until he might set every thing in due order, and he would not fail to go with him. The messenger did not deny him, and so they went up together into their chamber, whom ever after the messenger loved dearly for his proper behaviour, and personage, for indeed Wagner was a very goodly young man, being about the common stature, straight and reasonable slender, well trust, his hair very yellow, and his face fair, his beard which did but now express the blossoms of his lusty courage, of the like yellow, well mannered, as having been brought up amongst the finest and best sort of Devils: having a pleasant filed tongue, and would make the dainty rhetorick come as smoothly out of his mouth, as an arrow out of a piece of paper, well could he talk of amorous devices, and intreat the bravest ladies with sweet entertainment, in truth by report he was a gentle-like man, and accomplished with as many fine parts as a better man than he might justly vaunt of: he could play upon any fine instrument, and was not ignorant of any laudable exercises, carrying a brave lusty conceit even unto his death: and furnished with many proportions of art, there was nothing wanting in the man but a godly mind.

CHAP. VIII.

The Tragedy of Doctor Faustus seen in the Air, and acted in the presence of a Thousand People of Witten. An. 1540.

In a brave summer sun-shine day, the whole people of Wittenberg being gathered together, to behold certain matches for the garland, who could drink most, and also to see a match shot at a pair of butts with harquebushiers, as their order is, in a low meadow hard by the Elbe: which now being in his freshest pride, was full of fine and sweet flowers, being the latter end of the month wherein the sun departs from the last embracings of Gemini. On a sodain there was seen a marvellous bright and glorious rainbow, spreading its wide armes over the wide world, and straight was there heard a noise of trumpets, sounding a short flourish, and then another, and by and by another, all alike short, at the which the assembly was wonderful afeard, and listened, desirous to see the effects of this wonder and strange miracle, some of them fell to their Ave Maries lustily, thinking that the universal doom had been at that instant: As thus they beheld with great admiration, they might distinctly perceive a goodly stage to be rear'd (shining to sight like the bright burnisht gold) upon many a fair pillar of clearest crystal, whose feet rested upon the arch of the broad rainbow: therein was the high throne wherein the king should sit, and that proudly placed with two and twenty degrees to the top, and round about curious wrought chairs for divers other potentates, there might you see the ground-work at the one end of the stage, where out the personated devils should enter into their fiery ornaments, made like the broad wide mouth of a huge dragon, which with continual armies of smoak and flame breathed forth his angry stomachs rage, round about the eyes grew hairs, not so horrible as men call bristles, but more horrible, as long as stiff spears: the teeth of this hells-mouth far out stretching, and such as a man might well call monstrous and more than a man can by words signifie: to be short, his hew of that colour which to himself means sorrow, and to other ministers like passion, a thick lamp black, blacker than any paint, any hell, blacker than its own self. At the other end in opposition was seen the place wherein the bloodless skirmishes are so often performed on the stage, the walls not (so pleasant as old wives would have their tales adorned with) of pastry-crust, but iron, attempered with the most firm steel, which being brightly filed, shone as beautifully over the whole place as pale shining Cynthia, environed with high and stately turrets of the same metal and beauty, and hereat many in-gates and out-gates: out of each side lay the bended ordnance showing at their wide hollows the cruelty of death: out of sundry loops many large banners and streamers were pendant, briefly nothing was there wanting that might make it a fair castle. There might you see to be short the gibbet, the posts, the ladders, the attiring house, there every thing which in the like houses either use or necessity makes common. Now above all was there the gay clouds Usquequaque, adorned with the heavenly firmament, and often spotted with golden tears which men call stars: There was lively portrayed the whole imperial army of the fair heavenly inhabitants, the bright angels, and such whose names to declare in so vile a matter were too impious and sacreligious. They were so naturally done, that you would have sworn it had been heaven itself or the epitome of it, or some second heaven, and a new heaven it was: from thence like dewie drops wherein the sun layes his golden shine, making them to appear like small golden tears, the sweet odours and comforting liquor stream'd, and seemed always to rain from thence, but they never fell, but kept a beaten path from down on high wherein the descending angel might rejoyce. I should be too long if I should express this rare stage, especially in such sort and such like words as the like occasion in a more worthy subject would require, but of necessity we must barely apply our descriptions to the nature of the whole history. We must not fail in the first principle of art, according to that of Horace;

> Humano capiti cervicem pictor equinam
> Jungere si velit, & varias inducere plumas
> Undique collatis membris, ut turpiter atrum
> Desinat in piscem mulier formosa superne:
> Spectatum admissi risum teneatis amici?
> Credite Pisones isti fabulæ fore librum.
> Per similem.
> Non ut placidis coeant immitia.

I shall not need to turn back to declare the deep astonishment of the people, who are always in most small matters induced easily to wondering, but now this excellent fair theatre erected, immediately after the third sound of the trumpets, there entered the prologue attyred in a black vesture, and making his three obeysances, began to shew the argument of that scenical tragedy, but because it was so far off they could not understand the words, and having thrice bowed himselfe to the high throne, presently vanished. Then out of this representance of hells mouth, issued out whole armies of fiery flames, and most thick foggy smoaks, after which entred in a great battail of footmen devils, all armed after the best fashion with pike, &c. marching after the stroak of the couragious drum, who girded about, laid siege to this fair castle, on whose walls after the summons, Faustus presented himself upon the battlements, armed with a great number of crosses, pen and ink-horns, charms, characters, seals, periapts, &c. who after sharp words defied the whole assembly, seeming to speak earnestly in his own defence, and as they were ready to rear the ladders, and Faustus had begun to prepare for the counterbattery, determining to throw down upon the assemblies heads, so many heavy charms and conjurations that they should fall down half way from the ascendant: whilst these things began to wax hot from the aforesaid heaven there descended a legion of bright angels riding upon milk white chariots, drawn with the like white steeds, who with celestial divine melody came into the tower, to the intent to fight for the doctor against his furious enemies, but he wanting pay-money and void indeed of all good thoughts, not able to abide their most blessed presence, sent them away, and they returned from whence they came, sorrowfully lamenting his most wilful obstinacy, whilst he had all benointed the walls with holy water, and painted with blood many a crimson cross. At length the alarm was given, and the ladders cleaved to the walls, up the assailants climbed, up they lifted their fearful weapons. Faustus not able (destitute of help) to withstand them was taken prisoner, and his tower down rased to the earth, with whose fall both the large heaven and world shook and quaked mightily, whom when they had fettered they left there, they marching out and the forenamed chairs were presently occupied with all the imperial rulers of hell, who clothed in their holy-day apparel, sate there to give judgment upon this wilfull Faustus, whom two hangmen of hell unloosed, and there in presence of them all, the great devil afore his chief peers, first stamping with his angry foot, and then shaking his great bush of hair, that therewith he made the near places and the most proud devils courage to tremble, and with his fire burnt-scepter, and his like coloured crown all of gold setting one hand by his side, and the other upon the pummel of a chair, shook a pretty space with such angry fury, that the flames which proceeded from his frightful eyes did dim the sight of the Wittenbergers below. There was in this said Wittenberg, a gallant fair lady and a virgin, which now following her mother, accompanied with sundry gallant German gentlemen, had even now entred out of their barge, and seeing the whole world of people as they thought, gazing up into the heaven so very strangely, were partly strucken with wonder, some with fear, and some with sodain merriment, and hasting down the hill more than a round pace, asked some, what was there to do, and they bid them look up (for here is to be noted that they looked up afore but could see nothing but as always they were wont, until they shewed them it) which they did and at the same time wherein the great devil was in his red hot anger, this young gentlewoman looked up, whose most ugly shape so fear'd her, that even then there she fell down in a sown, whom they conveyed away very speedily, yet ere they could come home she was well nigh dead, and so she lay for two years without hope of life, or certainty of death: great sorrow to her parents and as cruel pain to her: but she at length recovered her spirit, and if by your patience I may, I will tell you how. There was a most learned and excellent doctor dwelling in the town who had great knowledge in the black-art, who being requested to use some physick to aid her in her great extremity, being promised for reward five thousand dollars; this doctor perceiving the cause of her malady was not caused of any distemperature of her body, but only of the aforesaid fear, knew that physick might well make her body sound, but her mind never. Wherefore not only for the reward but also to become gracious and famous at once, proceeded in his cure on this manner. One night having made his orisons and nine times combed his hair with tears of a pure maid, and nine times gone about a fire made all of pure Heben coal, and thrice nine times called upon the name of the most dreadful Hecate, he laid himself to sleep upon a pure white and clean unspotted maidens smock, and covered himself over with the ashes of a white hind rosted and burned altogether: he slept, and the next morning apparelled in white robes having often and often called, recalled and exorcised the three fairies Millia, Achilya, and Sybilla, at length the ground opened, and with them they brought a milk white steed, and did put upon his finger the ring of invisibility; when they were vanished, he mounted upon his horse, who with more swift flight than the winged Pegasus carried him throughout the wide air so fast and so long, that having passed over Bohem, Hungary, Thracia, all Asia Minor, Mesopotamia, and at length to Arabia Fælix, where he alighted upon a most high mountain, all the way from the top to the bottom of a just breadth and steepness, so that he that were on it, would think himself not in the world, and they beneath would deem him to be in heaven, upon the brims of it round about grew the high pines, and stately cedars, and always so green as the most fresh meadow: the height of this huge rock was two and twenty miles in even altitude, and half a mile of just circuit all the way; there he tyed his horse to a tree, and knocked at the castle gate, where afore was never seen any, so that no path could there be seen, so that a man might justly have called it the house of little hospitality; to him there came Neglectment, an old lady, and demanded what he would, who told her his errand, and withal a ring of fine gold from the three fairies, she knew the ring and his errand, and conveyed him into fair rooms wherein she shewed him many a worthy knightes memorials, many an antick monument heaped up; but inner rooms so monstrous dark and nightly, that no humane eye could perceive anything, and forth she brought him unto a garden, out of the midst whereof rose a little hill, from the summity whereof, there was a paved way of pure crystal stone from along whose bosom trilled a small water: this water an old man held, and indeed he had it as a patrimony, for therefore he could shew many an ancient evidence, and worn charter, his hair was all fled to his front, as if some enemy had scared the hinder locks from his scalp, on his back hung a pair of wings which flagged down, as if either they had been broken or he weary, and thus he over-strod a round world, from out of every part whereof gushed out this small river which was conveyed down in this cristal pipe: in one hand he held a long sythe, and in the other an hour-glass: here the Doctor seeing the old ruines of this sumptuous house, and all the fair walls and buildings overgrown with a deadly moss was much amazed, but because he could not tarry, he dipt a small vial in the spring and departed, and for because he was so peremptorily warned not to tarry, he could not behold the most stately galleries, in which he might see the worlds chief pleasures and monuments some wholly worn away, some half and some even now beginning, and some wholly quite overgrown with a thick earthy fur, for as he came by an old wall, he chanc't with his elbow to rub off the thick moss, and then might he see a fair piece of parchment gilded and painted curiously, wherein was truly described the antient tokens of a most brave and worthy gentleman: so having sped of his journey, he came by the same way again as he went. Neglectment shut the doors upon him, whilst he mounted upon his white swift-footed horse, and by the like time arrived at his own house, where having with the blood of a new slain heyfer thrice anointed the feet of his Cavallo, and tying at his ear with a string of fine silk, spun by the hands of a pure maid, the received ring of invisibility unto his ear, with many a cross and many an open

Ave Maria, dismissed him, who in the same moment returned to the place from whence he came. With this water the doctor came to the maid, and having used a certain incantation, gave her to drink of the water of deep oblivion, which she had no sooner tasted of, but straightways she had forgotten the terrible picture of the devil, and was revived out of all her infernal fears, the doctor called, winning him credit, favour and fame and richly rewarded for his medicine, departed, and coming home threw his vial into the deep river burying oblivion with oblivion: the parents of the young lady rejoicing exceedingly at their daughters recovery for ever after caused the place wherein their daughter was thus scared, to be unaccessable for man or beast, compassing it in with a high wall, and overthrowing the banks, so that now there is no mention of the meadow, nor of the wall.

The Devil, the great Devil Lucifer having finished his brief oration descended down out of his judgment seat and pointing unto all his nobles took Faustus by the hand and placed him just before him, taking him by the chin seemed to them to bid him speak freely, he mounted up again unto his high throne, and with a more mild madness expected the speech of the doctor, who having bowed himself submissively unto these damnable company: he began to speak, and yet not long, then he began to walk up and down, and to shew strange gestures, when sodainly for some bug words escaped by Faustus, all the devils there rose up, and with their swords drawn threatened with them the poor Doctor, turning all their bodyes and directing their faces to the king, who with a stern countenance commanded silence. When Faustus having long raged, of a sodain howling loud and tearing his hair, laid both his armes upon his neck and leaped down headlong off the stage, the whole company immediately vanishing, but the stage with a most monstrous thundering crack followed Faustus hastily, the people verily thinking that they would have fallen upon them ran all away, and he was happiest that had the swiftest foot, some leapt into the river and swam away; and all of them with great affright ran into the city and clapt the city gates together straight, and to increase this fear, they thought they heard a thing fall into the river, as if a thousand houses had fallen down from the top of heaven into it. But afterwards this was known to be Wagners knavery, who did this to show the pursevant some point of his skill.

CHAP. IX.

The messenger had not tarried above three days, when as Wagner had trust up his baggage, and was nowready to depart, when on the third day at night he caused his boy Arthur Harmarvan, (who was the son of a wealthy boor, witty above many, and praised for his notable waggery: his father dwelt at Malmesburg, a town hard by Wittenberg, in Saxony, in high Dutch-land, with whom Wagner being acquainted had obtained him of his father to serve him, and he to be taught of Wagner) him he caused to go to divers scholars of his acquaintance to sup with him at his departure, who being invited to this hated farewel, came speedily where they had a banquet and other courtesies which in such a time both customes and laws of their fellowship do prescribe: in the suppertime the scholars moved many questions, and amongst the rest one desired the pursevant to describe unto them his lord and master, for they heard say that the Duke Alphonsus was a marvellous qualified gentleman: the pursevant not willing to refuse their request told them that seeing their demands proceeded of a common good zeal, he could not but wrongfully refuse to satisfie: notwithstanding the truth might be better known of another than of him, whom duty bids to be partial, if any defect might breed partiality, but so much as I will tell you, the enemy will not disdain to affirm: and there he told them the very stature, proportion, and particular lineaments, concluding that he shewed the uprightness of his mind by the proportion of his body, and keeping in his outward shape the vertue which philosophers would have kept in the mind. There he told them the feature of his countenance, the colour of his hair, eyes, face, cheeks, &c. He told them his stature, favour and strength, which was such, that with pure cleanness of his force, he hath foiled a gentleman in wrastling, who besides whiteness of body, was very firm without affection, not as some do, which in performing any thing, will with such a ridiculous sowreness act it, as if the force of the body must be personated upon the theater of his face: he declared unto them that the gifts of his mind were such as then he could not for the number reckon up, but even as occasion shall serve might meet with them, being all such as were more ready to be admired than imitated, as if all vertues were gathered in him together, magnanimity, magnificence, affability, modesty, &c. Briefly he said, there were in him all those graces which adorn the subject with the title of vertuous. He likewise recounted unto them his studies, unto which he accommodated himself at vacant hours, which were partly poetry. A poem of his he said he had by chance gotten (and by greater chance had it there at that instant) which he had made in the praise of his excellent lady when he was but of young years, his father living, I dare say he would not for ten thousand florens have it seen, being such a one as on a dreaming passion he had let fall from his pen, and of many the most abject, but such as this is deserves commendations, because a prince made it, but if you saw his real devices, you would then say they were prince-like. And then he read it, which I was loth my good friends either to translate, or translated to present it here, for that it was not worthy your censure, considering the nice building of sonnets now a dayes, but according to Ariostos vein you shall find it very conformable, as also forthat I knew that if I should have left it out, it would have been more wisht for, then now admired. Yet for that I prefer your well known good wills afore any vain fear, take this with the rest, if there be any, with such favour, as if I were by you at the reading.

A mio solemente amandona.
Madonna; Donna nonparelia
L'Angelico sembiante e quel bel volte,
Fa l'odio, e l'ira va in oblivione,
Ch' a l', &c.

Thus have I harshly Englished them verbally.

Angel-like semblance, beauties ornament,
Whose vertue quells all wrath and rancor deep,
Whose life heavens grace and death would monument
Vertue thy life are . . . .*
How many wounded hearts thou makst to tremble,
And I of many one cannot dissemble,
How far into in . . . .* that eye-sore.

So were thy beauty but deserving praise,
So were thy beauty but as feminine,
Then could my quill his strain so high araise,
Then could with it compare the masculine,
Thy beauty praise thy bounty past divine,
No strain, no quill such wonderments assaies.
Then poets pen shall to thy power his power resigne.

What words may well express such excellence,
No humane thought thy beauties may comprise,
And words may tell all humane insolence,
All humane words and wit thy gifts surprize,
To satisfie my self in my pretence,
Our pen unto the heavens must wander hence,
And fill it self with dew of heavenly sapience.

* The letters were worn out in these places.

And I my life shall to your hands resigne,
Which live to serve a humane saint so past divine.

Se da colei
Che poco ingegno adhor adhormi lima.

This sonnet was ended with as much praise as it began with desire, and one of them copied it out and so it was made common to the rest, and made a good sort of them poets, rectifying their gross conceits, with so sweet a matter. He told them that this was but a preparative to wondering in respect of his choyce making. Then he shewed them this epigram, which he made when as before the duke his father a brace of fair English grayhounds fell down at the harts heels stark dead (the hart also lying not above six yards off dead too) with chasing, having outstript the rest of the dogs above half a mile.

Then he reckoned unto him the delight he took in limning, and shewed them very many fine devices of his own handiwork. The scholars singularly delighted with the view of the reliques of so great a prince, approved by silence that excellency which by speech they could not. In fine there he reckoned up enough to be praised, and peradventure more than was true, but not more than is desired. There he set forth with great and ardent emphasis other qualities, as his skill and hardy demeanour at the tilt, turney, how he could manage the sturdy steed, leap, run, vault, dance, sing, play on divers instruments, and talk with amiable speech amongst fair ladyes, which we call courting, in all his actions full of gentle familiar affability, still reserving to himself the due honour belonging to his personage. He concluded in fine that he was the most qualified prince, and absolute gentleman that day in all christendom: saying, if they knew his humanity, justice and liberality, you would say in him were all humanity, justice and liberality: and as the greatest thing that the world can shew is beauty, so the least thing that is to be praised in him, is beauty, you would say no less than I have spoken could be in his person if you did but see him Thus far the digression came in the commendations of this Alphonsus, which truly I was weary of, fearing the great insufficiency of the description, but yet he had not done. I would to God (quoth he) you would come to Vienna, and I promise you such lodging and entertainment, that next to the sight of him should be worthiest of your thanks. Wherefore you shall not sorrow that your friend Wagner departeth, unless you will seem to envy rather his felicity than his departure I would we were even all of us as we sit at the table in the dukes court, and here again with a wish, and here with there knockt one at the door: Wagner craftily feigning that he himself would rise to see him that knockt so desiring them all to sit still in any case, and opening therewith the door there entred two young lords of Tergeste and Moravia bearing torches, and next there came the duke of Austrich as they thought, and Wagner talked with him bare-headed, the pursevant thinking verily it had been his master, would have done his duty unto him, but that the rest hindred him: on his head he wore a little hat of blue velvet, with a rich band of pearle, stone and gold, and a long white feather, his cloak of blue velvet, round garded with gold lace, edged with orient pearle, and betwixt the gards eylet-holes, whereout hung by small silk threads long bugles, all the sleeves in the like order: by his side a golden hilted rapier, and on his rapier his hand, his buskins of fine Polonian leather, richly imbroidered on the turnings down with costly goldsmiths work, all his apparel whatsoever most beautiful and princely: he had no sooner passed by (which was not until he was distinctly viewed of them) but that Wagner spake unto them in such manner, saying that that honourable, this mans lord had sent for him, whose commandment I will in no wise repugn. Wherefore I beseech you to take it as you would my greatest advancement. This his description of his feature, judge how rightly he hath said, for my part I confess they are rather less than the truth, than not as he hath reported, and herein to satisfie you the more I have caused my spirit Akercock totake his shape upon him.

Now (quoth he) it is time to depart, but because it shall be the last night of our meeting, none of you shall depart, for I have lodging enough for you all, and because you shall not be forgetful of Wagner when he is gone, let every man wish his woman, and so to bed my masters. They began all to laugh merrily, not as hoping or wishing, but as if they had heard a merry purpose, and therefore they laughed because it was merry, and such mirth they always liked of. Wagner was almost angry, and yet for that he was almost, he was not angry, sending out a great oath as the prologue of his comedy, bidding his boy go prepare their beds and chambers, and bid them wish whom they would, he would their wishes should be performed. Then rose up one of the scholars perswading himself of Wagners earnest, and yet doubting, because he feared he was not in earnest. Why (quoth he) if you mean in very deed, my friend Kit, I would I had such a woman, I believe beside herself there is none fairer than the fairest in this town. Why meanest thou I jest, quoth Wagner, go thy wayes, yonder she is upon pain of my head, and so it was indeed: then every one strove who should wish first, and he that wisht last, had his first wish, so every one took his damosel, and for that night departed to their beds, who are witnesses of that nights great pleasures, and in the morning they arose wishing that every morning were the morrow of such a night. Every one gat him a hackney, and brought him on the way a dayes journey, where they with grief left him, who rode till he came to Vienna, and they till they arrived at Wittenberg. Thus still you see these pot-meetings are ended amongst these puft-cheek hannikins with bed dalliances, rightly describing their lives most bestial and epicure-like.

CHAP. X.

A lamentable history of the death of sundry Students of Wittenberg.

Not long after it was reported and blazed abroad, that Wagner was departed, divers scholars guessing that he had left his books or the most part behind, determined to sent for Harmarvan, which they did, who by no perswasions could be won to let them have his masters keyes, so they devised amongst themselves to bind the boy as he should go home to his inn whereas his master had put him to board till his return. And night drawing on Harmarvan went to his lodging, by the way scholars (to the number of seven) met him, and bound him, and beat him sore until he gave them all the keyes, which he carefully carried about him sowed in a wide German flop, which when they had (they being all mufled and disguised strangely with vizards) they loosed, and then they ran hastily to Wagners house, as if they had fled from followers, or else followed some hastily flying: where being come, they opened the gates, and being entred, shut them again, this being about eleven of the clock in the night, and in they went, where they found two barrels of mighty strong March English beer of two years old which they broached, and sat so long drinking till they were all well drunk. And then down they get into a black court, and having lighted tapers, having injuriously framed all the circles, squares, triangles, &c. and apparelled with all the conjuring robes that the art requireth, there they begin in a most dreadful confusion of hellish sillables to enform the fiend, and after these words followed (as if there needs must such things follow after such words) a terrible roar, and then so bright a smothering thick fiery fume ascended out of the earth as if it would have made an eternal night, then a vehement flame followed, which with continual motion ran about the brims of the circle, until as weary it left moving, (all this while they continued reasonably constant, and continued their invocations without any fear) then from beneath was heard most lamentable outcries, from above huge trembling, thunder, and round about nothing but fear and death in a thousand terrible divers shapes, then they began to quaile a little, but yet by incouragement grew hardy by reason of the number, then round about was sounded alarms with drums, and onset with trumpets, as if there all the world had conflicted, then the flame which all this while ran about the circle became a body, but such a body, as if it had been but a picture would have madded any one. At whose sight they wholly overcome with deadly fear forgat the use of the pantacles or any such gear, but even submitted themselves to the small mercy of the fiend, who with great violence, rent them, and tore them most lamentably. Harmarvan who had raised a great many to the intent to follow them, suspecting that which indeed was, was after long wandring (for they had caused a devil descryer to void all within a certain circuit) with his company brought to the house, where round about they might see in the court wherein these seven were conjuring, huge flames, as if some great pile had been made to the burial of a noble heroe, climbing up in huge volumes in the air, or if some great store of stubble had been fired, so vehemently furious was the flame that no man there (and there was above thirty) was able once to draw near to any part of the house, the cry was carried into the city of this fire, whereupon the whole town was assembled with hooks, buckets, ladders, &c. where in vain they emptied many a large well, till divers learned preachers falling down submissively on their knees, with good faith appeased this seeming fire, which indeed was none, but a mere diabolical illusion, then they entred into the house where they found the barrels brought to bed and delivered, the cups, the whole furniture clean destroyed, broken, and thrown about the house, but drawing near unto the most rueful and lamentable spectacle of all, coming into the yard or grove which was moted about and enclosed with a thick wall of trees very exceeding high, as fir trees are, so very thick that no light was perceivable into it, in the very midst whereof was a round plot of some one hundred feet any way from the centre, there found they the religious circles, there the strange characters, names of angels, a thousand crosses, there found they the five crosshilted daggers for the five kings of hell, there many a strong bulwark builded with rows of crosses, there found they the surplesses, the stoles, pall, mitres, holy water pots broken, their periapts, seats, signs of the angels of the seven dayes, with infinite like trash and damnable roguery the fruits of the Devils rank fansie. But the most lamentable sight of all, the seven scholars utterly torn in pieces, their blood having changed the colour of the ground into a dark crimson, all their bodies as black as any coal, as if they had been scorcht with a material fire, their flesh violéntly torn from the bones, and hanging down in morsels like the skirts of a side coat, their bones all broken, their veins cut in sunder, and their bowels broadshed upon the earth, their brains poured out, and covering the red grass all over, their noses stumped, their eyes thrust out, their mouths widened and slit to their ears, their teeth dasht out, and their tongues starting out betwixt their gummes, their hair clean singed off, in brief imagine with your selves in your minds, and propound a picture in your thought, the most deformed, torn and ill favoured that you can think on, yet shall it not compare to the most lachrimable sight and shew of them, surpassing as much all credit as my skill duely to describe them, whom when they had buried without tarriance, rased the house to the ground, and filled up the moats with earth, heaping upon the place of this murther the stones of the house defaced, then they returned home discoursing with lamentable judgment upon the high and severe revenge of Gods indignation upon them which durst presume to tempt his glorious majesty. And finally, unless repentance breed a more speedy remorse, such is the fatal end of such proud attempts. And surely this is most true, for

I my self have seen the ground where the house stood, and yet the moats damm'd up, and the water breaking through the stones even to this day, there did I see a scull and a shank bone of them not yet rotten: and there did I see the huge heap of stones wherewith they are covered, a fearful example of Gods wrath and justice against such infidel Christians.

CHAP. XI.

THE great Turk called Souldan, alias Cham, comprehending as many victories in his sword as some emperors in their thoughts, arrived at length before Vienna, having made his preamble with the destroying and burning of the country before him, thinking upon the ancient politick rule, "Better it is to have a spoyled countrey than a lost," with a brave prepared army of two hundred thousand Saracens, horse and foot, and so many it is certain he had, because they doubted not but there were 300000. The mighty Cham having erected his royal pavilions, and entrenched himself to besiege the noble Vienna, munified his camp with artillery and deep ditches, and then he sent a letter of defiance unto the honourable Alphonsus, as being principal in his own city, who was invironed within the walls of the city, expecting the day of battel, for to this intent the states of Italy and the Emperor of Germany, with the Dukes of Saxony, Bavaria, and the other provinces near, assembled (for now necessity bred unity) with a brave company of souldiers, to exterminate this monster out of their confines: unto the Duke of Austrich only (for he had no intelligence of their assembled forces) he directed his letters with defiance, meaning to conclude his long travails with a certain victory, fearing neither the peril which so many gallant souldiers throughly resolved might bring, nor that ever God or fortune (as they call it) would once shew him any disfavour, whose only favour is only in shew. Nor yet that the heavens great God would not with severe revengement chastize the Leviathans insolency and slaughter of so many martyrs, rather deferring then forgetting so just a punishment.

CHAP. XII.

About this time the messenger and Wagner arrived at Vienna very late in the night, and passed through the Turkish centinels, and arrived at the city, and for that night they lay at the pursevants house; no sooner had the approaching sun sent afore him the marshals of the morrow light, and a new morning ministred occasion of new matter, but up those two arose, and being ready departed for the court, and now the day was almost in the greatest beauty, when the messenger was admitted into the Dukes presence, unto whom he recited what ever was seen and done in that time of his absence, (only I forgot to tell you how Wagner raged and stormed, and thundred, when Akercock brought him word of the destruction of his house at Wittenberg, as he was in the way to Austria) wherewith the Duke was wonderfully both delighted and astonished. And having welcomed Wagner very graciously and accordingly rewarded, he dismissed them till further leasure, commanding the pursevant to shew him all the pleasure he might.

CHAP. XIII.

After all these most excellent princes were come into the council chamber, the herauld sounded his trumpet after the Turkish summons, then did all the states draw into the great hall, where in a high imperial throne richly ordered with shining cloth of gold, every noble and estate placed correspondently to his degree, where in presence of them all the herauld was admitted, who coming with his coat of armes lying upon the right arm into the bottome of the hall, made three obeysances with the right knee down to the ground, with a loud and distinct voice, spake unto the Duke only, telling him that his soveraign and master Soultan alias Chan, the son of Murad Chan, the son of Rabeck Chan, the son of Mahomet Chan, and so upwards till he came to their great prophet Mahomet, God on earth and emperour of all the east. And then he began to reckon the five hundred titles, with a long &c. unto thee Alphonsus, Archduke of Austrich, and there he declared the whole effects of his message, and at last with a great bravado ended, and then he did on his gay coat of armes, expecting their answer. When as the Duke craving licence of the Emperour to speak, answered the herauld in most gallant and triumphing terms, commanding him to say unto the proud Turk his master, that ere five days came about he would trample his victorious horns under his feet, and ride in triumph upon his stubborn neck, and that in defence of himself and of brave Christendom he would leese the uttermost drop of his blood, and to make it good he would not be in quiet till he had met his master in the midst of the field, and therewith he drew out his sword, and all they with him, crying God and Saint Michael for the right of Christendom: Then stood up the Emperour and avowed all that they had said afore him, commanding moreover the herauld to say to the proud usurper, that seeing the quarrel would breed great effusion of blood, and yet be never the nearer, that he a man every way equal to himself, not only for the speedier advance of his battels, but also to have a certain end to such an uncertain enterprise, he would fight with him body to body, armed at all points after their own guise, at any time within this fortnight, and herauld bring me word (quoth he) that he will so do, and by my honour I promise to give thee for thy tidings 10000 duckets. Then the herauld being highly rewarded was dismissed, and reported their brave answers unto the Turk, with all the great majesty of the Christian princes, who presently went to counsel together, and so continued till other like necessary business called them away.

CHAP. XIV.

In this Chapter (Gentlemen) part of the Dutch copy was wanting, and the other part so rent that it could not be read, yet by some circumstances I conjecture that the Duke of Austrich had divers and dangerous conflicts with the Turk, yet being supported by the English men and other Christians, with the help of Wagner, who standing on a high tower to see the conflicts, caused by his magick such a storm to arise that no man was able to abide, the Turk was still discomfited.

CHAP. XV.

The gifts of Wagner to the Duke, and three Devils retained for Souldiers to the same Prince.

In the next morning Wagner presented himself to the Duke in presence of all the whole princes of the Christians, whom very graciously he entertained as he might for his good service, and there in presence of them all he desired the duke to take at his servants hands a small gift, which he condescended unto, and then Wagner caused a chest to be brought in of fine iron, wrought and inamel'd with gold and colour most curiously, then he opened it and took out a whole armour of fine bright steel so light as a common doublet, but so subtilly and excellently framed, that it passed all comparison of hardness; there was a musket shot at every piece, whereon remained no great notice of a blow, but as of a little touch, plain, without any broidery work or otherwise carved but so exceedingly bright as would well have dazzled the long beholders eyes, a shield of the same fashion, made like a tortoise shell, a sword of the like fine temper, with all the furniture of a souldier, then took he out a plume, which he had no sooner put into the crest, but he that stood behind could not see any part of his back, nor he that stood before of his brest, so that thus it made him invisible, there he told him it was fetcht out of the great Turks Armory, which they say was Mahomets, but I say more truly Alias Chams which for himself caused to be made, having called together the most excellent philosophers and workmen that were to be found in all his wide empire. The great rewards the duke would have given him for it he refused, he was only contented with thanks and favor. And then might they see from the door of the chamber 3 most gallant men to enter, which were his three familiars, whom Wagner taking by the hands presented to the whole assembly of princes, but more directly to the duke, assuring them they were the most fortunate, most valiant, strong, hardy, and puissant men that in the world were to be found, and indeed they seemed to be as goodly swart men as any eye beheld, he told their several names, Mephostophiles he termed Mamri, Akercock he termed Simionte, Faustus he called Don Infeligo, shewing that they were born in those fortunate islands, wherein the poets feigned the elysian fields to be, joyned by the west upon the end of Barbary, being from Vienna to those fortunate islands, 35 degrees of longitude and eight minutes, and 48 degrees and 22 minutes from the Æquator or Equinoctial, in latitude not then found out. So were they most graciously entertained of all the nobles, and entertained in the dukes most honourable pay. Wagner said that they three left their countrey and sought adventures, and by chance coming this way, I knowing of it by secret intelligence, met them, and certainly assured of their high valours, thought good to shew them to you, for he that first had spoke to them had been first served, nor cared they whether to serve us or the infidel.

CHAP. XVI.

I SPAKE before of a challenge made by the Emperor unto the Turk, which when the herauld had reported unto the Souldan (who certainly was a very honourable souldier) there he vowed to perform it, and to set the emperors head upon the highest pavilion in view of all the city. And thereupon the next day after this skirmish, he sent the same herauld with purpose and commandment to declare in excellent gallant terms the acceptance of the combate, knowing that it depended upon his honour to shew his small fear in not refusing so equal a foe, whose profer proceeded from a most honourable resolution: when it was reported unto the emperour that the same herauld returned, he caused the hall to be adorned with most brave furniture, his high chair of estate placed, and all about seats for the other princes. The emperor having seated himself full of brave thoughts and gallant hardihood, expecting the answer of the enemy in such sort as it was in, very deed. In all brave manner the herauld in proud phrase uttered the purport of his message, requesting that a peace being concluded on both parts for the space of three dayes, and free egress and regress for the nobles on both parties, the one to view the camp, the other the court, and on the third day he would armed in his country manner, meet him in the lists, to shew that he never refused the combate of any christian emperor, albeit he knew his calling far superior to that of his. So then the message was accepted, the herauld had his ten thousand duckets carried to the Turks camp on horse, and they in the city began to keep feasts, and entertained the Turkish nobles in exceeding bravery, and they theirs in the like without damage or thought of treason.

CHAP. XVII.

During the time of this truce, these four companions, Infeligo, Wagner, Mamri, Simionte, cast how to abuse the great Turk most notably, and Akercock otherwise called Simionte he would begin first, and lead them the dance. Then he leaves them and gets me up unseen to the Turks camp, and in his camp to his own pavilion, and so into the place where the great infidel himself sate, he being then gone into the lavatory, which is a place wherein he three times a day doth bath himself, which by so doing he doth verily believe that all his sins are remitted and washed away, be they never so horrible, devilish, or wicked: then Akercock or Simionte, which ye will, goes invisible into the lavatory, where the great villain was bathing himself amongst three of his most fair concubines stark naked, swimming as much in their dalliance as in the water, mingling his washing with kisses, and his cleansing with voluptuousness. Akercock in the shape of a bright Angel appears unto him, and with a proud magnifico presented himself unto the slave, who straightwayes very reverently fell down upon his knees, and with his hands high lifted up, worshipped towards him in great humility, whilst Akerc. with good devotion fell aboard the concubines, and there acted them before his face one after another: when he had so done, he takes the great slave by the tip of his pickenovant, and shaking him fiercely (who all this while with great dread and fear lay half astonished and all naked on the ground) told him that he had prepared a more brave place for his so good a servant than so base a bath and no fairer concubines. (Now the Turk had seen how like a lusty rank fellow this Simionte had behaved himself, at which he wondred not greatly, because Faustus whom he thought to have been Mahomet, (as well as he did think Akercock) had also shewed the vertue of so great a God as Mahomet, twenty times more beauty than Jupiter.) Then the Turkish Emperor with more than half dying hollow voice, as if his breath had been almost gone, or else but now coming, said that he was all at his commandment, and so followed Simionte stark naked as he was born, who led him by the hand round about, and through every lane and place in his camp, to the great wonderment and laughter of his people, who verily thought Mahomet had commanded him to do penance before he fought with the christian emperor. But for all this the people fell into such a laughter that some had well nigh given up the ghost. At the same very instant divers christian nobles saw him all the while who effusedly laughed at so apparent foolery. The Turk for all this not moved, for indeed he heard all and saw nothing, went about wonderful mannerly, like as you shall see a Dutch frow with a handkerchief in her hand, mince it after the hopping German. Could a man devise a more notorious kind of abuse, than to make that man which will not be seen but in great secresy, and abundantly and richly clad, to be not only seen openly, but also stark naked, and become their laughing-stock, whose terror he is always? But Akercock had not yet so left him, but down he runs to Danuby (where there was ready Mamri or Mephostophiles to receive him) and there having turned himself and the vilest part of himself unto the Turks mouth, making him kiss and kiss it again, he took him and hurl'd him violently into the water, and then Akercock vanished away.

CHAP, XVIII.

The Second Mocking.

No sooner was he in but he saw then apparently how he had been misled and abused, and there for very shame would have drowned himself in very deed, had not Mamri come swiftly flying over and gave him a terrible blow on the noddle with a good Bastinado, that he almost made his brains fly out, and rapt him up by his long hair out of the water unto the land, where he buffeted him so long till at length he came to himself again, then Mamri fewtred himself to abuse him kindly, and there with sweet and compassionate speech comforted him, desiring his reverend majesty not to take any grief seeing it was done in the sight of all his men, in the knowledge of none. And therwith to shew the more pity of his misery he seemed to shed abundance of tears, desiring him to go with him and he would put upon his soft rayment. The Turk (who then had his crown upon his head or else it had not been half in the right Qu.) seeing one lamenting his case so affectionately, condescended unto him and promised him most large honourable promotion and reward, Mamri set him upon his legs and led him to a little muddy place by the river side, and there varnished the emperor over with most thick terrible excremental mud, not sparing either his face, nose, eyes, mouth, nor any thing, whilst the miserable man thought he had been in most divine contentment. Thus he led him in the view of five thousand people (for here is to be noted that all that ever saw him both knew him to be the great villain Turk, and could not but laugh most entirely at him, nor his own men could do any other nor once think of any rescue or remedy, by the working of infernal instinct) until he came to Vienna, and in Vienna to the most fair gates and where greatest resort of people are always togother, there at the city gate he drew out along taber and a pipe and struck up such a merry note, as the foolish ornament of all London stages never could come near him, no not when he wak'd the writer of the news out of purgatory with a shril noyse. There at the gate stood a carpenter who was then carrying a coffin to a certain house to bury one in, him Mephostophiles beat till he lay on the cold ground, and took the coffin, and caused the Turk to hold it in his hand. Memorandum that none of all these spirits were seen of any one but felt of them which saw them. Then from the gate he began to play, the Turk and the coffin skipt and turned, and vaunted and bounded, and leapt, and heaved, and sprung so fast and thick together, that the coffin rapping the miserable man sometime on the shins, breast, thighs, head, face, that the dirty colour was almost wip't away with the streams of blood. At this strange sight and the unheard noyse of that kind of instrument, all the boyes, girls, and rogues in the town were gathered with this troop, and this mirth, he conveyed them round about the streets, and all the way as they went, such eggs, such chamber-pots emptying, such excrements, odor, water, &c. were thrown down upon their heads, that it seemed all those vile matters were reserved for that tempest, until such time (then it being about two of the clock in the afternoon, when every one is busied in some pleasant pastance) as all this fair company came to the court where out at divers windows lay the chiefest of all the nobility, and the most brave gentlewomen, who seeing such a huge crowd of boyes, the great Turk and a coffin dancing, and a taber and pipe plaid upon, they were almost amazed, thus he marched finely round about the whole court, till coming to the court gate he entered in, (but the boyes were excluded,) with this merry morris there in the presence of them all the Turk fell down dead, whom Mamri laid in the coffin and then vanished away.

CHAP. XIX.

The Third.

THEN came Infeligo, or Faustus, and touching him revived him to the great wonder of the beholders, and covering him somewhat shamefully, went into his chamber with him, and there benotted him round upon the head and beard, which is the foulest reproach and disgrace that can be offered unto the Turk, which done he conveyed him into the presence of the emperor, where he made them such sport, that unneath they could recover their modesty in three hours space, to see the proud villain plastered over with such muddy morter, all over his head and face, his eyes and his teeth shewing like black Moors, or a pair of eyes looking through a lettice, or as they call it a perriwig, wherein if the eyes had feet they might be set in the stocks: all his lineaments were lineamented with this party, he stood quivering and shaking, either for cold or fear, like an aspine leaf (as they say) whilst every man buffeted him, he standing with a scour-gestick and an old shooe, as they do at blind mans buff to see who he could hit. Thus long he made them sport, till one told the emperor that it was the great Turk, at which he was exceeding wroth and sorry.

CHAP. XX.

The fourth and last.

WHEN Wagner seeing him grieved, came and kneeled down before him, declaring that he would undertake to heal all his wounds and other grievances whatsoever, yea and make him utterly forget all that was passed as if it had never been, and promised to carry him home himself safe and sound, which the emperor thanked him highly for, requesting him to perform it presently, for he would not for half his revenues that his foe should have any occasion to alledge against him, for to excuse the combate. Then went Wagner up into his chamber, and apparelled himself in white taffata, made close to his body, and then were they used to wear round hose half a foot deep, stuck with swans feathers, like the skirts of a horsemans coat, his hose, shoos, (for all were together) of the same white taffata, and within with white leather, at his heels two fine silver wings, and on his shoulders two marvelous large bright silvery wings, and on his head an upright steel hat (with a white feather of two or three ranges) of white taffata, and in his hand a caduceus, or a mercurial rod : in the same white silver colour, he entred into the presence-chamber afore all the assembly, to their singular contentation, for in his personated garments he seemed to be a very angel, for it was in doubt whether Mercury was half so beautiful or no. And there opening a large casement (as there they are very large) with a brave r'ingratio departed from them, taking up his flight in the view of them all into the air, as if he should have beat the azure firmament with his vast wings. Thus he carried him lower, and lower till he light upon a great elm, and there he opened his sight to see in what plight he was. The Turk seeing in what a trance he had been, began to swear, to ban and curse, and was even then ready to have thrown himself down headlong, but Mercury he stept to him and bade him be of good cheer, for it had pleased the great god Jupiter, whose servant Mahomet was, to shew him those great abuses, to the intent he should be more wary in his actions, and take heed how to tempt the Christians with vain battles and such like speech, but now (quoth he) come and give me thy hand and then will I lead thee to thy pavillion, whereas thou art not missed of the nobles, for in the place where thou were taken away, hath Jove sent one to bear thy shape. Then again he took his flight and all the way as he went he rapt his heels against the tops of high trees, and beat him pitifully upon the shins all the journey, upon the tents tops. Now they arrived at the same place from whence he was tane, and there he laid himself down, who perfectly recovered his former strength in full perfectness, and not only not felt it, but utterly forgot it. Then he continued his wonted solace and prepared himself to the battel, whilst he was made a laughing-stock of the world. Wagner returning through the same path which he had made in the air before, came not yet to the court before they had done laughing, for there the matter from the beginning to the end was rehersed.

CHAP. XXI.

The process of the Combate.

THE two days of the truce were passed, and the third morning was come, in which time many gallant feats of arms and activity were performed on both parts. Now the time of the combate was come. There was in the river of Danuby a pretty island of a quarter of a mile long or more as even as ground might be all the way, in this place were the lists prepared, and a scaffold richly hanged for the judges to determine in. In the evening about four of the clock (being then reasonable cool) the Christian emperor issued out above a hundred thousand Christians, the rest being above sixty thousand, were left to defend the city (for both the Christians and especially the Turks were increased) where he entred into the wide plain, and coming to the banks side he entred into a broad ferry boat, leaving his whole army on the other side of the river whilst he laboured to attain to the island. The duke of Austria with his attendants Mamri, Simionte, Infeligo, and Wagner, the dukes of Cleve, Saxony, Campany, and Brabant, with the like number, all bravely and gloriously mounted: the duke of Austria in his bright armor marshalled the field, and of the Christians sate as judges, the kings of Lussitany and Arragon, with their herauldss. Now the emperor is landed in the island and is mounted into his rich saddle, armed in armor so costly, strong, curious, and resplendescent, that it seemed all the beauty in the world had been gathered together in it, his courser so firm nimbly joynted, tall and large, such a one might have been the son of Gargantua's, more for the giant-like proportion. Then took he his strong and large ashen launce, bearing in his steel head iron death, at the top whereof hung a fair and rich pennion, the whole shaft of the spear double gilded over and curiously enamel'd, about his neck hung his horn shield, artificially adorned with his own atchievements, the belt whereon his sword hung, of beaten gold, his caparison of pure cloth of gold, whereon the rich stones were so ordinary that they took away the glittering of the mettal, only as if it had been the sun-beames, trailed along betwixt precious gutters. On his helmet was fixed a rich crown of the most excellent mettal. In brief, for I would fain have made an end of this idle news, there was all the richness in his empire, in that all the beauty of his richness, in them all the desire of each eye: when he had saluted the judges he trotted twice or thrice about the lists, then lighted at his pavillion which was there erected of cloth of gold, where he sate with convenient company and refreshed himself. Now in the mean the Turk he set forward with an army double the Christian, and 100000 and above still left in the camp. And here I must needs leave to tell you of his exceeding preparation unless I would make a whole volum, for besides the wondrous furniture of his souldiers, the most rare choice of ornaments, there was nothing could be devised, nay more than of set purpose could be devised was there: but briefly I will turn to the Turk himself, where if I had art according I should sooner weary you out with delight than words: but 100000 of his men having marched before to the banks, and there embattled themselves by the river all along, with such hideous noise of trumpets, horns, (for so they use) drums of brass, fluits, &c. that there was more heard than seen by far, then aproached the great Turk himself, before him rode 4000 Janisaries armed in their fashion, with a long gown of scarlet red, laced with gold lace, and long white sleeves, of a very narrow breadth, which was girt close unto them, under that a good armor, with a long high cap like a milk payle for all the world, of white sattin or such like gear, with a long feather enough to come down to a tall mans hams, very thick laced in the brims with gold and pearl, in his hand a short javelin, at his side his cemitar, at his back a great quiver of broad arrows, and by a string of silk hung his steel bow, over every 100 of these is a Boluch Bassa, a Centurion as we call him, and these be of the Turks guard, and are called Solaquis Archers, and they rode fifty in a rank: then came following them about 200 Peichers or Peiclers, all in one livery of very rich tissue after their fashion, and these are of the Turks laqueis which have a sharp keen hatchet sticking at their girdles, and the haft of Brasil, with this they will stand thirty paces off and cleave a penny loaf, or hit it somewhere, they will commonly stick an inch and a half deep into very tuff ashen wood or Brasil, or such like hard wood: there in great triumph upon an elephant richly trapped, stood a tower of two yards and a half high of pure silver, in the top whereof stood an image of beaten gold representing their Mahomet, round about which upon mules Azamoglands or Iamoglands, who are children of tribute exacted upon the Christian captives, and contributary, fine, sweet, and the most choyce picked gentlemen brought up to sundry dainty qualities, who with heavenly melody followed this elephant, the religious men going round about singing sweetly together: afore all these next to the Janisaries went above 200 trumpets, and as many followed the great Turk, who then approached, having his chariot of pure silver of above 20,000 pound weight, drawn with eight milk white elephants, round about rode and went bareheaded, Azamoglans Peiclers most gorgeously and resplendescent apparelled, under the Turks feet lay a pillow of clear crystal, embossed at the ends with huge golden knobs, on his head a wreath of purple, with a most rich diadem as it is commonly known the order of it, the stage can shew the making of it, but other things they differ mightily in. Here you must suppose the exceeding glory of his apparell, there he sate upright in the chair with such a majestical, proud, severe, warlike countenance, as justly became so high a throne, before him went Aga, which is the great captain of his Janisaries with the Hali Bassa, the captain of his naval expeditions, Bianco Bassa the captain of his Janisarie harquebushers, the Zanfyretto Bassa captain of his guard, with other of great authority bareheaded. After his chariot came sweet melody, and then five elephants of war (an elephant is well nigh as big as six oxen) gaunt and slender like a horse in the flanks, and of more swift foot than a man would think for, his fashion is like no beast in England, but the ridge of his back is like that of an horse, his feet hath five great horney toes, and a very long snout of above two yards in length, with which he will draw, by only snuffing up, a pretty good big lad, and deliver him to the rider, this long trunk falls down betwixt a large pair of teeth or tushes of above an ell and a half long (as ye may commonly see at the combmakers in London) bending like a boars, upwards, his ears wel nigh from the top to the neither tip of the hanging down above seven feet long. And after these five elephants, sadled and ordered for a man to ride on, came trumpets and all in the like manner as before, and then marched 500 in a rank, 100,000 footmen, and by their sides for wings 40000 horsemen, so that he came to the combate with 240000 fighting men, well accomplished in armes: then was the great Turk carried under a goodly canopy upon a black waggon on mens shoulders into the ferry, which was richly prepared, where in the view of both camps he landed, whilst the warlike instruments echoed wide in the air. In the island for judges sat (in armour as did the other) the king of Rhodes, and the king of Pamphylia, now called Alcayer. When the Turk was landed, there was brought to him by the hands of two kings, a great elephant of an ash colour, white embossed very glitteringly, whereon the great Turk mounted by a short ladder of silver, armed very strongly and most beautifully, then took he his javelin in his hand, and vibrated it in great bravery, (as he could handle his weapon well) and hung his quiver of long darts at his back, then his cemiter, &c. and so having saluted the judges, retired to the utmost part of the field, then mounted up the brave and puissant emperor so lightly in his heavy armor, as if either his gladness had lessened his weight, or the goodness of his cause, to the great rejoycing of the Christians and amazement of the Turks, at whom the Christians yeld so universally and hallowed, and other infinite kinds of gladsome tokens that the Turk astonished stood stone still till the Christians had done, and then as men new risen to life, with such an horrible shout, that their voyce rebounded to the air, at which time the Christians shouted again with them, as if they would have committed a battle with voyces, and surely their voices did fight in the wide coasts and shores of the air. This done, the emperors prepared themselves to the fight.

CHAP. XXII.

The Combate.

AND when they were sworn that neither of them had any magick herb, charm, or incantation, whereby they might prevail in their fight on their adversary, and had solemnized the accustomable ceremonies in like matters of combate. The herauds gave their words of encounter, then with loud voyce and shril trumpets couragious blast, whilst all the people were in dead night expecting the demeanour of these renowned princes. Now we have brought you to behold these two champions, arrived thither with their brave followers, ready to prove their valiance in the face of so great a multitude. Now if you will stand aside lest their ragged spears endammage you, I will give you leave to look through the lattice, where you shall even now see the two emperors with their brave shock press doubt betwixt their cruel encountrings. Now you may see the two combatants, or but as yet champions, coming from the ends of the field, the excellent Christian Emperor with incomparable valour, visiting his horse sides with his spurs, carrying his spear in the rest with an even level, so that the thundring of the brave steed presaged the dint of the greatest thunder clap. When Ali Chan, gently galloping with his huge beast, came forward with more swift space still as he drew nearer to the emperor. All this while you may behold them hastening in their course, like as you see two great waves galloping from the corners of the sea driven by contrary winds, meeting together by long randome, to make the neighbours shoars to quake and dimb'd with their boystrous carrier. The emperor being now with his greatest fury ready to fasten his launce upon his adversary, and his adversary ready to fasten his javelin on him, when the Turk sudainly stept aside, and the Emperor thrusted his void launce in the air, (for he might easily do it) for though the elephant be but low, yet he was higher than his horse by a yard, and yet his horse was the fairest and tallest to be found in all christendom, so that needs he must lay his spear in an uneven height to break it on him. Sudainly the Turk stopt, and with his nimble beast followed the Emperor as he had fled, whereat the whole army of Turks shouted horribly, clapping their hands, and the Christian stood still in great silence, struck with just wonder of this strange quiddity in combat, and ere the Emperor could make his stop, with a short turn, the Turk had hit him on the shoulder with his javelin, which being denyed entrance, for very anger rent it self in forty pieces, and chid in the air till they broke their necks on the ground, and had not then the horse started, the monstrous elephant had overthrown him with his rider to the earth. But then the horse incenst with ire for this injury, and his master more hotly burning with disdain and furious gall leapt, bounded, and sent outat his mouth the foamy arguments of his bitter stomach, but so fast the vile Turk followed that he had spent three long darts upon the barbed flanks of the horse, which all in vain returned to their master. The beholding Turks so eagerly persuing the stroaks with shouting, as if with a hidden sympathie their trayning had augmented the violence of the blows. At length the good emperor sorely ashamed came now to make him amends for his pretty falsery : and with great scope throwing his launce forwards just upon the Turks face, and when he was almost by him, the infidel as if he but made a sport of the fight, stept aside very deliberately thinking that he should have made him run in the like order as before, but he more cautelous marking of purpose which way he meant to decline, turned with him, and his learned horse could well do it, and indeed desire of revenge had so seated it self in his brave couragious breast, that now he even followed him as if he had been drawn with cart-ropes, the Turk seeing now he was circumvented, fetcht a pretty compass and trod a round, the elephant flying from the horse and the horse following the elephant, as you might see Seignior Prospero lead the way on Mile-end-green, in the ringles, this was a pretty sport to see the matter turn'd to a play.

Now the christians having like occasion to shew their gladness, gave such an applaudite, as never was heard in any theater, laughing so effusedly that they dasht their adversaries clean out of countenance, tickling again with the long loud laughter: when they had run not passing twice about the Turk seeing his time, conveyed himself out of the ring, and then got again on his back spending his cowardly darts upon his strong enemies armor, and so fast he followed and so quickly the good emperor turned back again, that his horses barb of steel out sticking in his front, met just upon the outside of the right eye of the elephant, that it sticking out a foot entred in above an inch, which the horse perceiving made the rest follow into his head, (up to the hilts as to say) laying his fore feet out straight, and his hinder legs in like manner, went poaking and crowded himself forward, still gathering upon the elephant, so that not so much with the horses force as the great beasts cruel pain, the elephant swaid back above a hundred foot. Now was the Emperor glad, and with both his hands lifting himself upon his stirrops, took his lance, and strook the Turk with the point full on the visard so thick and so many times, that some blood followed, with an hue and cry out of the windows of the helmet, to find the worker of his effusion: till the villain slave drawing his fine sword smote the lance very bravely in two, and casting his shield afore him, received the last stroke on the truncheon of it, which the gentle emperor with fell fury threw at him that he made him decline almost to the fall. The Turk sitting on the elephants back, could not with his semiter reach the Christian, nor he the Turk with his curtilar, so that now they sate and lookt one upon the other, and the people at them, and all at this strange coping. The good horse Grauntier by chance being gored a little under the mane betwixt the bendings of barbs with the sharp tusk on the elephant neighed with great stomach, and leasing from the beast which he had welnigh forced to the lists end, being thereto forwarded with the sharp spurs with so exceeding fury, that it was not only a marvail how the good prince could sit him so assuredly and also that he spoil'd not himself, but with more eager fury began to gallop upon the elephant again his mouth wide open, and horrible with the salt foam which in abundance issued from his great heart: for by how much the more a thing is gentle and quiet, by so much the more being moved he is iracund and implacable. But the emperor turning his reins carryed him clean contrary to the lists end, where stood launces for the same purpose as the manner is, of which he chose the two stiffest, longest, and rudest of their stature, and came softly pacing to the Turk: who stood even there still where he was, the elephant bleeding in such abundance, that by the loss of so much blood his meekness turned into rage, and began to rise and bary, and stamp, and with an uncertain sway to move, so that with much adoe the slave stayed and appeased him, then the brave emperor lifting up his vizor not only to take breath, but the more freely that his speech might have passage, he told the Turk that he had in a base cowardly manner by false fraud and unequal fight dishonoured himself and endangered him, for which he told him Malgrado suo he would be gloriously revenged: and now that they had spent a good time in uncertain fortune, he had brought two lances choose which he would, and either begin the fight anew or make an end of the old; promising upon his honour that if he refused so to do, he would fasten one in his beast, and another in his heart. And if he dared to do that, he bad him come down on foot, and there break a staff with him. The Turk as he was an honourable souldier then presently slipt off his elephant, bravely answering that he came to conquer him in sport, and not meaning to make a purposed battail, but sith he was so presumptuous as to dare him to his face, he should soon perceive how lightly he weighed his proud word, and then skipping to him, reacht a lance out of his hand, and went 100 paces backwards, so did the emperor very joyfully, when they are come so far as they thought they might trust to their breath, holding their lances in both their hands, began to run very swiftly, and desire brought them together so fast and couragiously, that their launces somewhat too malapart not suffering them to come together, hurld the Turk above seven foot off the launces length, so that not one there but thought that he had been either slain, or his wind dasht out of his belly: the prince reel'd backward above two paces, and yet fell down much astonished. The people on both sides exceedingly amazed and affrighted, especially the Turks who sent out such a doleful Sanutus that it would have moved the stones to ruth, but the dolor of the christians was not so great, for the moving of the emperor revived their spirits much. In a cause on which the beholders safeties do depend the ill success is much feared, for it may be seen by this, that they will with a certain alacrity and sympathie seem to help or to pity as the cause requires. On a sodain the emperor lift up his head, at which the christians gave such an universal shoot, as if even now they would have fray'd the mountains adjacent. The two couragious beasts, having lately heaped up red hot rancor in their disdainful stomacks, assaulted the one the other with all the weapons of nature, that it had been enough for to have delighted any one, but the horse had some small advantage by reason the elephants right eye was covered with the trailing down of the blood. By this time the emperor rose again, and the one went to his horse, the other to his elephant, having first splintred their spears, and fenced so long as any vertue remained in their slaughtered launces. When each had gotten to their beasts they began to forward them, who with equal ire moved, needed no incouragement, then did the emperor coming with full scope upon the Turk, smite the elephant just upon one of the teeth, while with great rage the horse had fastened his pike again in the jaw-bone, so that the elephant still swayed back, but neither of them being able to reach the one the other; the excellent prince casting his golden shield before him, and drawing his glittering curtelar, leapt upon the neck of his horse, and laying one hand upon one tooth of the elephant, with the other hand upon the thonge that went cross his forehead, vaulted up, and settling his feet upon the tusks, on the head of the beast, cast up himself, and laid his sitting place where his hands were, and there he rode by a little and a little, till he might buckle with the insedent. No sooner came he within the reach of the Turk, but he smote the Turk so freely, who was ready prepared for him, that he made him decline a little, there they fought so long that the elephant driven through pain was thrust up to the lists, hereupon all the christian people shouted, in a more free manner than ever at any time before, all the while the hard mettal'd swords play'd upon each others shields, so that the glory of their rare fight was so wonderfully pleasing to the eye, and so honourable to the combatants, that if they had jested one would well have been contented to view all the long day: but the good prince was too hard for the other, for with his ready blows he urged the great slave out of his cell, and made him sit behind the arson of the saddle, and if this accident had not happen'd he had surely made him sit behind the arson of his elephants tayle. For so soon as the elephant had but touched the lists, the Christian marshals of the field came gallopping and parted the combatants, holding the Turk as vanquished, whilst betwixt the contrary and adverse part there was four negatives, so that well nigh they had fallen to blows, for the case seemed to the Christian plain, to the Turk unjust. That because the beast whereon he rode went to the lists end, therefore the stopper should be blamed. Well, herauldes whose office it is to deal in such royal matters, had the discussing of it, and it was deferred to arbiters, with this condition, that if the Turk was found vanquished, he should be yielded as recreant (and miscreant he was.) So the matter was posted off whilst it never was concluded, and both the parties departed, the one to the camp, the other to the city, in no less solemn pomp than they entred accompanied into the sands, where so rare a chance fortuned betwixt so puissant emperors. And because the matter was as strange as true I have sojourned a little too long in it. But in the next inne you shall have a better refreshment or a newer choice.

CHAP. XXIII.

By chance a knight smote Faustus a box on the ear in the presence of a great company of brave ladies, wherefore he swore to be egregiously revenged on him, giving him the field, which the knight refused not, so the weapons, the place, the time, were ordained, and Faustus went out to the field, and no sooner was Faustus gone out of the presence, but Signior di Medesimo who was well known to be a valourous and courageous man in his kind as any was about the court, on a sodain fell down on his knees before all the ladies, shaking and quivering with a face as pale as him which was new risen from a months burying, desiring them if ever they tendred any Gentlemans case, to intreat Monsieur Infeligo to forgive him this trespass. At this the whole assembly burst out into a loud laughter, to see the man that was even now in his brave terms and vaunting words to come in all submissive manner to intreat for a pardon so ridiculously. He yet persisted with many a salt tear and hands lifted up towards the heavens, from whence his pitty came, when Faustus came blowing in like a swash-buckler with his rapier by his side, and his hand on his poynard, swearing all the cross row over. But when he saw the knight in such a pickle, he set himself against a wall and laughed so loud and so heartily, that all the whole rout could not chuse but laugh with him, and there was laughing, and here and there and every where. At length two ladies rose, to whom perhaps this knight owed some particular service, and desiring Don Infeligo with very mild sermon to be friends with Medesimo again, he told them that they could not demand the thing which he could not readily fulfil, marry he requested this, that as the disgrace, which he had received was too great to be forgotten without some such equal revenge that he might use some like injury, whereby he might be satisfied, and he might again come into his grace, which they granted. Faustus came to Medicimo and reared him up upon his feet, and then got upon his back, and so rid twice about the chamber, and when he had done he took him by the chin, who had not yet forgotten how to weep. Shaking worse than any schoolboy when he fears to climb the horse, and gave him a good box on the ear, and went his way. So the knight was utterly disgraced, and for shame durst not be seen all the day after. They which were there had sport abundance, and Faustus was feared for his brave valour, and with his continual delight in knavery got him foes enough too.

CHAP. XXIV.

Another time he by chance overheard a gentleman which was talking to a lady, and said that whatsoever she commanded him to do he would do it, if she would grant him grace. The gentlewoman belike willing to heare him speak so not to her, required him to build in that place with one word a castle of fine silver, at which the gentleman amazed went away confounded. Faustus followed him fast, and said to him that he had overheard the ladies unjust demand, wherefore go say (quoth he) thou will do it with one word. And so the gentleman did and it was done, whilst he ran laughing in to many nobles and lusty gallants, telling them he would shew them the strangest thing that ever they saw, and all they came running into the garden together, where they found the gentleman fast lockt in a pair of stocks, and an ugly foul kitchen wench in his arms. O lord what wondrous sport did he make them there. And when they had laughed their fill, he loosed the gallant, who went and swore all that he could he would be revenged on him. In such monstrous intolerable knaveries, Faustus took especial felicity.

CHAP. XXV.

These four honest fellowes Faustus, Akercock, Mephostophiles, and Wagner, went out together into the street, and walking there by chance espied four gentlewomen seeming to be sisters, them they cast to abuse, and they were never content to play any merry pranks for honest sport, but they must be so satyrically full of gall, that they commonly proved infamous, spareing neither their good name on whom they committed them, nor any kind of villany, so it might procure mirth: when they had talked sufficiently with them, they did so much that they were contented to ride abroad with them, and so each fetched his horse and came to them masked, and the gentlewomen were wimpled likewise, (for the men as well as women use there to wear masks.) Thus they rode to the common furlong where many Italian gentlemen were playing at the Baloun, and there they rode round about, whole armies of shoots accompanying them, they riding still backwards and forward, whilst these men-women had sowed their coats to their doublets, and pin'd upon their backs things of vile reproach amongst them, then rode they to the court not yet satisfied, where they were entertained with more merriment and laughter. And when these men-women saw the greatest multitude that was there likely to be, even upon a piece of ground which was higher than all the rest, they leapt down, and by reason of the friendship betwixt their petticoats and their doublets, they haled them down one after another, the horses ran away, and they lay upon them to their great confusion and reproach, yet they thought all well sith they were personated and masked, but the women stript off their womens garments and their head attires, and there they were well known to be four brave noble young gentlemen brethren, and each of them rent off the masks of Meph. and his mates, and detected them to their great shame, who neither durst revenge themselves for fear of further displeasure, nor of revealing what they were, nor could be moaned of any one for their notable abuses aforehand, so that whereas in others it had been but a common jest, on them it was wonderful strange and ridiculous. So they with shame enough went fretting in vain to their lodging.

CHAP. XXVI.

The emperor being some five or six days in rest within his walls, caused, as sloth cannot dwell in true noble breasts, the whole army to set forward, leaving a convenient garrison within the city of 30000 men, marched into the fields in sundry embattles with above 130000 men. And there in the view of the army Meph. Akerc.

Wag. and Faustus prick't up to the Turks camp, armed in compleat harness, and there challenged any four to break a staff with them, then came there forth four Janisaries horsemen armed at all assaies, and there they ran all together to the singular delight of the beholders, so gallantly they demeaned themselves, but in the cope all the four Janisares were run quite thorow and thorow (as they say) and there lay on the cold earth, then made these four fellows in arms their stop, and expected a fresh revenge, which came immediately thundring out of the entry of the camp, with whom to occur in time they met with the like success as before, to their singular commendations and high praises: then 'gan the Turk to stamp and fret, and commanded four of the best in his whole camp, and four more with them to run at these villains and to captive them, where they should rue the rashness of their presumption with long eternal torment. These eight came with all their power together and broke their launces very hardly upon their faces, and so did they four on theirs, then they drew their swords committing a brave turney, till two of the Turks were slain, and the six fled, which were immediately hanged: at which the Christians laughed heartily, and these four returned thanked highly, and for that the enemy would not advance himself to the general fortune of the fight, they marched in again into the city.

CHAP. XXVII.

About two a clock in the night the Turk approached with all his whole army unto the walls of the city causing particular bands and pyoneers to dig through the countermure, the sentinels which were on the walls, privily espying by reason the moon gave some slender light though she was but three dayes old, gave warning, without any alarm to the chief commanders: so that the whole power of the city almost was gathered into arms, without any stroak of the drum. The place wherein the Turk was entring, was right against a streets end of above two yards over, and not above thirty yards from the breach, they had digged a deep trench, and placed on the scarp nine double cannons throughly round and charged with chain and murthering shot, and on each side of the cross street they had erected forts of gravel, &c. like our barricadoes now, in each of which they placed above fifteen culvering and cannon. Now the breach being sufficient, the Turk having entered above 2000 men, gave the onset, and sounded the bloody alarm, when sodainly the flankers discharged and the bulwarks shot freely together, and utterly cut off all them that entred beyond the ditch, and betwixt those three mentioned forts with their terrible shot, they swept them all out of the place, then began the Turk to thrust his men forward upon the breach (having lost in this assault above 2100) and ever as they came up to the breach the cannon heaved them off, and the small shot from the loops so galled them that they durst not approach. But the Turk cared not, for the murdring of his men might weary the cannons insatiate cruelties at length. Then was alarm given through the city, and every one fell to their arms, getting to the walls, and the rest to the assembling places, whilst the Turk freshly filled the breaches with murthered men, he enforcing himself to his power to enter, and they to keep him out. When he saw that how he had stopt the breaches so with ded bodyes which almost made a new red sea with their blood, in great rage transporting above 30000 men over Danuby, furnished them with scaling ladders, whilst he with great store of cannon beat his own slain men off the forenamed breaches, for he was a merciless tyrant, and caused them to assault the wall it self, which they did. Now began the morning to appear, and the Christians came just upon the backs of the assailants, with the greatest part of the whole power of the city, and put them all to the sword, save those that escaped from them by water, but killed of their own fellowes. Then the Christians marched upon the Turk, who seeing his power greatly weakened, having lost at this unlucky assault above 23000 men, cursing and banning his disastrous fortune, and his gods the givers of it, retyred in a flying pace to his camp, whilst the plenteous spoils made rich the Christians, for upon the dead carkases were found store of jewels and gold in great plenty.

CHAP. XXVIII.

This new victory gladded the Christians exceedingly, as much as it greived the Turks. The breaches were now freshly repaired with all expedition. The Christian princes seeing the inconvenience that followed their keeping within the city, and how great shame it were for them to abstain from the enemy, considering their power to be not much inferior to that of the Turks in number, much more in brave souldiery, wherefore they made a general muster and determined to offer the battel to them in the plain field, which if they refused they would give them in their camps concluding all under one dayes valiance, then marched forth the English archers, of whom Wagner desired he might be with his fellows, which when they had taken their stand, they brought store of fletchery to them in carts, which were there disburdened, so every archer being five double furnished, the number of them now was 9000 the pike being converted into them, being thereto desirous, and having therefore made great suit, for the emperor was very loth to forgoe their first good service: Fau. counselled the captain to chuse a plot of above one hundred acres square, where it was open to each horseman, which they marvelled at greatly, but yet they easily granted to stand any where: they were so well placed, that they stood as well to defend the friend as to offend the foe. Then in due order marched out the whole army of the Christians, and so settled themselves, whilst the Turk brought forward his thick swarms. Now it had been a brave sight, to see the greatest princes of the whole world east and west, attended on by their whole forces set in aray, their gorgeous and bright armours and weapons casting up long tramels of golden shine to the heavens, the noyse of clarions, trumpets, &c. incouraging the fainting souldier, and increasing the boldness of the resolute. There was at once in this field all the terror of the world, accompanied with all the beauty. In the city you might have seen the remainders at the churches at prayer, solemn procession round about the town with great devotion, &c. Well, the time was come that the horsemen began to assault the pike, and attempting the ruptures of the aray, and the forlorn hopes fiercely skirmishing whilst with loud outcries the whole use of hearing was taken away: above you nothing but smoak, round about you the thundring cannon, and sharp horrors of sundry weapons, and at your feet death. There might you see the great use of the eughen bow, for the horse no whit fearing the musket, or caliver, as used to it nor yet respects the piercing of a bullet, by the thick tempest of arrows, hiding their eyes and hurting their bodies, overthrew the horse-master to the ground, on that side could not one horseman appear, but straight they fetcht him down, so that of thirty thousand horsemen of one assault, there was not one that came within five spears length of the battel on foot. The great Turk cursing heaven and earth, and all trees that bore such murthering fruit as bowes and arrows, caused a troup of five hundred barbed horses with twenty thousand more to run upon the archers all together, which they did, but when they came just upon a little ridge, not one horse but sodainly stopt, and the riders which now had rested their staves, lying close upon the saddle pommels, were thrown quite out of the saddle, and either their backs broken, or quite slain. All the whole archerie with the camp wondring hereat, as ignorant of the matter, every one suspending his several judgment, but Faustus laughed heartily, who knew the matter plain, for there had they buried in sand all the way wolves guts, which by natural magick, as authors affirm, suffers not the horse to come over it in any case, nor any force can carry him over with a rider on him. For the archers drew just upon, and so universally shot together, that all the troops were put to flight, and above half spoyled and murthered. To be brief, so much the Christians prevailed upon the Turks in three hours and a half fight, that all them were turned and fled, each one advancing forward in his flight, there were slain in this battel and flight above seven-score thousand Turks, the great Turk himself fighting manfully on his elephant, was by the emperors own hands slain, all his chief bassas and men of honour to the number of three hundred died manfully about him: now the retreat was sounded, and they marched home in most glorious pomp and rejoicing, where the souldiers made rich with the great spoil of the camp, were dismissed, and the princes returned home, and due order taken for the safety of the city. So the Duke of

Austria rid of his enemies, gave himself to his forepassed life, and the other princes with great joy caused general feasts and triumphs to be performed in all their kingdoms, provinces, and territories whatsoever.

FINIS.

CPSIA information can be obtained
at www.ICGtesting.com
Printed in the USA
LVHW101656010323
740520LV00002B/339

9 783375 148782